REGENCY
Courtship & Candlelight

Enjoy two sparkling Regency romances from
Elizabeth Beacon and Deborah Simmons

Elizabeth Beacon lives in the beautiful English west country and is finally putting her insatiable curiosity about the past to good use. Over the years Elizabeth has worked in her family's horticultural business, become a mature student, qualified as an English teacher, worked as a secretary and, briefly, tried to be a civil servant. She is now happily ensconced behind her computer, when not trying to exhaust her bouncy rescue dog with as many walks as the inexhaustible lurcher can finagle. Elizabeth can't bring herself to call researching the wonderfully diverse, scandalous Regency period and creating charismatic heroes and feisty heroines work, and she is waiting for someone to find out how much fun she is having and tell her to stop it.

A former journalist, **Deborah Simmons** turned to fiction after a love of historical romances spurred her to write her own, *Heart's Masquerade*, which was published in 1989. She has since written more than twenty-five novels and novellas, among them a *USA TODAY* bestselling anthology and two finalists in the Romance Writers of America's annual RITA® competition. Her books have been published in twenty-six countries, including illustrated editions in Japan, and she's grateful for the support of her readers throughout the world.

REGENCY
Courtship & Candlelight

Elizabeth Beacon
and
Deborah Simmons

MILLS & BOON

Mills & Boon, an imprint of Harlequin (UK) Limited,
Eton House, 18-24 Paradise Road, Richmond, Surrey TW9 1SR

REGENCY: COURTSHIP & CANDLELIGHT
© Harlequin Enterprises II B.V./S.à.r.l 2012

The publisher acknowledges the copyright holder of the individual works as follows:

One Final Season © Elizabeth Beacon 2011
The Gentleman's Quest © Deborah Siegenthal 2010

ISBN: 978 0 263 89772 2

052-0512

Harlequin (UK) policy is to use papers that are natural, renewable and recyclable products and made from wood grown in sustainable forests. The logging and manufacturing processes conform to the legal environmental regulations of the country of origin.

Printed and bound
by CPI Group (UK) Ltd, Croydon, CR0 4YY

One Final Season

Elizabeth Beacon

Chapter One

'Lord Shuttleworth!' Eiliane, the Marchioness of Pemberley and formerly Lady Rhys, exclaimed as she recognised with unaffected delight the vigorous young gentleman strolling towards them across Lady Finchley's ballroom. 'What a pleasure to see you again; it seems such an age since I saw you that I hardly recognised you.'

'I would have known you anywhere, my lady, and must offer my belated congratulations on your remarriage,' the most desirable viscount currently on the marriage mart replied easily, whilst briefly eyeing the lady at Eiliane Pemberley's side as if trying to place her. 'Miss Alstone, I trust you are well?'

'Very well indeed, I thank you, my lord,' Kate Alstone replied coolly, for if he hoped to fluster her by watching her with frost and mockery in his grey-green eyes he was doomed to disappointment.

'Nonsense,' Eiliane swept on, as if she had no idea

Kate and Lord Shuttleworth had the least reason to be awkward together and were being over-polite out of sheer perversity. 'You sent a very proper letter and a handsome present, one I didn't have to consign to the back parlour for my own peace of mind, either, in case it gave me nightmares. You should see the epergne my new sister-in-law chose, probably for that purpose! Kate saw it—isn't it a horror, my dear?'

'Indeed it is, but perhaps we'd better not let her know we said so.'

'Shuttleworth won't tell her, and he's sure to agree with me when he finally sees it anyway; such a pity you couldn't attend our wedding, my boy, although it was a very quiet affair as Pemberley and I were both married before.'

'Aye, a very quiet affair for about two hundred of your closest friends,' Kate muttered darkly, casting her far-too-innocent-looking friend and mentor a sharp look as she realised she'd invited Lord Shuttleworth to her wedding last summer and not told her chief bridesmaid.

Not that he'd condescended to accept, she added to her silent displeasure with both of them, because he doubtless knew she would be included in Eiliane's vast adoptive family and obviously had no desire to meet or converse with her. That much had become very clear when she'd glimpsed him exiting the first evening party she'd attended this Season very shortly after she had arrived with a group of friends. Then there had been a trip to the theatre when he'd chosen to visit a box no lady could dream of drifting into by design or accident and she wasn't fool enough to think he hadn't noticed her sitting in the one opposite. Watching him enjoy the company of one of the highest steppers of the *demi-monde* and her current keeper had, Kate told herself, been almost amusing. If his lordship wanted it to make it perfectly plain he hadn't been wearing the willow for Kate these last three years, he was quite welcome to do so. At the very least it would provide an antidote to the ennui yet another Season might have held for her without his antics enlivening it.

'And you know perfectly well that keeping it to even that number took the wisdom of Solomon and the tact of a whole diplomatic corps,' Eiliane reminded her friend, with a reminiscent shudder at the very thought of arranging her own wedding to her and her new lord's satisfaction.

'Oh, I do,' Kate agreed fervently, since she'd been caught up in trying to defuse far too many arguments once the Marquis's relatives realised their twenty or thirty closest friends would not be added to the guest list so they could boast of attending the most exclusive and fiercely anticipated society wedding of the year.

'Still, it's done now,' Eiliane said of her triumphant second marriage to a man who adored her as fervently as she did him.

Kate wondered how anyone could begrudge them such happiness and was secretly pleased that Edmund Worth obviously did not, at least if the warmth of his smile as he eyed her rather smug-looking friend was anything to go by.

'Again, I congratulate you on that fact very sincerely,'

he said as a prelude to moving on, but Eiliane wasn't going to let him escape so lightly.

'We will see you later, no doubt, as nobody could describe this affair as a crush and it'll be impossible to avoid bumping into one's friends all night, don't you think?' she said artlessly.

'I do my best to avoid anything so unfashionable,' he returned blandly, but Kate could see the tension about his firm mouth and the hunted expression in those silvery-green eyes even if her most partisan supporter wouldn't.

Eiliane deployed her most unexpected weapon, an awkward silence she quite failed to fill in her usual easy manner.

'I think I see Julia Deben over there, Eiliane; perhaps we should join her before someone else annexes the best seats in the room and you're left with a mere rout chair,' Kate managed in the hope of filling that horrible quietness and giving his lordship an excuse to go.

'Will you do me the honour of promising me a dance tonight, Miss Alstone?' The wretched man seemed to take perverse pleasure in asking her after all.

She silently handed over her dance card, refusing to gush or let him know the idea of dancing with him filled her with far more dismay than he could ever be allowed to know. Once they'd danced together so easily, their steps so harmonious there was no need to think about it. It had been the one thing they agreed on without any effort at all, and now even that would be blighted by his profound dislike of her. He handed the card back and she saw he'd put his initials beside two dances with a sinking feeling in the pit of her stomach. Now she must endure two cold and indifferent waltzes with him—the very prospect made her shiver.

'Until later then, Miss Alstone, Lady Pemberley,' he said with an elegant bow and a social smile that made Kate's heart ache for some odd reason.

She managed to curtsy with equal elegance and flash just as bland and indifferent a smile. 'Later, Lord Shuttleworth,' she managed to agree airily and kept that mere upturn of her lips in place for several moments after he walked away, lest anyone see her flinch at how her formerly impassioned suitor had grown so cold and distant towards her.

'Are you actually going to find yourself a husband this Season or not, Katherine Alstone?' Eiliane demanded with would-be carelessness that didn't deceive Kate one iota about which particular one she had in mind, despite Viscount Shuttleworth's obvious antipathy to the very idea.

They strolled across the room to greet friends and acquaintances, whilst Kate considered her answer and tried to tease Edmund Worth out of her errant thoughts. How very like Eiliane to ask the question nobody else dared, just when she didn't want to be asked most.

'Maybe,' Kate replied cautiously as Eiliane plumped down on an elegant sofa. She fervently hoped nobody else would be able to hear the conversation she'd been trying not to have for a week or more against the babel of noise caused by musicians tuning up and the general hum of greetings and gossip.

'Well, if you're not sure, I might as well make a

superb match for your sister Isabella while you make
up your mind if you want marriage and a family of
your own, or would prefer a lifetime of dull spinster-
hood and worthy causes. Miranda and I have wasted
three years of effort on you between us already, and
I'm not inclined to seek out a man you won't turn your
nose up at if you have no intention of marrying him
when I finally manage to find him,' Eiliane continued
relentlessly, just as if the most eligible gentleman Kate
had ever refused to marry hadn't just crossed their path
again mere minutes ago to remind them what a fool she
was.

'How kind of you to point out that I'm one and twenty
and almost on the shelf, Eiliane, but you'll have to wait
for Izzie to recover from the mumps first.'

Her so-called friend waved the exquisitely painted
fan her besotted husband of nearly a year had presented
her with before he'd left her alone in London for a whole
week—barring his entire London staff, Kate herself and
Eiliane's legion of friends, of course.

'The Season's hardly begun yet, so if your sister is a
week or two late in arriving it will only add to the sensation she'll cause when she does get here. I feel I can
safely predict that dearest Isabella will be proclaimed
a diamond of the first water the instant the gentlemen
of the *ton* set eyes on her.'

'Of course she will be,' Kate agreed equably, 'but I
still don't intend to snap up any available bachelor who
crosses your path before she arrives to eclipse me.'

'Sometimes, Kate Alstone, you make me completely
furious,' Eiliane accused contrarily. 'You just *will* not

realise your looks are out of the common run and none the worse for being unusual. You'd have been the toast of St James's ever since you came out if you'd just hold your tongue and simper winningly for once. The gentlemen quake in their shoes when they're rash enough to pay you a compliment and receive one of your waspish disclaimers instead of a polite smile for their pains.'

'And I suppose you always held your tongue and smiled until *your* cheeks ached when you were a débutante, your ladyship?'

'I was different,' her ladyship admitted with a reminiscent smile that made Kate wonder just how different her chaperon had been and envy her a little.

'You still are,' she replied with her real smile that always showed the warmth of her affection for the recipient and this time made Eiliane chuckle, despite the apparent urgency of her quest to marry Kate off.

'Well, if you say so, my love, although I never had any looks to speak of, and only got dear Sir Ned Rhys and then my darling Pemberley to look at me twice by being good company, instead of twittering at them endlessly as the mercenary females who flocked round like a pack of vultures insisted on doing.'

'And you're always so outstandingly modest with it.'

'Any woman who is wilfully ignorant of her own advantages constitutes a danger to herself and every sentient male who has the misfortune to set eyes on her,' Eiliane announced with queenly dignity and a significant look in her direction Kate managed to pretend she hadn't seen.

'Izzie hasn't the smallest chance of being unaware of her looks when most of the unattached gentlemen of the *ton* will line up to tell her what she can easily see in her own mirror,' she said cheerfully, for she'd never envied either of her sisters their spectacular looks. 'Not that she'll relish the sort of nonsense the silliest will pour over her at every turn when she does finally arrive. So the answer to your very rude question, Lady Pemberley, is that, yes, I must marry if I don't want to become an antidote, and finding me a suitable gentleman to wed will prevent you foisting some handsome idiot on my little sister out of sheer ennui,' Kate said, eyeing one such gentleman who'd proposed once, all too certain he'd succeed where others had failed.

'You've kept too many of his ilk at a distance for too long, Kate my love.'

'I'd certainly never encourage such a straw man,' Kate replied, but the prospect of her fourth London Season had made her think very hard about what she wanted out of life before she'd come to town this year.

Over the long winter months she'd decided mutual interests and a sincere friendship with her future husband would last longer than an uncomfortable heat and irrational passion disguised as love. Of course, she was too cool and sceptical a lady now to feel that sort of midsummer madness for a gentleman anyway and, imagining how that sensible decision would be applauded by most noble families, she gave vent to a long-suffering sigh.

Her own family didn't even seem to realise how tedious it could be to be watched with misty-eyed speculation whenever she met a new gentleman. 'Would this be The One?' they seemed to ask themselves constantly and Kate had even detected signs of such mawkishness in her brother-in-law, Christopher Alstone, Earl of Carnwood, of late. She'd always thought him far too hard-headed and cynical to think that because he'd made a love match, she must necessarily want to do the same.

His marriage to her elder sister Miranda demonstrated that passionate love *existed*, of course, and then her one-time governess had tumbled headlong into love with Kit's best friend and business partner, Ben Shaw, to prove it beyond all doubt. Ben and Charlotte clearly adored each other, for all they sparred constantly, and now even Ben's natural father and dear Eiliane Rhys had joined in the conspiracy and wed each other at last. Yes, love obviously wasn't a myth, but she'd seen the damage it could do as well and had no intention of succumbing to such an unreliable emotion herself.

'Any woman in search of an amenable husband should discount that one immediately,' she added distractedly, considering the idiotic man striking a pose nearby and wishing she could recall his name. Meeting Shuttleworth seemed to have interfered with her memory as well as her ability to think rationally. 'I want a gentleman good-natured and polite enough to make me an amiable husband, not one with too high an opinion of himself to treat me with any consideration.'

'Advantages we have wasted our breath pointing out to you in various gentlemen until we're nigh hoarse for the last three years and in all that time you've proved as indifferent as a marble statue. If you don't mean to fall in love, at least banish the thought of such a wicked travesty of marriage from your mind this instant, Katherine Alstone. You possess completely the wrong temperament for a cold and businesslike alliance and would be wretched within a month if you made one,' Eiliane Pemberley pronounced in a fierce whisper that spoke volumes of her disapproval and her new position, for she'd never harm her husband's public dignity, even if she had little concern for her own. 'Besides which, I couldn't bear to watch you belittle yourself and whomever you chose to make miserable for the rest of your lives. Most men deserve better than that from a wife, Kate, even if you don't seem to think you do from a husband for some odd reason.'

'Most of our kind think it perfectly normal to feel no more than friendship and a polite affection for their spouse,' Kate muttered mulishly, 'and all those deluded gentlemen must actually *want* to marry me, since they keep begging me to say yes.'

'Which is precisely why they're so unsuited to make a so-called convenient husband, although, given the way you treat them, I can't but wish the lot of them would come to their senses and teach you a lesson or two in humility.'

'I'm always perfectly civil,' Kate said defensively.

'When you don't happen to be busy, or would like a personable gentleman to squire you about a ballroom while you flirt and gossip with no fear of comeback. That's not civility; it's cynical exploitation.'

A strong sense of justice forced Kate to reluctantly

agree that she took her admirers for granted. Only one of them had ever tempted her to yield to his urgent wooing and marry him and she'd treated Edmund Worth, Lord Shuttleworth, so abominably in order to fend off his increasingly passionate demands that he'd left London before the end of her first Season and not indulged in another until now. Let Eiliane know that particular dark secret and she'd throw Kate at the unfortunate man's head and embarrass both of them beyond bearing.

Not that he fitted any description of an unfortunate man she'd ever come across. He was noble, wealthy and an unusually intelligent gentleman of wit and character. Three years ago his youthful intensity and fiery devotion had frightened Kate into insulting brusqueness, borne of an irrational fear that he could too easily steal her heart, just as her elder sister's treacherous first husband had cynically taken hers and then trampled on it ruthlessly and even gleefully, before callously deserting her in the most appalling circumstances.

Now she was one and twenty and still unwed, even if that was by her own choice. With the added disadvantage of flaming red hair she still found annoying after twenty-one years of living with it, even possessed as she was of the famous dark blue Alstone eyes and just enough height to render her graceful, Kate thought of herself as an oddity. She formed part of a close circle of family and friends who only wanted her to be happy, yet perhaps she just didn't deserve to be so after breaking a young man's heart so callously once upon a time?

Watching Shuttleworth avoid a matchmaking mama with a preoccupied nod, she wondered where her wits had gone wandering off to three years ago. If she'd only seen a hasty, impulsively passionate and rather callow youth in the man he'd been then, didn't that make her almost as headstrong and foolish as her sister Miranda had been at seventeen when she'd fallen in 'love' with a man so unworthy of her he wasn't fit to kiss the hem of her gown after a muddy walk? If she had been wilfully blind in her determination not to follow Miranda's example, could that mean Lord Shuttleworth might have been the love of her life and her ideal husband, if only she'd had the courage to say yes to him three years ago? Indeed, had the passionate sincerity of his youthful determination to wed her been the real reason her suitors ever since had seemed so colourless and interchangeable that she felt not a single qualm about refusing any of them?

His lordship had clearly got over any lingering infatuation he'd ever felt for her while he was away, since it had taken him two evening parties and a night at the play to find time to reintroduce himself to her after three years of absence. Tonight it would have been rude beyond anything his gentlemanly instincts could endure to ignore her in Eiliane's company, but all the time they'd been together he'd watched her with cynical grey eyes, their irises rayed with a silvery jade green that she couldn't recall studying quite so diligently in the past. Her heart had actually fluttered under his steely scrutiny; she'd felt it and cursed it for being so susceptible as she curtsied and observed his elegant bow and finely tuned indifference to whatever she might feel upon meeting him again.

'Perhaps I became useful to some of the eligible bachelors somewhere along the way,' she mused absently to Eiliane now. 'A safe habit we have fallen into on either side without noting it. They know I shall turn down their suit, so they feel safe declaring themselves my slaves and proposing to me in the certainty I'll refuse.'

'And you truly think that sort of habit would make a suitable basis for a lifetime commitment to love and honour a man if you broke it and shocked and perhaps horrified him by accepting him at last, Kate? It sounds a nightmare to me when you're young and full of promise and would do so much better if you'd only look for happiness within this theoretical marriage you're contemplating so coolly,' Eiliane retorted.

'Love can't always be a bolt of lightning.' Kate defended herself rather uncomfortably, because all of a sudden it seemed rather a sterile scheme to marry for less even to her. 'Sometimes I dare say it needs time to grow into something much more comfortable and this year I might meet a man I can respect for his integrity and honour as well as his sense of duty. Mama and Papa made a marriage of convenience, don't forget, and they seemed happy enough together.'

'They made the best they could of second-best, my girl, being people of wit and character. It was their love for their children that gradually bound them together, rather than any great passion for each other, and I know for a fact that your mother loved a man her family deemed unsuitable for her until the end of her days.'

'Oh, so it's all her fault then, is it?' Kate asked impetuously, finding someone to blame for the streak of passionate recklessness that ran through the Alstone sisters like a fault line in a mining seam, then she realised what she'd given away and could have kicked herself. Give Eiliane such a promising bone to worry at and she wouldn't rest until it was stripped bare of all sorts of possibilities.

'I knew it!' Eiliane exclaimed, as Kate winced. But at least her so-called friend's shrewd gaze had slewed away from Lord Shuttleworth, which was some consolation, for it now being centred so mercilessly on her instead, she supposed ruefully. 'You're terrified of falling in love with a handsome face, then bitterly regretting it, just as your sister did so disastrously, aren't you?' Lady Pemberley accused her triumphantly, as if she'd won a significant battle and Kate must now admit love was vital to a happy marriage after all.

'Of course not,' she lied hotly, but felt her cheeks flush and cursed her telltale redhead's complexion.

'You are, my girl, and you wouldn't be prattling to me about marriages of so-called sense if you were not cravenly terrified of letting your heart rule your head. What you should do if you possess even a sliver of good sense is use this Season to find the man you'll love and respect for the rest of your days together, before it's too late. If you meet that man after you've contracted some hollow alliance with another, you'll condemn both him and your unfortunate lover to a lifetime of suspicion and misery, as well as putting your very soul in jeopardy into the bargain!'

'Stop overdramatising everything. I possess a much colder nature than my mother or either of my sisters,'

Kate insisted and Eiliane just raised her darkened eyebrows sceptically and refused to be drawn. 'Because I was born with this unfortunate-coloured hair, everyone thinks I've got fiery passions to go with it, and you're all quite mistaken!' Kate told her crossly, wishing even her nearest and dearest would stop falling back on the ridiculous cliché that redheads always had temperaments to match their fiery colouring.

'Having watched you grow from a babe in arms into an intelligent, beautiful and often exasperating young woman, Katherine Alstone, I do believe I know your true nature far better than you do yourself,' Eiliane said slowly, as if she'd just discovered the key to a conundrum that had long been puzzling her.

'Then you'll also know how much I don't *want* to be engulfed by a grand passion, or become pale and interesting as I pine uselessly for a man who might well pass me by without a second glance,' Kate defended herself uncomfortably.

'I suppose we *might* find a gentleman who's either too preoccupied with another woman, or too blind or daft to be knocked all of a heap by your youth, beauty and usually shining intelligence and wit, if we searched the whole kingdom for him diligently enough, my love, but very few men will ever pass you by without a glance, I can assure you,' Eiliane said with a knowing smile. 'And love won't kill you, you know, Kate. I've endured it twice now and found it quite breathtakingly wonderful both times. Indeed, I consider myself exceptionally blessed to find it twice, even if I am rather a superannuated wife for poor Pemberley to lay claim to.'

'Nonsense, he was lucky indeed to win you and well he knows it,' Kate responded hotly, ready to argue black was white in order to see someone she loved as much as Eiliane happy again. 'It's just that I can't bear the idea of depending on someone else for my happiness, Eiliane, not that I don't believe in the possibility of love for anyone else.'

'Which is ridiculous if you'll only think about it a little harder, Kate. Indeed, it's totally illogical if we're going to go about this in the cool way you seem to favour.'

'I know, but I can't seem to change my mind, even with so many examples of wedded bliss in front of me to form a corrective,' she told Eiliane ruefully.

'I blame myself,' her friend replied gloomily, 'I should have insisted on wrenching the two of you from your grandfather's custody as soon as your sister Miranda turned up on my doorstep one morning with such woe and misery in her poor sad eyes that I knew he wasn't fit to look after a couple of kittens, let alone three vulnerable and lively young girls.'

'Don't do that to yourself, love, for none of it was your fault and how could you have removed us from Wychwood without kidnapping us? Once someone eventually noticed we were gone there would have been a fearsome uproar and my aunt would have insisted we return to even less freedom than we had to start with. Don't ever blame yourself for any of what happened when we were children, dearest Eiliane. And if not for you, we would never have been sent to school, so just think what we would have missed in dear Charlotte Wells, as we all thought she was then.'

'Aye, that's true, Charlotte is a darling girl and exactly the right wife for my new son, for all Ben wouldn't thank me for naming him so, since he's far too big and self-sufficient to stand in the least need of even an unofficial stepmother, but Charlotte couldn't make up for the neglect of your entire family, Kate. You have such a vast capacity for love, my dear, it seems an appalling waste that it might be lost or misplaced in some insipid and bloodless marriage when you could have so much more if you let yourself believe you could safely fall in love.'

If all three Alstone sisters had been born plain as porridge and wall-eyed, they'd still be beautiful to the Marchioness of Pemberley, and only the finest gentlemen in the land good enough for any one of them, Kate thought, affection overcoming exasperation as she acknowledged to herself how lucky they all were to have her. Eiliane was wrong, though, and if Kate wasn't to die an old maid, then she'd have to find a man she could respect in order to have the children she longed for, and what point was there in regretting what might have been?

Chapter Two

Her bridges could fairly be considered irrevocably burnt so far as Edmund, Viscount Shuttleworth, was concerned and Kate would have to look elsewhere for a convenient husband. Which was just as well, she reassured herself, considering she'd always sensed a huge capacity for passion and melodrama in herself and curbed it as sternly as she could, lest it lead her into some terrible tangle of love and fury and wanting that would damage all concerned beyond mending.

'I intend to make a list and, when I'm sure my choice of husband is quite suitable, I'll just have to find some way of making sure that gentleman agrees with me,' she asserted stalwartly, not quite able to meet Eiliane's eyes as her scheme sounded cold and rather depressing even to her when she said it out loud.

'Why wait?' Eiliane prompted sardonically, obviously at the end of her patience with such an implacably self-deluded idiot. 'If you're so very determined to go against your very nature, and God help the poor man you settle upon if you are, then why not begin straight away? Tonight's entertainment should make an ideal opportunity for you to start such a search—considering that most of the débutantes haven't yet arrived and those who have are still too overawed to offer you much competition. Why, you will almost have the field to yourself, my dear, apart from all the other not-so-young ladies who've been out too long and are desperate to catch a suitable husband, of course.'

'I'm only one and twenty,' Kate protested feebly, unable to keep a still tongue in her head in the face of what she knew perfectly well was deliberate provocation.

Eiliane gave an airy wave of her exquisite fan. 'No longer a sparkling young débutante, nor yet quite a faded quiz at her last prayers. How some of those vibrant young girls just out of their schoolrooms will pity you,' she went on relentlessly, seeming determined to provoke Kate into an argument that would disprove her claim to be chilly and passionless. 'To be so sought after initially, then left unwed three years on argues either that you're ridiculously finicky and far too high in the instep, or that the gentlemen have stopped asking you.'

'Then why do they still do so in such numbers, I wonder?' Kate defended herself absently, her eyes once again on Lord Shuttleworth as he seemed almost as if he'd felt her gaze on him and decided to allow her a closer look.

'Because the unattainable is always so very alluring,' Lady Pemberley replied, a little too seriously for

Kate's taste, 'and I don't want you to become a target for the less scrupulous rakes of the *ton*, my love. Better if only you'd accepted Shuttleworth years ago rather than take that primrose path to misery, I suppose. At least marriage to him would put the predators off until you presented him with a couple of heirs. Not that he'd make anyone a complacent husband,' she ended with a warning nod at the fascinating masculine figure they'd both been watching.

'Please don't turn all intense and Celtic on me just now, Eiliane dear,' Kate said absently, most of her attention on the nobleman forging a path towards them. She wondered fleetingly if he still felt more for her than he'd have her and the rest of the world believe—which only went to show what happened when she listened to her friend's ridiculous ideas about love.

'No, my love,' Lady Pemberley replied meekly and Kate shot her a rueful, exasperated glance, before going back to surreptitiously watching his lordship.

If only Shuttleworth had still been inclined to fall at her feet and beg her to marry him, they could be wed by the end of the Season and then nobody would be able to lecture her on the subject of love matches ever again. Except this older, grimmer Edmund Worth looked very unlikely to agree to an affectionate alliance with her, based as it would have to be on mutual interests and polite friendship instead of the flash and burn of love he'd once promised her. It seemed impossible to picture living at his side in such a temperate style, but was she capable of offering more even to him?

'Lord Shuttleworth,' she greeted him, oddly chagrined

when his expression became more guarded rather than less so.

She smiled awkwardly in the hope of establishing a polite sort of acquaintance between them, since nothing else seemed likely, and he eyed her cautiously, as if she might launch into a mad jig at any moment and embarrass him in front of the assembled company.

'Is it time for our waltz already then, my lord?' she asked clumsily and groaned inwardly at her own ineptitude. Obviously she wasn't very good at actually *encouraging* gentlemen, even if it was only to be a little more civil.

'And if only this next dance were to be one, how delightful that would make my evening,' he replied with an unforgivable glint of amusement in his grey-green eyes. He pointed helpfully to her dance card, which stated unambiguously that she was to honour another gentleman with the quadrille. Lord Shuttleworth must have been merely passing when she had made it impossible for him to do so without snubbing her even more crushingly than even he seemed prepared to do.

There was no point in stuttering and apologising, so she sent him a weak parody of a smile and stood silent and embarrassed, wishing she could think of a way to banish the suggestion of mockery playing about his mouth. It wasn't quite a sneer or altogether a smile and she found it flustered her ridiculously in a man who had once been her devoted cavalier. Anyway, she really didn't want him to kiss her—well, not that much—and, even if she did, it was probably out of sheer, perverse curiosity. He'd grown into a much more formidable man than she'd ever dreamt he would. What a shame if he'd cooled toward her just when her interest in him had sharpened, she decided, with an odd jar of panic in her stomach. And where had that ridiculous idea come from in the first place? Why on earth would she want this man-icicle to kiss her, ever? She must have run mad without anyone noticing if she thought being kissed by Edmund Worth would bring her anything but confusion and distaste, swiftly followed by their mutual embarrassment and an even chillier estrangement between them than there was now.

If only she hadn't had to leave him enjoying the company of her devious duenna far more than he did that of her charge, Kate might have found her dance perfectly agreeable. Her partner was an excellent dancer in direct defiance of the air of world-weary cynicism he seemed to think marked him out as a pink of the *ton*. Instead, she missed steps in her attempts to watch Eiliane and Lord Shuttleworth having a comfortable coze and silently dreaded what that unconventional lady might be saying to his lordship.

'Come now, Miss Alstone,' the gentleman beside her chided, finally losing patience with such an inattentive partner, 'either dance with me or pretend to be overcome by the heat, so we may be quit of each other and this dance without causing a scandal.'

'I beg your pardon, sir; I must be a little distracted by all this noise and bustle after so many months in the country, but I shall do better from now on,' she excused herself rather feebly.

'Good, for it does nothing for a fellow's good opinion of himself to dance with a lady whose attention is so patently on another man,' he told her with a frankness she found surprising in one she'd always thought dandified and affected.

Kate was very careful to mind her steps for the rest of the dance while she wondered if she had truly seen *any* of the gentlemen who had habitually sought her out at the balls and parties of the London Season. Until tonight she'd been able to flatter herself she was a reasonably intelligent and well-educated female who was also independently wealthy and up to snuff. So what hope was there of her finding that perfect husband for herself when she'd clearly misjudged herself so very badly?

'Thank you, Miss Alstone,' her partner said as the music faded and he bowed to her with jaded grace, 'you know how to depress a gentleman's pretensions most effectively,' he told her quietly and calmly. 'I shall not be troubling you with them again after tonight.'

'Sir, I have no idea of your meaning,' she protested rather faintly as that sense of nothing being quite what it seemed tonight haunted her again.

Was she asleep and in the grip of a nightmare where everything seemed normal, but in truth nothing was quite as it should be? Unfortunately not, for her dance partner was continuing and she doubted she'd allow him such an air of disillusioned cynicism in her dreams.

'Not your fault, Miss Alstone. I should have had the sense to listen to fair warnings when they were given me. Had I done so, doubtless I wouldn't feel so disenchanted now I've discovered they were correct.'

As they'd reached the sofa Lady Pemberley had annexed by the end of that crushing speech, the disillusioned gentleman bowed and took himself off to the card room to join his cronies, no doubt to confirm that Miss Alstone was a shameless flirt who lacked the courtesy to keep her attention on her conquests once she'd made them in order to eye up her next one. Kate's mind reeled. How odd that she'd got up this morning believing that she was a pleasant enough person to be with.

'Now *this* is our dance, is it not, Miss Alstone?' the cause of it all informed her suavely, getting to his feet as she approached and looking as if exchanging Eiliane's lively company for her own was a sacrifice he was most unwilling to make.

How did this confounded man ever delude himself he wanted to marry me so desperately when he's clearly revolted by the idea of spending half an hour in my company nowadays? Kate asked herself wordlessly as they joined the couples on the dance floor for a waltz that seemed more in the nature of a penance to him rather than a pleasure. 'So why *did* you keep asking me?' she finally questioned aloud, startling herself and shocking him into actually looking at her. His arm went across her back to take her other hand and a cool shiver of something untamed with an edge of warning ran through her like wildfire.

For an instant she felt strangely shaken by the intimacy of their locked gaze and the fluid, familiar movements of their bodies as his warmth engulfed her, taking the sense of chill and alienation out of her evening for a blissful moment as their bodies at least recalled how well they'd always danced together. She was strongly tempted to lean into his arms and let him guide her expertly around the floor without making much effort on her own part. Instead she made herself whirl and turn and glide as actively as he did himself, partly because he was a superb dancer and it seemed a waste not to, and partly because it gave each of them time to think of all the changes three years had made in the other whilst he considered that appallingly crass question she couldn't believe she'd actually asked him out loud.

'Maybe because you dance superbly,' he finally said with a faintly mocking smile, taking her remark at its lightest value and lobbing it back at her with a neatness that made her heart skip a beat in what felt oddly like panic.

Not because he'd once wanted to be with her above any other female then, or had dreamt of holding her in his arms from one waltz to the next, one ball to another? Not because he'd missed her sadly through all the long weary summers and winters since the last time he'd held her so close and danced with her, so superbly matched to every step as they had been so very long ago and ironically still seemed to be now when everything else was different between them?

'Thank you, my lord,' she replied a little stiffly. 'Luckily I can return your compliment without the least risk of flattery. Lord Shuttleworth has always been rated one of the finest dancers to grace the *ton*.'

'Now *isn't* that fortunate for him?' he parried sardonically, but his only response to her implied challenge was to make their dance even more energetic, perhaps to stop her finding breath to ask him any more inconvenient questions.

'Very,' she gasped and decided to wait for anything more until they stopped spinning about the room in this dizzying whirl.

He moved with a poise and latent strength she couldn't recall noticing before and a tingle of awareness shot through her when he tightened his grip on her to guide her past a dab of candle wax on the highly polished floor. Kate had to remind herself she was looking for a courteous and undemanding husband, not a disdainful and probably very demanding lover, and that Shuttleworth clearly didn't want to occupy either position in her life anyway. Her body remained unconvinced by such logic and troubled her with the most outrageous fantasies which her mind shied away from while they waltzed in apparent harmony. Kate did her best to ignore her own baser instincts and Shuttleworth's unspoken disdain while she smiled at nothing in particular as if her life depended on it.

Edmund George Francis St Erith Standon-Worth, keep your head, that gentleman silently demanded of himself as he held the ravishingly lovely Miss Katherine Alstone in the crook of his arm and tried not to think her being naked and passionately willing as she danced in his arms to an even more intimate tune, preferably without the interested gaze of the cream of fashionable society upon them, of course.

What on earth did the copper-haired torment mean by staring at him across the ballroom as if she'd never set eyes on him before, as if he'd finally come to her attention as something more than a dancing, talking marionette and she was intent on beckoning him to her side by sheer force of will? Could anything good be flying about her busy brain? he wondered, as he tried his best to pretend she was merely a polite acquaintance, despite the fact that his disobliging body and most of society knew he'd been besotted with her from the first moment he'd laid eyes on her three years ago. Unfortunately she knew it as well and, try as he might, he couldn't relax and just enjoy this dance with a graceful and accomplished partner who should now mean absolutely nothing to him.

He'd been far too boyish and silly to hide his infatuation with her three years ago. When she'd carelessly turned him down that last time as if she was waving away an annoying fly or a brash young puppy pestering her with unwanted adoration, he'd told himself his stupid obsession with her had been a youthful folly he would very soon grow out of, and that one day he'd look back on it with astonishment that he'd ever been so young and gullible. Well, he'd made it so at last by cutting her and all the dreams he'd had of her painfully and painstakingly out of his heart so he could come here again to find the woman he could marry and live with for the rest of his days, and that woman was *not* Katherine Alstone.

This spring, he'd assured himself as he travelled from his very substantial estates in Herefordshire to

his impressive house in Grosvenor Square, he'd look
about him for a quiet and biddable female to become
his viscountess. Marrying the too-clever, tricky and far-
from-biddable beauty his heart had once been set on
so uselessly would have been a disaster on both sides.
He'd told himself blithely that he was grateful to her for
saving them both from such a fate and he should thank
her on his knees for refusing him again and again.

It had seemed such a sensible plan when he was still
at Cravenhill Park, where Miss Alstone had refused an
invitation to stay for the summer and get to know him
better with a sweet, distracted smile and a brief assurance that they were too young and probably wouldn't
suit anyway.

How would she know? he silently quizzed himself as
he struggled with a strong urge to shake the slender, cur-
vaceous, infinitely desirable and utterly contrary female
until her perfect white teeth rattled even now, when both
of them were three years older and supposedly wiser.

He shifted uncomfortably to avoid making yet closer
contact with her and inflaming himself even further and
caught surprise in her blue, blue eyes as she turned to
look up at him questioningly. Turning the movement into
a demand that she spin fluidly past a less sure couple, he
fought a whole pack of demons at the feel of her body
so close to his, moving so gracefully to the steps of the
dance and reminding him, as if he needed reminding,
exactly who he held in his arms at last, warm and desirable and all too real.

No, he ordered himself as his body responded
instinctively to hers and he fought the magic fiercely,

he was done with self-inflicted torture. He'd wrung Kate
Alstone from his thoughts and routed her from his heart
and never again would he spend restless nights tossing
and turning as he was driven distracted by a bitter yearning for her in his bed, at his board and for ever by his
side. Knowing, for the simple reason of having tried it
in the throes of youthful desperation, that making love
with a *demi-mondaine* he'd fooled himself looked just
like her would never satisfy his ridiculous fantasies of
Kate, warm and shameless in his bed, with every inch
of her velvety skin and stubborn will in tune with his
desires at last, he utterly refused to become the besotted,
driven idiot she'd once made of him ever again.

Once he'd let himself see the gaping chasm between
heated dream and chilly reality, he'd contented himself with his estates and the odd trip to Bath to see his
elderly aunt, until the blessed day when he had finally
got himself under strict enough control to be indifferent
to Kate Alstone. By some benign fluke, it was in that
elegant and usually middle-aged spa town that he'd met
Therese, a lush and lovely widow ten years his senior,
who took him to her bed and taught him there were
other women in the world besides Kate, however little
his heart wanted to admit it at the time. Then, after
what he'd thought was a mutually satisfying association,
Therese decided to marry again. So she'd wed a man ten
years *her* senior after declaring herself quite ineligible
as the next Viscountess Shuttleworth when he offered
to make her so.

'You are too young, my love, too idealistic and intense
to be happy in such a lukewarm arrangement,' she'd told

him that last time they were together. 'We have been happy, but it's time for us to part. I shall wed my colonel and make him an excellent wife, but I'm not the woman you dream of when you cry out her name in your sleep. Either convince that one to marry you, dearest Edmund, or tear her out of your heart before you wed some poor girl who'll be for ever second-best.'

He'd protested, of course. Assured her that if she married him she and the family they could make together would always come first. But Therese had chided him for offering what he couldn't deliver and he'd hesitated too long before she gave him a sad smile and left to plan her wedding to her still handsome and rather rich colonel and to settle three counties away, which was probably just as well for all three of them. Therese was a fine woman with a quick wit and a kind heart and she now had a settled life with a man who adored her. Edmund liked and admired her, but he didn't adore her. Though nor, he told himself sternly, did he adore the redheaded beauty who'd once driven him half-mad with headlong, youthful love and longing for her.

So this year he'd quit Cravenhill for London, determined to find himself a wife who wouldn't drive him to the brink of insanity every time she smiled at another man. With her he would retire to his acres, where they'd live a life of quiet contentment and usefulness, spiced by an occasional visit to the capital to catch up with old friends. Such a pity that it all sounded so deadly dull just now.

No, it wasn't dull, it was sensible. He wanted to be at peace in his own skin and he wanted children, not just to inherit his title and lands, but because he'd been a lone, noble and therefore very privileged orphan ever since he learnt to walk. And he wanted sanity and routine and a sense of rightness about his life, not insanity, uncertainty and a mess of passion, frustration and exasperation that Kate Alstone would offer her long-suffering husband, when she finally condescended to admit one to her bed, if not her heart.

Easy enough to weigh his hopeless passion for Kate against that yet-to-be-born tribe of children and the faceless, sweet and loving Lady Shuttleworth, who would give them to him and love every single one as much as she adored him, and be quite certain he was cured. Now none of it was quite so clear-cut and he felt thoroughly out of sorts and nearly as deeply exasperated with Kate as he was with himself.

Curse the contrary female for looking at him tonight as if she liked the man he'd become far more than the foolish boy he'd once been. Trust her to reawaken the slumberous, wanton siren he'd once made of her in his obsessed, Kate-tortured dreams and remind him how lifeless his sweet wife sounded by the side of the rich and passionate promise Kate could offer a potential husband. If, of course, the lucky devil succeeded in awakening the sensuality she managed to hide so well from herself. For he doubted she had any idea with what heady promise her delightfully curved lips and very pleasing form tantalised an idiot like him.

'She—is—not—what—she—seems,' he intoned under his breath, enduring the feel of her delightfully formed body brushing his tension-tightened muscles as he shifted her for the final turn and prayed for a rapid end to this torture. *She is everything she seems and more*, the faint waft of her rose-perfumed skin in his oversensitive nostrils taunted him back, the soft shift of woman-warmed silk tantalising his guiding fingers even through his supple evening gloves, as if every sense he had was uniquely attuned just to her. But she's not for you; she's not part of your domestic idyll. She doesn't *want* to love you, the argument began again in his head and he was relieved when the music finally wound down and he could let his hand drop with what might seem unflattering haste to someone who couldn't read his mind.

Three years on he was more mature, cynical and tried and tested by life than he had once been, but she was three years lovelier, three years away from the eighteen-year-old débutante she'd been then. Then she'd been a girl close to being unformed compared with the gorgeous creature she was now, all rich curves and slender, elegant limbs that carried the usual Alstone height with a panache all her own. He forced himself to remember she was also haughty and cold as he finally made himself step away from the unattainable siren she really was.

What she really was just now, he observed rather ruefully, was an offended goddess who considered herself slighted by some mere mortal who'd dared turn his back on her extraordinary beauty. He caught the hint of suppressed fury in her indigo gaze, the tightening of her lush lips into a line and then a brief pout that warned him his danger wasn't over, as if he didn't already know it from his dratted body's reaction to her proximity. He so desperately wanted to kiss those rosy, lushly discontented lips of hers that he had to clear away an imaginary frog from his throat to manufacture an excuse not to offer her his crooked elbow for a precious moment of respite from her touch.

It was either that or stalk off and abandon her to the giggles of the avidly watching gossips and seek less incendiary company. Even to avenge himself for all those broken nights and wasted days, he couldn't do it to her. She still had no idea what she did to a man, he decided. High time she wed some unfortunate idiot, who could then spend his time rescuing her from her own folly and leave Edmund to find his sweet, nebulous viscountess and an easier life. The sooner the better, he assured himself and finally decided he was cool enough to offer Miss Alstone that arm and escort her into the supper room after all.

What a fool he'd been to be so full of misplaced confidence she meant nothing to him any more that he'd written his initials on the supper dance to prove he was cured. Evidently something about her called to him on a deeper level than he'd realised, but there was still time left this Season to effect a complete cure. Legions of débutantes would soon arrive and might even be lovely and amenable enough to put Kate Alstone out of his head entirely. He frowned as an inner voice informed him that rumours of such a fabulous paragon would have reached him by now, if such a creature existed outside the covers of a highly coloured novel.

Such an impossibly ideal girl would cause riots if she

so much as set foot in the capital, but instinct informed him lugubriously that he'd still prefer the woman at his side to such an exquisite creature. No, he told himself doggedly, he'd choose his kind, pleasingly pretty and so far purely mythical wife, and just managed not to pull his arm away before Kate could settle her hand gingerly into the crook of his elbow, as if he might bite her if she didn't keep a strict eye on him.

Suddenly Edmund's sense of the ridiculous reawakened and he made up his mind to distract himself with the heady task of confusing the lovely Miss Alstone, whilst searching for his true quarry. It would do the redhaired witch good, he assured the doubter within. He wouldn't be cruel, heaven forbid, but someone should make her realise she existed in the same world as the rest of faulty humanity, not on a higher plane where everything was ordered to her convenience.

Chapter Three

'How is everyone at Wychwood, Miss Alstone?' he asked in a tone even he knew was insufferably indifferent to her answer, although he liked the Earl of Carnwood and his spectacularly lovely wife. Now he came to think of it, if Miss Kate Alstone resembled her fiery sister as strongly in character as she did in outward beauty, he couldn't walk away from her to wed a less unique woman. Thank you for not being made in your elder sister's extraordinary image, he silently praised the beauty at his side, but even he wasn't yet a bitter enough man to say it out loud.

'All very well,' she replied stiffly, as if she could read his thoughts, and he made himself look into her intriguing indigo eyes to make sure he was mistaken.

No, he informed himself sternly, he refused to cave at the hint of wistfulness in her gaze, the faint droop of discontent and perhaps a hint of longing in the curve of her rosy-lipped mouth. It was an illusion, he reminded himself. She might look as if she longed for a tithe of her sister's passionate and mutually loving marriage for herself, but she didn't have the least intention of following Miranda Alstone's stormy path through life. After enduring her chilly lack of attention for a whole Season, he'd concluded Kate had no heart to lose. Trust her to decide to feel piqued that she'd finally lost his adoration tonight, just when he was starting his hunt for a very different female.

'My sister is expecting to present Lord Carnwood with another pledge of her affection very shortly,' she added to her terse assessment, again with that hint of wistful longing in her voice he wished she'd learn to conceal a little better.

To anyone else he supposed it might seem a tone of rueful irony, a discreet nod towards the fact that her sister and brother-in-law were deeply in love and therefore made insufferable company for a rational human being. Too many months spent learning her moods and interests from avid observation, he thought crossly. What an irony if she so longed to carry brats of her own that she was prepared to take him as her husband after all, just when he'd realised he couldn't tolerate such a marriage to a wife he'd once longed to adore until his dying day. Compassion threatened as he wondered why she thought it safe to love her children and not her husband, who could be her equal and her passion. No, Carnwood and his countess were unique and he was done with dreams; Kate was not the wife for him.

'Ah, well,' he replied carelessly, 'your brother-in-law is sadly in need of an heir.'

'Kit will feel the need for whomever my sister presents him with, my lord. Not even the most cynical and uncaring spectator could deny that.'

Now he'd really offended her, just as he'd intended to. What a shame, then, that the fleeting vulnerability of hurt he glimpsed in her eyes, the not-quite-hidden wince as he pretended indifference to two people he liked and envied, pained him as well. Better this way, he reminded himself and smiled encouragingly at a certain Miss Transome he'd been introduced to earlier and her hovering swain. With any luck, they would join them at supper and break up any suggestion of a tête-à-tête between himself and the beauty at his side before too many people recalled that he'd once been mad, deluded and desperate for her.

'La, my dear Miss Alstone,' Miss Transome spouted so fulsomely so that Edmund almost regretted encouraging her, even to save himself an intimate supper with a woman he couldn't have and didn't want. 'How finely you two do dance together. It quite put us off our own feeble attempts, did it not, Mr Cromer?'

'Yes, quite,' poor Cromer replied as if his throat was parched after all the monosyllabic replies he'd made this evening to his voluble companion. 'Get supper for the ladies, eh, Shuttleworth?' he managed in a magnificent feat of oratory.

'Quite,' he replied, apeing his old school friend's sparse conversational style and they resorted to the groaning supper table to procure enough refreshments to silence even Miss Transome for a few idyllic moments.

Edmund decided both he and his taciturn friend had been rash to attend a party so obviously organised for the benefit of single ladies who'd survived too many Seasons unwed, before fresh débutantes arrived to outdo and outflank them. It was perhaps the last chance for such ladies to catch the eye of a potential husband before open season was declared on them. One glance at their hostess for the evening and her superannuated eldest daughter should have any sane bachelor saying a hasty farewell and dashing off to his club in order to survive and fight another day. He, of course, had a reason to attend any party where he might meet his elusive future viscountess, but what on earth had led Cromer to risk it?

'She's m'aunt,' Cromer explained obscurely and Edmund must have looked almost as puzzled as he felt, because his friend added a brief explanation. 'Lady Finchley, she's m'aunt.'

'That accounts for it then,' he conceded.

'Your excuse?' Cromer asked morosely.

'Idiocy,' Edmund replied, borrowing some of his friend's abruptness.

'Must be,' Cromer commiserated as they turned back with their booty. 'Though the Alstone icicle's a beauty,' he conceded generously.

'Aye, but is she worth enduring the frostbite for, I wonder?' Edmund asked in a thoughtful undertone as he watched her nod regally to an acquaintance.

'M'father wants me to wed. Always liked Amelia Transome, but the thing is that she *will* talk. Much better tempered than my cousin Finchley, though,' Cromer risked waxing lyrical.

Scanning the room and finally spotting Miss Finchley seated at a flimsy table with a widower of at least five and forty, who still looked hunted and not very willing, Edmund sympathised. Miss Transome was open and amiable, but the thought of being fluttered at over the breakfast table for the rest of his life must make the strongest man hesitate. Neither female bore the slightest resemblance to his dream wife, so he turned his attention back to Kate Alstone with a sneaking feeling of relief that he didn't stand in Cromer's shoes and could at least please himself whom he brought to supper, so long as she wasn't the woman who pleased him all the way to the altar.

'Oh, how perfectly lovely,' Miss Transome gushed at the loaded plates.

'Quite,' Kate said with much less enthusiasm, and Edmund wondered if she'd been talked into a headache by Miss Transome's busy tongue and dreaded carrying the burden of conversation with her on his own.

Kate nibbled unenthusiastically at her supper, despite poor Lady Finchley having pushed out every boat she could launch in the hope of netting her daughter a husband at long last by hiring an excellent chef. To be fair, the headache she felt tightening her hairpins and nagging at her temples had nothing to do with Miss Transome's prattle, so the blame for that must lie at Lord Shuttleworth's door. Wretched man, she decided, as she surreptitiously surveyed him with a disillusioned gaze.

Once upon a time he would have fallen at her daintily shod feet given the slightest hint of encouragement, but now that she'd finally steeled herself to accept a husband, he certainly wouldn't be one of her suitors.

She hoped she was too proud to wilfully mistake his indifference to her tonight for a fleeting headache or a black mood on *his* part. There was too much distance about him to lay his behaviour at such a random and socially convenient cause and gaily expect tomorrow to bring amendment. He no longer desired her, now she finally wanted to become a wife and mother, and it was the frustration of it all that had caused her headache. It wasn't as if she cared for him, other than as she might for any man she'd once known and come to value for his integrity and the dry sense of humour that had once lurked under his youthful enthusiasm.

Now it was gone, she decided guiltily that she'd always secretly revelled in Edmund's apparent obsession with her and the certainty that he'd always long for her, even if he couldn't have her. Had it been a guilty pleasure she knew she ought not to feel to know one person on this earth probably still thought of her as uniquely desirable? She really hoped not, since that would make her a tease or a shrew, then and now. And he certainly didn't want her now, so why did it feel as if someone had taken away the most promising treat she'd ever pretended she didn't really want in the first place?

So all in all it was little wonder that she was nursing the beginnings of a fine headache and an inexcusable grievance against Edmund Worth, just because he no longer felt inclined to make a fool of himself over the

Honourable Katherine Alstone. Now that there was no chance of him offering for her ever again, she supposed she could acknowledge in her own head that it would have been wrong to accept him anyway, when he so obviously wanted to love his wife and she certainly didn't want to love her husband. However, she wondered uneasily if she would have found it so wrong to accept him on such terms if he hadn't made it so very clear they were no longer on offer.

Kate surreptitiously scanned the room under cover of Miss Transome's interminable prattle for any likely bachelors, now the most promising one of all was struck off her list. Not one of those present made the idea of sharing the intimacy required to bring her children into the world seem anything other than a nightmare. There would be other balls and routs, of course; ones where the gentlemen were both more plentiful and a little more willing to be charmed, although the other ladies would also be both more sparkling and more innocent, if also more tongue-tied.

Most eligible gentlemen had spurned Lady Finchley's rout for their clubs, which severely limited her choices. Sensible gentlemen, she decided, as she noted her fellow quizzes dotted about the supper room, trying their best to be all the things their desperate mamas bade them be. Miss Transome was projecting vivacity with such determination Kate wondered if she might sprout wings and fly up to the ceiling and circle about them all, still twittering frantically as she did so. Nearby, Miss Wetherby had cornered the market in pale and interesting and was reclining gracefully on a fragile chair that looked to be her only support in a failing world. And just what was Miss Alstone doing? Wilting too, Kate decided crossly; she was drooping like a wallflower and refusing to even try to be civil to those about her, just because she'd been disappointed in hope, if not in love.

'Do you attend Mrs Flamington's ridotto, sir?' Miss Transome asked Mr Cromer with apparently artless curiosity, and Kate could have told her just from reading Mr Cromer's hunted expression that it was unlikely.

'No,' he managed reluctantly, before courting even more silence by popping a bite of lobster patty into his mouth and consuming it very slowly as if to stop his reckless tongue committing him to something the rest of him didn't agree with.

'Are *you* planning to be there, Lord Shuttleworth?' the lady asked earnestly.

Yes, how about you? Kate asked him with silent malice as she watched him swallow his chicken puff with gallant determination and even manage not to cough while he did so. Seeming to read her very thoughts, he cast her a repressive look and Miss Transome a warm smile that probably gave her far more encouragement than he ever dreamt it would, if the flush of sudden colour in her cheeks and the pleased sparkle in her eyes was anything to go by.

Kate sympathised with the foolishly romantic nature concealed under all the fluff and froth, even as she had to fight a primitive urge to ruthlessly crush any hopes of capturing Shuttleworth's interest that might be stirring in Miss Transome's receptive breast. He wasn't hers to be possessive about, and had made that abundantly clear tonight. If he wanted to land himself with a wife who'd foolishly long for his love and affection for the rest of their days together, then that was his problem. Except that some annoying part of her argued it was hers as well, however hard Kate tried to ignore it.

'I fear I'm otherwise engaged that day,' he said with apparent regret.

'Yes,' Kate said with a hint of malice, 'Lady Tedinton has a waltzing party, has she not?'

When she'd heard rumours that a lady with a French-ified name, who might or might not be Selene, Lady Tedinton, had shared a lot more than a mere friendship with young Lord Shuttleworth while they were both in Bath one spring, Kate had dismissed them as mere gossip, even if the thought of him sharing that exoti-cally beautiful lady's bed had pained her with surpris-ing sharpness while she did so. An honourable young gentleman like Shuttleworth wouldn't cuckold a man of Tedinton's venerable years and genial temper, she'd assured herself, even if her ladyship was twenty or thirty years younger than her lord and reported to hold to a conveniently elastic interpretation of her marriage vows. Since neither had confirmed or denied the rumour, it had flourished on and off and Lady Tedinton was even said to preen to her friends for having fascinated such a potent young lord.

Now Kate was nowhere near so certain Edmund would refuse the invitation in the lovely Lady Tedinton's somnolently knowing sloe eyes and could see how his leanly handsome face and fine form would appeal to a jaded wife of her ladyship's sybaritic nature. In that lady's position, with a much older husband preoccupied with affairs of state and his estates, as well as his children from his first marriage, would she be tempted to dally with a vigorous young gentleman who'd be sure to make her a passionate and considerate lover? She hoped not, but eyeing Viscount Shuttleworth surreptitiously now, Kate knew she'd find him nigh irresistible if she stood in Lady Tedinton's expensive Parisian shoes, even if she wouldn't much like the fit of them.

Anyway, it certainly wasn't jealousy that pricked at her as Edmund explained himself to Miss Transome far more warmly than he'd spoken to her all evening. It was merely pique that one who had once seemed to adore her had returned to town looking as if he couldn't imagine what madness had come over him to have ever thought her the centre of his universe.

'I am engaged on business that day, Miss Transome, but most of my acquaintance seem set on going to the ridotto, so you certainly won't lack for companionship if you intend to go yourself.'

If only because Mrs Flamington was rumoured to possess a very pretty daughter it would abound in eager young gentlemen, Kate thought cynically, then ordered herself not to be such a sharp-nosed nag and to sympathise a little more with her new friend when she was only intent on the same outcome as herself. In fact, she informed herself ruefully, she and Miss Transome were sisters in adversity.

'And you, Miss Alstone,' Lord Shuttleworth asked at last, as if she were only a polite afterthought, 'are you bound for Hill Street or Cavendish Square that day?'

'Neither, Lord Shuttleworth,' she replied uninformatively.

'How unfortunate for your admirers.'

'I dare say they will endure it.'

'Ah, but endurance and enjoyment are so distant, Miss Alstone, that I wonder you don't at least try to pity your disappointed admirers a little more,' he taunted her, and drew Miss Transome's attention by doing so, which felt far worse to Kate than enduring his contempt unnoticed.

'I intend to enjoy my visit to an old friend who is currently bereaved and therefore does not seek out such bright company, but I wish both hostesses and their guests well in my absence of course, my lord,' Kate managed coolly.

'Beautifully put,' he acknowledged with a fencer's bow and Kate felt tears prick her eyes at the thought that where once upon a time they'd almost been friends, now they were very much more like bitter enemies.

The air of chilly politeness between herself and Lord Shuttleworth hadn't escaped the notice of the gossip-mongers and Kate felt every speculative gaze and insincere enquiry after her health like little darts. Longing to be securely among family and friends once again, Kate realised how privileged she was to have escaped the attention of the more vicious gossips until now.

'I knew you were feeling low for all you denied it, my love,' Eiliane scolded gently as they rode home in the carriage at long last. 'So why on earth did you insist on staying so late at that very dull party?'

'Because to leave early would have provided even more food for the gossips,' Kate admitted wearily and silently thanked her friend for not rubbing her nose in tonight's many humiliations, especially after their earlier discussion. A conversation that now seemed so arrogant and misguided on her side she could hardly bear to recall it with hindsight and squirmed in her comfortable seat. If he'd managed nothing else tonight, Lord Shuttleworth had taught her how little she mattered in the great scheme of things and most especially how little she meant to him.

'Oh, don't concern yourself about them,' Lady Pemberley said cheerfully, 'they're so hungry for something juicy to chew over after so many months away from the capital that if they can't find a real scandal they'll make one up out of nothing. Give them a few days for a real one to erupt and they will soon be distracted from trying to make trouble where it doesn't already exist.'

'And it's not exactly a scandal if a gentleman who once admired me no longer does so,' Kate replied rather hollowly, not sure if she was reassuring Eiliane or herself.

'Of course not, but don't forget most of the younger ladies present tonight have been found wanting in comparison to you over the last few Seasons, my dear, and feel a little pity for their plight. Many of them will never climb off the shelf fate has left them on so pitilessly, the poor dears.'

'I'm not sure I will now and I do feel for them, even if I can't admit they were ever measured by my low standard and found wanting. I never intended to set myself A1 at Lloyd's and everyone else at nought, Eiliane.'

'Ah, but that's the problem. Not only are you beautiful, graceful, well born and surrounded by people who love you, but you're also astonishingly unaware of how unique and lovely you are. No wonder half the ladies of the *ton* secretly envy you and the other half want you to fall flat on your very pretty nose, Kate dear. If I didn't love you so much, I might dislike you myself for being so unreasonably beautiful.'

'How can anyone possibly be so appallingly mistaken, let alone you, Eiliane? I'm the least perfect person you'll ever encounter, even if you live to be a hundred, and I'm certainly *not* beautiful.'

'I know none of us are perfect this side of heaven, but you really are fortune's favourite, my love, even if it doesn't feel like it just now,' Eiliane replied with that depth of understanding that always floored Kate at unexpected moments. As Lady Rhys and now the Marchioness of Pemberley, her friend had set up so many humane schemes for rescuing the poor, the unfortunate and even the plain criminal, that Kate could only wonder at her energy and try to respect her judgement.

'It certainly doesn't,' she admitted as she stepped out of the carriage, glad of the comfort Eiliane had managed to bring into her husband's lofty town mansion as they were welcomed home after a trying evening. 'Although I do feel blessed to exchange Lady Finchley's ballroom for your fine residence, Madam Marchioness,' she managed to tease her friend and hostess lightly.

'It's nice enough now, I suppose,' Lady Pemberley

conceded rather absently as she set eyes on her new lord, gracefully sauntering out of his library as if he hadn't galloped his poor horse back to his London home almost mercilessly, then waited with restless impatience for his lady's return once he finally got here.

'I thought you were meant to be away for a whole week,' Eiliane chided, eyeing her tall, upright and still very handsome lord as if checking him for any sign of damage.

'I soon got my business over and done, so there seemed no point lingering to me when I could be more comfortable at home,' he replied, gazing at his lady as if he'd not set eyes on her for a month.

Watching them with exasperated affection and faintly amused by their refusal to admit they were happy as larks together, Kate left them to it and went up to bed, allowing her maid to fuss over her with such unusual docility that the girl finally asked if her mistress was sickening for something.

'No, it's just the headache,' she explained as patiently as she could.

'Oh, then you're not in love, Miss Kate?'

'Certainly not. I can imagine nothing worse,' she replied with such revulsion even Eiliane might have believed her, if she wasn't otherwise occupied.

'I can, and I think it would be wonderful,' came the dreamy reply.

'Bah! For heaven's sake, take yourself off to bed and stop bothering me with such absurd notions, before I feel compelled to scream.'

'You'll see,' her maid informed her with sharp nod

and, deciding there was no more to be done to change her young mistress's mind, took herself off to bed, presumably to dream of a nebulous lover who'd take her for granted and father ridiculous numbers of babes on her before neglecting her for someone less careworn, Kate decided, with a cynicism that seemed excessive even to her.

Maybe it would be better to have the illusion of loving someone to look forward to though, at least until cold reality broke through and spoilt it all, she thought wistfully while she climbed into bed and extinguished her candle. Before she succumbed to exhaustion, she thought that for as long as the enchantment lasted, a person might be deliriously happy with the one they thought they loved, before real life proved what a fairytale it all was and that so-called love faded away as if it had never been.

Chapter Four

However much she wanted to, it somehow seemed impossible to make her excuses and stay home when Kate received an invitation to the ball Lord and Lady Tedinton were holding to launch his lordship's daughter into society. Of course, it wasn't jealousy of lovely Lady Tedinton and whichever gentleman she might or might not have taken as her lover in the last couple of years that had made her so reluctant to come, but Kate couldn't help wishing the evening over and done with before it had scarcely begun now she was here. Her ladyship was looking exotic and sensuous and strikingly beautiful, and Kate supposed it was no surprise that Lord Tedinton had succumbed to her youth and voluptuous figure and seductive smile, even if he clearly should have known better at his age.

Either others didn't share her reluctance to be here, or were so curious to see how her ladyship would behave towards a stepdaughter barely seven years younger than she was herself that they couldn't bring themselves to stay away, because it seemed to take for ever for the parade of coaches drawn up at the Tedinton town house to reach the front door. Kate wondered why this particular party was so popular, when Lady Tedinton made so little effort to court her own sex and the patronesses of Almack's and one or two other *grande dames* could make or break any social event. Obviously his lordship's good character and generous opinions commanded loyalty from his peers, but Kate thought many of those present were here in expectation of hearing or seeing something scandalous and would be acutely disappointed if Lady Tedinton failed to provide it.

Kate took one look at Miss Tedinton and decided the poor girl knew exactly what was in the minds of many of those who were so effusively wishing her well. As Eiliane had pointed out, the gossips were eager and primed for mischief after a dull winter and Kate heartily wished she didn't have to be here to witness the poor girl's obvious embarrassment. Yet if she'd stayed away it would probably cause even more speculation about Shuttleworth's defection from the ranks of her admirers and her reaction to his coolness toward her. Too many people knew, or thought they knew, that Lady Tedinton might have captured Lord Shuttleworth's very close attention if the rumour mill was to be believed. How gleefully they'd all have talked tonight if Kate had played the coward and not come when they also knew Shuttleworth had once been her most devoted cavalier. As she waited with Eiliane to be announced and greeted as effusively as a marchioness and her protégée must be, even if the words must stick in Lady Tedinton's elegant throat, Kate wished someone would wave a magic wand and telescope time so she could be at the other end of this evening in the time it took to snap her fingers.

'You look splendidly,' Eiliane murmured reassuringly and Kate was cross with herself for betraying any hint of her feelings. 'That new gown is a triumph and you'll cast all the débutantes into the shade in it tonight because, although it's white and perfectly proper, none of them could carry it off with such *élan*.'

'Thank you. It seems there may be something to be said for being one and twenty after all, then,' Kate managed to reply as she smiled ruefully at her chaperon and wondered yet again why she was still feeling so nervous about tonight.

It was true that her white silk gown with its corded and looped trim and belled-out skirt was considerably more sophisticated than anything a débutante would dare wear and she felt a little better at the sight of her looking elegant and surprisingly assured in one of the long mirrors probably placed to throw more light on to the stairs. The style was a little fussier than she liked, but as the dressmaker had informed her, when she'd tried to order it made up in a plainer style, that was the mode and it was unthinkable for Miss Alstone to be thought dowdy and behind the times. The belled skirt and very high waist undoubtedly suited her figure and one of the few advantages of red hair was that even the most severe critics could never accuse her of being insipid. Being one and twenty, she could also wear her mother's pearl-and-diamond set without being informed she was fast and the fact of them at her neck and wrists and ears felt both reassuring and right.

Funnily enough, it wasn't the débutantes she was most concerned about, but Kate smiled brightly and tried to look eager for the delights ahead of her when they finally reached the head of the receiving line and she met Lady Tedinton's apparently sleepy-eyed gaze. Her ladyship's dark gaze chilled and Kate was tempted to seek out another of those well-placed mirrors to check there wasn't a knife plunged between her shoulder blades she was, as yet, too frostbitten to feel.

'How lovely that you could both attend our humble little entertainment,' her ladyship cooed as if utterly delighted they'd come.

'Oh, we wouldn't have missed it for the world,' Eiliane responded just as insincerely and Kate wondered once more at the polite lengths the great ladies of the *ton* would go to in order to best their enemies. 'Such an interesting use of flowers and drapery to accentuate the colouring of such an angelically fair girl,' Eiliane added with a pointed glance at his lordship, who suddenly looked thoughtful about the unsuitable cerise-silk swags that festooned the ballroom at such an innocent affair as a débutante ball.

'Dear Philippa is such a passionate lover of this particular shade of dusky rose silk that nothing I could say would change her mind about ordering yards of it to drape the ballroom with. Wise heads are so seldom found on young shoulders, don't you agree, Lady Pemberley?' their hostess parried sleepily.

Kate saw 'dear Philippa' conceal a frown and shoot

a helpless, hunted glance at her papa behind a fan that
was also dark rose to match the silk draped behind her
and quite the wrong colour for any débutante to carry,
let alone a blonde and blue-eyed girl like Miss Tedinton.
The expensive and elaborate fan looked distinctly odd
against the stark white simplicity of the ball gown even
her ladyship hadn't been able to argue against buying for
such a young girl, as if she'd been given it to hold while
someone far more sophisticated was busy. After all,
Kate thought cynically, why spend a penny more on her
stepdaughter than necessary, when her ladyship could
pass on her cast-offs to her and spend it on herself?

Lord Tedinton looked pitifully relieved at his wife's
implausible explanation and was obviously too blinded
by his beautiful countess to see beyond the end of his
own nose. Kate ardently pitied the children of his first
marriage and smiled encouragingly at the unlucky
Philippa while Eiliane exchanged insincerities with their
hostess. Receiving a shy smile in return, Kate made a
mental note to bully the more pleasant youths of her
acquaintance into demanding Philippa Tedinton's dance
card, before her stepmama pushed her into more venial
hands in the hope of getting her off her hands more
swiftly, and cheaply.

'Dreadful woman,' Eiliane whispered as they walked
down into the ballroom and paused to take a discreet
survey of the company.

'I doubt most of the gentlemen present would agree
with you,' Kate murmured, watching a few of the fascinated males and searching for one in particular, although

she chided herself for being such an idiot all the time she did so.

'Some have sense enough to see through the obvious,' Eiliane said, sounding as if she was trying to reassure her protégée that Edmund was one of the wise who'd already done so, although why she should when he meant nothing at all to Kate was quite beyond her.

'And some do not,' Kate said bleakly, her eyes briefly pausing on Edmund's golden-brown head. He was bending over one of the prettiest of the current crop of débutantes to initial her dance card. Then he gave her a gallant bow and an altogether too charming smile of farewell, until later.

'Not that you care what he thinks,' Eiliane continued blandly and Kate stopped pretending not to watch Lord Shuttleworth long enough to give her so-called friend a long cool look instead.

'No, not that I have so little sense as to do that,' she agreed silkily.

'Liar,' Eiliane murmured softly, then spying out the best seat in the house, again managed to procure it with a polite, ruthless smile that suddenly made it hers by right. 'I'm far too old to stand about like an exhibit at a fair and too young to sit on a chaperon's bench,' she said placidly when Kate raised her eyebrows at her tactics.

'And you only ever lay claim to whatever age you're admitting to at the time when it suits you to make use of it.'

'One of the few gifts middle age offers is the opportunity to exploit it at regular intervals.'

'And your rank?'

'Oh, yes, that, too, of course. A sensible person must make use of any unfair advantages the good Lord gifted them in support of a good cause, don't you agree, Shuttleworth?' Eiliane asked the one man Kate didn't want to see until she'd got over watching him either court an overgrown schoolgirl, or be eyed by their hostess as if she were a hungry cat intent on catching the finest prey she could spot.

Kate told herself she was merely disappointed not to be given the chance to avoid him all evening and greeted him with the brusque nod he deserved for all the self-doubts and turmoil he was putting her through. She then could have cheerfully hit him—if she weren't such a rational person—when he returned it with a distant bow.

'That depends on the circumstance, your ladyship,' he replied with an easy smile Kate envied her friend as she felt her own face stiffen into a chilly mask so she'd be ready for the contrast when he finally deigned to meet her eyes.

'Always so cautious, Shuttleworth?' Eiliane teased.

'Not always,' he parried rather dourly and Kate would have been a fool to read his cool glance as approving of her in any way. 'But I always agree with *you*, your ladyship, as it saves me so much energy,' he said with a lazy smile that did such unfair things to Kate's breathing she wondered if she was coming down with more than just bruised pride and dented self-esteem. A severe cold? Influenza, perhaps?

'The rest of us have to live with the consequences when she becomes more certain of her own omnipotence than Madame Marchioness here has any right to be though, my lord,' she reproached him lightly, wondering why she was bothering to speak to him at all when he didn't seem to welcome either her presence or her conversation.

'Neither of us will ever attain such a happy state whilst we have the corrective of your abrasive tongue available to put us right, Miss Alstone, isn't that so, Lady Pemberley?' he parried.

'It is,' Eiliane said with such heartfelt sincerity that Kate felt her confidence in her own judgement falter once again.

'Am I really so brusque and disagreeable?' she asked unguardedly.

'Only when you're not being right all the time. It really is most annoying in you,' he said, openly taunting her now and Kate told herself she was a fool to feel shaken and deeply unsure of what she'd built on the wreckage she and Izzie had been left with after the collapse of their once-safe little world.

'Just because you happen to think it's your divine right to be correct instead?' she asked him smoothly enough, refusing to even try to meet his eyes this time.

'Of course,' he said with the hint of a frown between his dark brows, so perhaps her avoidance of his eyes had given away her uncertainty and, yes, just a touch of hurt that he seemed to think her so arrogant and self-satisfied.

'I won't allow masculine superiority as a defence, just because the rest of the world suffers from the delusion it actually exists, your lordship. To claim it, you'll have to prove you possess it,' she challenged him and finally managed to meet his silver-green gaze as if it cost her nothing but a coolly ironic smile.

'I'd be delighted to do so, when you finally manage to screw up sufficient courage to risk defeat at my hands, Miss Alstone,' he replied, making no attempt to mask a heat in his look that echoed the wolfish, challenging smile on his suddenly very tempting masculine mouth.

Feeling as if she'd already suffered a loss when her wildest fantasies centred on his lips as if they could unlock the secrets of the universe, Kate clenched her fists resolutely at her sides. Seeing the threat of an easy victory in his intent and suddenly very green gaze, she made herself hold it steadily, as if doing so cost her no effort at all. Hopefully only she knew her fingernails were threatening to bite through her kid gloves and into her soft palms as she clamped down on her more primitive instincts in the hope they might give up in the face of bleak reality.

'Don't flatter yourself, my lord,' she warned him softly.

'No need, when you've done it for me by refusing to pick up any of the challenges I cared to throw out in the past.'

'I am not a coward, and you're the one who retreated from the fight.'

Suddenly the air was crackling with something more than the slightly bitter teasing of two people who'd once had such promise of linking and entwining their lives, yet failed to take that vital step together. Kate's mouth felt inexplicably dry and her pulse was racing, but she made herself meet him glare for dare. Half-conscious they were in all too public a space for such a contest of wills and wishes, she still couldn't let her eyes fall modestly and step away from him. Giving an involuntary sigh as she continued to hold his jade-and-steel gaze without flinching, she allowed herself the small concession of licking her lips to slick their inexplicable dryness and marvelled at the feral heat that flared in his eyes as he changed from confident, taunting challenger to offer a darker and deeper world of sensual threat instead.

'I think you're going to miss the first waltz if you don't hurry, my dears.' Eiliane intruded a little too brightly on their silent, too-significant struggle for some victory Kate didn't even understand wanting to achieve so desperately in the first place.

'And what a shame that would be,' she managed to say as acerbically as everyone seemed to expect her to, even if her lips felt numb and her tongue oddly stiff in her parched mouth.

'Have you already promised yourself to someone else, Miss Alstone?' Edmund asked relentlessly, for some reason best known to him refusing to do what she fully expected him to and walk away to find the pretty little miss he'd been talking to earlier.

'No, but I dare say you have.'

'You'd be wrong and not for the first time then, so perhaps you'd best hurry up and join me for it, before we attract even more attention to ourselves,' he replied.

'I never dance with noblemen who order me to do so, attention or otherwise.'

'Then pray do us both the favour of joining me on the dance floor, before the tabbies make all sorts of mistaken assumptions about our tardiness, Miss Alstone,' he demanded more than asked.

Seeing that he was right and they were attracting far too much notice for comfort, she took his offered hand and let him lead her onto the floor, as if she could imagine nothing more pleasant than to dance with the rude, contradictory, disturbing man. Instead it felt as if he'd just snapped the tethers of the polite pretence that should have held them both in check and left them perilously adrift in a world where she had no bearings or familiar landmarks to chart it by.

'Why do you suddenly seem to hate me, my lord?' she heard herself ask as soon as they were launched into the dance. She was silently cursing herself for agreeing to be held so close to him, so curiously in sympathy considering their new antipathy and the odd fact that he'd never affected her like this in the past, when he'd just been a skilful partner who didn't tread on her toes.

'I don't hate you, Kate, would that I could,' he answered her with no hint of a smile to soften his hard-eyed scrutiny of her upturned face.

'Perhaps it would be easier,' she agreed rather wistfully.

'For you or for me?'

'For both of us.'

'Then you *are* a coward,' he murmured, but still he held her as if she was precious and their steps harmonised with such ease it felt as if they'd been born to dance together.

'How so?' she managed to murmur, fighting a stupid urge to lay her head on his shoulder and dream her way through this waltz, as if all that mattered was being held so close to him nothing could come between them. At least imagining how that shocking spectacle would appear was enough to stiffen her spine and make her set a little distance between them.

'If you ever find the courage to really look into that guarded heart of yours, Miss Alstone, you might find your answer to that question and a few others as well,' he informed her even as he twirled and confused her in time with the dance.

'I don't know what you mean,' she said, wishing she was in a position to cross her fingers against that uneasy lie, for she was beginning to wonder herself.

'I know, that's the pity of it all,' he responded rather grimly and they spent the rest of the dance in uneasy silence.

Their waltz was over too soon and not soon enough, so they could step away from each other at last with more than just physical space yawning between them. Kate marvelled at herself for being such a fool as to have refused to marry him so often in the past, even as the guarded part of her drew back and whispered he'd always ask too much of her, however many times he asked and she said no. She told herself to be grateful he'd had the sense to slash through whatever bonds bound them to each other three years ago. Yet it didn't feel right that they should now go their separate ways as if they'd never once mattered to each other. She hesitated ridiculously when he offered her his arm so distantly at the end of their dance, as though he were about to conduct someone he barely knew and didn't much like back to her chaperon.

She laid her fingers on his immaculately tailored coat sleeve and did her best to look undaunted and serene while a flash of hot and confusing warmth shot through her at the feel of such latent power beneath her fingertips. It was utterly ridiculous to feel intrigued by even so light a touch on his muscular arm, when she'd been more or less immune to his physical allure on first acquaintanceship. She was still struggling with this odd twist to their relationship that now left her more conscious of him than he was of her when they were rudely interrupted.

'What a delightful display that was, don't you agree, my love?' Lady Tedinton greeted them with apparent laziness as Kate and Edmund unwarily stepped off the dance floor and straight into her path.

'Oh, they'll need to practise for a few more years yet before they're even half as good at it as you are, my dear,' her husband replied and Kate could see how little her ladyship relished being lumped in with those who were accomplished and experienced, but no longer young, even if her husband seemed oblivious to her quick frown of displeasure.

'Practice makes perfect, don't you agree, Lord Shuttleworth?' the lady responded, avid hunger brazenly obvious in her heavy-lidded eyes as she ran them over him, as if testing his power as a lover and liking the idea of taking him as her current one a little too well, whatever their past relationship might be.

'Only until that perfection is achieved, my lady,' he said with a supremely elegant bow Kate thought was more an attempt to distance himself from the woman than offering her even a hint of encouragement.

'But if it's not properly maintained, even perfection can fade away from lack of application,' the lady murmured and Kate wondered at her daring, at the same time as she marvelled at her husband's wilful blindness to her true nature as she tried to joust with a potential lover under his very nose.

'A little imperfection always seems so much more human to me,' Edmund replied with a surprisingly warm look in Kate's direction that she decided was his way of subtly informing Lady Tedinton she was much less to him than she thought herself to be, since he'd just put Kate ahead of her and everyone knew they were no longer even friends.

'Yet no doubt surprisingly tedious after a while. A person of taste and refinement, not to mention experience, cannot find it easy to be burdened with a bungling amateur forced to strive for mastery of a set of skills that comes to others with almost instinctive ease. It must be tedious indeed to endure such gauche fumbling at such times,' her ladyship responded.

How so much malice could be directed at her with one heavy-eyed, apparently amused glance was almost beyond Kate. She was tempted to shrug her shoulders and make a polite excuse before drifting away with an absent farewell, but she owed Edmund more than that, even if he was confounding and confusing her more than she'd dreamt he could when she was three years younger and even more foolish.

'If one takes lessons from a fine teacher, they can be enormously stimulating for both pupil and educator in my experience,' she managed to defend herself as coolly as if she had no idea their three-way battle concealed a nasty set of double meanings that were all going straight over Lord Tedinton's head.

'Since I hear that your former governess used her position in a noble household to gain a rich and powerful husband, one can only suppose the less wary gentlemen among the *ton* need to be very careful indeed of those lessons, Miss Alstone,' her ladyship said with a faux smile only her husband would ever trust.

'Would it be her position as my governess, or that of the only grandchild and sole heiress to the Duke and Duchess of Devingham you intend to cite, my lady?' Kate said with such apparent pleasantness she was sure she heard her adversary's perfect white teeth snap together with impotent fury.

'Since the odd creature foolishly renounced the latter, then it must be the former, and what a very fine scheme it turned out to be,' Lady Tedinton said, letting temper flash out recklessly, as if she sensed her most coveted lover slipping out of her grasping fingers when Edmund's eyes iced over in obvious contempt.

'Sometimes,' he said with such chilly calm even Kate shivered, 'it takes an inveterate schemer to spot a careful plan where none ever existed, my lady.'

Since he also bowed to the apparently noble couple

with ceremonious elegance and an empty social smile, Lord Tedinton laughed and seemed as unaware of his lady's fury as he was that she was being subtly accused of being devious and spiteful.

'Indeed it does—now, are you going to honour me with that dance or not, my dear?' he said as brightly as if they were all getting along famously. 'After all, you lured me away from our duty of greeting belated guests on the promise of one, so we'd best join the next set and let them see exactly why we deserted them, eh?' he urged his wife indulgently.

Kate smothered a chuckle at her ladyship's barely masked impatience with his doglike devotion. The obnoxious female was already watching them with ill-concealed fury; presumably she wanted Edmund to share that devotion and hated Kate for being there to rescue him from her witchy wiles. If only the deluded female knew how little Edmund actually wanted Kate herself now, the awful woman would probably triumph and crow unbearably over her, she decided, sincerely hoping she could escape such an unpleasant encounter when Edmund's engagement to some dewy-eyed débutante was finally announced.

'What did you ever see in her?' she asked unwarily once their host and hostess had taken to the dance floor and the music was loud enough to mask her voice from an interested listener.

'Since you refused to become my wife more times than either of us care to be reminded, you have renounced all right to ask me that impertinent question, Miss Alstone. So I suggest you keep your arrogant opinions and any other ill-informed and ill-natured gossip you have garnered about me to yourself in the future,' he told her as icily as he'd just set down her ladyship and Kate knew she'd be on the verge of tears if she let herself risk such a public loss of control.

Biting her lower lip to keep it from wobbling, she nodded to him regally as words deserted her, but she refused to let her steps falter under his icy silver-green gaze, or show any sign that she was even conscious of Lady Tedinton's darts of dark-eyed resentment, as that lady barely even bothered to pretend her attention was centred on her husband or the dance.

'I wish you a good evening, my lord,' she managed to say expressionlessly enough as they neared Eiliane, who was gossiping happily with one of her cronies on the dark rose-coloured sofa that now reminded Kate almost insupportably of their hostess for the night.

She curtsied to him with formal grace, he bowed with almost as distant a hauteur as he'd used to depress her ladyship's pretensions and they parted before Eiliane had even spotted them returning together and been able to come up with a pretext for keeping them so.

'This must be one of the most tedious parties either of us ever had the poor judgement to attend, Kate,' her mentor greeted her cheerfully, once the friend she'd been so absorbed in pumping for the more interesting secrets of the *haut ton* had departed to bully some hesitant youth into dancing with her débutante daughter.

'Indeed,' Kate managed as she resorted to the small amount of cover allowed by her fan to conceal some of her confusion.

'You're overset, my love,' Eiliane exclaimed, even more concerned when the hectic colour in Kate's cheeks ebbed as she recalled Edmund's cold fury with her at even the mention of his rumoured *amour* with their hostess.

'I'll do well enough once I've got my breath back,' she managed to say calmly enough as she wondered why on earth she'd let her tongue run away with her in such an appalling fashion just because the very idea of Edmund making love to that vixen had made her feel ill.

'Nonsense, we'll call for our carriage and go home. I'll be glad of an early night and you look as if you could do with a week of them all of a sudden.'

'No!' Kate thought of how insufferably Lady Tedinton would triumph and smirk if she was weak enough to turn tail and go home like a whipped dog after that obnoxious encounter. 'I would rather stay a little longer and perhaps go on to Mrs Farnborough's as we had planned. That last dance was quite a vigorous one and I shall be perfectly fine in just a moment.'

'Will you, my love?' Eiliane asked shrewdly and Kate wished her a little less acute for once, but hoped her friend had no idea of the real reason why she was feeling so out of sorts and low spirited.

'Yes, I shall feel quite restored once I've had a rest. It would never do if I gained a reputation for giving myself die-away airs after all, for you'd never get me off your hands then,' she joked weakly. She refused to even consider the fact that it felt as if she'd never look at another man for the rest of her life and feel the least desire to marry him, or even stand up with him for a waltz after her bittersweet ones with Edmund had spoilt her expectations of any other partner.

She certainly refused all invitations to waltz for the rest of the evening, but brazened out the remainder of the pantomime it rapidly became to her. Seeing the daughter of the house dance with the suitable young gentleman she and Eiliane managed to throw into her path helped and, from Lady Tedinton's petulant expression, Kate thought her new enemy was probably having an even less satisfactory evening than she was. She allowed herself a brief smile of triumph when they finally left the Tedintons' ballroom, quite certain there was a metaphorical dagger in her back this time.

Chapter Five

'There it all is then, shipshape and neat as you like,' Ben Shaw, the other half of the firm of Stone & Shaw Shipping that he and Kit Alstone, now the latest Earl of Carnwood, had set up long before his lordship even dreamt of inheriting the family wealth and titles, informed Edmund the next day. As this came after an exhaustive tour of the warehouses and the new enclosed dock Stone & Shaw were building by the side of the one they'd already outgrown, then a return to the elegant offices they now kept in the City for a résumé of the firm's finances and projections for future profit, Edmund could only agree with him.

'Even I can see that for myself, thank you,' he told his formidable friend and business associate and wondered why Ben Shaw thought he needed reassurance that, while he was at the helm, Stone & Shaw would turn a fine profit for any investors lucky enough to be admitted into the select ranks of their stockholders.

'If you didn't come and see it all for yourself every now and again, I wouldn't have much respect for you as a man or an investor, and I dare say we'd never have done business together in the first place,' Ben told him.

'So long as I don't try to interfere in the way you run the enterprise from day to day, I presume?'

'Aye,' Ben admitted wryly, 'you've the measure of me on that front, my fine young lord, and that's plain to see.'

'Not as young as I was,' Edmund defended himself automatically, although such teasing bothered him much less than it had when he was first admitted into the august boardroom of Stone & Shaw, probably because he had been thought likely to become part of the family Ben Shaw protected and loved as fiercely as if they truly shared ties of blood, by marrying Kate Alstone.

Would his refusal to become part of that family, now he'd finally returned to the *ton* with the aim of taking a suitable wife who wasn't Miss Alstone, mean an end to such an unexpectedly comfortable and profitable friendship? If so, he'd regret it deeply, Edmund decided, and settled down for an excellent glass of burgundy and a companionable cigarillo, determined to enjoy them and this unlikely friend while he still had the chance.

'Speaking of your relative youth, or lack of it, when are you going to get down to the business of finally wedding and bedding that stubborn girl of ours?' Ben came straight out and asked the question Edmund had been dreading all morning.

'I'm not,' he admitted bravely, considering Ben was the largest and most formidably tough man Edmund had ever encountered and could probably mill him down without even having to break his stride.

Coming under the steady examination of a pair of grey eyes that suddenly looked as if they were determined to see into the very depths of a man's soul wasn't the most comfortable experience of Edmund's life, but he held his ground and managed not to sigh with relief when Ben sat back in his chair and watched him blandly instead of reaching for his neckcloth and attempting to strangle him with it. 'Because?' was all Ben said while considering this new state of affairs.

'I can't imagine a worse fate than being in love with a woman who merely tolerates me, especially if we were to be bound inextricably together for life, can you?' Edmund replied, thinking of the Tedintons and barely managing to hide a shudder at the idea of being trapped inside a marriage like that one.

'No,' Ben admitted, 'but it beats me why you've now decided she won't do when last time you were in town you were so madly in love with her you couldn't even consider wedding anyone else.'

'Beats me as well, but maybe I finally saw the truth of the matter, before she got so bored with turning me down that she decided to accept me just for a change of scenery.'

'I think you would have discovered you had underestimated her if she did so,' Ben said sagely and Edmund wondered if the unconventional giant did indeed know Kate Alstone far better than he did. He'd once lavished such minute attention on her every mood and gesture that it seemed a sad reflection on Edmund's judgement and so-called powers of observation if he'd failed to understand her after all that effort.

'No, for I won't ask her again, so the situation will not arise,' he insisted, denying himself the luxury to hope that he was wrong about her after all. 'I lost my taste for being a tame lapdog to her some time over these last three years.'

'Then if she weds another man, you'll be entirely indifferent?'

No! The certainty of it roared through him like a sudden bitter tempest on a summer day. He'd hate her, and the cur she married, until his dying day.

'Not entirely,' he admitted out loud.

'Not in the least, you young fool,' Ben informed him roughly. 'Had my Charlotte even threatened to promise herself to another man, I'd have torn him apart limb by limb and danced on his lousy body, then taken her to bed and loved her until she saw some sense. So either you don't love Kate and never have, or you still do and owe it to yourself and her not to end your life in Newgate dangling on the end of a hangman's rope. Although, I suppose in your case, my lord, it would be a jury of your peers and a silken noose at Tyburn instead of a hempen collar.'

Despite Ben's mockery of his rank and what he'd make of the stern resolution Edmund had made to find himself a suitable wife this year and forget Kate Alstone if he ever found out about it, Edmund didn't feel excluded from the select ranks of Ben Shaw's friends. Either the unconventional giant didn't believe Edmund could turn his back on his passion for the wretched female he'd once thought so firmly lodged in his heart he'd never shift her, or Ben was determined to stand his friend, irrespective of those other loyalties.

'I've no taste for martyrdom,' he admitted at last.

'As well Kit Alstone's occupied elsewhere, then, for he's a damned idiot when it comes to his precious family and those he truly loves. He might decide you've dishonoured Kate's good name and challenge you to a duel if you don't wed her after all, for if ever I met a hot-headed fool when he's in a temper, it's my lord Carnwood.'

'She's the one who turned me down time and again, not the other way around,' Edmund protested.

'Well, I did say he was a damned fool, didn't I?'

'And you think me one as well?'

'I never claimed to understand any of you great lords of creation and I can't say that a closer acquaintanceship with the two of you has improved what I already had very much.'

'And I don't see how you intend to get away with that hackneyed line any more, considering we all know who your father is now,' Edmund said with rash courage, for it was also common knowledge that Ben Shaw was no respecter of titles and ancient privilege.

'Let's hope the Marquis of Pemberley stays so busy with his new wife that he won't interfere with your plans then, whatever they are, for he's devilish fond of Kate as well,' Ben warned, discussing his natural father with an ease neither of them had ever thought to hear when he'd still been so convinced he hated his lordly sire.

'Aye, it's bad enough having his wife's attention fully fixed on me, without adding Lord Pemberley's eagle-eyed scrutiny to the mix—along with Lord and Lady Carnwoods' thrown in for good measure,' Edmund admitted ruefully.

'Don't delude yourself I'm too busy to interfere myself, will you?'

'I never delude myself that badly, but what beats me is why,' Edmund said.

'Because I don't believe you can really turn your back on the headstrong minx after you fell in love with the little devil at first sight, and don't forget I was there to see you behaving like a mooncalf when it happened, so don't try to deny it. I've met men who could cut themselves off from a woman they once cared for like that, as if she'd never existed or was cold in her grave, but you're not one of them. Kate cares for you more than either of you seem to know, and I don't think you're fool enough to turn aside from the magnificent female she'll become if she weds the right man, if only she'll just throw caution to the wind and accept you at long last.'

'Thank you for thinking I am that man, but I'd have to be fool enough to ask her first. So what holds her back from being that woman anyway then, Ben?'

'And you once claimed to be in love with her?' Ben said with a hint of scorn in his deep voice that made Edmund flinch, despite knowing it was Kate who had been so set against falling in love once upon a time rather than he. 'I can't but marvel at fine young gentlemen who call infatuation love, then flit from girl to girl, like strutting peacocks waving their tail feathers, with not a worthwhile thought in their silly heads.'

'I certainly thought myself in love with her three years ago, until she convinced me it was hopeless; if that makes me vain and idle, then so be it.'

Ben gave Edmund another of those searching glances, then nodded as if making up his mind about something. 'I never really thought you guilty of those vices, so Kate obviously made a fine fist of whistling your mutual happiness down the wind, but have you ever stopped being furious with her long enough to wonder why?'

'No, I just realised my one-sided love would make our lives a farce, even if I managed to persuade her to say yes instead of no in some moment of weakness.'

'If you really loved her, you wouldn't have given up at the first hurdle.'

'Hardly that.' Edmund was stung into justifying himself as he looked back over that wild springtide when they'd both been painfully young and he'd been alternately effervescent with hope and cast into the depths of despair by Kate's inability to see how finely suited they could be, in bed and out, if only she'd open her eyes and see the rich possibilities of it all.

'I grant you she's stubborn and can be damnably difficult to either drive or lead at times,' Ben conceded.

'Difficult? She's nigh impossible,' Edmund told him with a bitter exasperation he thought he'd conquered, but it seemed that his friend was right and he still had strong feelings toward Kate Alstone, even if foremost among them was currently vexation, closely followed by something darker and angrier and born of three wasted years apart that he refused to examine more closely right now.

'There are one or two good reasons why she's not exactly the easiest female to live with at times,' Ben said almost apologetically, which in itself was enough to render Edmund momentarily speechless.

He shook his head over what those reasons might be and must have looked as puzzled as he felt. 'I can't imagine what they might be,' he replied at last.

'Then apply the brains God gave you and use your imagination, Edmund. Have you ever stopped to wonder how you might feel if you were brought up as a much-loved and indulged child of a happy family instead of a noble and indulged orphan? Then imagine that, one by one, you lost every person in the world who was dear to you one way and another, all but your little sister, whom you then had to fight like a tiger to protect from the suddenly hostile world around you. Kate and Isabella Alstone lost their parents, their brother and, to all intents and purposes, their elder sister in quick succession when Kate was little more than ten years old. Their grandfather, who should have protected them both and loved them all the more, was so wrapped up in his own selfish grief and fury at the fates that he abandoned those two little girls to the so-called care of his daughter, Lady Ennersley, and *her* daughter, and I wouldn't trust either with my pet dog, let alone the comfort and education of two innocent and supposedly helpless young girls.

'Take my word for it, Edmund, those two unnatural females are the worst harpies I ever met, and I was brought up near the rookeries and certainly know a harpy when I see one. They constantly belittled and even beat Kate and threatened to do the same to her little sister, except Kate used to get in their way so they couldn't reach her, which of course meant that they chastised her instead. They also robbed them of all those two little girls held dear, refusing to let them even see Eiliane Rhys as she was then. I know my darling stepmama tried time and again to wrench them both out of their icy grasp, but old Carnwood ignored the plight of his own grandchildren and refused to do anything to stop his daughter or the devil's spawn she gave birth to making their lives a misery for far too long.

'Those two heartless witches told them he hated them for living when his son and then their brother died and maybe they were even right, for he never made any effort to look to their welfare until it became more comfortable to act on Eiliane's constant nagging to at least send them to school rather than to refuse to do so. Their aunt and cousin also managed to convince Kate that nobody but the servants cared what became of them, and that even they only gave a damn what happened to them because they were paid to. If not for my darling wife, Shuttleworth, those girls would have remained alienated and adrift even at the school their old fool of a grandfather eventually sent them to, solely to get them out of his way and to stop Eiliane's constant letters and enquiries about them, and calm the hornet's nest she stirred up among his wider family to shame him into action.

'Now *I* respect Charlotte's judgement and my own instincts well enough to be certain there are very deep and passionate feelings hidden behind Kate's cool façade, even if you can't see it. To the wider world she's a confident and desirable young beauty with riches and privileges at her fingertips most young women would envy her, but if that's all you see when you look at her, Edmund Worth, maybe you don't deserve her after all. You might be better off with a less complex and difficult woman if you're merely in search of an easy life with a conformable wife who'll exclaim over your cleverness hourly and give birth to a pack of spineless brats you can hand your wealth and titles on to before you finally die of boredom.'

Perhaps as a fortunate, if often lonely, orphan he *had* been guilty of envying Miss Katherine Alstone her loving family and so had failed to look beyond the cool indifference with which she met the eyes of the world. He knew better than to dismiss the counsel of a man he respected, Edmund decided, and neither could he ignore the opinion of Ben's wife, a woman of such extraordinary character, integrity and unusual looks that he couldn't help but admire her, from a safe distance.

'Maybe I'm *not* the man you take me for, and perhaps I don't deserve Kate Alstone as I should if I can't gain her love, but I never managed to knock down that wall of touch-me-not indifference you claim she's hiding behind, Ben, even when I was trying my damnedest to demolish it.'

'I suppose you know what they say about faint heart not winning fair lady?'

'All very well, but three years ago my doglike devotion did nothing to win her affection or convince her she can trust me. I hope you don't expect me to sit at her feet for another three, risking being kicked aside every time she wonders if another pet might not suit her better.'

'Maybe she doesn't want a pet in the first place, then.'

'What does she want then, man? I'm damned if I know any more.'

'Just that—she wants a man and not a lapdog. She's a sensible female and finds them pettish and yappy and who can blame her? I'm relieved my wife has never shown any sign of falling for the breed.'

'From what I can tell she just adopts strays, and the larger and uglier the better.'

Edmund recalled his visit to their eccentric household last week with a reminiscent grin. Mrs Shaw had lately taken in a hound of very mixed breeding and huge size, who bayed at all her visitors and buried his bones under her best furniture, whilst protecting her and hers from all and sundry, even though she didn't actually stand in need of any protection so far as he could see.

'My point exactly,' the lady's husband agreed smugly.

Edmund wondered what the *ton* would make of the son of a marquis, even one born the wrong side of the blanket, who smugly claimed kinship with a mongrel of the most mixed variety and dubious origins. Possibly Ben's very indifference to his own blue blood, and most of his father's peers along with it, explained why he wasn't just tolerated, but lionised by all but the most stiff-necked of them. It seemed to him that there was nothing quite so intriguing to most of the *ton* as someone so genuinely unimpressed by their elegant show and lofty traditions as Ben Shaw appeared to be.

'So next time I call on Miss Alstone, you think I should growl menacingly at all other visitors who dare to enter Lady Pemberley's drawing room?' Edmund asked with a rueful grin. 'Then perhaps I could pin any gentlemen I don't like the look of up against the wall with teeth bared, whilst I attempt to bay loudly at the same time and dribble down their shirt fronts or all over their precious Hessians while I'm doing it?'

'If you could leave out the drooling, that will probably go down better,' Ben said with a reminiscent shudder and Edmund almost pitied him that aspect of the over-enthusiastic Prometheus, as Charlotte had christened her latest waif.

'Maybe, but I am what I am, Ben, and have never been good at pretending to be otherwise, I'm afraid,' Edmund admitted ruefully, almost ashamed of himself for lacking the guile to storm and bluster sufficiently to gain Kate's attention at last.

'No need, you're rich, titled and personable, Shuttleworth, so why would you need to be other than what you are? Just show Kate how much you've grown up since you fell all of an adoring heap at her feet three years ago. Make her see that you've become your own man while she wasn't paying attention before you give up on her, that's all I'm suggesting.'

'All?' Edmund echoed faintly, but he grinned at his unexpected mentor just the same and left after an interesting as well as an enlightening morning in a thoughtful frame of mind.

It might have been possible to set his face against the very idea of loving Kate and abhor her inability to see what was in front of her pert nose when he was a hundred miles from her and spare her incendiary presence, Edmund admitted to himself as he walked away from Stone & Shaw's neat offices. He might even have found a sweet and biddable wife to put in her place if only she'd stayed away this Season. Kate was too near now; too real and right in front of him night after night, proving how much less life with that sweet little wife would be than one with her. Maybe it wouldn't be fair to offer another woman so little when she might find an untainted young spark to make little paragons with instead. And how could less ever be good enough, despite his three-year-old resolution never to let Kate Alstone trample roughshod over his dreams again?

Despite the vow he'd made to himself to forget her, he still yearned for her in his bed and at his board night after night in his dreams and in his deepest, darkest fantasies. If he couldn't beat his obsession with her, why not use it to trap her with her own scheming? He'd seen her summing up the young bloods and even the personable widowers in search of a wife to look after their restless and motherless broods and had wanted to strangle her for looking about her for a suitable, coldly selected, unloved husband. Still, he might be able to use her stubborn misreading of her own character and get her up the aisle before she realised they could never be so little to each other if they both lived to be ninety.

Hadn't apparent indifference got him a lot further already than devotion ever had? He recalled the feel of the sway and dip of her lush but streamlined body against his in the dance and gave a reminiscent grin. If she was to be lured out of her ivory tower, wasn't he already halfway to tumbling her into his arms instead? With such a promising start he'd be a fool if he failed to draw the real Kate even further out from behind those defensive barriers of hers.

The prospect of a future he'd resigned himself never to achieve was heady, but the last thing he wanted to do was risk more humiliation at Kate's hands. Next time he asked her to marry him he'd make quite certain the skittish redheaded torment was ready to say yes at last. So there had to be a very long way to go before he could be sure his last offer was met with eagerness, rather than the absent-minded kindness she might show a boot-boy who'd spilled lamp oil on the furniture and was being tiresomely emotional about the whole tedious business of clearing it up.

Edmund had walked through the City and into Mayfair, probably only escaping being robbed because he'd dressed plainly for his trip round Ben's empire. Potential thieves took one look at such a distracted gentleman and decided he was either mad and too much trouble to bother with, or a poet or an artist caught up by his muse and therefore too poor to be worthwhile. He'd experienced such a revolution of feelings since he'd set out from it this morning that he got back to Worth House in Grosvenor Square only to find he couldn't settle to anything, so he took his favourite hack out in an attempt to calm his seesawing feelings instead.

Did he really love Kate Alstone? That was the question that trumped all the others, he decided, as the black gelding finally won free of the mêlée and Edmund allowed him a little more freedom. Deciding it wasn't too late to ride into the countryside to avoid the curious and the sociable when the evenings were drawing out and there was a moon tonight anyway, he set the powerful animal on the road to Richmond and tried to keep at least half his mind on their going.

When he'd first met her, perhaps he'd still felt less than other men, because he was the last of his line and couldn't join one of Wellington's regiments to fight Bonaparte, or follow Ben Shaw and the Earl of Carnwood's example and forge his way by his own efforts. Even as a boy he'd known he couldn't leave his land and his people masterless and abandoned to the uncaring hands of the Crown as the Prince Regent, with his voracious appetites and gargantuan debts, would strip every asset the Worths had built up so diligently over centuries, then sell it piecemeal to whoever offered the most money.

Had his secret insecurity, when he'd been forced to turn his back on the army he'd once longed to join and dutifully go to Oxford instead, made him doubt himself, until he'd felt Kate's rejections were all he really deserved? If it had led him astray about himself and the woman he wanted to love for life, then he cursed it. Ben Shaw's shrewd summary of Kate's well-hidden fears and insecurities had made him see at last why she might hold back from love, or any other emotion that would leave her vulnerable to hurt. He raged against the very thought of how badly hurt she had been and fervently wished he'd been the one to punish those two she-devils instead of Kit Alstone. Everyone knew he'd banished the old earl's daughter to a remote estate and ordered her to stay there on pain of losing even that, and the lady's daughter had been told to live abroad with the secret husband she'd apparently been wed to ever since her seventeenth birthday, despite her subsequent and bigamous marriage to another man.

So why hadn't Edmund had the confidence to see through Kate's almost absent-minded tolerance of her eager court and him in particular when they'd first met? What excuse did that young sprig have for not looking into her dark blue Alstone eyes and finding the real Kate she still hadn't dared to fully become lurking under all that wary indifference? That Kate was lion-hearted and passionate and he wanted her fierce protection and all that pent-up love she was so wary of giving for his children, and a share of that last commodity for himself as well, or he'd end up envying them and that would never do.

Well, he could see her now and had her firmly in his sights at last. He was his own man now, too, and if not the dashing hero he'd once dreamt of being, he was strong enough to shoulder his responsibilities and even enjoy them most of the time. He'd got his estates running at a healthy profit and restored the depleted fortune managed, or mismanaged, by his various trustees until his majority, so if he could take on all that and succeed, why not have one last, reckless throw at winning the woman he's always wanted above all others as well?

He grinned at the memory of how he'd managed to confuse Kate recently without even trying; now he was in earnest, keeping her off balance and paying attention long enough to claim her heart and her hand suddenly didn't seem so unlikely after all.

Chapter Six

'*What* a brilliant catch Lord Shuttleworth will make some lucky girl, now he's obviously looking out for a more *suitable* wife,' Kate heard one of the chaperons behind her whisper rather loudly to her crony a week or so later and knew perfectly well that she was meant to hear every word. After all, she had refused to marry the lady's impecunious elder son in no uncertain terms at the end of last Season and that did put a doting mama off a girl rather badly.

It was true, of course, that she'd watched Edmund dance with all the prettiest and most eligible débutantes the Season rejoiced in night after night and could vouch for the fact that, while all seemed to agree he was a very fine gentleman and would make an even finer husband, some were shamelessly eager to march him up the aisle of St George's, Hanover Square, at the double.

'Indeed, my dear—he's so rich, so well born and *so* handsome that he's without a doubt the finest catch to be had this Season,' another lady, who persisted in thinking Kate had deliberately eclipsed her elder daughter's début, and blamed her for that poor girl having to marry a mere mister with only two large country estates and a town house to his name, asserted. 'The Tedinton woman seems quite set on cuckolding her poor husband with him, but that won't bar him from marrying well. My dear little Felicity is too young yet, but your girl hasn't made enough effort to captivate such an eligible young lord up to now, my dear; you should remind her of her duty to her family.'

'Darling Charity is quite determined on her Mr Holt and he on her, so Henry will agree to the match in the end, I dare say, and Lord Shuttleworth can marry where he pleases so far as I'm concerned,' the first lady replied placidly enough, since Mr Holt was commonly held to be a very wealthy man and she was obviously a realist.

'It's a well enough match, I suppose, but Shuttleworth would make a very fine feather in any mama's cap,' the second said wistfully.

'Especially Lady Tedinton's,' the first lady said with a shrewd and significant nod in the languorous and lovely Countess of Tedinton's direction.

'That, my dear, rather depends on whether she's intent on wearing him on her bonnet or her sleeve,' her friend replied with heavy significance.

'Surely not even she would do that, especially during her daughter's come-out Season when it would be more fitting if he caught the chit rather than the mother?'

'The girl's only her stepdaughter, don't forget, and

not ten years younger than the painted hussy her father married in some fit of madness. Tedinton should have known it would end in disaster once he'd made such a ridiculous second marriage.'

'That woman can't pull the wool over the ladies' eyes, even if the gentlemen hang on every word that falls from her painted lips. She's little more than a strumpet and not a very well-bred one at that.'

'I pride myself on always being able to read a person's true nature, despite any shoddy façades they may care to throw up to confuse people. Even Tedinton won't be able to fool himself her affairs and her low appetites don't exist for ever, for all that she's a beauty.'

'True, but she's nowhere near as clever as she thinks she is. The woman has risen too high and now thinks she can have whatever, or whomever, she wants. Such arrogance will prove her downfall one fine day and it won't be a moment too soon for me when she tried to condescend to me last time we crossed each other's paths.'

'Well, I doubt she'll try it twice, my dear, but there's no mistaking exactly what, or rather whom, she wants right now,' the other lady replied meaningfully. Lady Tedinton was watching her stepdaughter chatter animatedly with Lord Shuttleworth whilst reclining on a nearby sofa and eyeing him as if she'd like to pounce and never mind how many spectators saw her do it.

'Her thoughts are written all over her face, for all she thinks we're too stupid to read them, yet he looks more entranced by the girl. Tedinton would be a fool to turn down such a match on the say-so of a wife who wants Shuttleworth herself. So that match would put the cat among the pigeons, and set others with their eye on him in their place once and for all,' the first lady said sweetly.

Kate did her best to look serenely unconscious of their spite while she fervently hoped they were wrong. She wasn't well acquainted with the girl, but she was pretty enough and might be charming as well for all she knew. However, she was clearly no equal match for Edmund Worth. He deserved a woman who wouldn't bore him before the honeymoon was over and, if he met that lady, Kate supposed she'd have to shrug her shoulders and look about her for that perfect husband a little more diligently than she was doing at the moment.

'Certain ladies need to realise that it's never wise to be too finicky and risk coming back Season after Season, don't you agree, dear?' the second of her detractors continued relentlessly, with a significant nod in Kate's direction she pretended not to see.

'Luckily our darling girls are in no danger of finding out that pert opinions and overweening vanity will almost certainly land them on the shelf for good.'

'Quite—I never could abide such precocious chits myself,' her friend agreed while Kate planned their imminent demise in minute and purely theoretical detail, to keep from verbally grinding them under her chariot wheels as her restless temper demanded she must.

'Our dance,' pronounced Mr Cromer concisely at just the right moment to stop her leaping to her own defence in a reckless fashion.

'Indeed,' Kate replied gratefully, having come to

value his sparse conversation over the last weeks, as he
began to court Miss Transome in earnest.

Who would have dreamt a few years ago that Amelia
Transome and Kate Alstone would ever come to enjoy
each other's company so much, when each had eyed the
other during their début and decided they had little in
common? Now Kate valued Amelia's kind heart and
generous nature and wondered at herself for not seeing
past her chatter and fluttery manner before. And at least
Amelia regarded Mr Cromer dancing with Kate as the
lesser of two evils, since she couldn't dance every dance
with him herself. In her company at least he wasn't being
giggled over or eyed speculatively by one of the eager
newcomers or their husband-hunting mamas, and Kate
felt at ease with at least one of her dancing partners,
so all three were content. Yet Mr Cromer had a good
friend in Lord Shuttleworth and every now and then
Kate would glance up and find him standing by the
other gentleman's side and watching her, as unreadable
as he was unsmiling while he did so. His lordship hadn't
asked her to dance again and she told herself that she
was relieved.

'Shuttleworth ain't serious about that chit, y'know?'
Mr Cromer informed her during one of the country
dances.

'He gives a very good impression of it, then,' she
replied, just as if she had every right to feel bitter, which
she most certainly did not.

'Chivalrous to a fault, always was. Easing her path
into society quiets his conscience, I suppose.'

Then it was true. Edmund *had* been Lady Tedinton's

lover and evidently he still felt guilty about that and, considering the wretched woman was another man's wife, so he should. How could he have fallen for that heartless female's overblown charms? No, there was no need to wonder about *that*; Kate only had to flick a look at the sultry beauty doing her best to look faintly amused by her stepdaughter and his lordship to know exactly why a gentleman would find such lazy sensuality irresistible.

Yet Kate thought from the downward curve of her pouting lips that the lady was secretly furious at his defection. Turning the situation over in her mind, Kate shivered as she contemplated the sort of marriage she'd fooled herself she wanted. The very idea of casually following in the footsteps of Lady Tedinton and taking lovers once she'd borne Edmund's heirs made her want to weep now. Then, imagining how she'd feel if they'd actually wed and she'd found out about the exotic Lady Tedinton afterwards, she felt a strong temptation to go into strong hysterics. So maybe it was as well this was neither the time nor place to consider what her revulsion at the very idea said about her own feelings toward Edmund Worth.

'Bestholme,' Mr Cromer remarked obscurely after they'd finished their dance and he was escorting her back to where Eiliane and Miss Transome were sitting.

'Yes?' Kate said encouragingly.

'Fortune hunter,' he warned with a shake of his head for emphasis.

'Ah, I thought so,' she said with a grateful smile.

It set the cap on a hateful evening that Mr Bestholme

seemed even more desperate to corner her attention when she refused to take to the dance floor with him. He besieged her with sly comments and overfamiliar touches whenever he could force himself closer to her by using the crush of guests as an excuse and if she didn't get away from his damp, cruel hands and hungry eyes soon she was going to be sick. Eventually she disgusted herself by taking to her heels and fleeing his far-too-persistent and public pursuit, even resorting to the ladies' withdrawing room where even he wouldn't have the gall to follow her.

Sure the man would think nothing of compromising her into marriage if that was the only way he could get his repellent hands on her fortune, she quit her temporary sanctuary and trespassed into the private part of the house to plan a rapid retreat to Derbyshire and the safety of Kit's fearsome protection, if her determined evasion of Mr Bestholme didn't persuade the human leech she wasn't going to be tricked, pressured or just plain forced into marriage.

It seemed a coward's way out even to her, but it sounded so tempting after the last few weeks of disappointed hopes and mistaken dreams. To be in Derbyshire with spring softening even the starkly beautiful peaks with its lovely bounty, to breathe in good clean air and be able to ride all day without having to be civil to a soul if she didn't choose to meet one, seemed like heaven just at the moment. And what a relief it would be to escape the nagging feeling that three years ago she'd turned away the one man who could have made leaving her beloved Wychwood for a new life as his wife and mother of his children a wonderful adventure, rather than an impossible sacrifice.

Yet even while she was searching through possible excuses for running away, mentally planning her journey and thinking up a story that would convince Kit and Miranda when she got home that she was perfectly well and happy, just jaded with London and the social Season, she knew she couldn't do it. There were her detractors to outface and, more important than any of them, there was Izzie, who would be here very soon—how could Kate not be here to witness her little sister's social triumphs and enjoy her lively company once more? It might hurt far too much that Edmund had decided to look elsewhere for a bride and a lover, but she was an Alstone and would not turn tail and run at the first setback put in her path by unkind fate.

There was Eiliane to consider as well, of course, and, come to think of it, she was oddly distracted tonight and unlike her usual sharp-eyed self for some reason. Her chaperon had hardly seemed to notice Bestholme's increasingly bizarre behaviour tonight and Kate frowned as she wondered belatedly if there was something seriously wrong with her dear friend and mentor. Then she had her two newest friends to see safely wed, of course, and Amelia Transome had gallantly deployed her most determined chatter on Kate's behalf tonight in a selfless way that commanded equal loyalty. Even Mr Cromer had put his stalwart silence between her and Mr Bestholme as often as he could without seeming too particular himself, but nothing had put the awful man off his single-minded pursuit of her fortune.

Kate could practically hear the ill-natured gossip breaking out all around her if she went back into the ballroom to make sure her chaperon wasn't sickening for something. Awarding herself five minutes of peace and quiet would do no harm, she assured herself cravenly, and stole on through the half darkness of the private rooms of their host and hostess's town house with a guilty sense of playing truant from reality and fortune hunters, as well as intruding on their privacy.

Edmund eyed the assembled company and almost wished he'd stayed in Herefordshire this Season after all. Yet the fine hairs on the nape of his neck were prickling as if trying to warn him of some danger the rest of him was slow to pick up. Lady Tedinton, with her silly pretence that he had already been her lover and would shortly be so again, was a damnably inconvenient complication he'd certainly not bargained for and he'd had to waste far too much time tonight avoiding her very obvious lures and any hint he might be susceptible to them. He did his best not to meet *her* gaze as he searched the room in vain for a glimpse of Kate's glorious red curls, but something told him he'd soon have to take the time and trouble to convince Selene Tedinton once and for all that she meant nothing to him and never would, in terms even she couldn't misinterpret as part of the game she so loved to play.

'Something's amiss,' Cromer informed him brusquely as he joined him with a worried frown on his face.

'There's always scheming afoot at affairs like this

one,' Edmund responded coolly, even if his friend's unease only added to his own.

'Miss Transome claims that Lady T. and Bestholme are up to something,' Cromer said with resigned acceptance that Amelia's sayings and doings were more important to him than he'd dreamed they could be until recently.

'Any idea what?' Edmund asked, suddenly very interested in them as well.

'Don't know. Unholy pair at the best of times. Welcome to each other, except the Tedinton woman keeps looking at Miss Alstone as if she'd like to kill her slowly, then stamp on her grave. Miss Transome's convinced the woman's hatching a scheme to put Miss Alstone out of the picture for good so far as you're concerned.'

'She's mistaken her adversary then,' Edmund said curtly.

'Or her quarry.'

'Yes, she couldn't be more wrong there,' Edmund replied softly.

'Going to stand here gossiping all night, then?' Cromer prompted.

'No, I'll deal with the harpy in my own good time, after I've tracked down Miss Alstone and seen her safely back to her chaperon's side once more.'

'Aye, she's been gone too long for her own good. You go and find out where she's up to and we'll cover your backs as best we can.'

'Thank you, the confounded woman is a damned nuisance at the best of times and this isn't one of them,' he said grimly. 'Sometimes I'd like to strangle her.'

'Better marry her as soon as possible instead—obviously made for each other,' his friend said with understated irony that was currently wasted on Edmund as he fumed at Kate's protracted absence.

'I'll think about it,' Edmund said tersely and with a casual look about him to locate the Marchioness of Pemberley and Bestholme, who was, luckily for him, still in the ballroom and not pursuing Kate around the half-lit gardens or goodness only knew where else she might be hiding herself.

Satisfied Kate's chaperon was engrossed with old friends now and blissfully unaware that anything was amiss, he left by way of the card room as if he hadn't a care in the world, even as he fought an irrational fury that Kate hadn't come to him for help instead of bolting for the shadows. After searching the quieter rooms of their host's residence, he was beginning to think trouble existed in Miss Transome's overheated imagination when he caught the faint, unmistakable scent of Kate Alstone lingering in an otherwise deserted corridor leading towards his host's library. He stilled his already near-silent footfall and listened for any further sign of the elusive, overly independent female.

Despite knowing very well she should return to the ballroom and prepare to endure a whole evening of dodging Bestholme as stoically as she had it in her to manage, Kate had wandered furtively on through private rooms she knew very well she shouldn't intrude into. The farther she got from the ball, the more she felt like a hind with the noise and threat of hounds and huntsmen fading behind her and the harder she found it to turn about and go back. She scoured a dark room for unexpected fortune hunters and allowed herself a huge sigh of relief once her eyes adjusted to the darkness and she still found no sign of the repulsive creature—nor any hidden galleries or dangerously secluded corners he might spring out from.

Sinking into a snug high-backed chair by the unlit fire, she wondered if the lady of the house sat there to embroider or read whilst her husband laboured over his speeches in the House of Lords, which were apparently earnest, detailed and well intentioned, but guaranteed to empty that august chamber almost as fast as a cry of fire. It made a rather appealing picture of two lives entwining over the years so that, even if she didn't share his interest in politics, her ladyship sat and kept her lord company whilst he pursued one. Shifting in her chair, Kate wondered if Eiliane had been right all along. Maybe marriage wasn't a military campaign from which all emotion must be sternly banished and all hope of anything better shorn ruthlessly away in case it proved false.

Too late for such a conclusion to make any difference to her situation, she decided sadly, but she still felt irrationally betrayed by Edmund's defection when she had absolutely no right to. Such a shame that she'd spurned him so emphatically during her first heady Season, when she'd been too young to realise just what wonderful possibilities were being offered her and grab them with both hands. Now he was so indifferent to her it felt as if some long-anticipated treat had been withdrawn and her life was suddenly limited and dry for the lack of it. Squirming in her comfortable seat, Kate braved an answer to so many of the questions troubling her and it only made matters worse. Edmund, who no longer wanted her, who despised her for turning him away, who seemed determined to court a sweet and suitable wife not in the least bit like Kate Alstone—somehow he mattered uniquely to her and it was obvious to anyone who had two eyes to see with that she no longer meant a thing to him.

Cursing her younger self for refusing to see that he'd make her an ideal husband and lover, Kate felt unable to just sit and contemplate her own idiocy and jumped to her feet to pace restlessly. She couldn't put her hand on her heart and admit it was irrevocably his and therefore broken beyond mending and, as he now watched her with hard disillusionment instead of adoration in his silver-green eyes, that was just as well. Yet Kate had an uncomfortable suspicion she'd been testing Edmund's devotion from the moment they first met, and considering it had proved such a chimera, maybe she'd been right not to trust it enough to agree to marry him.

Doing her best to be honest with herself now her future looked bleak, Kate stopped her perambulations and tried to face her own faults as unflinchingly as she was prepared to pick over Edmund Worth's. Impatient with herself for being unable to consider him, or her feelings for him, with dispassionate coolness, she was about to pace her host's fine Persian carpet when a sound in the corridor outside made her freeze in her tracks. Just making out the soft tread of a gentleman's evening shoes on the marble floor outside, Kate muted a huff of impatient fury and turned to face the wretch who'd been chasing her all evening with defiant determination and the fireside poker.

'Preparing to beat me off with more than just words this time, are you, my dear?' the intruder asked her blandly and relief and something far warmer than that ran through her at the very sound of Edmund's voice. It made her feel young and silly all of a sudden as she had to put her hand over her mouth to stifle a chuckle.

'Only if you really annoy me, Lord Shuttleworth,' she said, her heartbeat thundering in her ears for a very different reason now and her fear flying as wild curiosity about darkened rooms and their unknown possibilities took its place.

'Maybe you should carry it at all times to fend off importunate suitors then?' he said as he took it gently from her and returned it to its stand.

'I can think of at least one person I'd like to leave with a few good bruises,' Kate said darkly and saw him frown even in the semi-darkness.

'Just say the word and I'll do it for you.'

'And then be forced to meet the repellent man at dawn as if he deserved to be rated a gentleman after all, my lord? I rather think not,' she told him crossly and just the thought of him risking all he was to a pistol ball made her insides go as cold as if she'd swallowed an icicle.

'I can take care of myself,' he told her abruptly.

'I dare say you can, but I'll manage without your assistance on that front all the same. I do like to sleep at nights, you see?'

'So do I, although you've robbed me of a great deal of that commodity since we first met,' he informed her softly and Kate realised how close he suddenly was to her only at the instant when he slid a strong arm round her waist and pulled her against his muscular frame so easily it hardly even occurred to her that she might resist him.

'Have I? How very inconsiderate of me, Edmund,' was all the response she seemed able to offer, which was very odd of her, considering she'd come in here to avoid similar attentions from another man.

'Yes, it was. So don't you think it's high time you shared a little of my sleeplessness to make amends?' he murmured huskily.

'Maybe…' she began, but it was too late and he stopped her mouth by the simple strategy of kissing it until she forgot what she was going to say and almost everything else as well.

Chapter Seven

At the advanced age of one and twenty Kate had experienced only the most respectful of chaste salutes to compare this one with and they were no help at all, she decided hazily. She supposed having such a powerful guardian hovering like Nemesis in the background must have kept her ignorant of such dangerous delights until now. If Edmund had kissed her like this three years ago, she'd almost certainly have been married to him virtually ever since, but had either of them been ready for such heady enchantment then? It was a question she'd never be able to answer since he hadn't kissed her until her wits were shot and her body singing with some wild hope she didn't dare name until tonight. Abandoning any effort to reason with herself, she snuggled even closer to him, whilst raising too-willing lips to lure him back to her the moment he seemed about to recover his senses and back away.

'Edmund,' she murmured his name reproachfully,

protesting any distance between them and wantonly hoping he could be persuaded to do it again.

'Katherine?' he replied, lingering on the syllables of her name as if it was a sensuous luxury in his mouth.

'Kiss me again?' she begged shamelessly.

So he did and this time there was nothing reverent and respectful about his wickedly knowing mouth as it opened hungrily on hers and, as soon as she echoed him in instinctive response, he plundered it ruthlessly. For the first time Kate felt the true allure of being seduced as well as seducing, with a man's firm mouth and hot demands suddenly a wonderful promise, rather than a threat of terrible vulnerability or base subjection. She shivered in anticipation of something even more mighty, a force that could take her under and drown her in passion and sweetness, so she did her best to make sure she attained it by sneaking her hands up and about Edmund's strong neck, then shocking them both by moaning against his lips when his tongue invaded her mouth and her knees turned to water.

It was heat and light and sustenance and she couldn't currently imagine ever needing any other. He ran lingering, approving hands down the supple line of her slender back and she all but purred with satisfaction when he reached the firm swell of her buttocks and settled there for a hot, breathless moment before he swept that incendiary touch back up to mould her even closer into his kiss. Gasping with delight as his wicked tongue darted in and out of her wanton mouth in a rhythm even she recognised as primal, for all her ridiculous innocence, she clung as if he was her rock in a very stormy sea indeed.

Then he allowed them the sumptuous treat of lowering his hand to cup her breast and Kate wondered how she managed to stay standing for the rush of heat and temptation that rocked through her like a force of nature. She heard his breath catch at the willingness of her tightened nipples, obvious under the richness of silk and his exploring fingers and she stuttered out a sigh of delight when he explored one of them further until she moaned once again. All thought of where they were and what risks they were taking of being discovered fled as even the distant sound of music faded from her consciousness and all that mattered to her was him. Edmund, her almost-promised lover, hers. At last there were no questions in her head except for how soon the searing ache at the heart of her could be appeased with something he and no other could grant her. Caught up in her first taste of headlong, driven passion, she keened softly at the bolt of demand for more that ran through her like hot fire.

Head reeling from her innocently erotic responses to his runaway loss of control, as soon as he felt her mouth respond to his with untutored enthusiasm, Edmund tried hard to draw back, to let his longing hands fall from her magnificent body and put distance between them that his own harder, even more eager body certainly didn't want.

'No, stay,' she urged, her voice husky and shaky and utterly in tune with every one of his feral instincts to possess her and carry her off to his lair and keep her there for ever. 'Kiss me again,' she demanded, so lost in what they'd set alight between them that he doubted she remembered her own name, let alone his.

'If I do there will be no going back for either of us,' he managed to grate out between lips stiff with wanting and needing to do exactly what she demanded.

'Edmund,' she whispered and it was an agreement, not a denial.

Triumph roared through him as his body tightened even more painfully. He struggled to leash his own out-of-control instincts and the need he'd kept under such a mighty curb ever since he'd met her in the face of her suddenly so wild, so natural, so truly Kate-like urgency. The lure of lowering her on their host's fine carpet and thrusting into the warmth and welcome she was innocently laying out for him tempted him until it felt like too much of an effort, too much of a betrayal not to give in and take her to their mutual ecstasy.

He tensed to do as they both wanted and seize her by that ridiculously slender waist of hers and soothe and stoke her passion until neither of them had any choice but to let themselves sink onto the floor of this room in a stranger's house and rut like a pair of spring-tortured animals. He'd always known she would be matchless and sweet and impulsive and unashamed in her wants and needs, if she ever let herself be the passionate and extraordinary woman she had it in her to become. Now that Kate was free from the restraints the miseries of the past had forced her to curb her true, passionate self with, she was utterly breathtaking as she took fire in his arms and demanded an intense seduction neither of them would ever want to forget.

And here they were, exactly where they should not be, with risk and scandal dogging every step along the way, and all it would take to set it off was someone else feeling the urge to wander as she had wandered and find them out. They were trespassing in the shadows of their host's private rooms, with an open door at their back and hundreds of curious guests far too eager for any slight scandal that presented itself to their eager ears and eyes a matter of mere yards away. Reluctantly he restrained the ravenous wolf within him bond by painful bond, until he could gasp in a huge breath of cooling air and set his forehead to hers, drawing on an unexpected stock of true tenderness that surely only she could unleash in him at such a time.

'Not here, lover,' he murmured, 'and certainly not now.'

'Where then, and when?' she demanded, the tremble in her low-voiced demand threatening to undo all the good he'd managed to do them.

'In our marriage bed, after all is made right between us in our own eyes.'

'It *was* right,' she protested bitterly, drawing away from him as if his touch repelled her now and he cursed her contrary, headstrong nature, even as he knew very well it was one of the things that made him want her so unbearably that he'd take her on virtually any terms.

He wondered if he'd made a mistake after all by not seducing her as if she meant no more than a quick and lusty roll in the hay to him. Yet every instinct that wasn't primitively crying out for her and a release from this nigh-overwhelming frustration shouted just as loudly that he'd have lost a crucial part of her if he'd sunk into her and brought them both to a quick and savage climax on the floor in a virtual stranger's house with so much risk all around them.

'Not until you know exactly what you want from me and why,' he told her implacably.

'I want *you*, and I want you *now*,' she challenged him furiously.

'But *why*, Katherine, *why* do you suddenly want me so much?'

'Because…' She almost let something betraying slip out, but stopped herself just in time, as she always had when it came to her feelings for him, whatever they might be, and now he doubted she knew any better than he did.

'Because I'm irresistible, because I make your world shift and then brighten whenever I come into the room? Or is it just because I'm the first man to get past your ice-queen defences and make you feel the possibilities of being a real woman?' he made himself ask in a voice husky with wanting to do just as she urged, to forget anything else and let the devil take care of afterwards.

Luckily she was far too innocent, far too confused to read his true state from that gruff enquiry, for if she truly ignored the scruples that had backed them away from the precipice and rubbed her roused body against his, butted her mouth against his and demanded more, he knew he'd be beyond controlling his response to her, beyond fighting this reckless need that tore at his self-control and snapped at the fetters he was trying to put on both their demons.

'I really can't imagine,' she told him with such a superb attempt at frosty dignity he almost applauded, except that would drive her further back behind her defensive ramparts and he couldn't allow that now they were so close to getting where he'd wanted them to be for so long.

'Oh, I think you can, Kate,' he murmured.

'So you can prove to me I'm just a foolish woman like any other you might care to kiss in the dark? I think you just did that,' she said quietly and all hope might have drained out of him, if he hadn't reminded himself that everything about their recent encounter argued the exact opposite, if only she wasn't so innocent. She didn't know the difference between mere lust and the nigh-overwhelming passions and heady emotions they'd just lit in each other.

'If that was all I wanted, I could have done it perfectly well three years ago and got it out of the way,' he said flatly.

'Arrogant, boasting braggart that you are?' she gritted furiously.

'Adult, realistic man that I am now,' he corrected and did his best not to grin at her as she sucked in a mighty breath in order to denounce him comprehensively enough to slake her wounded pride. 'Quiet!' he ordered abruptly.

All Edmund's senses were alert again as he remembered the world outside this silent, darkened room and cursed himself. He shouldn't have taken such a reckless risk with Kate, shouldn't have got so close to seducing her and himself in this risky, hole-and-corner fashion. His ridiculous susceptibility to her hadn't withstood the purely tempting fact of her, alone and unguarded and almost sad in the darkness. She'd gone straight to his head like fine wine, just as she had the first time he'd ever set eyes on her, and it tore so painfully at his heart to see her pensive and lonely that he finally accepted Ben was right. He could never turn his back on her and all she meant to him, despite the nearly three years of effort he'd wasted trying to evict her from his heart. He cursed himself for making that discovery in such a place as he heard another whisper of sound from outside his host's study.

'Don't you—' She never quite managed to counter his abrupt order since he clamped an impatient hand over her mouth and forced himself to at least try to ignore the feel of it, soft and moist under his palm, since he wanted his senses alert for whoever was creeping about outside.

He saw a wicked glint come into Kate's eyes even through the gloom, as if she knew very well that the connection between them had not been severed and probably never really would be now. She narrowed her gaze and let her sharp and sweet tongue lick his palm, even as she breathed in quite happily through her nose and watched him like a houri. No, he couldn't succumb to her mischievous allure, the gnawing temptation to kiss and take and to hell with the consequences. Evidently he was as fast under her spell as ever, but he wasn't going to be discovered here with her, because the decision to marry him or not would then be sidestepped and void as it became inevitable, and that would let her off the hook of having to admit how she felt about him. Marriage of convenience indeed! he scoffed silently. How could she be so wilfully blind to her own passionate nature?

'Someone's coming.' He risked getting even closer to murmur in her ear and felt her senses jar and her mouth tense enough for him to risk taking his hand away.

Casting about him for any avenue of escape, he noted the locks on the long windows into the garden with something like despair. For a moment there seemed nothing for it but to face whoever was coming and announce his immediate engagement to the woman he'd wanted for so long, but he wasn't inclined to let whoever was coming dictate their fate. Seeing a door into some lesser office ajar, he towed Kate inside before she could protest, or dig her stubborn heels in and brazenly await discovery, so he'd have to marry her without the admission of love he was determined to wring from her.

Kate peered through the crack in the door that was all Edmund had left them by rushing her in here and could just make out the faint glow of a single candle. She blinked against even that much brightness after the virtual darkness of the shadowed room and flinched away from the idea of being discovered cowering in here like a guilty felon. It would make so much less of what they had been doing, until Edmund had recalled what a gentleman he was, and even now frustration and awe tugged at her newly awakened senses. She swallowed an unladylike curse that they'd been interrupted, just when she'd been hoping he might seduce her after all. Instead they'd only gone a heady, headlong stride forwards, then sharply back to dull respectability again. She was undoubtedly fast and wanton, and maybe in the morning she'd feel suitably ashamed of herself, but just now she'd trade the last three years of dull respectability for three hours of sensational discovery in Edmund's far-too-noble bed.

Her rebellious reverie was interrupted by the noise of a candlestick being carelessly plunked down, then the unmistakable sound of a man pacing. She should have been relieved that Bestholme had stopped searching for her, but wished whoever was marching up and down the book room at Jericho instead. Releasing a pent-up shush of breath in an exasperated sigh earned her a sharp nudge from the annoying man at her side. Even as she stung at his silent rebuke, she caught the sound of two voices murmuring and realised someone else had entered the room while she was working herself into a fine rage against fate and Edmund's overactive conscience.

Then she heard Bestholme's rather nasal tone after all and shuddered, but could hear little more until the furtive pair came closer to their side of the room and she hoped it wasn't because of some give-away sound she or Edmund inadvertently let slip. Wondering why, if this was an assignation, they didn't just shut the door and be done with it, or go and bother some other clandestine lovers with their unwanted presence, Kate shifted from one foot to the other to ease her cramped limbs and longed for them to leave.

'I'm sure there's nobody out there and I vow it's like

making an assignation with a little old lady who's afraid of her own shadow, meeting you in secret and pretending all night that we mean nothing to each other, even if it does relieve the boredom of a very dull evening, but why won't you do just this one little thing for me, George?' Kate heard a distinctive husky voice murmur.

Whatever was Lady Tedinton doing here, risking whatever scraps of her tattered reputation she had left to her? And what on earth could she be asking an apology of a man like Bestholme to do for her? Deciding she was fated to overhear other people's conversations tonight, Kate listened shamelessly, but when Edmund's strong hand felt for hers in the darkness she clasped it gratefully and clung to the warmth and comfort he was silently offering.

Suddenly she didn't need him to tell her the rumours of him and the unscrupulous woman standing only yards away from them being lovers were merely lies; a tale the peculiar female had no doubt thought up to puff up her own consequence. Not that Kate suddenly thought him a perfect Sir Galahad. No doubt he'd taken at least one or two willing beauties into his keeping in the past, since he wasn't a monk or a saint, even if the mere thought of him doing so hurt far too much for comfort. There was a core of integrity about him that would not let him couple with a woman who held her husband and his family in such contempt that she didn't care if most of society knew she'd cuckolded him repeatedly.

'It's a hell of a risk, Selene,' Bestholme replied at last after considering whatever that 'little thing' might be for a very long moment to two listeners, forced to breathe so shallowly that Kate for one felt almost suffocated by her desire not to be heard and discovered by so unattractive a pair.

'But I'm so very weary of warming an old man's bed, Georgie. Please, say you'll do this for me, lover? I so long to be free,' her ladyship wheedled in a little-girl voice that somehow made their discussion all the more sinister.

'No, I'm not risking putting my head in a noose to set you free in order for you to try to wed a man who has no more interest in you than a stone statue might have. Tedinton's fortune would go to his heir anyway and I dare say your jointure would be tied up so tight not even the Lord Chancellor could get his hands on it. You'd end up worse off and alone, and I can't afford to keep you, you're far too extravagant and altogether costly a creature for me, my dear.'

'That repellent brat is a minor and makes no effort to ingratiate himself with anyone and I'm certain you're quite wrong about my jointure. Algy thinks the world of me and will leave me a rich woman.'

'He might be a ridiculous old fool, but he's far more possessive than you choose to realise. He won't leave you a target for men like me after he's gone, and the boy has a pack of embittered relations all longing to avenge the slights you've heaped on them these last ten years. The truth of it is that you've grown lazy, Selene. The world doesn't revolve around you and what you covet for now, despite your belief you only have to scheme for whatever you want to get it.'

'Just do this one little thing for me and I'll make sure

that high-nosed Alstone bitch has no alternative but to marry you,' the woman cajoled and even as Edmund's hand tightened on hers to offer comfort and denial of what the scoundrels were discussing so coldly, Kate had to put her other hand over her mouth to stop herself shouting out a protest at such a repulsive strategy and add the furious caveat that she wouldn't marry Bestholme if her very survival depended on it.

'And precisely how do you propose to do that?' Bestholme asked.

'I'll whip up such a scandal she'll beg you to wed her by the time I've finished.'

'You don't have the power, Selene my dear. Haven't you realised by now that nobody as heedless as you are will ever hold sway among the *ton*? I doubt they mind your blatant peccadilloes with other men, or even the fact you married a fool for money for most of them did the same when it comes down to it, but you're about as subtle as a town crier about your contempt for your husband and his cronies and he's widely liked, for all he's a senile old fool, and you, my dear, are not.'

'Never mind preaching me a sermon and to hell with what a pack of pompous fools think, will you do it?' Lady Tedinton replied in her lazy, malicious drawl as if they were discussing some minor favour instead of cold-blooded murder.

'I'm still listening,' Bestholme replied as if bored, but indulging her.

And so am I, Kate was tempted to shout and step out of hiding to confound the unlovely pair, but she shuddered at the very idea of confronting such a sordid pair of rogues and wasn't it as well to know exactly what they were planning?

'Quiet,' Edmund mouthed a warning against her ear, but how had he known?

Kate was so busy struggling against the incendiary effect of just his breath on her ear lobe, his mouth so close against her neck she could almost feel the words form on his lips, that she missed Lady Tedinton's first few words and frowned fiercely at him in the pitch darkness. How could she be so wrapped up in her response to his closeness that even the small matter of the murder of Lord Tedinton faded against the fierceness of the fire Edmund had lit between them with those few passionate kisses?

'All you'll need to do is be found with the silly chit in a scandalously dishevelled condition, then you can inform everyone you were just celebrating your engagement a little prematurely,' she was saying in a scornful tone. 'Even Carnwood won't gainsay you when the silly wench is obviously in need of a husband.'

'And you think I'm incapable of thinking up such a simple scheme myself, Selene? I'm almost insulted,' Bestholme responded in that cold, indifferent voice Kate now knew was not an affectation, but reflected his true self.

'You're still being dunned and always begging so-called loans off me to pay off your endless debts, so you evidently don't have the nerve to carry it out.'

'Whereas you have the nerve and not the brains?'

'Think so if you dare,' Lady Tedinton hissed and Kate shuddered at the casual evil of it all.

'I do dare, but that's why you keep coming back to me, isn't it?' Bestholme demanded and there was the sound of a brief scuffle and then a horribly needy moan as Lady Tedinton demonstrated the truth of what he said.

'Take me now,' she growled.

'No, it's too risky,' her lover argued and gave a low chuckle that made Kate shiver at the cold lustiness of their loathsome need for each other, 'and I like you desperate, Selene. By the time Tedinton has pawed you all the way home and tried to mount you like a man, you'll be glad to meet me in that very convenient summerhouse he's had built in the garden for us, if he only knew it, and feel a real man between your legs again at last.'

'I hate you,' she informed him throatily and there was another of those horrible interludes as Kate heard them kiss noisily and even caught the sound of fine cloth tearing as they went at each other like beasts.

'I like the way you hate. Now tidy yourself up, then get back to the ballroom and persuade that old fool to take you home early. I'll go the other way and come back through the garden, so nobody will know you were with me. It's only the fact I'm supposed to be courting a fortune that keeps my creditors off my back as it is, so who knows what they might do if they found out about you, my lovely doxy?'

'Foreclose?' Lady Tedinton asked as if discussing the weather and Kate felt sickened at the sound of her lover's flat-handed slap, presumably to somewhere that didn't show. 'I could come to you in the Fleet,' she offered throatily, as if violence made her more eager and Kate wondered if she might disgrace herself and Edmund by actually being sick, then considered the consequences and managed to control her revulsion after all.

'No, try informing on me to get me sent there and you'll rapidly discover what a mistake you've made. Just behave yourself and go on keeping that senile old idiot sweet, then be where I told you to be by dawn, Selene, or I'll take my pleasure elsewhere. There are plenty of younger and more obliging mistresses than you who can be had for a lot less trouble than you cause me,' Bestholme warned carelessly.

'I'll be there,' Selene Tedinton replied urgently.

'I know,' her repulsive lover drawled huskily and Kate heard his footsteps recede while the light faded as he ungallantly took his candle away, leaving his mistress still in the dark.

A few moments later there was the swirl of silk and satin and an exasperated curse, then softer footsteps receded towards the ballroom until all seemed silent and empty in the room beyond this airless office they'd been trapped in.

Chapter Eight

'Have they really gone?' Kate whispered as quietly as anyone could whilst making a sound at all.

'I hope so, since you're restless as a cat and nowhere near as silent,' Edmund grumbled back.

'I was quiet as a mouse and resent your aspersions, my lord,' she informed him with as much dignity as a lady could assemble whilst shut in this cupboard of a room with the unbelievably infuriating Viscount Shuttleworth and forced to listen to murder and her own forced marriage being planned outside it.

'Then for heaven's sake do it softly for a change.'

Kate stamped a soft-soled foot on the runner and hoped Bestholme really had left and so wouldn't hear the faint thump it made against the oak floor underneath. If being angry with Edmund for very little reason helped keep her from falling into hysterics over what she'd just overheard, then Kate was all for it.

'Virago,' he chided impatiently.

'Tyrant,' she flashed back at him.

'Come on, I've had enough of lurking in the dark like a thief,' he growled in an exasperated masculine rumble and towed her as abruptly out of their hiding place as he'd hauled her into it in the first place.

'Just as well they really have gone,' Kate carped even as she clung to his hand like a lifeline. 'We'd have been in a fine pickle if he'd stayed here in order to give her a head start for the ballroom.'

'He's not that much of a gentleman and we're in a fine pickle anyway,' he told her seriously.

Thinking back over the last however long they'd now been away from the ballroom and propriety, Kate could only agree with him. 'How are we going to stop them?' she asked shakily.

'We aren't.'

'Then you're prepared to let that harpy and her disgusting paramour murder her husband without even lifting a finger to stop her?'

'No.'

'Then what are we going to do?'

'*We* are going to do nothing. When you cease your incessant nagging and let me think, I dare say *I* will eventually find a way to stop them without a scandal.'

'And I just sit about simpering while you stamp about brooding and proving what a clever gentleman you are?'

'You're a single female with a reputation to consider.'

'Bah! If I were a married woman without any shreds of one left to me, you'd still find a way of excluding me,' she fired back at him, struggling to free her hand from his at last, although it felt very comfortable in the misogynistic, contrary man's hold and part of her really didn't want to stand alone after such an evening.

'Yes, I would,' he told her implacably.

'Why? I'm not a fool or a hysterical female given to fainting and die-away airs.'

'No, just because you're you,' he told her rather obscurely, 'and you'll be busy,' he added by way of a diversion.

'Busy?'

'Planning our wedding,' he said and Kate felt the odd sense of detachment she'd been suffering ever since he'd stopped kissing her finally threaten to overwhelm her.

'I thought you just said "our wedding",' she said faintly.

'I did.'

'But how can I do that when we aren't going to be married, Edmund?'

'Because we are, Kate.'

'Solely because you just kissed me in a private room where nobody could see us? That's complete nonsense and nobody will know what we've been doing if we don't tell them.'

'They will when we return to the ballroom together in a state of disarray and hint very strongly that we'll shortly be announcing our engagement. I may despise Bestholme and his whore, but I'm not above borrowing that scheme now the devil's in the driving seat.'

'Nonsense, if you go ahead and I follow you into the ballroom a little later, nobody will dream we were together all this time, or that either of us heard anything we shouldn't have tonight. Nobody need be any the wiser.'

'You have a simple-minded faith in the gossips suddenly turning incurious about all you say and do that I could find almost admirable, Miss Alstone. If only it wasn't so misplaced and silly,' he told her, suddenly back to the aloof and superior Lord Shuttleworth he'd been towards her since returning to town and Kate refused to ask herself why his icy tone hurt and the hard look she could imagine in his eyes cut through her so coldly. 'You have now been absent for far too long to just shrug it aside and pretend you've been innocently drifting about, and I don't want those two black-hearted villains realising you overheard their assignation,' he went on relentlessly and Kate felt her palm itch to slap some sense back into him.

'Then what do you suggest that I do instead, you infuriating man?' she gritted through clenched teeth.

'Be thoroughly compromised by me, or prepare to embrace life as a social outcast,' he informed her so laconically she felt that odd sense of not being quite connected with the real world threaten her again.

'You can't do this, Edmund, you'll be dragooned into marrying me if we appear together in such a state as you suggest and we both know that you don't want to wed me any more,' she protested in a fierce whisper.

'Better that than risk that unsavoury pair realising you were wafting about listening to out-of-the-way conversations, Kate,' he declared not very encouragingly.

'How flattering,' she told him crossly, wishing she

could turn her back on the infuriating monster and walk away.

'Find a bit of steel to stiffen your backbone, for goodness' sake, Miss Alstone,' he chided like some large and handsome gadfly sent to plague her by a malign fate.

'Why should I resign myself to such a fate when you obviously don't have the least desire to marry me?' Kate managed to say in defiance of her inner idiot, who was demanding stridently that she accept eagerly and be glad he felt honour-bound to marry her after being so sternly set against it.

'Needs must when the devil drives,' he said coolly and must have decided he was done with useless words and it was time for action before things got worse.

He hustled her out of a side door and into the garden proper before she could find breath or words to protest with and urged her inexorably closer to the long windows of his lordship's fine ballroom, but not close enough for propriety, of course. The further they got from that darkened room the better, even if it was leading them closer to marriage, Kate decided numbly, and cursed herself for not fighting this more strongly. It was hard to fight temptation when it beckoned so wickedly.

'You could leave me here alone,' she whispered softly in defiance of her own eagerness for any sort of marriage with him, even this forced one.

'So you could be quizzed from now until next Christmas on the identity of your cowardly lover?' he murmured back, and anyone watching them would probably mistake them for fellow moon-led idiots lured out here by such promising darkness, she decided crossly. 'Go back in that room alone after spending such a long time away from it and your chaperon, and you'll be ruined without anyone having to plot against you,' he continued relentlessly, 'and in acute danger once that harpy realises you could have overheard her plot to murder her husband, whilst you wandered about in the shadows so carelessly that anything might have happened to you.'

'And being a perfect gentle knight you're sacrificing yourself instead?'

'No, being a pattern-card of perfection was so dull that I gave it up,' he declared flippantly.

'Along with me?' she murmured, then could have kicked herself for letting him know how much his recent rebuffs had hurt her.

'I thought I'd save myself the pain of enduring another crushingly polite refusal,' he told her and Kate hurt at the careless apology in his deep voice. 'I dare say marrying you won't be so bad once I get used to the idea again,' he added.

'And if you think I'll stand by idly while you have affairs with other women you will be sorely disappointed, Edmund Worth,' she informed him in a fierce undertone.

'That's entirely up to you, dear Kate. If you keep me otherwise occupied, I probably won't have the time or the opportunity to stray,' he observed and silenced her with another mind-stealing kiss.

Furious, she did her best to bite him, so he deepened his kiss and dared her give whatever she might have had the wits to withhold until now. Defeated by her own need of him, her body seemed to meld itself to

Edmund's powerfully lean one of its own accord and wild heat burst into instant life again. She angled her wanton mouth to his in a way she should think appallingly fast but didn't. *Never mind fast*, her deepest buried instincts warred with her training, *he'll still marry you now, even if he doesn't really want to.*

She couldn't make herself break away, even with that chilly thought in the back of her mind, but she clenched her hands at her sides and refused them the luxury of his lithely muscled body. It didn't abate the searing wildfire flaming through her like a force of nature, but it made her feel a little better about herself and the self-control she'd once prided herself upon.

Unimpressed, his hands ran over her in an unashamed exploration and she loved it. She'd always denied being capable of deep feeling, in her ignorance of how elemental and out of control she would be with the right man. Now he let his wicked hands find a way between them, despite her body's ridiculous efforts to plaster itself against him like a poultice, and Edmund ran an approving thumb over a raised nipple that immediately hardened and begged for more without permission from her. She had to fight not to moan and cry out a frantic demand for more, for everything. If not for the half-painful gnaw of need, the half-wondrous goad of heat at the heart of her, of course she would put distance between them and escape the purely physical spell he'd cast over her, yes, that was just what she would do, in a minute.

This was the wild and passionate Kate he'd always known existed beneath that façade of serenely composed beauty. Edmund managed to find enough willpower from somewhere to put a distance between them and convince himself painfully that he'd discovered enough about her most secret passions for now, in public or almost public as they were. He forced his hands away from her delicious body before his fascination with it broke his self-control. She was flushed and breathless, her soft gasps for air drawing his attention to her lush, but firm, young breasts, rising and falling rapidly against the low neckline even a single lady could wear by her fourth Season without being considered intolerably fast.

Her eyes were wild and more beautiful than he could ever recall seeing them even in his dreams as they blazed with feelings he would give half his fortune to read fully. Her lips parted as she fought to get her breath back and his eyes lingered on them with hungry fascination as she slicked them with her sharp little tongue. If he wasn't to throw himself on her and ravish her on the lower terrace of his hostess's garden, he must get their engagement rolling relentlessly on before she lost that starry-eyed, just-kissed look and remembered all the doubts and fears that inhabited her contrary thoughts whenever he wasn't in a position to haze them with merciless passion. An image he'd best not dwell on if he wanted to get the next few minutes over with without causing an even bigger scandal than the one he had in mind.

'Come,' he ordered brusquely as he towed her back to the shark-infested waters of the *ton*, before she balked.

'I still can't see why…' Miss Alstone seemed about

to take over from his wild Kate, so Edmund summarily tugged her into the ballroom and put an end to her nonsense.

'Good heavens!' Cromer exclaimed at the sight of a stormy-eyed, very thoroughly kissed Kate on Edmund's arm and just managed to suppress a grin. 'They're quite right about that dangerous moonlight,' he mumbled as he stepped back to let the company see what it had done to so cool and collected a couple.

'Good heavens, indeed, and yes, very right,' Edmund replied calmly.

'I don't think they had much to do with it,' his Kate mumbled tartly and Edmund wondered if he was suffering from shock and hallucinating when she didn't just tear herself away from him and flounce off. It wasn't every day a man heard murder plotted, and with Kate pressed so close he'd struggled to listen to a word of it. He'd wanted her so mercilessly and now he nearly had what he'd longed for so deeply within his grasp at long last, what had happened so far tonight almost seemed unreal to him for a few moments.

'I hope you'll congratulate us, Cromer, for I refuse to wait any longer after three years of waiting for a yea instead of a nay, even if her former guardian and brother-in-law hasn't agreed to it yet,' he said with a possessive look at Kate.

'Carnwood cutting up rough, is he?' Cromer asked obligingly, managing to look astonished while his eyes told them he didn't believe a word.

'You see? Everyone thinks I'm your ideal husband,' he whispered in Kate's ear and felt her tense, as if she might jump away and deny every last truthful hint of how they'd been amusing themselves since they left the ballroom that he was building up so carefully. 'Try it and I'll kiss you right here,' he threatened softly.

'I hate you,' she told him between clenched teeth and he met the heat and fury of her furious glare with a satisfied smile.

'Hate away, my fierce Kate,' he murmured and heard a sentimental sigh from somewhere close by.

'Mountebank!' she condemned in a spitting under-tone, but still made no effort to pull away or give his apparent devotion the lie.

Looking as if he was trying very hard to come down to earth, Edmund considered his friend's previous question. 'No,' he replied to the clever lead, 'but I can't tear myself away long enough to go up to Derbyshire and ask him.'

'Should think you've obtained his permission often enough in the past,' Cromer said.

'So I keep telling Miss Alstone, but it took me until tonight to convince her I can't endure to wait and be wed with the full fanfare and fuss of a grand wedding. I'll have to go and beard Carnwood in his lair now she'd agreed at last that our wedding must be soon, then maybe we can get on with being my lord and my lady at long last.'

'Short notice, gossips bound to twitter like starlings in an apple orchard,' his taciturn friend warned sagely and Edmund gave an expressive shrug before looking significantly about him at the eagerly whispering throng.

'I've waited long enough,' he said loudly enough for

most to hear him and enjoy a fresh wave of delighted speculation.

He smiled wolfishly at Kate, hoping his eyes conveyed a warning to back him up now this was all but irrevocable. She really had the most extraordinary eyes, they were truly ultramarine, he decided distractedly, savouring the word on his tongue as he almost murmured it aloud. Very blue, he translated, and was in grave danger of falling into the wondrous depths of them and not caring where it took either of them. Most blue, he corrected in his head, and freed himself of their spell just in time to stop himself kissing her passionately in public.

'Well, here's a fine to do,' Lady Pemberley observed, apparently torn between laughter, delight and a chaperon's duty as she hurried towards them. 'Impatient children,' she chided as if mildly exasperated.

'You could hardly expect me to be patient when Miss Alstone finally agreed to wed me at last, my lady,' he responded, fervently hoping Kate would play up to his act and not revert to that contained sceptical aloofness she used so often to set the world at a distance just at the wrong moment.

'Yes,' she managed rather lamely instead, 'his lordship is *most* impatient.'

'So I see,' Eiliane Pemberley responded drily, with a comprehensive scrutiny of Kate's wildly curling hair and scandalously creased gown before her sharp eyes met Edmund's with a challenge.

'Perhaps we should send that notice to the *Morning*

Post and so on soon, Lady Pemberley?' he asked with apparent satisfaction before she could speak it.

'I believe that might be for the best,' her ladyship agreed blandly, despite the dagger look his Kate shot her. 'Imperative even,' Eiliane added implacably, giving Kate just as sharp a warning look in return. 'It's high time we ordered Kate's bride clothes to be made up and St George's, Hanover Square, isn't at all easy to book at this time of year, even for you and this haughty young woman, if that's where you decide you both want to marry in the end.'

'I'm not haughty,' Kate protested hotly.

'No,' he drawled, caressing her hand as it rested in his with a rightness he hoped she wouldn't deny any more, even when they were alone. Playing with her gloved fingers absently, he smiled with sleepy-eyed approval. 'You're very far from it if I remember rightly, and I have an excellent memory,' he murmured intimately.

'Forgive us, ladies and gentlemen, but all will become clear to you when a certain announcement is published shortly. I cannot say more now, I fear,' Edmund announced to nobody in particular with as elegant and ironical a bow as a gentleman might with his tawny locks still awry from his lady's fingers and his neckcloth askew.

'Since you wicked children decided to pre-empt proper formalities, perhaps you should have your betrothal dance now?' Eiliane suggested just loudly enough for the cool clear sound of her voice to rise over the hubbub.

Lady Wyndover looked as if she might be considering

the unlikelihood of it all, then nodded, before indicating the orchestra should play a waltz for her scandalous guests. Kate let her steps shadow Edmund's as closely as usual. She was so confused by the suddenness of it all she couldn't say what her feelings were at gunpoint, but most of their fellow guests evidently thought it a love match.

'Keep dancing,' Edmund scolded softly as her steps began to falter as weariness threatened to make her wilt like an overheated lily. 'Don't you dare flag and let Bestholme and that witch suspect everything is not exactly as it should be between us,' he berated in a stern whisper.

Sympathy might have made her collapse in his arms and require to be taken home, but he could be a little gentler, Kate decided. He was looking at her now as if it was only a matter of time before she swooned or did something equally feminine and therefore foolish, so she glared at him instead.

'You're the most irritating male I ever came across, Edmund Worth,' she informed him even as she smiled up at him as if the sun rose and set in his eyes.

'At least I'm pre-eminent at something, then,' he drawled back, as if he found her stubbornness and bad temper mildly irritating and amusing all at the same time.

'I really and truly hope that you're one of a kind then, my lord, for I'd hate to think the human race was afflicted with two such.'

'Didn't your long-suffering relatives teach you it's

rude to abuse your acquaintances in such a forthright fashion, Kate?'

'You're not an acquaintance, you're my betrothed.'

'I can see why you put off gaining one until now if this is how you intend to treat me from now on,' he countered, giving her a supposedly warm smile even while his cool willow-green eyes warned her he wasn't joking.

'I could jilt you at the altar if you'd like me to,' she offered half-seriously.

'Banish the idea from your mind right now that you can escape this marriage, Kate, or I'll walk off and leave you standing here with your mouth open. You made an idiot of me once too often three years ago for me to let you do it again.'

'I never meant to make you feel an idiot then, my lord,' she said and a heavy feeling of regret chilled the pit of her stomach as he looked unconvinced.

He looked at her austerely, as if seriously wondering what she was currently using for brains. 'That's moot, but there's no going back for either of us after tonight, so all we can do is get on with it,' he said brusquely.

'I'll do my best to make you a good wife,' she said stiffly.

'And that's all a convenient husband can ask of his lady, is it not?' he seemed unable to resist saying as the dance finally came to an end and he bowed over her gloved hand as gallantly low as if he was utterly besotted with her and thought her a queen amongst women.

'Quite,' she replied repressively and just about managed not to kick him soundly on the shin, or tread very deliberately on his toe.

The noble effort it cost her must have shown on her face if only because he was close enough to see more than anyone else. He grinned at her, that old, infectious grin she'd once taken so carelessly for granted, and it gave her a bittersweet heartache for the ease there could have been between them, if only she'd been less of a fool when they'd first met.

'I wish we could be friends again,' she said wistfully, only to see laughter fade from his unusual silvery green eyes and the chill return, as if she'd no right to ask.

'I want you, Kate. I'll be faithful for as long as you return the compliment, but I'll never be your lapdog again.'

'I can't imagine you as anyone's willing slave nowadays, my lord, but I would have us be comfortable together at least.'

'Do you think your elder sister and her husband find mere "comfort" in their marriage?' he asked her as if the very word offended his mouth.

'No, I think they each consider that the sun rises and sets in the other,' she informed him steadily, 'but I doubt they'd thank me for saying they were anything so mundane as merely comfortable together.'

'Then why should we settle for less?'

'Because we're not in love,' she was goaded into declaring exasperatedly.

'My point exactly,' he murmured in her ear as they returned to Eiliane's side and she couldn't glare into his challenging eyes, for fear of letting the world see this wasn't the fairytale romance they'd just been at such pains to pretend it was.

'You don't fight fair, my lord,' she murmured instead as she met his eyes with every appearance of dewy-eyed wonder.

'No,' he breathed for her ears alone as he raised his hand to let it whisper down her cheek in a regretful, lover's salute as if he couldn't bear to completely let her go whatever the conventions, 'that would be because I fight to win, Miss Alstone.'

'Win what?' she asked with genuine puzzlement as he let his hand drop and she shivered as her every nerve seemed on the alert and desire almost made her shake with the effort of resisting a foolish driving compulsion to be in his arms again.

'You, Miss Katherine Alstone, body, heart and soul,' he murmured as he once more leaned towards her as if he might kiss her and Kate was sure she heard several of the ladies huddled nearby to get the best view of them sigh sentimentally.

'First you'd have to want me,' she whispered.

'Oh, I most certainly do, sweet Kate, make no mistake about that,' he drawled and she could see the truth of it in the flash and burn of such raging hot desire in his eyes that it made them look intensely green all of a sudden.

Involuntarily her mouth opened and her lips were so dry she just had to lick them, watching him gaze at her tongue as if he wanted to catch it with his own and then... Best not to think of that then, not with such a very interested audience hoping to see the self-possessed Miss Alstone melt into boneless idiocy in front of their eyes.

'I suppose we'll see you tomorrow then, my lord?' she said foolishly, so muddled by the mix of fiery passion with that edge of angry desire that kept flaring between them that falling back on platitudes was the only option open to her.

'You can be very sure of that,' he replied, 'but the night isn't over yet.'

'It is for me. Do you think we could leave now, Eiliane? I'm so very tired,' she turned and asked her friend, eager for some peace and quiet in which to gather her scattered thoughts.

'And at least I can accompany you home without arousing speculation, now we're engaged all bar the shouting,' Edmund said with an ironic smile.

'Oh, I suspect there might still be shouting,' Lady Pemberley said, evidently considering Kit Alstone's reaction to the news that his sister-in-law and former ward had behaved so scandalously. 'But, yes, we can go home now and your escort is always welcome, Lord Shuttleworth, especially in these strange and uncertain times.'

'What it is to be wanted,' he said with a smug look of *faux* self-importance that made Kate smile and Lady Pemberley inform him she'd always known he wasn't the straightforward young man he too often pretended to be.

'If I were that simple, I'd have stayed on my estates nursing my broken heart and missed the prospect of a lifetime of marital strife with your lovely charge, Lady Pemberley,' he parried lightly.

'Just as well you didn't, then,' Eiliane replied as he handed her into the luxurious carriage her husband had brought on the occasion of their marriage.

'Yes, isn't it?' he said with such cordiality Kate eyed him with suspicion.

'My love?' he prompted with such bland patience she once more felt her foot itch to kick him as she looked at him with a sharp question in her eyes. 'Could you get into Lady Pemberley's splendid equipage before the horses collapse from boredom or one of us catches an inflammation of the lungs, do you think?'

'Oh, yes, of course,' she replied, doing so with such haste she nearly fell over her own feet. 'I'm so clumsy that I seem to constitute a danger to myself and others tonight. It really is most irritating.'

'I don't know,' he murmured as he managed to climb into the carriage with all the grace she'd failed to find. 'I quite like it, and perhaps it's a sign that I've finally knocked that exquisite balance of yours out of kilter at long last.'

'And that's something about tonight's events I certainly need to hear about in more detail, my lord,' Eiliane informed him in her sternest chaperon's voice.

'Later, if you please, my lady. We have a great deal to explain and only a short carriage ride to do it in, if you won't consider letting me come inside to enlighten you properly when we get there,' he cautioned and Kate could feel the tension in his powerful body as he sat opposite her, but evidently couldn't bring himself to relax into the generous squabs of Eiliane's carriage.

Chapter Nine

'If I were a proper chaperon I'd probably occupy the whole drive back with a stern lecture about your disgraceful behaviour,' Eiliane said ruefully and then fell silent.

Kate thought of all that had happened since she'd left her temporary home tonight and all hope of relaxation left her in a heavy sigh she hoped was inaudible above the noise of the horses' hooves and the rattle of iron-rimmed wheels on cobbled streets. Obviously not, because Edmund's strong fingers reached for hers and his hand engulfed hers to offer simple comfort before the sound of it had hardly left her lips. She felt at least some of the horror of hearing two conscienceless rogues scheme murder, then almost couple with each other, subside under the warm reassurance of his touch as he massaged the chill stiffness from her fingers.

'Thank you,' she murmured as they drew up outside the Marquis of Pemberley's town mansion.

'No need for thanks when I intend enjoying a very thorough exploration of everything about you before we're very much older, my Kate,' he breathed into her ear before he jumped down to hand them down with such elaborate ceremony she wondered crossly if he was trying to infuriate her, or if it just came naturally to him.

Considering the smug look he gave her after she stiffened her shoulders and marched up the shallow steps in front of him, she concluded he knew exactly what he was doing. Nobody watching them would suspect she'd suffered anything more shocking than an impetuous engagement tonight, and she swept into the cosy and private sitting room Eiliane had annexed for her own use, unsure whether to be grateful or furious that he'd manipulated her so easily once again.

'You're clearly a master of strategy, my lord,' she informed him when the door was finally shut and that fact alone made her realise that Eiliane already thought of him as family.

'Edmund,' he corrected as if it really mattered. 'But I'd never lay claim to so much guile,' he denied with an unreadable look she found oddly disturbing.

'Never mind that, I demand an account of your adventures,' Eiliane said with a sharp look at Kate's dishevelled gown and Edmund's disordered locks, 'or should I say *mis*adventures?'

'The latter,' he affirmed. 'Tonight Kate decided to wander off and explore Lord and Lady Wyndover's personal rooms, with far too little consideration for their privacy I feel I must point out, as that fact seems to have escaped her.'

'I *was* being harried unmercifully by Mr Bestholme,' she argued.

'You could have looked to me to remedy that, but you risked far worse instead of lowering your pride. I found her sitting in his lordship's book room in the pitch dark, Lady Pemberley, where we had a slight altercation before I heard someone padding furtively about in the proscribed fashion for the evening,' he explained, then raised an eyebrow at Kate as if waiting for her to argue. He nodded when she didn't, as if that confirmed an idiocy she plainly couldn't defend and proceeded to explain whose tryst they had overheard to her shocked chaperon.

'Oh, heavens above,' Eiliane gasped, 'what did the two unprincipled rogues say while Kate was listening to every word?'

'For goodness' sake, Eiliane, I'm not a child,' Kate protested.

'You are an unwed female,' Edmund answered as if that explained everything.

'But not an unfledged one,' she argued.

'So you might think, Miss Alstone, but I beg to differ.'

'Really, my lord? Pray what would you ask of a *fully* fledged lady then?' she asked with as much irony as she could fit into a few short words.

'I'll tell you after we're married.'

He was undoubtedly the most infuriating, self-satisfied, would-be superior male she'd ever come across and with a brother-in-law and guardian like Kit and his best friend, Ben Shaw, lurking like a man-mountain in the background, she'd met a fair few of them.

'Never mind quarrelling, what did they actually say?' Eiliane asked and Edmund explained distractedly, as if his mind was suddenly busy elsewhere. 'What a truly awful person that woman must be at heart,' Eiliane said hollowly.

'My reaction exactly,' Kate said, getting to her feet with a resentful glare at her newly affianced husband, who ignored her and solicitously poured Eiliane a restorative glass of brandy.

Considering the stark contrast between his gentle way with Eiliane and his abrasive manner towards her when she'd actually heard the whole horrid conspiracy for herself, Kate blinked back inexplicable tears and eyed his broad back resentfully.

'I should have chosen my words more carefully,' he reproached himself as he handed Eiliane the glass.

'I don't see how it could be wrapped up comfortingly, but could you see them, Kate?' Eiliane asked shakily.

'No, because, if you remember, I was immured in pitch darkness in little more than a cupboard with Lord Shuttleworth,' Kate explained patiently. 'If I had known how densely populated his lordship's book room might become tonight, I would have stayed in the ballroom and endured the evening more gladly.'

'A lot of nonsense is talked about premonitions and portents,' Edmund said rather grumpily, as if hurt by the idea that she would rather have come home tonight a free woman than his affianced bride in all but a few formalities.

'Forgive me for finding my situation less than enjoyable, my lord,' Kate replied sarcastically, for suddenly she felt very tired and didn't know how much longer she could endure his impatience when all she wanted to do was nuzzle her head against his shoulder and seek any comfort he cared to give her.

'I might if I wasn't part of it,' he explained with a rueful look that understood too much about her ragged emotions.

'I didn't ask you to declare yourself in front of several hundred people,' she defended herself wearily.

'I suppose you expected me to just abandon you to the condemnation of all those who thought you'd gone sneaking off to meet some lover? I was the one who compromised you, after all.'

'It wasn't your fault,' she said, trying her best to get him to see that it was his loss of freedom she found so intolerable, not her own.

'That's odd, because it felt as if it was to me,' he said with a flash of sardonic humour that warmed her, despite her resolution to resist his charm, at least for the rest of the evening.

'Aha!' Eiliane said with what sounded to Kate like rather a contented sigh for a supposedly outraged chaperon to utter. 'So you forgot to tell me the most pertinent details of the whole affair, did you? Somehow I thought you might have done.'

'Maybe,' Kate admitted warily, seeing the I-told-you-so glint in her friend's eye.

'Almost certainly, considering the state you were both in when you appeared out of the garden looking as if you'd taken up where Adam and Eve left off, Katherine Margaret Alstone,' Eiliane scolded.

'We are engaged,' Kate defended herself recklessly, 'so surely Edmund and I can kiss each other without you and half the *ton* getting all of a-flutter about it.'

'You were certainly *not* engaged, nor anywhere near it until tonight and well you know it, my girl.'

'That's a private matter between the two of us, don't you think, Lady Pemberley?' Edmund said gravely and Kate wondered how her friend felt about being on the chilly side of his exquisite manners for once.

'It might be if you hadn't made such a fine show of it in public, young man,' Eiliane parried bravely, but Kate could have told her from the resolute set of his jaw that she'd get no more from Edmund about their more intimate affairs.

'Do you actually want us to wed, your ladyship?' he asked coolly.

'It's been my dearest wish since I first set eyes on you together, my lord, for some odd reason that escapes me just at the moment,' Eiliane admitted.

'Then why not leave best alone, ma'am?'

'Because Kate and her sisters are the daughters of my heart, despite their headstrong ways and knack of getting into any trouble that's brewing.'

'And we all love you so very much, Eiliane,' Kate assured the woman who'd done her best to mother her since her own mama died.

'Something in my eye,' Eiliane explained gruffly to

Edmund as she returned Kate's fierce hug. 'I hope you intend to make her very happy, my lord.'

'It will be my duty as well as my pleasure,' he promised quite solemnly.

'Then I'm content,' she said, as if he'd just made a vow she intended to hold him to for the rest of her life, and that she might even come back and haunt him if he broke it after she'd gone.

Edmund nodded and tried not to wish Kate was resting her fiery head so trustingly against his shoulder instead of Lady Pemberley's. Maybe one day she would be that unguarded with him, but for now he had her promise to wed him, and her passionate response to every sensual demand he'd made so far.

'You should go to bed and rest,' he told her abruptly and wasn't surprised when she raised her head to glare at him as if he'd suggested she take poison.

'Why?' Kate asked, standing up in order not to be towered over. 'I've only endured the revolting attentions of a fortune hunter, overheard his repellent clandestine assignation with a so-called lady of my acquaintance and then been forced to listen to their murderous schemes, before narrowly escaping ruin by a man who would rather marry virtually any other woman in England than me. So the last thing I want is to sleep while you and Eiliane plan my life without so much as a by-your-leave.'

'I wouldn't like to wed any of the royal princesses,' he said with unpardonable levity and Kate seriously considered throwing the contents of Eiliane's glass at him, since her friend had left it untouched, but she decided he didn't deserve even that much acknowledgement of his ill-timed humour and drank it off in one swallow instead. 'Can't take her drink very well, can she?' he observed as Kate choked and spluttered on that reckless gulp of fine cognac and incandescent fury.

'I should be thankful for small mercies if I were you,' Eiliane advised sagely, 'and if you intend to go on like this, my lord, I'd learn to duck very swiftly indeed if I were you,' she warned, with a cautionary look at Kate's flushed cheeks.

'I shall not lower myself to throw anything at *him*,' Kate snapped even as she felt the warmth of the strong spirit seep into her cold belly. 'He thinks he's going to get his way by making me so furious I'll forget to be horrified by what I overheard tonight and storm off to bed so you can arrange my wedding without any inter-ference from me, and it's *my* future, too,' she ended. Yet even she had trouble following the logic of her own argument.

'Did it work?' Edmund asked with what looked like academic interest.

'Nearly,' she gritted between white teeth and forced them apart as she willed her hot temper to die down and her fists to unclench.

She *wouldn't* be ruled by her passions. No, that hope didn't work after tonight. She'd lived by them all evening and there was little prospect of getting them back in a neat box and throwing away the key.

'I'm perfectly recovered now, so shouldn't we be dis-cussing this rationally?' she managed to ask as if she thought it was true.

'I suggest we send appropriate notices to the news-papers and hope Carnwood won't take offence when I explain what took place tonight,' Edmund said far too calmly, considering she was still in turmoil.

'That's not what I meant and you know it,' she snapped.

'Planning to jilt me even before I manage to get our names on a special licence, my dear?' he asked and met her eyes with a bland look before shaking his head. 'Not possible, I fear. We could have a pair of potential murderers on our tails as well as an assured scandal if we don't go through with it.'

'This isn't what I meant by rational discussion of our future and you know it.'

'I long ago gave up on being rational with you, my dear, so let's return to our plans, shall we?'

'We could if only I knew what they were.'

'I suggest getting ourselves up the aisle before the tabbies have time to work themselves into a frenzy and Bestholme realises we might not have been seducing each other the entire time we were absent from the ball-room tonight should be our priority.'

'And if he does realise it, then it will all be for nothing.'

'Oh, surely you exaggerate? I can say without undue vanity that you'll be marrying to advantage before the end of this Season. Which is exactly what you planned to do at the outset of it, rather than endure ending another Season unwed, is it not, Miss Alstone?' he observed coolly and Kate blushed under his ironic gaze.

Was she so transparent, so lacking all subtlety? She

felt bitterly ashamed of her scheme to secure a convenient husband even as she was asking herself why.
After all, arranged marriages were often made between
eligible *partis*—except they were usually made by the
families and not the victims. Now why had that damning
word suddenly sprung into her mind?

'I would have been just as advantageously wed three
years gone by if you'd had your way at the time,' she
pointed out.

'Oh, the follies of extreme youth, Lady Pemberley,' he
said, unfairly dragging Eiliane into their argument and
Kate had no doubt which side of the line that turncoat
would jump. 'Moonstruck young cubs such as I was
then should be ordered out into the world to discover the
realities of life, instead of being left to make idiots of
themselves at the feet of capricious young ladies, don't
you think?'

'Maybe if the Continent had been less chaotic, we
could have sent you on a grand tour until Kate came to
her senses,' Eiliane replied.

'Traitor! We could send him on one now instead,'
Kate muttered darkly.

'In the hope you'd escape your fate when I came
back?' he said sardonically.

'No, in the hope you wouldn't come back at all.'

'This is no time for petty quarrels,' Eiliane chided
and Kate fumed all the more.

'No, we have the rest of our lives to indulge in them
after all,' Edmund replied.

'How I look forward to it,' she replied with an artis-
tic sigh.

'Then at least we'll never be bored,' he said with a rueful grin.

'At the moment a nice, comfortable attack of *ennui* would suit me very well, but will it work?' she said rather obscurely.

'Will what work?' he asked warily.

'Throwing dust in their faces.'

'Oh, that—it depends on what they decide to do next, I suppose.'

'How reassuring.'

'You're not the sort of female who wants a pat on the head and a parcel of pretty lies, my dear.'

'I'm not *your dear*.'

'I think we'd better hope you are, Kate. We'll endure an unhappy marriage if it turns out that you're not.'

'Then why marry me at all?'

He watched her as if fascinated. 'I never took you for a fool, however I railed at your obduracy when I begged you to marry me and got a polite "no, thank you" for my trouble, but maybe I'd have been better off respecting your intelligence less from the outset,' he said as if in the grip of a startling revelation.

'Are you telling me I'm *stupid*?'

'I'd never be so ungallant. Lady Pemberley, I appeal to you—did I even hint that your protégée is a lack-wit just now?'

'No, and I should have to reproach you for such a slur, my lord.'

'It won't work, so you might as well stop provoking me,' Kate said.

'Have you got anything interesting to say about

our betrothal, then?' Edmund asked as Kate reminded herself she wasn't going to indulge in a redheaded temper.

'I believe it takes a proposal from the gentleman, then acceptance on the part of the lady to constitute a betrothal. At no time tonight can I recall receiving a formal offer of marriage from you, my lord, or accepting it.'

'Knowing that I laid myself at your queenly feet more times than either of us care to remember in the past will just have to suffice. I promised myself that last time that I'd never beg you to marry me again and it's one vow I fully intend to keep.'

'Which doesn't bode well for our future,' she said quietly.

'I dare say we'll rub along well enough,' he said with a careless cheerfulness she hated. 'You're a fine woman and I'm in dire need of an heir or two, so you'll hear no complaints from me. Just see to it that you abide by your vows and I think we'll suit like ham and eggs at the breakfast table.'

'How very reassuring,' she answered faintly, wondering if she was meant to be flattered.

'You wanted a marriage of convenience,' Eiliane reminded her sneakily.

'I did, didn't I?' she replied numbly and tried to comfort herself with the memory of Edmund's fiery kisses.

How silly to find she wanted an impassioned lover after all and not the detached and sardonic husband he promised to be. Regret threatened once more, along with bitter nostalgia for the ardent, love-struck young aristocrat he'd once been. That Edmund had bombarded her with flowers, thoughtfully chosen trinkets and sent with them fervent assurances of his enduring love. Fool that she was, she'd brushed him aside as if he was an importunate boy, instead of a young man who'd one day become this mature Adonis and break too many susceptible feminine hearts, including her own if she let him. Some Adonis, she reminded herself as she straightened her shoulders and met his unreadable grey-green gaze. And some enduring love when, three years on from swearing she'd break his heart for ever if she refused to marry him, he was watching her as if she were a specimen he was studying for a paper at the Royal Society.

'Have we got a bargain, Miss Alstone?' he asked mercilessly.

'It would seem so, Lord Shuttleworth,' she agreed, refusing to let her eyes fall while she admitted he was to be her fate, for good or ill.

'Then I'll take a kiss to seal it with, saving your presence, Lady Pemberley?'

'Oh, I'll turn my back, never fear,' Eiliane said blithely and Kate glared at her friend as she did just that. 'I swear I can feel that furious glare of yours, Kate,' her ladyship murmured irrepressibly.

'I'm quite sure you can,' Kate muttered vengefully.

Then she forgot her annoyance with her inefficient chaperon as Edmund's lips once more took hers in a potent, passionate kiss that rendered her breathless and defenceless before Eiliane had hardly finished turning away. Shock, she assured herself. That was why she melted into his masculine arms as if formed to fit them. Yielding to the pressure of his firm mouth on hers, she opened her lips and let him invade the softness within. Her breath caught and her hands clenched in a vain attempt to stop them creeping up to caress his strong neck and ruffle his vital golden-brown hair, where it curled irrepressibly into his nape and tempted exploration.

He knew all the same; she felt it in the smile he let form against her willing mouth, the way he shifted to bring her body so close even she couldn't mistake his arousal. It was blatant, startlingly explicit as she felt melting heat threaten to rob her of the use of her legs until she clung to him and yielded everything. His passionate enjoyment of her femininity made her feel unique and special, and she needed to know there was something more in their future than duty and the mutual respect she'd once thought so important.

'That's enough kissing to seal half a dozen bargains,' Eiliane observed, even though she was staring appreciatively at a portrait of her husband as a young man that hung in pride of place over the mantelpiece and obviously not at all bored with the sight. Kate could have sworn she heard a satisfied sigh as Eiliane added another triumph to her matchmaker's tally.

'I've had enough of everything for one day, so you may do as you please about announcements, my lord. I'm tired and confused and I can't do this any more,' Kate confessed with a catch in her voice she hated anyone to hear.

'Aye,' Edmund agreed. 'Go to bed now and ring for

a posset to help you sleep. You need rest after such a day, and the one we'll face tomorrow.'

She must be exhausted for his concern to threaten tears, Kate decided. 'I'm not a child,' she managed to remind him shrewishly when she turned at the door to take one last, incredulous look at her new fiancé, not quite sure if she'd dreamt up such a handsome one after the last weeks of uncertainty and self-doubt.

'That much is blatantly obvious,' he drawled, letting his eyes wander over her flushed cheeks and heavy eyes, now the darkest of blue with the richness and potential of what could be between them left over from that last kiss. He went on with his scrutiny of her supple young body in a way that left her in no doubt he relished every single slender curve and elegant line of her and couldn't wait to take his bride to his bed and begin his marital duties.

'I fear there's a great deal to be done in the morning,' Edmund added when he finally managed to tear his gaze from her tingling form.

'A very great deal,' Eiliane agreed gravely.

'So you will call on us, then?' Kate asked and could have kicked herself for sounding so betrayingly eager.

'I don't know, I thought I might go and order a new pair of boots, or perhaps a visit to my tailor and then a stroll to my club to see if I could meet up with a few old friends to pass an idle hour or two reasonably pleasantly instead,' he was stung into replying. 'Of course I'll be calling on you as soon as I decently can and, if you're still asleep after such a wearisome night as this one has been, I'll wait until you're awake and plague Pemberley instead,' he added roughly as soon as he saw she was half-inclined to believe him.

'Oh, very well then,' she said and found herself wishing stupidly that he was coming upstairs with her, to kiss her gently into sleep as a lover might after they'd worn out the night with loving, even if he only slept chastely beside her for the brief sliver of night still left to them now.

'Until tomorrow, ladies,' was all he could say or do until she really was his to take to bed whenever and wherever they chose, his jade, silver and wildfire gaze told her, as it lingered on her once more and it boldly caressed and promised her all that and more until she shivered with anticipation.

'Goodnight then, Eiliane, Edmund,' she muttered and made her legs carry her away, before her wicked desires led her to say something foolish.

'Goodnight, lover,' he murmured intimately as she went past.

Almost as if, she reminded herself indignantly as she heard the echoes of the door closing behind her, *almost* as if he already had the right to strip her of her ball gown and explore every inch of woman underneath it bit by sensuous bit, while he worked her into an incoherent mess of passion and eagerness for his ardent attention. Trying not to agree with him, she ordered her weary feet upwards and went to bed dreaming of him instead of the evil she'd overheard or the scandal their betrothal would probably be entangled in by morning.

Chapter Ten

'Was teasing and tormenting poor Kate after such an extraordinary evening as she just weathered altogether fair of you, Lord Shuttleworth?' Eiliane mused as she was left facing a rather self-satisfied viscount.

'Not at all, but it made her forget those two villains and their foul schemes. I could hardly take her to bed and divert her with a night of untrammelled passion under your respectable roof instead, now could I, Lady Pemberley?'

'Not from want of trying, so far as I could tell just now.'

'You mean you didn't position yourself cunningly enough so that you could see everything that went on between us in yonder mirror without Kate knowing it, my lady? How very noble of you.'

'You're so sharp you run the worst risk of cutting yourself I ever came across in a man,' she condemned with a strong hint of admiration.

'If I were that clever, I'd have taken myself off on that tour of the Continent the instant Boney set out for Elba in the year fourteen and it was open to travellers again for the first time in years, my lady.'

'Since you're about to become an adoptive godson to me, you really must call me Eiliane from now on instead of all this my-ladying, but do you mean it?'

'Do I mean what, Eiliane?'

'You have a very annoying habit of answering a question with a question that could make me regret taking your side in all this after all, I hope you know?' she said with gentle malice and he grinned back at her as if they understood each other perfectly. 'I meant, of course, do you truly regret not leaving the country before Kate made her come-out? If you really don't wish to marry her, you'd best confess it straight away so we can get you both out of this betrothal without ruining Kate's good name, or putting you beyond the pale.'

'Is that even possible after tonight's almost-announce-ment? It sounds beyond the wisdom of Solomon to me.'

'Most things are possible if one goes about them in the right manner, but one has to know first if they are also desirable, my lord.'

'Back to that, are we?'

'If necessary,' Eiliane replied implacably, letting her absolute loyalty to Kate show, even if she would think her protégée illogical as a London mob if she thought about letting this fascinating young lord slip through her fingers once more.

'No, I'm very satisfied with the outcome,' he replied

seriously enough, 'if not exactly delighted by the way it had to be achieved.'

'Good—it's my belief Kate doesn't know her own mind.'

'I doubt I'll ever know what goes on in her contrary head, but I intend to guard her happiness with my life. How else would I behave towards my wife after all?'

'Being a man of honour?'

He shrugged and looked as if honour was the last thing on his mind, but she could believe it if she chose, and Eiliane hid a smile of catlike satisfaction. None of this had happened quite as she'd expected, but Kate was engaged to a man of wit and character who wouldn't let her lead him about by the nose at last and, for now, that would do her very well.

'You'll have a fight on your hands, on more than one front,' she warned.

'I dare say I'll weather it.'

'Remember that Kate's really a very different creature under all that stubborn reserve and contrary coolness, Edmund Worth, one who could be badly hurt by a husband who didn't understand her.'

'I'll never willingly hurt her, I can promise you that at least.'

'Then I'm content.'

'Would that I were, too,' he replied obscurely, before bowing and wishing her a good night. Lady Pemberley retired to her splendid bedchamber just before her lord ran lithely up the stairs at a speed many men half his age would envy to join her and diverted her attention from anyone's marriage but their own.

* * *

Edmund chose to walk home, despite the offer of his carriage from the Marquis of Pemberley when that gentleman returned home very late and found him about to depart. Apparently his lordship had been dining with some obscure official who probably had more real influence than the Prince Regent and his entire circle of raffish friends put together. The marquis obviously moved in the most exalted of political circles and, if he didn't watch his step, Edmund might be at risk of joining them. He reported his engagement and received his lordship's hearty good wishes, as well as a half-serious threat to horsewhip him if he ever made Kate unhappy, which he took in good part as he silently agreed that he'd deserve it if he didn't, before he finally set out for home.

He wasn't as weary as he should be after such a night and took a convoluted route home through Mayfair, where dawn was already stealing into shadowy corners and town-bred blackbirds and song thrushes were chirruping in readiness for performing a dawn chorus in the parks and gardens along his way like an orchestra tuning up. He needed to walk himself into at least a few hours' sleep against the day ahead of him, so he strolled on through the dawn and the already stirring city, considering how different his life was now from when he set out for an evening spoilt by the familiar frustration of watching Kate dance and flirt with other men.

Kate had responded to him with such headlong enthusiasm tonight, or last night or whatever it was now, just as she had in his wildest dreams so many times in the past. Not being able to take that passionate response to its logical conclusion had left him with an inevitable burn of frustration and a spike of exhilaration that would keep him from sleeping properly until his wedding night if he let it. After all, self-restraint and denial were feelings he should be all too familiar with, but now Kate had tacitly agreed that their becoming lovers would be the most wondrous thing this side of paradise and it was newly minted.

Fighting both of them until he'd got his ring on her finger at last would be a gargantuan struggle, but in the meantime, he intended to make her think harder than she wanted to about that blazing attraction. Yes, if he was to suffer weeks of longing for her until he could finally slake it in their marriage bed, she could spend them considering why she belonged in no other bed but his. The very idea of her marrying another man made him so angry that his staff tiptoed about him when he finally got home and whispered knowledgeably that his lordship must be disappointed in love again to return home looking so grim.

'Good gracious, Welland, where on earth is everyone?' a familiar voice in the corridor outside Kate's bedchamber demanded next morning.

She did her best to bury her head under the pillow and pretend last night had been a disturbing dream, but her memory told her she was undoubtedly engaged to Edmund Worth and nobody could have imagined those deeply sensual kisses they'd shared so enthusiastically that her body throbbed eagerly at the very memory, before she told it sternly to behave itself.

'Surely they're not *still* abed on such a lovely morning, especially when I managed to rise from my sickbed with the dawn to post here hotfoot,' the annoyingly happy and altogether too-awake voice outside asked again.

So her sister Isabella really was yelling wrongheaded observations as unsubtly as ever and it wasn't a nightmare as she'd hoped, Kate decided grumpily. She reluctantly removed her head from its down-and-fine-linen sanctuary and rang the bell. If she was going to have to cope with Izzie in what sounded like tearing spirits, then getting dressed seemed not only called for, but just plain essential.

Evidently Eiliane agreed with her, for half an hour later all three ladies were installed in the morning room, drinking tea and eating breakfast while they came to terms with the day.

'Don't tell me you travelled all night just to get here at such an unearthly hour and badger us out of our nice, comfortable beds?' Kate queried as Isabella continued to look rudely healthy and annoyingly serene whilst tucking into an enormous plate of ham and eggs.

'Then I won't, sister dear. Being a proper and sensible young lady now that I must make my come-out at last, and knowing what a life of dissipation you two lead, we stopped in Windsor last night and came on this morning in an attempt to cosset my failing strength, rather than arrive scandalously late to an empty house last night.'

'You don't look very weak to me,' Kate said with a sceptical sniff, wishing she had half as much energy as her little sister, who was glowing with her accustomed health and vitality once more after her recent illness.

'I either had to promise to behave like a Bath breakdown and coddle myself all the way here, or submit to setting out on my journey with the entire Mausley family in attendance, with most of Richard's university friends threatening to act as outriders. Agreeing to spend a couple of nights on the road was a small price to pay for escaping such a ridiculous fuss. We would have taken for ever to get here, what's more, and I'd already had enough of Bath and all those silly young boys.'

'Proving importunate, were they?' Kate asked cynically, knowing the effect her sister's deceptively angelic countenance had on susceptible young gentlemen.

'Maddening,' her sister agreed without any sign of vanity or gratification.

'Never mind all that,' Eiliane put in impatiently and Kate braced herself for the announcement she was sure to make. 'I hope Lady Mausley didn't send you all this way alone, however much fuss you kicked up about being properly accompanied,' she said anxiously, confounding Kate's fears she was about to describe last night's misadventures and unknowingly putting her in her place at the same time.

Isabella rolled her eyes at the very idea and sighed. 'Would that she had,' she said disgustedly. 'If you care to look upstairs, you will find that Emily's maiden aunt is currently lying down in your best guest chamber, doing her best to recover from the extreme fatigue of driving here from Windsor this morning at a pace quite suitable for the average funeral. Her companion, who also happens to be Miss Mausley's former governess and as ancient and formidable a lady as you'll ever encounter, is attending her along with Miss Mausley's maid, who could sour milk with a single glance at the best of times and apparently this isn't the best of times. The Mausleys' coachman, two footmen and a postillion are being stowed wherever they can be found room even in your grand residence, my lady, and they are all awaiting what I hope will be a very speedy recovery and a swift return to Bath of the whole caravanserai.'

'Well then, Fanny Mausley certainly sent you off in style, so I'll grant she's a proper and caring hostess, even if she did carelessly allow you to get the mumps in the first place, love.'

'She certainly didn't have anything to do with that, as I picked them up all on my own and, so long as she did actually send me off at last, that was all I really cared about,' Isabella said ungratefully and went over to investigate the covered dishes on the sideboard for further sustenance.

'She was probably worried you'd eat her out of house and home after so many weeks of ransacking Bath and the surrounding area for supplies,' Kate observed with a shudder as she watched her sister pile her plate with yet more ham and eggs.

'I'm hungry and I'd dearly like to know just what's put your hair so out of curl this morning, sister dear,' Izzie demanded. 'I hope you haven't been overindulging?'

'Of course I haven't and, if I had, it would be my business and none of yours.'

'Now there you're quite wrong, for it won't help my

début if I have to go about London apologising because my older sister's become a toper and could disgrace us at any moment.'

'I don't think many are rash enough to think any of us all that respectable in the first place and I certainly haven't taken to the bottle in your absence, little sister, and therefore I'm not feeling in the least bit liverish,' Kate replied, the temptation to enjoy a refreshing family argument threatening to topple her dignity at any moment.

'Then you must have got out of the bed the wrong side, sister dear, for you look about as happy about my return as a lion with a thorn in its paw.'

'Of course I'm pleased to see you, I was really worried about you,' Kate admitted gruffly and almost let herself weep lachrymosely over her little sister when Izzie jumped up to hug her fiercely.

'There really was no need to be,' Izzie assured her cheerfully as she plumped down on her chair once more and looked genuinely delighted to be back with her family. 'In fact, it was downright embarrassing to catch such a childish illness and have to go about looking like a gargoyle for a week or more.'

'I wager you managed to look lovely despite it, considering you have an annoying habit of coming out of any potential disaster smelling of roses,' Kate assured her and traded an indulgent smile with Eiliane as Isabella returned to her abandoned breakfast with vigour.

'And so do you,' Izzie assured her absently between mouthfuls.

'Not this time, I didn't,' Kate muttered darkly, but her sister's hearing was famously acute and Isabella shot Eiliane an interrogating look when Kate became so absorbed in buttering a slice of toast she somehow couldn't spare time to meet her sister's eyes.

'It's not my tale to tell,' Eiliane observed with a shrug, so Kate glared at her instead.

'I accepted Shuttleworth's hand in marriage last night,' she announced baldly in order to get it over with and proceed with weathering her sister's much-too-acute scrutiny of her averted face.

'Then why are you being so cross-grained about it? In your shoes, I'd be jumping up and down with joy to secure a fine husband I could love and respect, instead of growling and grumbling into my breakfast as if I'd just lost a guinea and found a farthing.'

'Then *you* marry him,' Kate snapped, then wished she could climb into a hole in the floor and pull the carpet over her when she realised Welland, Eiliane's usually imperturbable and meticulously correct butler, had opened the door after only a brief knock in order to admit her new fiancé to this supposedly joyous family occasion and just in time for Edmund to hear her disastrous comment.

He paused at the sound of her defensive remark and watched her blush with cynical eyes, before he raised his eyebrows to let her know he'd heard. He turned to smile at Isabella, as if seeing her again had put the sunlight into his morning. Maybe it had, Kate thought in complete horror at the very idea of Edmund falling under her enchanting little sister's spell. Something even

more uncomfortable than horror jagged under her confusion as well, but she wasn't prepared to think about
what it could be, not while her ridiculous remark still
echoed between the two of them and the possibility she'd
just hurt him again, or even that he might now think
twice about wedding her after all, dragged painfully
at her thumping heart. Even Eiliane looked unusually
daunted.

'Well, I'm delighted to welcome you as a brother,
even if my sister is feeling as grumpy as a bear with a
sore paw this morning, Lord Shuttleworth. You're going
to make an excellent addition to the family in my opinion,' Isabella declared brightly and bounced out of her
seat again to give him another of her impulsive hugs, as
if she had no idea her sister had just dug herself a tiger
trap and fallen headlong into it.

Kate scowled at her cooling piece of toast and hoped
he wouldn't take that embrace as anything more than
an exuberant expression of joy and sisterly solidarity on
Isabella's part.

'At least gaining a sister, and such a lovely one, by
marrying into your family will go some way to soothing
my wounded soul after your sister's begrudging acceptance of my suit, Miss Isabella,' he told her with one of
those old, unaffected smiles as he returned her sister's
embrace and Kate tried to pretend neither of them were
there while she fought off a ridiculous, primitive stab
of jealousy even she couldn't pretend was indigestion
after such an interrupted meal.

He might have kissed her with sensuality and passion
last night, but somehow the sight of him looking so

genuinely pleased to see Isabella again made her long for the days when he'd greeted her with such warmth as well. Reminding herself she'd always returned his delight with either suspicion or indifference, she felt ashamed of her eighteen-year-old self and did her best not to regret the passing of the eager youth Edmund had been then. She had nobody to blame but herself if her attempts to set him at arm's length had worked so well he probably believed her ridiculous invitation to Isabella to marry him herself just now had been sincerely meant.

'It's not begrudging, precisely,' she qualified, waving her toast in the air in what she knew was a most ill-mannered fashion to emphasise her point. 'It's more a matter of being annoyed that you considered me so compromised that you must marry me whether you want to or not,' she explained earnestly and made Isabella more interested in her sudden engagement rather than less so.

'I should have got the coachman to whip up his team and get here last night after all, despite Miss Mausley's delicate nerves, for it sounds to me as if you two had an evening I'm sorry to have missed. Are you going to tell me what you got up to, or leave me to speculate wildly?' Isabella asked, wide-eyed and eager for any detail she could coax or trap them into providing.

'It's got nothing to do with you,' Kate intervened hastily, before Edmund could yield to the melting appeal Isabella suddenly managed to add to her wide-eyed and supposedly innocent stare.

'We left the ballroom for half an hour, quite separately, then re-entered it looking scandalously dishevelled by

one another after a very improper interval, so I broadly
hinted to the company that an announcement of our
engagement would follow very shortly,' Edmund told her
flatly and, shorn of all its twists and turns and the dizzying, unexpected seduction of his kisses, Kate hoped it
sounded a workaday enough explanation to halt Izzie's
rampant curiosity in its tracks for once.

'You did all that?' she asked Kate incredulously as
it became plain her curiosity was bolting headlong for
the wide-open spaces after all. 'No, Kate, please don't
tell me that you got carried away by *passion*? I really
never, ever did come across anything quite so shocking
in all my life, sister dear, and you, Lord Shuttleworth,
are obviously a very superior kisser indeed.'

Kate shot her sister a furious look, then spared one
for her new fiancé when she saw him appear ridiculously
pleased by that accolade, then try to look modest and fail
abysmally. It was true enough, so perhaps he had some
reason to preen himself on his skill in that dubious art,
but he could at least try to pretend to be ashamed of the
bad example they'd set her sister.

'Charlatan,' she muttered as Eiliane made room for
him to sit at the breakfast table, then rang for more
coffee as if he was already part of the family.

'Shrew,' he countered and, plumping down in the
seat next to her as if there was nowhere he'd rather be,
he gave her a casual hug and pressed a quick, hard kiss
on her open mouth that unfairly shot straight to her legs
and rendered her incapable of getting up and walking
away with dignified hauteur after all.

'*Very* superior,' Izzie observed approvingly and Kate

came back to her senses to find all three of them staring at her as if expecting something spectacular.

'Can I eat my toast now?' she asked sarcastically and hoped they were safely put in their places by her feigned indifference.

'No,' he denied her ungallantly and, seizing it, made a show of biting along the surface she'd absently nibbled at, as if eager to put his mouth everywhere hers might be even in the mundane act of eating her breakfast instead of his own.

She might have found his posturing of the devoted lover seductive and warm, promising so much for their marriage she'd instantly forget his enforced captivity. Unfortunately she knew he was putting on a show for Izzie and his ability to parody a lover's devotion made Kate feel edgy and, contrarily, a touch betrayed.

Watching Edmund and Isabella determinedly plough their way through a mountain of food as if they'd both just walked here from Windsor, Kate tried to consider if her sister would make Edmund a better wife, but found the idea horrifying. Then she wondered numbly when she'd become so jaded she refused to indulge in even the simplest pleasures without examining them for flaws? Food could be one of those pleasures, when not indulged to excess. So it must be sheer perversity that was making the coddled egg she absently helped herself to taste like dust and ashes in her mouth. Swallowing coffee hastily to help it down, she joined Eiliane in watching the experts at work instead.

'I'd rather keep either of them for a week than a

fortnight,' Lady Pemberley observed with a smile that understood too much of Kate's seesawing emotions.

'It's just as well that the kitchens are restocked from your marquis's vast estates at such regular intervals,' she said with a wry look back that agreed, yes, she did stand in need of a little sympathy and support. Yet if this was an ordeal, how could greeting the legions of callers they must expect this afternoon with a serene countenance and an unrevealing smile be described?

'I'll tell them to send an extra cartload every week if we're to entertain a pair of hungry wolves for breakfast each morning,' Eiliane joked.

'Nonsense, I was only sharp set after so many weeks of being offered nothing but invalidish pap,' Isabella emerged from her coffee cup to inform them. 'If I ever even see a bowl of gruel again I swear I'll throw it out of the nearest window.'

'You poor thing,' Kate said blandly, 'did they lock you in a garret as well?'

'They might have wanted to, because I made a sight sure to frighten small children, but Emily's mother really did offer me a bowl of gruel one day, I swear it.'

'Only the once, I suspect,' Kate observed wryly and Izzie grinned back with a nod that somehow re-established their usual easy accord, one they'd surely need in the face of the changes about to take place.

'She's usually quite a sensible woman, so, yes, only that one time.'

'Mrs Mausley was probably terrified what my lord Carnwood would say if his ward went into a decline in her care. I expect you were looking pale and interesting at the time as well,' Kate teased her sister.

'Probably—most inconsiderate of me not to have had the mumps when everyone else did at school, was it not?'

'Yes, especially as I remember you being unbearably smug while *I* went about looking like a gargoyle instead, so maybe I should have caught the first stage to Bath to soothe your fevered brow and gloat just a little after all, little sister.'

'Not if you ever wanted it to become un-fevered you shouldn't.'

'True.'

'And if you'd come to stay with the Mausleys as well, you wouldn't have had the opportunity to scandalise the *ton* outrageously as well as finally becoming engaged to Edmund at long last, so I for one am very glad you stayed away.'

'As am I, dear sister-in-law-to-be,' Edmund said with such politeness Kate couldn't say whether he actually meant it or not.

'Well, of course you are,' Eiliane said as if there was no question about it, and for once Kate wanted to live in dreamland as well and smiled her thanks at her. 'That being established beyond doubt, I think we should retire somewhere a little more private and discuss strategy, don't you?' Eiliane added with raised eyebrows and Kate wondered which of them she was intending to exclude.

'Oh, very well,' Isabella said with a sigh, 'it's perfectly plain you wish me to go away so you can discuss all the interesting things you won't tell me, so I'll just go and annoy my maid by getting in the way of her unpacking instead, shall I?'

'If you would, just for half an hour or so, my love. Then all three of us really must visit Celestine as a matter of urgency and never mind preparing for morning calls. The *ton* will just have to wait.'

'We must?' Kate asked with a sinking heart, for ordering a bridal gown and her trousseau seemed so inappropriate just now, when she'd said such a foolish thing about her marriage, just as if it wasn't exactly what she'd wanted all along and perhaps now even needed.

'Of course we must,' Eiliane said implacably and Kate avoided Edmund's eyes, unsure if she would see mockery or fury at her apparent reluctance in them.

'And I dare say I'll need a new waistcoat or so as well,' he said blandly and she was no closer to knowing his true feelings towards their upcoming marriage.

'Half an hour, then?' Isabella said with a sympathetic look for Kate that told her what her sister thought of his lack of enthusiasm.

'At the most,' Kate replied, thinking she could very likely stand no longer.

'It's like pulling teeth; anticipation is almost always worse than the act itself,' Edmund assured her with a perfectly straight face.

'Except for the small fact that it's also painful almost beyond words.'

'Not necessarily and, even if it is, the agony is brief, then comes the euphoria of finally being rid of it.'

Now why did Kate suddenly think they weren't

talking about dentists at all and why should his eyes take on such an intensely silvery light until she wasn't quite sure if they were green at all any more? Which was all very confusing of him and his eyes; she was almost sure she wanted him to go back to being polite and reliable, instead of the mocking devil he'd become some time in the last three years.

'I really hope you two know what you're talking about, because I certainly do not,' Eiliane interjected.

Chapter Eleven

As they were about to be sucked into the whirlwind of relentless activity the Marchioness of Pemberley generated whenever a new project presented itself to be organised, Kate wondered if this was the time to mention any doubts, but Eiliane sat down at her husband's impressive desk and drew a blank notebook out of the top drawer as if everything was set in stone.

'Not a new one, we'll have to get married now,' she joked feebly to Edmund.

'We had to get married the instant we appeared in Lady Wyndover's ballroom in a state of disarray. Don't even think about backing out and leaving me to explain you preferred social ruin to becoming my wife,' he said in an unamused undertone.

'It was a feeble joke, not a declaration of intent.'

'Never joke about our marriage,' he said dourly, as if near the end of his tether as well as his patience with her.

'I've endured enough taunts about your repeated refusals these last three years to last me several lifetimes.'

Kate flushed and mumbled something vaguely apologetic.

'If we might get on with the business in hand, then?' Eiliane asked, her expression almost as impatient as Edmund's. 'Isabella will not give us long, so if you two intend to marry with indecent haste we'd better get on with arranging it.'

'I'll have to go into Derbyshire and ask Carnwood's permission before there's an official announcement,' Edmund said with a frown.

'Shouldn't I accompany you to tell him I've changed my mind?' Kate asked.

She felt distinctly unlike herself in far too many ways and had done ever since Edmund had kissed her last night. So what did it say about her that stumbling on a pair of very guilty lovers and a plot to murder a man had left her feeling distressed but reasonably composed, yet one sensuous kiss from Edmund Worth had sent her floating in such a cloud of unreality she still didn't recognise herself next morning?

'Certainly not,' he countered sharply.

'Why?'

'Because we've scandalised enough people already without adding to it by infuriating your brother-in-law and former guardian and upsetting your sister,' Edmund said with exaggerated patience, as if addressing a slow child who probably wouldn't understand him.

'But we need not go alone.'

'And what about your other sister?' he asked, as if she

was confirming all his worst suspicions by suggesting they uproot Isabella now she was safely returned at last and obviously in robust health as she prepared to make a spectacular début.

'Isabella will stay here, of course, even Lady Pemberley can hardly present her if she's not here to be presented,' she replied patiently, as if he was the idiot.

'Then who will chaperon *you*?' he asked, still with such insufferable reasonableness she felt her temper rise and forced herself to count to twenty.

'There's sure to be someone,' she said with a shrug, 'some proper and respectable female who'd be willing to lend us countenance if she thought it would avert even more scandal. Emily Mausley's aunt might even be prevailed upon to do so in such a worthy case for an instance, or what about Miss Carton, she's certainly respectable enough for all three of us,' she said brightly, glad she'd recalled the stern and efficient lady who came in three days a week to help Eiliane with her many good causes and her correspondence.

'I need Miss Carton here,' Eiliane protested. 'I couldn't think of managing without her for the fortnight it would take you to post to Derbyshire and back with any degree of comfort. It's folly to even think of going, Kate. Shuttleworth can ride there and back in a few days if he's unburdened by coaches and luggage and your maid and his valet, as you'd have to take them with you if you were to travel in that sort of state. No, it's a ridiculous idea. You must stay here and face the intrusive questions until your betrothal is officially announced. It will be unpleasant, but you're not one to shirk a task because you don't like to make an effort to deal with it, I hope.'

'That's really not fair, Eiliane, you know I take my responsibilities seriously,' Kate defended herself.

Being heiress to a large estate in Ireland, as well as owning several smaller holdings in England and the small fortune invested in funds left her in her parents' will, weighed heavy on her shoulders now she was one and twenty and felt obliged to make decisions she'd been very happy to leave to Kit in the past.

'I agree that you're as good and concerned a landlord to your tenants as anyone can be when a few hundred miles and the Irish Sea keeps you from meeting most of them, my love, but it's high time you stopped being such a coward where your own life is concerned, Kate. You must learn to deal with more personal problems like a mature adult instead of a frightened child.'

'I have, I am,' she defended herself stubbornly and glared at both of them.

'Then let's get on with that list of things that must be done which you're so eager to begin, your ladyship, before I must set out for Wychwood,' Edmund intervened with a sigh that told Kate he disagreed with her about the emotional maturity she'd just claimed for herself, but wasn't inclined to dally and argue just at the moment. 'I should probably have left already if I'm to get as far as I'd like to with my journey before it's dark,' he added impatiently.

'Surely you don't intend leaving without a letter from me to explain everything to Kit and Miranda and assure them of my agreement to your offer?' Kate objected.

'Absolutely not,' he barked as if she'd suggested sending a primed bomb in his saddlebags. 'First you want some unfortunate lady who has just travelled here from Somerset, probably against her own inclinations and purely out of duty to a guest in her family's care, to pack up again and hare off to Derbyshire at your say-so and at a few moments' notice. Now you think it's a perfectly sound idea to blithely inform your pregnant sister that I've compromised you to the point where a marriage between us is a more or less foregone conclusion among the *ton* and presumably you then intend to rely on her to prevent Carnwood killing me in a duel when he finds out how upset she is about just how close to the wind you sailed with me last night on the Wyndovers' terrace?'

Feeling that horrible sinking in her stomach again that had plagued her on and off since Edmund appeared in town this spring, suddenly as indifferent to her as if he'd never begged her to marry him in the first place, Kate decided she'd weathered enough for one morning.

'No, I'm not,' she snapped, 'for if Kit kills you, at least it'll save *me* the trouble.'

'Vixen,' he informed her with a wry smile, but at least that frozen look had left his eyes, so did he still care for her after all? This was hardly the right time or place to find out.

'So what does that make you?' she asked snootily instead.

'A fool, I suspect, considering I'll be setting out to ride my poor horse into the ground in order to beg your brother-in-law and former guardian for your hand, Kate Alstone. Despite the fact I'd probably do better to buy a

passage for the Americas and a new life in exile, instead
of staying here and marrying a stubborn, ill-tempered
termagant who'll do her best to lead me a fine old dance
for the rest of our days.'

'Much better, so why don't you?'

'Because annoying you for the rest of our lives promises to be so much more amusing, and my estates and
tenants need me, even if yours apparently don't. Now,
I believe we've used up half our time with arguing
already, so shall we occupy the rest by doing something
useful?'

'You two may do so, but I'm going to find my younger
sister. Remember her? The other sister I don't consider
whenever I'm putting my own selfish needs before
anyone else's? So I'll bid you goodbye, my lord, and
leave you to plan the rest however you please and tell
me about it afterwards. I suppose I'll see you after your
epic ride to Derbyshire and back, whether I want to or
not?'

'That you will, my love, that you will,' he informed
her suavely and escorted her to the door and bowed over
her hand, as if they'd been discussing their wedding in
delighted harmony for the last quarter of an hour.

'One thing I do know after the last few weeks, my
lord, is that I'm certainly not your love,' she muttered
as Eiliane became ostentatiously absorbed in her list-
making.

'All the last few weeks have proved conclusively is
that you, my lovely Kate, don't know your own mind,
let alone whatever happens to be skulking about in
mine.'

'And that you think you're very clever,' she informed him crossly.

'You wrong me; only a complete idiot would marry you after what you put me through three years ago and expect any peace out of it.'

'Then I suggest you decide now whether you're capable of such a noble self-sacrifice after all and a long ride with all the bother of a visit to my brother-in-law to no useful purpose.'

'I never said I wanted anything as humdrum from life as peace and quiet though, did I? So it will serve a very useful purpose to me,' he replied in a low voice that sent an unwanted shiver of desire down her back, despite her threatening temper and secret reluctance to part from him. 'Stop teasing me with such un-Kate-like shilly-shallying when we both know the die is cast,' he added.

'But I wasn't teasing, Edmund,' she said silkily and he laughed.

'I know and that's what makes it so irresistible. Most men prefer to fight for what they want most from life, sweetheart, and you really ought to remember that very pertinent fact in your dealings with my sex and adjust your behaviour.'

'As I'm fated to marry you in a matter of weeks, I won't be dealing with any other gentlemen now, so their peccadilloes can be of no importance.'

'But *I* am a man, Kate, and expect my peccadilloes to be vital to you for the rest of our lives. So important that they completely exclude any other gentleman's,' he said smoothly, but there was an implacable purpose in his silvery green eyes that made her shiver.

'As *I* am a true lady, I will certainly never be aught but faithful to my husband, your lordship,' she told him stiffly, but something flashed between them as his gaze heated and promised her such untold intimacies when they truly became man and wife that her head spun and her breath came short and shallow.

'And I'll be as devoted to my wife as you allow me to be, Kate,' he promised ambiguously and she shivered as he bent over her hand and kissed it as formally again, as if society were watching, and not an unconventional marchioness pretending to be fascinated by the view out of the window and her notes for a spring wedding.

'Goodbye then, Shuttleworth,' Kate managed to say as if it was three years ago and she was as indifferent to his staying or going as she'd managed to pretend even to herself that she was then.

'Goodbye, my dear,' he corrected her gently enough, before surprising her by pressing another of those hard, hotly uncompromising kisses on her softly opened lips after all.

Whilst his mouth on hers was all she wanted to explore, enjoy and seek more and yet more intimacy with, as he drowned her senses in infinite possibilities until she was oblivious to everything else, Edmund calmly opened the door behind her back. Then he relinquished her mouth with a lopsided grin that admitted yes, kissing her was a very pleasant, if time-consuming, occupation before he gently pushed her out into the corridor. With jolted incredulity bordering on fury, she numbly watched him turn and face Eiliane's bland smile of enquiry as if he'd just put the cat out, even as he gently shut the door in Kate's face to exclude her.

Never before had one of the Marquis of Pemberley's finely crafted and highly polished mahogany doors been subjected to a glare of such burning hatred. Never had Kate wanted to kick one of them so badly that her foot hurt in sympathy and anticipation until today. Simmering with fury and righteous indignation, she stood on the other side of that satin-smooth door and clenched her fists to stop herself beating them against it in a tattoo of wild frustration. Instead she turned smartly on her heel and tried to contain her rage and wounded pride as she marched up the stairs and sought her own spacious bedchamber to pace in agitation, until she was fit to seek out her sister without snapping Isabella's nose off when she didn't deserve it.

Isabella greeted her with a determined expression on her lovely face that told Kate she hadn't escaped an inquisition. 'If you think I'm going to tamely accept the tall story that you and Shuttleworth just fell into each other's arms last night like a belated Romeo and Juliet, Katherine Margaret Alstone, you've never been more mistaken in your life,' her sister informed her sternly.

'We might easily have done,' Kate defended herself, deciding she'd have to do better than that if she was going to escape having to tell Isabella the whole story.

'After he asked you to marry him so many times that first year even I stopped counting, and you refused every single offer he made when he was more romantic and ready to love you than he appears to be now? I wasn't born yesterday or even the day before that, sister dear.'

'I've had a change of heart.'

'Unconvincing,' Isabella declared and tapped her foot impatiently.

Kate sincerely hoped she was wrong and wasn't it almost true? 'He's grown into more of a man than the rest of my suitors put together,' she heard herself say and it was true and yet a little less than the whole truth. She'd spent several weeks metaphorically measuring eligible bachelors against her requirements of a perfect husband and failed to be impressed by any but Edmund, but there had been others these last few years who would impress the most finicky and discontented of ladies, and none of them had made her heartbeat flutter and her knees go weak with need, which right now seemed most unfair of them.

'Well, that can hardly be considered difficult, since you've turned away every overtly masculine and poten- tially demanding man you met since you made your come-out,' Isabella echoed her thoughts mercilessly. 'Little wonder they gave up on you and decided to marry someone less challenging and a lot more amenable after a few weeks of your ice-queen act, Kate. I suspect Lord Shuttleworth only ever seemed an acceptable escort to you in the first place because he wasn't yet the mature and rather impressive man he is now when you made your come-out. He's certainly nothing like the love- struck youth you met three years ago any more, is he?'

'I said all along it was a mistake for Miranda and

Kit not to find you a new governess when Charlotte married Ben, for you've obviously been spending far too much time minding my business for me and too little on your lessons these last three years. I'm sure that I never got left to my own devices in London far too much when *I* wasn't even out. You must have been given far too much liberty to know so much about eligible bachelors now and you're only just making your début and should therefore be innocent and sweetly naïve, not a budding fishwife who thinks she knows everything there is to know about other people's private business,' Kate snapped.

'Heaven forbid I should ever be as innocent as Miranda evidently was when that worm lied and wheedled and seduced her into eloping with him in that scrambling fashion,' Isabella said with an expression in her eyes that made Kate's heart sink.

She'd fought so hard to shelter her little sister from the full impact of their elder sister innocently believing Nevin Braxton's self-serving, cynical lies. Even now she shuddered to think of the terrible consequences of what should have been just a silly youthful infatuation, when Miranda eloped with a villain before being abandoned by him, after being stripped of her innocence, her pride and even her health while he gaily spent the quarter-day rents for the whole Wychwood estate he'd somehow managed to steal away with her on wine, women and more unspeakable pleasures that Miranda would never dream of discussing with her little sisters.

'Both of us have her example in front of us to make us wary, Izzie, but you only need to watch Miranda with

Kit, or Charlotte with her Ben, to know that not all men are lying villains.' With incredulity Kate heard herself defend that overwrought emotion some called love, the very one she'd spent so long avoiding and refusing to truly believe in.

Only yesterday she would have probably applauded Isabella's hard-headed refusal to be taken in by passions that threatened to fog the intellect and blind a person to all the faults the object of that passion might possess.

'Suddenly you're singing a very different tune,' Isabella confirmed with some satisfaction and Kate wondered if her devious sister had manufactured this whole scene to get her to do just that. 'About time, too,' she added and smiled smugly.

'I'm just making observations,' she excused herself lamely.

'Liar.'

'At least I'm not a precocious brat who thinks she knows far more about other people's business than they do themselves,' Kate retorted, infuriated that her sister was right. The moral high ground she'd thought so settled and immutable under her feet shifted every time Edmund gave her one of those hotly assessing looks, or a provoking smile that promptly sent her wits to the four winds.

'Neither am I,' Isabella replied with annoying, very conscious calm in the face of the childish provocation Kate had just resorted to in order to change the subject.

'Neither are you what?' Kate asked shortly, already

having had her temper severely tested by her betrothed this morning and deciding she'd had enough.

'A precocious brat,' Izzie replied coolly and proved it.

Arrested by the truth of that declaration, Kate finally took in the absolute certainty that her whole life was about to change for ever. Isabella was a beautiful and composed young woman, almost guaranteed to become the toast of London society as soon as she stuck her nose inside the first ballroom and Kate was going to marry a man who'd thought himself in love with her what seemed like for ever ago, just when he seemed to have decided he didn't want to wed, or perhaps even like, the woman who'd cost him so much wasted time and frustration. Edmund had certainly cooled towards her during those three years of absence and, before last night, had seemed more intent on watching her with cynical amusement and a lazy smile than begging for her closest attention and her hand in marriage.

He'd obviously found little enough to like about her when he was subjecting her to that mocking scrutiny these last few weeks and it was obvious even to her that he'd been hunting for a wife whose greatest virtue would very likely have been *not* resembling Miss Katherine Alstone. Apparently he'd learnt to distrust her since they'd parted on his last passionate offer to love her and her refusal of that offer. She recalled a few more heated memories from last night and decided he'd managed to overcome it long enough to kiss her senseless and want her almost ravenously all the time he was doing it. The whole topsy-turvy situation was enough to give any female the urge to fall into hysterics, she decided, and met her little sister's gaze with some of her confusion probably all too evident in her own.

'Edmund's clearly no longer a besotted youth, eager for any kind word I care to offer or a duty dance or two when I'm not otherwise engaged, and you obviously don't need me, either,' Kate admitted hollowly. 'Nothing about my life or that of most of the people I care about is as I thought when I came to town this year.'

'Shuttleworth's certainly not a youth, and whether or not he's besotted with you largely depends how you treat him, I suspect, but I'll always need you, Kate. Perhaps in a different way now I'm not the vulnerable little girl you fought so hard to protect, although just a child yourself. We're both women now and all three of us Alstone sisters could be closer than ever, if you'll let yourself need us as deeply as we'll always love and need you.'

'Whatever do you mean, Izzie? I've always loved you both so much.'

'Only that you did what you had to do when Miranda ran off with that awful Nevin Braxton and Grandfather refused to even hear her name mentioned again, let alone allowing her any contact with us at all, despite you being so very young yourself. When our dear brother, Jack, died, it left us at Wychwood, grief-stricken and lost as we were, and you stood up to Aunt Ennersley and Cousin Cecelia's bullying and carping and even somehow persuaded Grandfather to send us to school to get us away from them. Both Miranda and I needed you to be far more grown up than anyone had the right to ask you to be at such an age then, but I'm a woman now, Kate, and Miranda is so blissfully married neither of us need worry about her happiness ever again, with Kit there to see to it so ably.

'You can stop worrying about me, and it's plain as the nose on your face that Miranda is almost insufferably delighted with her earl. Maybe one day she'll even stop feeling guilty that such a youthful folly took her away when we needed her most. What I'm trying to say, and probably making a ham-fist of it, is we love you deeply and heaven knows you've proved you love us, but you don't need to fight the rest of the world any more. Miranda and I want you to be *happy*, Kate, so please let Edmund Worth love you as ardently as he's wanted to from the first moment he laid eyes on you, and make sure you are just that for the rest of your days.'

'It's too late,' Kate said bleakly.

'Don't be ridiculous, you're about to marry the man.'

'Only because he thinks he compromised me beyond repairing while rescuing me from my folly. He's been doing a very good job of ignoring me all Season whilst he flirted and danced with the prettiest of the current batch of débutantes. He was obviously trying to make up his mind which one to marry and it certainly wasn't me he expected to walk up the aisle towards him at the end of the festivities, Izzie.'

'Yet he gained *your* attention by proving himself not to be an eager young puppy to be kicked away or taken for granted any longer, if he was ever as tame as you thought him to be in the first place, of course, which I doubt.'

'I really don't think that was what he was trying to do, Izzie. Indeed, Edmund made it very plain to me from the instant he set eyes on me again this year that he no longer cared one way or the other *what* I thought of him. He was seeking a pretty and conformable wife, and he certainly wasn't looking in my direction to find her since I am patently neither pretty nor conformable.'

'No, you're beautiful and spirited, which makes you far more interesting and exciting to be around, but did you really care what he thought of you, Kate? You didn't seem to during that first Season when he followed you about like an overenthusiastic dog guarding a bone.'

'I've missed him,' she admitted rather grudgingly.

'And if you'd been caught behaving improperly with any other man than Edmund, you'd have meekly married him instead?' Isabella demanded ruthlessly.

'Perhaps,' Kate mumbled as if she were the younger of the sisters by several years and didn't want to own up to some iniquitous deed she was ashamed of, even while her mind screamed an unequivocal 'No!' So apparently she'd rather face disgrace and social exclusion for the rest of her days than wed anyone but Edmund, Viscount Shuttleworth, which seemed close to disastrous when he could put her out of the room with such breathtaking arrogance, then go back to discussing details of their wedding with Eiliane as if they didn't concern her in the least.

'Then you're an idiot.'

'Well and so I am. Eiliane thinks me one, you obviously agree and Edmund hasn't stopped glowering at me since I was stupid enough to agree we have no choice but to marry each other after all.'

'And you're just meekly accepting the majority decision on your sanity, are you, sister mine? That really doesn't sound at all like you.'

'It's not, but I don't *feel* at all like me at the moment, Izzie,' Kate admitted her confusion at last and surprised herself by feeling considerably better for doing so.

'Good, then there's clearly hope for you yet.'

'I fail to see why my feeling confused about it could mean my marriage to Edmund is any more likely to succeed.'

'I know, that's what makes the whole situation so irresistibly amusing,' Isabella said annoyingly and refused to expand on her cryptic statement any further.

Chapter Twelve

'The Earl of Carnwood and Viscount Shuttleworth, your ladyship,' the Pemberleys' butler announced solemnly six days later, then he reluctantly shut the door after that noble pair before he could observe the full effect of his announcement on the ladies.

'Good heavens, whatever are *you* doing here?' Kate demanded of her brother-in-law as soon as he stepped into the room. She noted that, even though he was as tall and powerful and full of life as ever, the Earl of Carnwood quite failed to overshadow Edmund as he should have done just with his impressive physical presence.

It wasn't much for her to ask of a brother-in-law and ex-guardian, she chided him silently. All he'd needed to do to make her feel a lot better about her seesawing emotions and uncertain temper was to put a pampered young aristocrat in the shade for her with his effortless poise and that air of barely contained energy Miranda obviously found so irresistible. Not that she had the least desire to lust after her sister's husband, of course, especially now he was no longer her guardian and she'd come to regard him as an elder brother, but Kit could at least have done her the favour of putting her betrothed back into the Edmund-shaped slot she'd once managed to make him fit into so neatly.

'Where else did you expect me to be at a time like this?' Kit replied harshly, as if only just restraining himself from shaking her, which might well be the case since he'd probably hated travelling every last mile that now separated him from Miranda and their children, both born and still just about unborn.

'We were managing perfectly well without you,' she defended herself, unable to conceal the fact that her gaze was locked on Edmund as if she was waiting for whatever danger he posed to reveal itself so she could jump the other way.

Except he was her affianced husband now and shortly she'd no longer have the luxury of avoiding anything about him. The delicious shiver that accompanied that inescapable truth distracted her so shockingly that she heard Kit's impatient reply as if from a vast distance.

'So well that you got trapped in such a deep hole by drifting about someone else's house as if you owned it, that Edmund was forced to dig you out of it at the cost of his own freedom,' Kit accused her crossly.

'I take it you both had an unpleasant journey then,' Eiliane finally managed to say with the manic cheerfulness of a hostess doing her best to cope with an impossible social situation and two travel-stained noblemen.

Both evidently thought their business too important to go to their respective homes so they could bathe and change before they strolled into a lady's private sitting room. Which made Kate's heart leap with apprehension for what they thought so urgent it couldn't wait just an hour to be dealt with in a more leisurely fashion.

'Indeed we did, Lady Pemberley. It was infernally damp and ridiculously hasty and I'd very much prefer to be at home with my wife, not caught up in some ridiculous bumble-broth of my sister-in-law's making,' Kit told Eiliane with only a slight softening of the formidable frown knitting his dark brows.

He continued to watch Kate as if she was about to add something equally silly and dangerous to the misadventure that had forced Edmund to pay him a hasty visit in the first place. She squirmed under his condemning gaze, despite feeling Kit was being ungracious and unfair, and that she'd done nothing particularly awful. It wasn't as if she'd gone into that room for any other reason than to avoid an importunate suitor and a nasty public scene when she would have been forced to repulse his obnoxious advances in no uncertain terms. Kit wouldn't have liked it if he'd been forced to gallop south to extricate her from Bestholme's predatory clutches and bear her home in disgrace, instead of agreeing for her to wed Edmund as he'd always wanted her to.

'Pray come and sit by the fire,' Eiliane invited soothingly and Kate knew she owed her friend fervent thanks for trying to deflect Kit's rarely aroused temper, before he gave her the full benefit of his pent-up frustrations.

'I allowed myself the luxury of ordering one lit today, despite it being springtide according to the calendar, so you can both enjoy my extravagance and I won't have any standing on ceremony from you, dear Edmund, now that you're almost a member of the family.'

Now one storm at least had been averted, Kate almost caused another by nervously giggling at the contrary effect Eiliane's invitation had on her two visitors. Kit relaxed enough to mutter something about all his dirt and had the very idea of him going across the square to change before he could sit down and recover from his hasty journey summarily dismissed. He shrugged wearily and subsided into the comfortable chair by the fire before gratefully stretching his long legs towards the warmth with a long sigh of relief. Would that Edmund followed his example, Kate decided wistfully, as he stood aloof instead. He was watching her like a cat at a mouse hole, which seemed rather harsh of him when she was still trying to conceal the rush of pleasure her first sight of him after several days apart had provoked in her fast-beating heart and very confused mind.

How very unfair of the fates to allow her immunity to his looks and charm three years ago and now make her so ridiculously sensitive to his every look and gesture, when he was far less charming, if even more formidably handsome, than he'd been then. The fates had a great deal to answer for, she decided bitterly, and pretended to be absorbed in the list in front of her. Unfortunately it was one of Eiliane's interminable ones concerning their hasty wedding and she blushed foolishly at the very thought of the future looming inexorably nearer with every day that passed. It really wasn't ladylike to feel so wickedly curious about becoming a wife in every sense of the word.

A little maidenly shrinking at the unthinkable intimacies ahead of her would be far more proper, then she could forgive herself for being such a fool as to turn him down so often and so emphatically in the past. She shivered at the very thought of such incredible closeness between a man and his new wife entering the marriage bed together and wondered if it was possible to conceal her innermost thoughts and secret hopes from an intelligent and observant husband. She'd have her answer to that question all too soon and tried to look inscrutable when she glanced at him.

Edmund seemed more concerned with trying to read her deepest secrets in her face than with his own comfort, even after the hard ride he and Kit must have endured to get here so quickly. Kate squirmed under his examining gaze, just managing to meet it with more of an effort than she liked and she tightened her betraying fingers on her notebook lest he see how they were trembling.

'Was the journey so very bad?' she finally managed to ask.

'It was cold and wet as well as unpleasantly muddy,' he admitted at last and Kate couldn't dismiss the idea he might have enjoyed it far more if he'd been bound for Wychwood on any other errand.

'I'm sorry,' she offered stiffly.

'I really have no idea why,' he said with a ghost of

a smile, 'even you can hardly be responsible for the vagaries of the weather.'

Oh dear, none of this was going according to plan and how would they ever get on as man and wife if even a conversation about the state of the roads and the weather could turn from innocuous to personal in such a stilted, unpromising way?

'I was being polite,' she informed him crossly and had to control her temper when the contrary man evidently found the notion amusing and actually managed to look as if he might like to know her after all.

'Forgive me for not recognising the effort it cost you,' he teased with such a warm smile she couldn't resist a ridiculous need to grin back at him, just as if she'd been sitting here twiddling her thumbs since he'd gone and waiting for him to get back so she could simper at him like a besotted milkmaid.

'I'm not really so ill mannered, am I?' she asked.

'No, I recall being crushed by your exquisite manners on more than one occasion.'

'Then I shall endeavour to treat you with excessive rudeness from now on.'

'I'd certainly prefer that to the impenetrable politeness you once used to depress my pretences,' he said wryly.

'Then for goodness' sake sit down, you're giving me a crick in the neck as well as keeping the warmth of the fire from the rest of us.'

'Much better,' he murmured as he sat down cautiously on the sofa beside her with an apparent docility that no longer deceived her in the least.

Quite aware that very little about their supposedly private interaction had escaped either Kit or Eiliane, Kate decided a front of apparent serenity would serve her best against their rampant curiosity about her relationship with Edmund.

'So how is my sister?' she asked Kit as she handed him a cup of tea while Welland rounded up his acolytes and left the room once more, surprised not to have it thrust back at her while he demanded something more potent after such a journey. The Earl of Carnwood was in danger of becoming civilised, she decided wryly, and met his self-conscious glare with an innocently enquiring look.

'Well enough,' he admitted gruffly and sipped the fragrant Chinese blend Eiliane always insisted on having served with carefully concealed appreciation. 'It's quite refreshing after a long ride,' he defended himself and Kate saw Edmund grin at Kit's discomfiture with an openness that told her they'd reached a new equality on the road somewhere between here and Wychwood.

'Never having been overburdened with female relatives nagging me to forsake my wicked ways, I've always had the liberty of choosing which ways to pursue for myself, until now of course,' Edmund said with a polite bow and a bland look Kate didn't altogether trust.

Despite not believing she'd ever be allowed much say with regard to his behaviour, it occurred to her that she'd never seen him drunk, nor heard it whispered that he indulged in private debauchery even the gossips dared not be specific about, for fear of polluting their own tongues and reputations. Well, apart from that annoyingly persistent murmur about him and Lady Tedinton that she didn't believe for a moment, of course. Unfortunately she didn't have much faith in Edmund's implication that she alone would have permission to plague him about his foibles in future, let alone believing she'd be listened to once he'd made his mind up on any course of action he considered important.

'Lucky you,' Kit responded and Kate wondered how much difference even Miranda's opinions made to him once he had determined on something.

Since Kit's two sisters must have been responsible for any feminine nagging done before he and Miranda married, and her elder sister was a very decided female under all that serene beauty of hers, Kate supposed it was therefore just about possible for a strong woman to influence a masculine force of nature like Kit. The question being, of course, whether she had any chance of altering a course of action the equally stubborn male she was to marry might choose to embark on.

'One thing I'm not going to be moved so much as an inch upon, though, is the subject of your marriage,' Kit declared with the rock-hard set to his chin indicating a state of mind Miranda had learnt to circumvent rather than try to change.

'Then you disapprove?' Kate heard herself ask squeakily, even desperately, as if marrying Edmund had become the be all and end all of her entire existence.

'Of course I don't,' he replied and Kate wondered if she was the only one who heard the unsaid aside that she was an idiot to even suggest he might.

'What about our marriage, then?' she asked, and had

to physically stop herself reaching for Edmund's hand as if she needed his strength and support to face her brother-in-law's weary irritation with cool self-command.

'It won't take place in London,' Kit informed her bluntly.

Kate annoyed herself intensely once more by looking to Edmund for his opinion of that ultimatum before expressing her own. 'But what about Isabella?' she managed to say, unable to read his silver-green gaze and having to do all the work on her own after all.

'What about her?' Kit asked.

'It's her début Season and she's been late enough beginning it already, without her being dragged north to see me married and make it even shorter for her.'

'I propose that we ask her opinion of the idea before we start galloping off on wild-goose chases in either direction,' Eiliane suggested with the exquisitely breakable serenity of a lady who'd just spent the last few days hastily planning a fashionable wedding at St George's in Hanover Square that now looked very unlikely to take place.

'Well, where is she then?' Kit asked impatiently, as if Isabella had been deliberately obstructive in not refusing to stir an inch outside the front door until he reached town, especially when she hadn't known he was coming in the first place.

'Shopping—the Mausley family arrived in town the day before yesterday and you know very well that Fanny Mausley has always been Izzie's bosom-bow, Kit,' Kate said as pacifically as she could manage when she was beginning to feel rather impatient with her brother-in-law's weary irritability herself.

'And if only she wasn't such a breathy, overeager female, I'd be a lot more ready to forgive her for carrying my ward off on a hunt for fripperies when all I want is to get all this nonsense settled and go back home as fast as a pack of hired nags can carry me now I've worn out my own, and that won't be nigh fast enough for my taste,' Kit grumbled.

'It's not nonsense, it's my *wedding* and you sound just like the crabby guardian out of some Drury Lane comedy, overeager to get back to your acres and forsake the hurly-burly of the town for ever.' She managed to swallow her own annoyance to tease him and won a reluctant smile and a self-deprecating shrug.

'That's what the love of a good woman can do to a man, Shuttleworth, so be warned by my example and start *your* married life as you mean to go on,' Kit warned.

'Oh, I'll do that, never fret,' Edmund replied with a mocking glance at her that jolted Kate out of her mood of half-contented acceptance of her new lot in life and left her struggling to control her temper again.

'And *I* shall be forewarned,' she pronounced haughtily and had to conceal her ridiculously oscillating feelings for a very different reason when Edmund's smile turned openly sceptical. He seemed more intent on challenging her on every front than wooing her into accepting this marriage with good grace and it was just stupid to feel the least bit tearful about it.

'I do enjoy a refreshing tussle to whet my appetite,

especially when I know exactly how and where the engagement will end,' he murmured for her ears alone.

Kate marvelled at the conspiratorial glance she intercepted between Kit and Eiliane when she managed to tear her gaze from Edmund's and pretend to disregard his double-edged teasing. Surely they weren't deluded enough to think she and Edmund were in the midst of some besotted lovers' tiff just for the pleasure of making up their quarrel at the end of it? She could see nothing but some implacable purpose that involved his supremacy and her submission in his eyes, even if he was doing his best to use the sensual heat that had flared up between them as soon as their gazes clashed to get his own way. Struggling with a morass of contrary emotions, she wondered idly where cool and composed Katherine Alstone had gone, just when she needed her most.

This older, infinitely wiser and far more dangerous Edmund Worth called irresistibly to her senses and threatened to override her promise to herself never to fall in love, never risk her very soul for the traitor emotion that had lured her big sister into an elopement that had broken up their family and cast Miranda into a terrible limbo where she was excluded from everything she'd held most dear for five long years. Kate didn't love him, had promised herself *not* to love him from almost the first instant she'd laid eyes on him, she now realised. Yet just because she suddenly longed to learn the intimacies between a man and a woman that had previously been too secret and dangerous to risk exploring with him, that didn't mean she had to change her mind about everything else and become a meek little cipher to an unexpectedly powerful husband.

'Don't flatter yourself, my lord,' she managed to hiss back almost soundlessly.

'Oh, I don't, and I certainly never promise what I can't deliver, Kate. Surely you know me well enough to have realised that by now, my dear.'

'Well enough to know I'm not *your dear* any more,' she muttered.

'The longer our acquaintance goes on, Kate, the more I become convinced you've little idea what really goes on in your own head, let alone mine.'

'I certainly don't have a clue what goes on in yours,' she told him as fiercely as anyone could when trying not to be overheard by two very interested listeners.

'No, I really don't think you have,' he replied with such a delighted smile he almost charmed her into abandoning her cross-grained mood and smiling right back at him, before the implication of his words hit her and she frowned instead.

'Nor do I want to,' she told him ungraciously.

'Ah, but you will, Kate. You undoubtedly will, once we're finally husband and wife and I have you all to myself at long last.'

'That sounds more like a threat than a promise,' she faltered in a most un-Kate-like fashion.

'It probably is; you've made it into one by your own stubbornness over the years since we first met.'

'Nonsense,' she managed to scoff unconvincingly, all those spurned offers and ignored courtesies he'd once wooed her with so vainly piling up to mock her. Now she was to marry the wretched man anyway, she would welcome just a tithe of that worshipful dedication to her lightest whim he'd shown all those years ago.

'Luckily for you I can hear the sound of a small tempest arriving home, even through Lord Pemberley's substantial walls and fine doors, so no doubt your sister has arrived home from her excursion at last and we can find out if she chooses to stay here or remove to Derbyshire to witness our wedding.'

'At least she's got a choice,' Kate mumbled grumpily, but he didn't bother to reply.

'I told Fanny and her mama we would meet them at the theatre tonight, Eiliane,' Isabella announced even before Welland had the door open properly. 'I hope we're not engaged for some silly waltzing party full of giggling girls and spotty youths, for Kean is playing Hamlet and Fanny's brother has hired a box.'

'No need to ask if you're fully recovered, minx,' Kit told her, getting to his feet with a warm smile of welcome. 'And being as contrary as ever from what I can see. I can't help wondering why we bothered to go to all that trouble to arrange your début so carefully, since you're finding it all so tedious.'

'Kit! Oh, how lovely,' Isabella exclaimed, throwing the bonnet she was carrying by its strings into a corner and herself at her not-very-stern guardian, who caught her, then swung her round in an exuberant bear hug.

Kate couldn't help but contrast Kit's bad-tempered greeting for her with his delight at seeing Isabella. She didn't feel jealous of the open affection between them because she loved her sister too much to begrudge her the security of loving her guardian and brother by marriage, but it hurt a little that she didn't share such a warm relationship with him. Yet Kate realised fairly that she alone was responsible for keeping Kit at a distance, even if he had taken her aloofness at face value and stopped there.

'Contrary female,' Edmund muttered and she marvelled that he could read her so easily, while her shrewd brother-in-law and usually perceptive little sister were apparently quite unable to, which was probably just as well at the moment.

He smiled and shrugged as if he didn't know quite how he did it, either. Kate suspected that, as an orphan, even a very privileged and wealthy one, he'd learnt to watch and weigh up the feelings and motives of those around him from a very early age. He'd grown up with as little reason to trust others as she had learnt much later in childhood, yet he'd won his battle for his own unique place in the world and she felt as if she was still fighting for hers. Edmund George Francis St Erith Standon-Worth, Viscount Shuttleworth, really was an extraordinary man, she decided, and she wasn't quite certain she deserved him.

'Annoying man,' she replied placidly enough.

'And I couldn't possibly comment on your state of mind or temper,' he teased. Perhaps it was just as well Kit recalled he was weary and interrupted them before Kate could stare besottedly at her own fiancé, as if he meant more to her than he rightly should if they weren't marrying for love.

'Now we've got all that over with, and before I cross to my splendid mansion and change into equally splendid evening dress in order to escort you to Drury Lane tonight, brat, let's settle what's to be done next between us all, at long last, shall we?' Kit said as soon as they were all back in their seats and he and Edmund and Isabella were working their way through plates of scones and several cups of tea.

'Apart from Kean?' Izzie asked between mouthfuls.

'Of course, no waltzing party could ever compare,' he reassured her approvingly, probably as pleased as the rest of them that Isabella was so deeply unimpressed with her many social triumphs and showing no signs of letting all the admiration and fulsome compliments she was receiving go to her head. 'It comes down to you deciding what you wish to do most, Isabella,' Kit went on.

Kate was surprised that Edmund had let him take charge, until she concluded they'd already decided what the absolutes were between them and she did her best not to be irritated by such masculine arrogance when there were more pressing matters to be irritated about, like planning a wedding around the projected arrival of Kit and Miranda's very imminent baby. She and Miranda should never have become entangled with two such strong males if they wanted an easy life or to get their own way all the time, she supposed ruefully.

'Your sister and Shuttleworth are determined to be wed inside a month,' Kit went on, explaining the situation in his own inimitable manner, 'although some

of us could call that indecent haste when they've been
shilly-shallying about it for the last three years. Maybe
he thinks if he doesn't get the contrary wench up the
aisle very soon, she'll change her mind and jilt him.'

'Don't be ridiculous, Kit,' Eiliane intervened with a
visible shudder that made Kate very glad she wasn't in
the least inclined to follow such a course. 'None of us
could show our faces in society for a very long time after
such a lapse of courage and good manners on Kate's
part.'

'You almost tempt me to do my best to persuade her
to do just that then, my lady Pemberley,' Kit remarked
ruefully.

They all knew that he had never done much more
than tolerate the social whirl, probably mainly for his
family's sake, and much preferred the company of the
clever men and women he'd moved amongst before the
ton ever dreamed of admitting the son of a bankrupt
drunkard to their select ranks.

'Which would almost sway me to try to call you out
one fine May morning, Carnwood,' Edmund almost
joked in return.

'An interesting way to begin a closer relationship
with your prospective bride's family, don't you think,
Shuttleworth?' Kit replied and Kate was tempted
to throw something at both of them for being so
provoking.

'And, as I have no intention of reneging on my word
now it's given, also totally hypothetical,' she chided both
of them.

'True, and you're also right to glare at me in truly

Kate-like fashion. We're wasting time and there's precious little of that with the great lover here determined to march you up the aisle in double-quick time. The dilemma is, Izzie love,' Kit went on a little more seriously, 'that Miranda would dearly love to see our Kate married, which means the wedding will have to go to her since she is far too big with child to come here. Wychwood is Kate's home as well, of course, and therefore the right and proper place for her to be married anyway.'

'And Kate has no say in the matter, I suppose?' she asked, largely because she felt it was expected of her rather than out of any real disagreement with that assertion.

'Kate always has something to say about whatever matter is being discussed,' Kit replied drily, 'but is she going to argue that black's white, before agreeing to do exactly what she and everyone else wanted her to in the first place this time, or can we take that part of the proceedings as read and get on with planning this wedding of yours instead?'

'Why does everyone seem to consider me contrary to the point of mania all of a sudden?' she asked with what she hoped was a creditable attempt at lightness.

'I can assure you it's not sudden,' Isabella muttered darkly.

'Nor is it true,' Edmund defended her. Kate took in the lovely solidarity of being half of a couple for the first time in her life as his hand in hers, his warmth next to her, reassured her that even when her strong will clashed with his immovable conviction that he was right, they would still be more than my lord and my lady to each other.

It might not be love, it might not equal the almost headlong passion and devotion Kit and Miranda had for each other, or the deep, almost surprised joy Ben Shaw and his wife, Charlotte, her former governess, took in each other, yet her once-convenient marriage was going to become a far better thing than the shadow she'd aspired to at the beginning of the Season, Kate realised. She was so glad to have avoided such a dull travesty almost by accident, but not altogether sure she deserved what she had instead, which was Edmund Worth, probably the most eligible bachelor formerly on the marriage mart. The question was, did he deserve Kate Alstone, also very eligible on paper, but perhaps a little too distrustful and shrewish in fact?

Chapter Thirteen

'I should love to be wed at Wychwood, but as I want both my sisters to be there as well, perhaps we should wait until the Season is over?' Kate suggested.

'You are not putting off marrying Lord Shuttleworth for a minute longer on my account, Kate,' Isabella told her sternly. 'Besides which, I'll be completely weary of this whole silly business by the end of a month, and I certainly can't endure the prospect of waiting another to breathe some clean air and hear some reasonably sensible conversation again at last. Whenever you set the date, I will find a way to be there, Kate, even if I have to walk to Derbyshire dragging Eiliane and the marquis away from her balls and soirées along behind me.'

'You won't have to drag me. I'm feeling strangely jaded with them all myself this year for some odd reason,' Eiliane admitted and shrugged when they all stared at their famously sociable hostess. 'I suppose I'm just not as young as I used to be and lack the energy I once had,' she told them, which made Kate meet Izzie's concerned gaze with a shrug and a frown of her own.

Eiliane usually had almost boundless vitality and could outstay most of the younger set at the balls, concerts and soirées the London Season abounded in.

'Anyway,' Eiliane insisted, 'Pemberley and I will be there whatever date you decide on, Kate, my dear. Lord Liverpool will just have to manage without my husband for a few days while he attends to more important matters than the tedious affairs of state that wretched man keeps bothering him with.'

'Perhaps we'd best consult his lordship about when would be the best time for him all the same,' Kate suggested, reeling slightly at the idea that her wedding was more important than the fate of nations and Lord Pemberley's work for the government. 'And we must consult Mr Draycott about dates as well, because there's no point in us settling on one if Wychwood Church is not available when we want it.'

'Draycott sent a list of possible dates for us to argue about,' Kit recalled. 'Shuttleworth has it, I believe.'

'I do. Kate and I will meet with Lord Pemberley and discuss them, after we've decided which ones would suit us best for ourselves,' Edmund said, his eyes cool and challenging as they met the Earl of Carnwood's.

'Then everything is well on the way to being settled,' Eiliane interrupted brightly as if she really thought they might argue or worse in her sitting room, when Kate knew both were too gentlemanly to risk upsetting a woman they both held in such strong affection.

'So it would seem,' Kit said wearily and ran an

impatient hand through his unruly dark locks. 'Now I'm for Alstone House and a much-needed bath and shave, then a quick nap,' he said gruffly.

'And let's hope you come back in a better mood,' Isabella dared to tease.

'We can only hope so, as I still have to draft a suitable notice announcing Kate and Edmund's betrothal to send to the papers before I can bring about that wonderful transformation, don't forget, so I'll have to rack my brains and consult Lord Pemberley's secretary about the correct form first. You have no idea how much easier my life was when I was a carefree black sheep of the family, nor how much I look forward to shuffling off at least one of my responsibilities on to you, Shuttleworth,' he replied with a rather wicked grin before he took himself off to bring about those wonders.

Edmund bowed and left with a more conventional farewell to transform himself into the perfectly turned-out nobleman they were more familiar with than the travel-stained pirate he resembled just now.

'Well, really,' Isabella said indignantly once the three ladies were alone again, 'you'd think Kit would be a little more civil on the subject of Kate's nuptials and her future happiness, wouldn't you?'

'He's concerned about her,' Eiliane explained and surprised Kate herself with such a reason for his gruffness with her.

'Why on earth would he be?' she betrayed herself into asking as if she couldn't imagine why Kit cared one way or the other, so long as he was rid of all responsibility for her. Which was untrue, as she knew he cared deep down that she should be well and happy with whatever husband she chose to wed.

'Because he's not sure you and Edmund are marrying for the right reasons.'

'But that's ridiculous; Shuttleworth has been wildly in love with Kate ever since he first set eyes on her,' Isabella argued.

'But was Kate equally wild for him?' Eiliane asked with a steady look.

'I should have been,' she replied with a self-depre-cating grimace. 'I could have been, if only I'd let myself see how different he was from all the others.'

'And from Nevin,' Izzie said and this time it wasn't a question. 'You were always afraid of doing as Miranda did and falling for a man who turned out to be nothing like he appeared, Kate. It's a problem we both have to face after watching that monster cajole and flatter and creep until he had Miranda believing black was white, after all. I was only a little girl at the time and far too wrapped up in myself to take a lot of notice of him, but Kate was always too acute for her own good, Eiliane, and much too easily hurt by everything that happened to us after he came.'

'I know, I should have been there, I should have come as soon as your parents died and certainly when I heard that your poor brother had been sent home from school after that wretched fever,' Eiliane condemned herself, as if everything that had happened to the Alstone sisters since before Nevin Braxton eloped with Miranda had been her doing.

'No, I've already told you that you're not to do this to

yourself!' Kate ordered furiously. 'Your first husband was ill at the time. In fact, the poor man was dying, so how could you just up and leave him while you came to Derbyshire on a fool's errand? You loved him, Eiliane, and he needed you. You must never again blame yourself for something my damnable cousin Celia and infernal aunt were responsible for.'

'You're ordering me about like some warrior queen, love, and do mind your language in case something like that slips out in public, even if it's a perfectly good description of the repellent creatures,' Eiliane said.

'It just makes me so angry to hear you blame yourself for not anticipating the evil those two thought up and carried out, as if you should have known about it all along,' Kate replied brusquely.

'And it's so very hard to make her angry, don't you agree, Eiliane?' Izzie put in with an angelic expression of sisterly patience on her lovely face and laughter lurking in her eyes.

'It was, at one time, far too difficult, Isabella,' Eiliane said as if it had been something that worried her far more than Kate thought it should have done, considering how wayward her emotions could be when she gave them full rein. 'But at last it seems much easier to goad her into all sorts of passions again, which is a blessing I'm profoundly thankful for.'

'And one I shall suspend judgement about until after she's wed and Shuttleworth can cope with her tempers and her wild ideas instead of us.'

'Why, thank you, sister dear,' Kate said ironically. 'I *am* still here, you know?'

'I do; you're hard to ignore.'

'Then kindly remember I'm still your big sister and that I know exactly where and when all your darkest misdeeds occurred.'

'Sometimes a person's memory can be too good,' Isabella replied with a very steady look that told Kate she wasn't referring to her own childish mischief.

'Yes, I'm finally beginning to realise that,' she admitted at last and felt as if a huge weight was lifting off her shoulders, along with the dark memories that had perhaps been allowed to shape her view of the world for far too long. 'I almost let them win, didn't I?'

'So long as you don't now, that's all that matters,' Isabella replied and Kate wondered how her little sister ever got to be so wise.

'I forgot one small detail before I left for Wychwood, Kate,' Edmund said when she came into the small drawing room of Pemberley House that evening. Kate finally realised why Eiliane had lost a glove, asked Izzie to go and fetch it for her and then suddenly recalled something else she'd forgotten, and had simply had to go and fetch it herself, leaving the newly affianced couple alone.

'Apart from my missing proposal?' she dared to joke, because treading on eggshells with each other for the rest of their natural lives was a prospect she couldn't endure, when one of the things she'd always liked the most about him was his wry and often self-deprecating sense of the ridiculous.

'No need for you to garner another of those when you already have a full set,' he told her resolutely. 'I've told you already that you can't have that, Kate, but maybe this will go some way for making up for the lack of it?'

He handed her a ring box and within it was the most lovely sapphire-and-diamond ring she had ever laid eyes on and she'd seen Miranda's, which until tonight had seemed unsurpassable.

'It's completely beautiful, Edmund,' she said, staring down at the amazing depth of colour the sapphires held and the pure clarity of the fine diamonds that sinuously curled around them in a lover's knot.

'I saw it years ago and knew then that it could have been made for you,' he told her uncomfortably, as if he was ashamed of the headlong youth he'd been then. She could have stamped on her own toe in fury at herself for doing that to him, except it would have made her fall over in a heap at his feet and, she reminded herself, she'd already promised herself that she wasn't going to do that.

'Thank you, but can I wear it?'

'I'd be highly insulted if you didn't,' he said with a wry grin.

She fumbled as she tried to take the lovely thing out of its bed of finest velvet with shaking hands and he did what she'd secretly hoped he might and took it from her to extract it neatly from its box and place it on her finger, presumably so she didn't drop it and condemn them both to an undignified search on their hands and knees.

'There you are, you see, I told you it could have been made for you,' he said as he played with her fingers and suddenly very little of Kate's attention was on the masterpiece of the jeweller's art on her ring finger.

'Edmund,' she said huskily and even she heard the note of yearning in her voice, but somehow no longer cared if it gave away how much she'd missed him.

'Did you really long for me so much that you're actually prepared to admit it, sweet Kate?' he murmured and drew her even closer.

'Yes,' she admitted, because as she was almost in his arms, her eyes heavy with longing and her lips parted and doing their best to invite his kisses, there seemed very little point denying it. She had missed him ever since he arrived in town this Season and she saw how changed he was from the lovelorn youth she remembered, then realised what she'd lost three years ago by refusing him so persistently that he'd finally listened to her and gone away.

'Good,' he said with exasperating masculine superiority and stepped away from her as Eiliane called something back to Isabella and they both stood on the stairs, very obviously pretending not to listen, but doing their best to hear every word.

'Good?' she muttered with a bitter glance in his direction. 'About as good as finding cherry-stones in a pie.'

'I *like* cherries, Kate,' he said in a ruthless undertone, his eyes on her lips as he licked his own, as if anticipating the ripeness of her mouth moist and eager under his. 'I long for them when they're so red and ripe and luscious, picked just fresh off the tree. Then I just want to bite into them and feel their sharp sweetness on my tongue again so very badly.'

'Very nice,' she said aloud, her tone flat and her eyes on his, flaring defiance at him for attempting to seduce her with words, under her supposed chaperon and her younger sister's very noses.

'Not just nice, Kate, but also delicious, pleasurable and compulsive,' he told her, placing a wicked emphasis on each description that made a shiver of anticipation run through her. 'We really must order sweet cherries at our wedding breakfast; I would so hate to do without their unique and piquant flavour at our celebration when we'll be setting out on our lives together at long last,' he concluded.

'I will order a tart especially for you.'

'What an obliging wife you're promising to become,' he parried and, even as he picked up her evening cloak, he took elaborate care to enjoy every chance to touch her as he caressed it into place over her nearly naked shoulders and exposed neck. Somehow he managed to drive her half furious with him and half inclined to swoon with frustrated passion at his feet all at the same time.

'And what a disobliging husband I seem to be chaining myself to,' she managed to say lightly for the benefit of their audience.

'You flatter me.'

'That was not my intention.'

'At least I'll soon be in a position to give you a few lessons in how to tell truth from fiction, Kate,' he said, looking inexcusably pleased with himself.

'First, my lord,' she informed him snippily, 'you'll need to find out what the differences between them are for yourself.'

'I thought we could do that together,' he said so smoothly that she glared at him in frustration, not quite sure if she wanted to slap him or kiss him.

'Come *on*, you two,' Isabella interrupted them impatiently, 'the farce will be over and the first act as well before we even get to the theatre if you don't hurry yourselves, instead of casting sheep's eyes at each other in that nauseating fashion.'

'Really, Isabella,' Eiliane rebuked her, 'that's such a vulgar turn of phrase.'

'But apt, they're nigh as annoying as Kit and Miranda and I never thought I'd be able to accuse Kate of thinking the world well lost for love.'

'I doubt you can now, either,' Edmund said with a wry smile as he finally took his hands away from Kate's shoulders and left her feeling horribly cold and bereft all of a sudden.

'Whether I can or not, please would you two kindly hurry? Even if you don't mind me glowering at you both for the rest of the evening for causing us to be late, I doubt very much if you'd endure Kit doing it with half as much detachment.'

Eiliane shuddered theatrically at the very thought and chivvied them all down the broad steps to her luxurious carriage before Kate could even think of a sufficiently crushing reply to annihilate her little sister with. Then, once they were ensconced in the carriage, she had the fiery consciousness of Edmund sitting next to her to struggle with, so they managed to arrive in Drury Lane with Isabella still uncrushed and almost unbearably smug as a consequence.

'I'll pay you back for that,' Kate managed to mutter to her when she thought the others too busy with polite manoeuvring as they descended from the carriage to hear either of them.

'You can try,' Izzie said before accepting Edmund's gloved hand to help her descend with more grace than she deserved to have at her command, at least in her older sister's opinion.

'Oh, you *really* should have known better than to say that,' Kate said menacingly, then promptly forgot the inventive punishments she'd been planning as she placed her hand in Edmund's in her turn.

She marvelled that her sister could do that as coolly as if it was just an everyday courtesy, which she supposed dazedly that it was between Edmund and her sister. Fire seemed to shoot through their joined fingers and along her oversensitive nerves to render her so open to the promise of it all that she was almost beyond using her legs in their accustomed fashion, let alone her sharp tongue.

'Now then, children,' Eiliane said reprovingly, as if she had no idea Kate was moonstruck, or bewitched, or whatever it was Edmund had done to her with that first kiss in Lord Wyndover's darkened book room. 'There is a time and place for nursery squabbles and such tit for tat and this is neither. There will be no lemonade spilt with apparent clumsiness over each other, nor will either of you step contritely on the other's hem as you climb the stairs to our box. Nor will Carnwood be further tried with your childish bickering after his wearisome ride to get here just when we all need him so badly, do I make myself clear?'

'Abundantly, I should think,' Edmund said, looking unforgivably amused that both sisters were trying not to look as chagrined as a pair of naughty schoolboys up before their headmaster.

'As a mountain stream,' Kate muttered.

'*I* wouldn't dream of behaving so badly,' Isabella asserted with such angelic innocence not one of them believed her.

'Then don't,' Kit greeted them as he strode forwards. 'Whatever it is Eiliane is threatening you so magnificently over, just don't.'

Isabella sighed. 'Oh, very well, I suppose we are a little too old for such things now,' she said regretfully.

'I very much doubt it, but I've had a long and rather trying day and am over a hundred miles away from my wife to make it all much worse, so I think I can safely admit my temper is currently on a fine trigger. So do you actually want to see this interminable rigmarole of a play or not, brat?'

'I do,' Isabella agreed with a look of such charming docility Kate wondered if her little sister should not be on the stage playing Ophelia to Kean's Hamlet, instead of just watching some less talented actress do it instead.

'You have no idea how lucky you are,' Edmund informed Kate as they were finally welcomed into the box the Mausleys had hired. She turned and looked enquiringly at him. 'You belong to such a close family that you can fight with your sister, be at outs with your brother-in-law and earn a mighty scold from your much-tried chaperon and mentor all in one evening.'

'And that's a privilege?'

'It is from where I'm standing,' he said with a smile of acknowledgement that, yes, it was an odd thing to envy her. 'I want my children to have it, too.'

'Have what?'

'That closeness, the chance to be knit into a family that will bicker and snipe at each other one moment and unite against the world the next to protect and love all the members of it as fiercely as tigers.'

'I don't think...' she began and then the implications of what he was saying finally sank in.

His children would be hers as well now and, through her, part of the wider family she was fortunate indeed to have grown up in. A family she'd failed to appreciate fully these last five years, since Miranda had come home and found Kit, then put the deep bond all three sisters had with each other at the heart of her own new family.

'I really don't think often enough, do I?' she continued with a rueful smile.

'Never mind, I dare say I've had more than enough time to do it for both of us these last three years,' he replied with an answering one that was much gentler than any he'd given her all Season.

'Oh, come *on*, you two,' Isabella summoned them impatiently, rolling her eyes in a pantomime of resigned exasperation at Fanny Mausley which she doubtless thought Kate couldn't see. 'Have you both become deaf as well as daft for each other?'

'Isabella Alstone, you will keep a still tongue in your head on the subject of your sister's private business, or risk being taken home before the curtain even comes up on the first act,' Eiliane snapped irritably and Kate spared a moment to wonder what ailed their usually even-tempered friend.

'Aye, be quiet, brat,' Kit drawled warningly and Isabella subsided onto the seat next to her best friend and managed to be silent for all of two minutes.

Once the main performance of the night began there was none of the usual murmurs and interruptions from the audience, who were as caught by the menace and turmoil stalking the state of Denmark on the stage as Isabella, who sat still and spellbound by the whole performance. It was a *tour de force*; even Kit had to admit that when the curtains closed for the interval. Kean had held his audience completely in thrall from the moment he stepped onto the stage and Isabella was voluntarily silent for all of a minute before she came out of her drama-induced daydream.

'Better than any ball,' she said as she finally left Elsinore for London.

'Don't look to me for an argument,' Kit said and even Fanny Mausley agreed it had been a very fine start to their evening, if a little gloomy, and now she could see why her brother had dragged them here when they could have danced all night instead, which was high praise, considering she adored the social whirl and all the glitter and gossip that went with it.

Young Mr Mausley had ordered refreshments delivered and looked very pleased with the success of his plan to please Isabella, even if her equally besotted suitors and friends of both families flitted in and out of their box to compare notes on actors and audience alike. Kate's ring was eyed enviously by ladies she knew would eagerly tell everyone who'd listen that the elder Miss Alstone had indeed captured the most eligible and desirable bachelor on the marriage mart as soon as they set foot outside the door. She did her best to be amused by her current notoriety and wondered for at least ten seconds if Isabella might one day discover her match in the obviously besotted but still painfully young Frederick Mausley, just as she had in Edmund, then dismissed the idea out of hand. Frederick had neither the strength of character nor the promise of grace and mature power Edmund had possessed at a similar age, if only she had let herself see it.

Chapter Fourteen

'So here you are, Miss Alstone,' Lady Tedinton drawled as she insinuated herself into the box and sat herself down in the chair next to Kate while she was still busy wondering how the woman's presence tonight hadn't registered with her until now. 'What a costly bauble you're wearing tonight, and how fortunate for you that you managed to catch such a fine fish in your net before your sister arrived in town to eclipse you.'

It must have been self-protective instincts that kept her ignorant, Kate decided, as she froze a visible shudder of revulsion in its tracks and faced her enemy as if having trouble recalling who she was. She managed a curt nod of acknowledgement and fought a hollow feeling in the pit of her stomach when she realised Edmund had left the box for some reason while she was having her ring inspected once more.

'Most young ladies who transgress the limits of acceptable behaviour pay for it with their reputations.

You are fortunate to belong to such a rich and powerful family, Miss Alstone,' the woman said silkily and how could Kate fight back, when she was supposed to be ignorant of the repulsive and possibly criminal behaviour her enemy indulged in when she thought nobody was listening?

'Indeed,' she said distantly instead.

'I was not so lucky,' her ladyship went on melodramatically.

Kate raised her eyebrows and allowed herself a pointed stare at the glitter of diamonds decorating her ladyship's throat, ears and wrists and the finest silk gown that clothed her and she hoped she managed to convey her incredulity, as well as her indifference to anything else the spiteful creature had to say.

'Tedinton rescued me from my encounter with a certain gentleman when I was much younger and probably more foolish than even you are now,' she went on, as if warming to the picture of herself as the *ingénue* she'd probably never been. 'As the sixteen-year-old daughter of a mere country squire with no fortune or aristocratic connections, I was easy prey for a cold-hearted seducer, although he was barely two years older than me when he got me with child and laughed in my face when I begged him to marry me.'

'How affecting,' Kate said expressionlessly.

'You won't look so smug when I tell you his name,' Lady Tedinton leaned forwards to whisper venomously.

'Will I not?' Kate asked carelessly, finding the whole

performance distasteful and a lot less convincing than any she'd seen on the stage tonight.

'It was Edward Worthington—such a neat alias for a nobleman to go carousing under away from his own nest, don't you think?'

'It might be, if I believed a single word you have to say.'

'Do you think I care what you think?' her ladyship asked with barely veiled hatred.

'Then why are you here?'

'To let you know exactly who and what you are about to wed.'

'How altruistic of you, Lady Tedinton, but I don't believe you care a snap of your fingers if I marry a paragon of all the virtues or Bluebeard himself.'

'Very well then, you tell me why he should be allowed to get away with what he did to me. He fully intends to marry you and pretend that his honour forced him to do so. How can he act as if he's so noble and upright and correct when he left me outcast and pregnant so young as if he had nothing to do with it? Well, I won't have it. I refuse to sit by and let him behave as if he never seduced me, then left me so friendless and alone that I had to wed a man thirty years my senior to give our bastard a name.'

'How strange, then, that when you were sixteen my fiancé was probably just beginning at Eton and was therefore far too young to compromise anyone, and that your stepdaughter told me just the other evening that her eldest half sister was but four years of age and her little brother a mere babe in arms. While only you can truly

know their provenance, your ladyship, I doubt even you
are so remarkable a freak of nature as to have endured
such a remarkably long confinement it must have entered
the annals of science,' Kate said coolly and stood up to
withdraw to the back of the box where they would be
less easily overheard, so Lady Tedinton was forced to
either carry on sitting and crick her neck as well as lose
much of her dignity, or stand and let Kate look down on
her from an equal footing.

'I am barely four and twenty and I miscarried his
brat,' the woman claimed impatiently, not even bothering to look particularly convinced by her own tall
tale as she only just managed to keep her tone low and
venomous. 'You're clearly besotted with the duplicitous
coney catcher, which makes you even more of a fool
than I thought you. If you don't believe anything else,
just ask him about his little interlude with me at the
Crooked Man on the road to Oxford last year and see
if he doesn't give himself away for the villain he is.'

'To me Lord Shuttleworth's integrity is beyond question, madam, whilst yours is dubious to say the least.
Nothing you can ever say will make me believe him
the villain you're trying to paint him for some perverse
reason of your own,' Kate said in so frigid a tone the
others finally realised she was fighting off an enemy
rather than just another veiled interrogation about her
marriage plans, even if they were too far away to hear
any details.

It warmed a cold place in Kate's heart when Isabella
and Eiliane moved to flank her and Kit stood fluidly
to emanate menace and power as effortlessly as most

men breathed. Even Lady Tedinton paled under his fathomless dark stare while she did her best to look unconcerned by such a united front.

'I've been meaning to have a few quiet words with your husband, Lady Tedinton,' Kit said at last, and didn't even dignify her as a foe by pretending it was a threat rather than a promise. 'Does he escort you tonight, or are you in other company as usual?' he asked silkily.

'My lord is from home.'

'How singularly inconvenient, but I really must seek him out before I return to Derbyshire, so we can discuss certain acquaintances we have in common.'

If Lady Tedinton wasn't trembling in her satin evening slippers, then she certainly ought to be now, Kate decided, as she felt an instinctive shiver run down her back at the contained danger in Kit's dark eyes, even when it wasn't directed at her.

Yet somehow even Kit's menacing presence wasn't as chilling as Edmund's voice as he re-entered the box and saw Lady Tedinton confronting Kate. 'Ah, now I see why that supposed urgent message from Cravenhill failed to materialise. I know you like to be forward with the gossip, madam, but I'd no idea you were so desperate for it that you'd contrive a meeting with my fiancée behind my back by such devious means.'

'We have had a very interesting coze, but my patience with the infantry is limited at the best of times,' she snapped and tried to back towards the door without it seeming like a retreat.

'I hear that when it comes to actual infants it's not just limited but non-existent; your husband has my sympathy,' Edmund said, standing in her way with such a blandly social smile it only made the contempt in his eyes more telling. Surely that should kill off any lingering hope she had of engaging him in her illicit affairs?

'Neither my husband nor my children are any business of yours.'

'You consider taking too close an interest in another person's private affairs could prove dangerous to the enquirer then, do you, my lady?'

'I have no idea what you mean.'

'No, then I must be thinking of someone else likely to discover it shortly—an old friend of yours, perhaps?'

'You speak in riddles, sir.'

'Do you understand me, Carnwood?'

Kit nodded and his smile was every bit as chilling as Edmund's. 'I have the advantage over most of our kind in being brought up in a very different sphere, so I learned from a very early age to see the truth behind the false front.'

'You are fortunate in your friends, Lord Shuttleworth,' Lady Tedinton managed to reply as if she wasn't in the least bit intimidated. 'They seem to speak in the same sort of riddles as you specialise in yourself.'

'I am *very* fortunate in my friends, and even more so in my family,' Edmund said as he stepped casually past her to take Kate's cold hand in his. Just as though the vicious virago who'd just done her best to ruin that family for him was a trivial obstacle in his way to what really mattered in life.

'You two deserve each other,' she hissed venomously.

'They do,' Kit intervened before her ladyship could escape with the last word. 'Anyone foolish enough to try to come between them now they have both finally realised that very pertinent truth, Lady Tedinton, will discover how very unlucky such an intervention could be for the one who attempted it.'

'You can't touch me, you're only a counter-jumper,' she spat back, no longer looking in the least bit beautiful as her true nature glared out of narrowed eyes and a mouth suddenly hard as a steel trap.

'I'm also the Earl of Carnwood,' he replied almost mildly, 'but I'm not ashamed of what I made of myself before I became a lord. How about you, your ladyship? What had you made of yourself before your besotted lord came along, I wonder?'

'I am the daughter of a country squire,' she said like a child reciting its catechism, but Kate could see the glint of fear in her dark eyes all of a sudden and the sheen of sweat on her upper lip.

'No, you're the daughter of a country vagrant, born and raised in the workhouse. Did you think you could threaten me and mine and fear no retaliation? I make it a rule to know my enemies, Lady Tedinton. Those among them who have as much to hide as you do are reckless indeed to join their ranks in the first place.'

'You lie, and even if you didn't, you'd have to prove it.'

'My agent took copies of the parish register, descriptions of you and your mother from the superintendent and the milliner you were apprenticed to at the age of seven. You had a very hard start in life, madam, one I

would never have held against you if you hadn't sought
to damage my innocent sister-in-law, who also happens
to be my former ward and very dear to me on both
counts. I pity poor Tedinton when he finds out what
you really are and had made of yourself before he wed
you. How hard he fell for your charade of the genteel
innocent fallen into bad company and what a triumph
for you when he wed you to rescue you from them.'

'I was gently born,' she insisted lamely.

'You were the daughter of a criminal's moll and she
used you as a lure to catch unwary fools, then fleece
them of everything before moving on to the next. Except
you tired of sharing the proceeds and informed on her
and her former colleagues, so you were free to set up
on your own and catch far bigger game.'

'And a fine coney I caught myself,' she admitted
brazenly at last. 'My husband's a fool and deserves to
pay for his endless stupidity with his life, but he'll not
believe a word a shop-soiled earl like you has to say
against me, especially when I tell him how sadly spiteful
Miss Alstone has become towards me, and how she's
even managed to turn her whole family against me, just
because she heard some vicious and untrue rumours
about me and her lover and is a jealous little cat intent
on destroying me as a consequence.'

She rounded on Kate, who eyed the spitting fury in
front of her with acute distaste. From where she stood,
she could see something, or rather someone, standing
half in and half out of the door, looking frozen and
distraught, as if the floor had just dropped out of the
world.

'Nothing to say?' the woman demanded and Kate watched her serenely for a moment.

'There's nothing I need say that you haven't just said for me,' she replied as coolly as if her fiery temper wasn't begging for release until she'd finally told the venomous creature exactly what she thought of her. No need to demean herself by falling to such a base level, at least not now.

'Indeed you have, Selene,' Lord Tedinton said wearily, as he finally opened the door he'd cracked open and discovered so much that he really didn't want to know. 'Indeed you have.'

'Tedinton, we were practising a scene from a little play we're all getting up. You know how I adore arranging evenings of dramatics for the amusement of our friends and family,' her ladyship exclaimed as if she knew she would get away with it, which was, Kate supposed, her finest weapon against her rather gullible lord.

'No, Selene, you were not. You hate them and say so every time they are suggested to alleviate your boredom with me and mine, and how odd if you suddenly acquired such distinguished friends and failed to tell everyone who would listen all about them and whatever you are planning.'

'They are *not* distinguished, they are adventurers and liars,' she said in a sudden switch from assured lady to little girlish, misunderstood victim. 'They have been plotting to bring me down and now you're letting them succeed.'

'No, I'm not. You're the one who's been plotting and

I'm the fool who stood by and let you meet your lover in dark corners to plan the downfall of an innocent young girl. I couldn't bear to believe Philippa when she came to me the night after the Wyndovers' ball and told me what she'd heard when she followed you out of the ballroom that night with your lover. I have hoped and prayed ever since that she was wrong; that she misheard and it was another man's wife who she'd heard meeting with that wastrel Bestholme and planning to kill her husband. You have no idea how fervently I've hoped and prayed for that delusion to be true ever since, Selene.'

'The little snake, I'll murder her with my bare hands!' Lady Tedinton finally betrayed herself utterly and Kate gave a horrified gasp, almost wishing she could erase the last few minutes from her memory and feel clean again.

'When Shuttleworth came to see me this afternoon and told me that he'd overheard you, too, I still didn't want to believe it, although I know him to be an honourable young man not given to making up such melodramatic tales. I badly wanted you to be vindicated, so I agreed to listen tonight, if Philippa would get you here and Shuttleworth persuade you to talk to him about his suspicions, unfounded as I thought them to be, but how very wrong I was. How could you behave so viciously towards a young woman who has never done you any harm, Selene? Miss Alstone, I really cannot apologise enough for my wife's ill-bred spite and that ridiculous pack of lies she just tried to spin you.'

'None of it was your fault, my lord,' Kate replied.

'Ah, but it was, I have been bitterly to blame in

236 One Final Season

all this,' he said sadly and she could hardly meet the sadness in his eyes as he admitted how mistaken he'd always been in his much younger wife, until tonight. 'Can I trouble you for your help, gentlemen?' he went on with resigned dignity. 'The wretched woman is too cunning for me and will escape before I can work out what must be done about her.'

'Of course,' Kit agreed with equal resignation. 'Shuttleworth?'

Edmund nodded and, with a brief smile for Kate, stepped forwards to face a task no true gentleman could ever relish.

'We will all remain here for the rest of the play,' Mrs Mausley said, stepping forwards from the shadows where she'd been standing, horrified and silenced by the whole ugly tableau even the best-mannered lady could hardly pretend not to hear when it was taking place in her own box. 'Frederick will accompany Lady Pemberley and the dear girls home at the end of it, and the rest of us will follow their carriage to make sure no harm comes to them,' she added, as if that arrangement would prove a match for a veritable army of ruffians.

'And I'll ask Pemberley to join you as soon as possible,' Edmund said shortly. Since they knew the marquis would be here as fast as his noble legs could carry him if he thought his lady was in danger, all three lords and one supposed lady left the box and trusted the remainder with the delicate task of keeping up appearances.

'Well, it's a shame her infamy is probably going to be covered up,' Eiliane said comfortably enough as she shifted her chair so as to get a better view of the stage.

'But these things have to be done,' Mrs Mausley agreed, with a significant glare at her son and daughter, who hastily nodded and looked horrified at the idea they should be the route by which such news got out. 'I suspect the woman will be found out to be mad anyway. I've thought for some time that nobody could be quite so blatantly unconcerned about her own misconduct being discovered if she wasn't unhinged, and now it seems I am proved right.'

'For the sake of her unfortunate children and poor Tedinton, I'm not quite sure if that's better or worse than her just being bad,' Eiliane put in with a sad shake of her head and Kate marvelled to see what had been a rather wary acquaintanceship between two women who had little in common becoming a firm friendship in front of her eyes.

'What will they do, then?' Kate asked.

'We must trust the gentlemen to make sure she can't do any more damage,' Eiliane said, smiling brightly at an acquaintance in a box on the opposite side of the theatre as if nothing untoward had occurred.

'One of those gentlemen married her in the first place,' Kate couldn't help muttering her dissent.

'Yes, but dear Kit and your Edmund won't allow him to ignore the way she's tried to destroy your engagement and plot to murder, however unlikely that creature she's been meeting was to bestir himself on her behalf if she did but know it. Now do be quiet, Kate dear, for Isabella and I wish to see the rest of this fine play, even if you lack the stamina for it.'

'Great ladies,' Fanny Mausley murmured as she sat down next to Kate and gave her a mischievous smile that made her realise just why Isabella liked this flighty girl so much. 'So essential to the proper regulation of society,' she parodied some former teacher mercilessly, 'but, oh, so wearying to live with,' she added in her own voice and Kate gave a splutter of laughter and earned a fine crop of glares and hushing as the curtains drew apart and Kean stepped onto the stage once more.

'Lucky it was Kean and not some lesser actor tonight, because otherwise we would have been fidgeting in those hard seats for hours wondering what their lordships were up to and not being able to leave and find out for appearances' sake. I for one am extremely grateful to him for diverting us so royally tonight,' Eiliane admitted once her own particular lord had handed them up into his fine carriage and climbed in, before ordering the door closed on the world.

'Lucky, indeed,' Kate echoed faintly and sat back in her seat to watch darkness and light flash past the windows as the coachman did as he'd been bid and got them home as quickly as possible. 'Poor little girl,' she muttered as she watched the shadows where any footpad or streetwalker or saint might walk unseen by the hurrying throng rushing home to their comfortable homes and cosy hearths after an evening of enthralling drama.

'Indeed,' Eiliane replied sadly, knowing perfectly well who Kate was talking about. 'And if she'd only behaved herself and not tried to lash out at so many others, I for one would never have begrudged her stellar rise from such appalling beginnings.'

'Don't waste your pity on her, love,' said Lord Pemberley, who had evidently been informed of what had gone on tonight by Edmund or Kit. 'It's poor old Tedinton I feel sorry for, and his unfortunate family. All he ever did was fall foolishly in love with a lovely face, and the rest of them did nothing at all to deserve a crazed harpy being thrust into the midst of their family.'

'All the same—' Eiliane began.

'No,' he stated firmly, 'I'm not having you find her some place where she can abuse the trust of those who gave it to her and worry you half to death while she does so. No, Tedinton was fool enough to marry her, he can find a way to feed, clothe and house her while somehow keeping her away from him and his at the same time. You are not getting involved with that heartless vixen in any way.'

'Very well, my love,' Eiliane said with such mild agreement Kate nearly leaned over and felt her friend's forehead to see if she was running a fever. 'I shall be very glad to get back to Pemberley after Kate's wedding,' she admitted and Kate met her sister's eyes as the coach finally pulled up outside Pemberley House and the flare of torches gave them enough light to see each other.

'Are you quite well, Eiliane dear?' she finally asked when they were all four of them inside the cosy parlour Eiliane always resorted to after a busy night to relax and reconsider the evening, and what an evening this one had been.

'Very well, Kate,' her hostess said with a dreamy smile. 'Very well, indeed.'

'Good,' she replied rather hollowly, at sea about Eiliane's distracted manner and the rather odd mix of incredulity and shock and pleasure that she seemed to be able to see in Lord Pemberley's usually humorous grey eyes even after hearing such a tale.

'I just *can't* keep it quiet, Pemberley, even if you can. Not from my own family,' Eiliane burst out at last.

His lordship looked at her, smiled and rolled his eyes to the ceiling as if consulting Jupiter, who was painted on it, even in this relatively small private room of his grand town mansion. 'Very well, love, I should have known better than to ask it of you in the first place,' he agreed at last.

'It was such a shock,' Eiliane said, blushing and looking almost girlish and confused about whatever 'it' was.

'It was that, indeed,' he replied and, distinguished peer of the realm whom the government consulted about their more insoluble problems as he was, he gave Kate an enormous schoolboy grin and laughed delightedly at some glorious joke only he and his wife were privy to at the moment.

'You know I have been out of sorts lately, Kate?'

'Yes, even I have noticed that, Eiliane,' she said solemnly, but she was beginning to add two and two and make four at last and couldn't suppress a broad smile of her own even while Izzie looked more puzzled than ever.

'Pemberley badgered me into seeing a quack as I was so tired and my stomach was uncertain and I even felt a little sad now and then, which is just not like me, as you know. I thought I needed a tonic or perhaps even a week or two in a nice quiet seaside village where I could rest and breathe in good sea air for a while, but it seems that I was wrong.'

'Oh, my!' Isabella finally burst out, eyes round and mouth half-open as she recognised those symptoms from Miranda's confinements at last. 'You're going to have a baby, Eiliane?'

'I am,' said Eiliane blissfully.

'We are,' his lordship put in, as proud as a peacock.

'I'm so pleased for you both that I don't have the words to describe it,' Kate said joyfully and hugged Eiliane gently, then threw caution to the wind and hugged his lordship as well.

'Can we be godmamas to him or her?' Isabella asked eagerly and danced up to repeat Kate's hugs with interest.

'You can, my love. Kate might be busy with her own…husband by then,' Eiliane said on a stumble that had Kate blushing nearly as much as she was herself.

Eiliane meant of course that she could be *enceinte* herself when the time came to christen my lord this or my lady that in Pember Hall's ancient chapel. The thought was so heady she could quite see why her host and hostess were acting like a pair of besotted teenagers at the prospect of becoming parents so late in life.

'I'm far too old, of course,' Eiliane claimed suddenly.

'Then what does that make me, love?' Lord Pemberley asked genially.

'Distinguished, which is most unfair of you,' his wife answered. 'I'm four and forty; that's much too ancient an age to be becoming a mother for the first time.'

'What did the doctor say about that?' he asked patiently, as if they'd already had this conversation several times already.

'That I'm healthy as a horse a good many years younger than whatever the equivalent age to me in horse years might be and that learning to sit still for a few moments a day in order to give my babe a rest would do me a world of good.'

'Sensible man,' her doting husband told her.

Kate met Isabella's eyes and they nodded to each other before leaving the room without Eiliane or her lord even knowing they'd gone.

'They're so happy,' Kate whispered when they were both in her bedroom with the door shut to keep out interested ears.

'So happy and so in love. I don't care what anyone says, Kate, even if I have to be Eiliane's age to find a man I can love like that, I'll stay single until I do.'

Kate was silent, contemplating love and good fortune and the merits and drawbacks of a civil contract of marriage.

'Anyway,' her sister said as she reviewed her declaration and evidently decided it might not be altogether tactful in present company, 'I'm going to ask Fanny's mother if I can stay with them until I come north for your wedding, Kate. It really is high time Eiliane stopped flitting about town every night as if she's got to fill every hour she's not with his lordship with constant activity. They need a week or two at Pember Hall together to enjoy it and relax a little before your wedding as well as after it. After all, dear Lord Pemberley works far too hard as well and now at last they'll both have a reason to look inwards instead of outwards for fulfilment.'

'Mrs Mausley will want to know why,' Kate cautioned, wondering when her sister had become so perceptive and just what she perceived about her.

'I doubt it; neither she nor Fanny is as scatterbrained as they pretend to be.'

'I realised that tonight,' Kate said thoughtfully. 'Indeed, I realised quite a lot of things tonight.'

'High time you did, big sister,' Isabella told her with a cheeky smile, then happily went off to plan her life for the next few weeks and probably that of Lord and Lady Pemberley and the entire Mausley family as well.

Chapter Fifteen

Kate sat down on her very comfortable feather bed, smoothed the delicate silk brocade of the cover and ran a hand over fine linen and lace-covered pillows almost as if apologising to them for something. Then she slipped out of her fine cream silk gown and laid it carefully aside, before divesting herself of all her evening finery. She donned a very plain dark gown, her heaviest and most concealing cloak and a dark jockey cap she some-times wore for riding to cover her give-away hair, then sat down on the bed to wait for stillness and silence to overtake the household.

Edmund left Lord Tedinton's house in Green Street along with the Earl of Carnwood and was very glad to be doing so at last. Neither of them had a spring in their step after such an evening and Edmund shook his head wearily when Kit invited him to Alstone House for brandy and perhaps a cigar because, he informed

Edmund wryly, 'I'll get damned little sleep tonight without Miranda in my bed.' Love, Edmund thought as he bade Kit Alstone goodnight, was a hard taskmaster. It drove his friend and future brother-in-law to bark and growl at anyone who came between him and his Miranda, even when it was Kate. How would it feel to know the lady you married longed for you, waited for you so impatiently every minute you were gone, hungered for you in her bed as much as you did for her in yours until neither of you could sleep very much at all if the other wasn't there?

Like a triumph and a banquet and a victory parade all rolled into one, he decided wistfully and told himself Kate was just as unique in her own way as her passionate sister. He could hardly complain if what made her so also rendered her more aloof and in control of herself than her elder sister. It was ironic that she was the true redhead of the pair, he decided, as he let himself in through his front door with the neat key he'd had made for himself when he finally persuaded his doting staff not to wait up from cellar to attic every time he was out late at night. Miranda, Countess of Carnwood, had a thick mane of parti-coloured hair that had brown, blond and red all mixed up in it somewhere, but it was Kate who'd inherited her famously lovely mother's rich red locks. Kate, who did her best to fight the passion and intensity and sheer beauty hidden in the depths of her deep blue Alstone eyes. His Kate, who would never let her heart rule her head, or tell the world with unguarded gestures or intimate touches and gazes and stolen kisses

when she didn't quite care if anyone was by or not, how
very much she loved her lord.

Still, he would have her in his bed and gracing his
house, or houses, and she would be the woman who
birthed his heirs if they were blessed with any. Kate
would be the mother of his children, the mistress of
his estates and the lover of his dreams. He was a happy
man, and in a few weeks' time he would be an ecstatic
man with a redheaded enchantress in his bed who had
no idea of her own power, or the possibilities she held
once she became fully a woman and not an innocent,
however she might argue with that description.

She'd walked into his heart when she'd been that
unfledged beauty three years ago and now he was quite
resigned to the fact that he'd never manage to remove
her from it, whatever he tried. Back then, her height
and those lovely bones of hers had hinted at the promise of even more startling beauty to come, even deeper
enchantments to entrap the unwary. Well, he'd been
unwary; he'd stumbled headlong at her feet in a tongue-
tied confusion of rampant youthful lust and idealistic
worship of the goddess she was too human to be. No
wonder she'd looked on him so warily, as if he might
embarrass them both with some public display of devotion and make them into a laughing stock; no wonder
she'd refused to marry him when he'd begged her to do
so as if his life depended on it. Idiot, he castigated himself as he impatiently ordered any of his staff he caught
lurking in corners, just in case he needed a twenty-five-
course banquet or a suit of bespoke armour in the middle
of the night, he supposed whimsically, off to bed.

At last he reached his bedchamber and shut the door on the world with a heartfelt sigh, squashing the urge to indulge his household by ringing his bell and ordering someone to come and relight the candles that were usually left burning in one or two sconces ready for his homecoming, however often he told them he was quite capable of lighting them himself when he got home. After the day and night he'd just endured he felt the need for light and a fire, even if it was nearly June, and then he'd sip a leisurely glass of cognac in front of it as he tried to come to terms with all that had happened since he'd left it last.

Stretching and giving a mighty yawn, then rubbing a weary hand over his stiff shoulders and up to the rigid muscles in his neck as he felt the effects of that long and demanding ride to Derbyshire and back, he wondered about just tumbling face down onto the bed fully dressed and letting sleep and blessed forgetfulness overcome him for a few hours. He was about to force himself to reach for the tinderbox and shed some light on his undressing and ablutions when a stir of movement from the direction of the bed set his senses prickling and his thoughts racing wildly. He cautiously let them reach out, explore possibilities as he made what he could of the information available. No hairs were rising on the back of his neck, or at least if they were it was not in fear but exhilaration. His skin wasn't crawling, but an incendiary flush roared over it that he was glad only he knew about in this heavy darkness.

'What the devil are you doing here, Kate Alstone?' he demanded as he finally found that tinderbox. It only

took him about half a dozen strikes of the flint with suddenly very unsteady hands to get a spark and produce
flame enough to light a candle, then a spill to put to the
fire they were surely going to need.

'If you need me to explain that, my lord, then we're
both in trouble,' she joked sleepily as she sat up to stretch
and yawn and send his heated imagination into the ether.
'You're very late in coming home, Edmund.'

'Had I known you were awaiting me, I certainly
would not have been.'

'Well, that's good,' Kate replied, still feeling rather
astonished that she'd fallen asleep on his very comfortable bed and trying hard to gather senses that were only
concerned with his presence and all the possibilities
it raised. 'You don't look terribly pleased to see me,
Edmund,' she finally managed to inform him a touch
inadequately.

'You really don't want to know about that,' he muttered darkly and she smiled to herself as she just caught
the tail end of an even softer, really inventive series of
much-tried curses.

'Oh, but I do,' she murmured in what she hoped was
a sensual drawl, but feared might have come out as a
doubtful whisper, not doubtful about being here, just
dubious about whether he actually wanted her to be.

'Never mind me, this is about you, Kate,' he told her
far too seriously.

'No, it's about us.'

'What sort of "us" had you in mind?' he asked cautiously as if he wanted her to spell it out in humiliat-
ing detail before he took up all the implications of her

being here in the first place and did something about it, be it yea or nay to her implied and perfectly shameless proposition that he take her to bed and ravish her until the stars faded and she must steal home with the dawn.

Now there was enough light to see as well as sense him, she watched his face for a few clues as to how he was feeling about her intrusion and saw the strained tension about his mouth, the weariness of his shadowed eyes and wondered if she'd chosen the wrong night to come here after all. Then she called on all she knew of him and sensed the avid hunger in him, probably laid bare by that very tiredness, and saw the slight shake in his hand as he fed the fire he'd lit. No, it hadn't been wrong, she decided triumphantly, it had been perfectly right. If not, he'd have sat by it, so tired and jaded by the events of the evening that he couldn't sleep as he brooded over the whole wretched business detail by detail, just in case he could have done something differently, something that would have saved such bitterness and despair for Lord Tedinton and his unfortunate family.

'This sort of us,' she informed him huskily and she surged up off the bed and came to stand in front of him with shameless boldness, meeting his gaze with everything she'd come here to tell him tonight in her eyes.

'Stay here like this, Kate, and I won't be able to keep my hands off you for much longer,' he warned, as if that was a threat to her and not a promise and she put out a tender hand to outline his face as if still learning him in the darkness he'd just dispelled.

'I'd be highly insulted if you could,' she told him as she got to his mouth and felt it firm even more under her butterfly touch, as if that was the only way he could keep it from doing exactly what she wanted it to, which was ravishing her from her fingertips to her toes and back again—even if she was a bit foggy about the most intimate details in between.

'I can't control the need I have of you enough to be restrained and careful with you tonight. You must go, Kate, while I can still let you,' he whispered as if to speak out loud might snap his leash and let out all the pent-up desire for her that he'd subdued for so long and she'd been so afraid they'd finally killed between them.

'I don't want your control any more, Edmund,' she told him through lips that were so ready for him they'd gone full and pouting and soft and eager for the matchless taste and feel of his against hers in anticipation.

Deciding he could have all the explanations and justifications and logic his male mind needed afterwards, but not now, she impatiently breached the gap between them and let her body argue for her. At least it knew what it wanted, even if he was too much of a gentleman to do as she longed for him to and seduce her until she was mindless, beyond thought and caught up in this huge new continent of experiences she and her lover had what felt like for ever to explore.

'I just want you, my love, so please will you seduce me before dawn breaks and this all gets a lot more complicated and public?'

'Even more complicated than it already is?' he said

would-be coolly, but she felt the shock jar through him at those two words, the sudden change from that weary edge in his husky voice to an energised, utterly present lover without a tired bone in his body. At least that eagerness soothed her jumping nerves at making that bold statement of fact. *'My love?'* he echoed as if unable to quite believe his ears.

'Yes! Now will you just kiss me and get on with making me and you into that "us" we just talked about? We only have a week for our clandestine affair, because if you think we'll have any chance of loving in every sense of the word under Kit's roof once he gets me back to Wychwood, then you have far too sanguine a nature, Edmund Worth.'

'I have a very hopeful temperament,' he told her with the hint of a laugh back in his voice. 'Heaven knows, I've needed it badly enough these last three years.'

'Edmund!' she protested and glared up at him with demand and need and just that slight edge of temper in her eyes.

'Kate,' he breathed her name as if it was a promise; 'Kate,' he repeated as he brought his lips so close she actually heard herself keen an inarticulate invitation. 'My lovely Kate.'

Impatient for now of the reverence in his voice, even while she took it in and stored it up to gloat over later, she licked her lips and slyly brushed his with her tongue as she did so. Instantly she was engulfed in fire and need and joy as he took her mouth in a kiss that abolished thought for both of them.

She had those transforming, sensually matchless

kisses from the night of the Wyndovers' ball to warn her, and entice her, of what a difference making love with Edmund might make to the very essence of her life, but that night she'd still been unaware of so much. Now she felt the heat of him, the hardness of him and wanted everything, all of him, all over her. She stretched against him, blissfully butting curves and long, lushly sleek limbs against the dense-packed muscle he somehow managed to fit on to his deceptively lean frame. With nothing held back, she had the sheer luxury of being able to explore him boldly. Running her hands over his powerful shoulders, she felt those muscles loosen and unknot under her hands, then change again and flex as he shifted to hold her even closer and smoothed his own exploring hands over her eager body.

He melded her even more intimately to him by widening his stance, bringing one leg round to draw her explicitly against the hard maleness he made no effort to disguise from her. Wriggling wantonly against him, she gasped an inarticulate, greedy moan against his plundering mouth and let her hands wander lower, over the cleanly streamlined narrowness of his waist to appreciate the tight male buttocks that were braced with the weight of both of them as he curved her even more closely, yet more intimately together. Even this wasn't enough, this wasn't someone else's book room or a terrace where other lovers might be too close by; this was my lord's bedchamber where nobody would interrupt them until morning, and probably not even then. The presence of that wide feather bed lured and promised and intrigued her more than any other bed ever had in her life. There they could explore, discover and experience so much more that she almost wished he'd stop kissing her and learning her inch by tantalising inch long enough to get them there without any further ceremony.

'Hmm,' she managed inarticulately when he raised his mouth from hers long enough to gasp in an unsteady breath.

Feeling his lips curve against hers, she wondered what the infuriating man could find at all funny about a perfectly sensible comment. She frowned, then pouted, then paid the price by having her lower lip oh, so gently nipped, then soothed with his tongue and explored until that inarticulate murmur turned into a long feminine moan of pleading she'd never even thought could leave her own mouth before she realised she was all his and he was hers.

'I can just about stop now, if I have to, Kate,' he told her huskily, even as his lips seemed unable to put more than a half-an-inch gap between his and her mouth to say it. 'I've waited so long for you, I could still just about wait another month until we're married,' he told her and the words sounded as if he had to think about shaping every one with truly Edmund-like determination, because any words but love words and lovers' murmurs had no real meaning between them in his half-lit bedchamber in the still watches of the night.

'You might be able to manage that titan feat of self-control, my lord, but I can't,' she told him, her turn to feel the foreignness of everyday language on her tongue as she wriggled against him as seductively as she could with only instinct to go on, her hands busy again all the while as her fingers tugged incompetently at buttons as if they'd never felt or heard of them before. 'Ham-fisted,' she scolded herself grumpily.

'Just as well if you never seek employment as a valet, then,' he joked distractedly, but seemed to abandon his over-gallant attempts to save her from herself as he used the gap created by her attack on his waistcoat to palm her firm, high breasts and light another level of conflagration within her.

Through the workaday cambric of a dark morning gown she had no idea why either she or her maid had packed at the time, she felt her breasts seem to rise and swell under his fascinated hands. Nipples already peaked and tingling seemed to heat and pebble even more under his sensitive touch and all she wanted was to feel his skin on hers, his hands hardened and calloused from the reins as he rode these last few days for her, for her hand, for her promises, for her as his wife. But tonight, this was for her as his lover, his woman, his blatant, burning desire for her and hers for him and that had nothing to do with all the pomp and panoply of aristocratic alliances and settlements and contracts and stern-eyed trustees.

At last she fumbled enough buttons free and triumphantly shucked the two halves apart, even making the sacrifice of losing his wicked exploration and the awesome stimulation of his spread palms, and the delicious almost pressure of his fingers padding against her nipples until the quicksilver heat deep inside her was becoming almost an unbearable pleasure pain.

She would have twisted her body and pressed her legs together in an attempt to appease it, if his very obvious arousal hadn't been too temptingly already there and hard against for her to relinquish. So instead she moaned again and her shallow pants of breath made a light descant against the urgency of his deeper breathing as he searched for control of himself and her wriggling and shifting against him in protest made that arousal even mightier.

His turn to forget what buttons and buttonholes did as he fought the wretched things into submission where they ran down her back. Luckily she'd had to helpfully leave some undone when she'd put the dress on, since she couldn't reach so high up her own back, so at least it didn't take his fingers as long to learn how to undo the rest again as it had hers. But she was making up for it by divesting him of most of the buttons his shirt had ever rejoiced in before tugging it from his evening breeches and forcing him to stop his attentions to the rest of her wretched gown in order to shrug out of the fine lawn and draw it over his head to throw it somewhere it certainly deserved to be sent for coming between Kate Alstone and her compelling lover's intriguing torso.

Content to explore the delicious novelty of satin-smooth skin over iron-hard muscle, and play with the light dusting of golden-brown hair that adorned parts of his torso in such an interesting way as she'd never even let herself dream of, she felt him push, persuade and tug her gown off her shoulder, then slide it off her fingertips until even the sleeves finally gave in to his touch and fell away. With the gown a heap of soft fabric at her feet, it took him mere seconds to shuck her out of the flimsy chemise that was all she'd thought necessary for this particular nocturnal visit.

All but naked, she stood a little apart from him to let them both appreciate the fact. Shockingly, she didn't feel in the least bit shy to have his hungry eyes devour every detail of her as if he couldn't learn her fast enough or comprehensively enough for his taste. His hands were on her even as her arousal and the burning, wet heat between her legs protested that, whilst she was naked all but for a pair of soft-soled slippers, he was still an impeccably dressed, if very obviously aroused, gentleman from the waist downwards. Then the feel of his roughened palms on her bare skin spun all thought of anything else but the pleasure of his touch away.

The pad of his strong fingers now tantalised her narrow waist, then moved up to rest just below the swell of her breasts and he must be able to feel the shallow breathing the sweet tension of waiting for more provoked in her, because his hands were suddenly warm on her rib cage, almost as if he'd share the very process of breathing itself with her. At last he moved and those tantalising forefingers of his outlined the curve of her lower breast against that rib cage and then went up around to test the rich swell of them without allowing them the luxury of touching her nipples, until she thought she might burst into flame if he didn't put his hands to work on them at last. Then he was there, still exploring delicately, still with one finger, to outline an amber areola as if describing female perfection, if the awed wonder in his willow-green eyes was anything to go by.

He flicked a fingertip across her pebble-hard nipple and she gasped and lost the use of her legs. Luckily he knew, knew what he was doing, what he'd just done and plucked her out of her fallen skirts and her satin slippers and into his arms, against that delightfully hair-roughened chest, so this time it was her turn to feel his breath stutter and then hurry under her skin, except her skin was not an interrogating, arousing, tantalising digit; it was a peaked and already overheated breast and the vulnerable indentation of her waist and she couldn't even think to where the curve of her bottom was brushing against him, inviting and anticipating so much more.

'Stop wriggling, woman,' he demanded in a voice so husky she hardly recognised it, and promptly wriggled a whole lot more in the hope of hearing it rasped and hoarse with need of her once again.

'I like it,' she told him, casting him a look of heavy-eyed invitation she really hoped he couldn't refuse.

'Maybe you do, but there's a time and a place for everything,' he husked and the sound sent shivers down her exposed spine and made her snuggle against him even more determinedly. 'And this is it,' he told her as he set her on the bed and stood a little back to watch her with such a blaze of need and fierce joy in his eyes that she felt any last maidenly qualms melt away unmourned.

'Oh, it is, it is indeed, love,' she said softly.

'Love indeed,' he echoed and finally shrugged out

of his breeches and stripped off his fine evening stock-
ings and kicked his elegant evening shoes into some
corner his valet would doubtless tick and tut about in
the morning.

Chapter Sixteen

If the sight of her had made him gasp, her first sight
of a naked man, a living, breathing naked man who,
unlike the famous classical marbles at Wychwood, was
very obviously and very fully aroused, should at least
have made her blush, she supposed, in a brief nod to
her otherwise very proper upbringing. He stood, all
narrow hips, long strong limbs, leanly muscular torso
and wide shoulders, his muscles taut and golden-brown
skin stretched smooth and warm over them, and looked
at her with eyes that asked her not to find him alien or
impossible now they were so far along their road that
turning back would probably leave him racked with pain
and frustration, as well as doubting them as lovers and
unsure of her all over again.

A rush of love hit her and something much more
earthy and passionate, and perhaps yes, that was part of
love as well, she decided as it scorched through her and
she let her awed, delighted eyes meet his and describe

it all for her. She met his gaze with all the feminine pleasure she felt in rousing him so emphatically absolutely on display; the urge to move under his gaze like a blatantly sensual wanton shook her for a moment and she considered the more modest alternative before dismissing it and writhing against the silky velvet under her sensitised skin, as if the feel of it might compensate her just a little for the lack of him there instead. She raised a hand to caress the long line of her own waist, leg and hip and heard a feral growl as he sank down beside her, face savage with need and dominant with denial that anyone should pleasure her tonight but him, even if the one doing it was herself.

She gave him a smug smile and a look she hoped said, 'Well, and what *are* you waiting for then?' and withstood the answering storm with a delighted welcome. Now his fingers were intent on stoking her arousal as high and hard as his own was obviously driving him, for they didn't play and tease so much as rouse and imprint her with his touch, his longing, his possession and she revelled in it all. His mouth was ravenous on hers, as if he'd somehow manage to quench years of longing for her into one storm of wanting, for now. She met it, set her tongue to dance and flirt with his, spared a hand from learning his broad back to stroke it down the side of his face as they kissed as if they couldn't bear to stop.

She knew his face so well, had thought she had his features off by heart, and yet learning them with her fingers was so much more intimate, so much more than just looking. He watched her eyes with his as their mouths melded and moved. She felt the way his taut skin stretched over high cheekbones and lean cheeks, traced his determined jaw as he flexed it to take their kiss even deeper, to tangle up her senses in him even more potently. Willing and active in her own seduction, she raised that finger to trace the edge of one eyebrow, the silky tips of his unfairly lush eyelashes, and her insides melted at the intimacy of it, the power of it. She loved him, and at last she knew it, so she let it show as openly as she could, along with the heat and wanting, the delicious burn of arousal and the thrill of sensual curiosity. Seeing the way his irises contracted, then expanded again as he blinked in the face of her unguarded gaze, she wasn't at all surprised to feel him shift her against him as if he couldn't wait any longer, had lost the ability to be infinitely patient with such a wanton virgin when she clearly didn't want him to be patient any longer.

He lowered his head to trace open-mouthed kisses over her jaw and down the slim throat that stretched and luxuriated in every touch; meanwhile he slid one hand down her waist and spread it over the springy curls at the vee of her thighs, sending a confident finger to explore the hot wetness between her legs, the intimate ache he knew would lie at the heart of her. That touch suddenly seemed a delight and a torture as he stroked and thrust and her body took up a rhythm she hadn't even known it knew by instinct alone. She writhed against the silky bedcover, tried to lock her legs together to hold back the tearing heat within, but he raised his head from sucking on her mercilessly aroused nipple and his eyes asked for her to trust him, even if he seemed as beyond words as she was.

Reminding herself that she would very likely follow him into hell itself if she had to, she relaxed her muscles, let his wickedly knowing hand work its magic and her head fell back as a melting rush threatened to overwhelm her, even while his fingers drove her even further along an urgent, sense-stealing journey to something beyond any words she had to describe it. Striving against it even as she wanted to plunge straight into that hot compulsion for more, she mewled in protest so he seized her mouth again and echoed the driving rhythm of his fingers against her most secret core and she shattered. Her body plunged and bucked under his touch and her heart pumped and sang as she shot into a new world of shattering pleasure, but she came back from it feeling oddly lonely, fulfilled yet not quite full of joy.

'Now,' he promised hoarsely as he positioned her pleasure-soaked body to accept as much of the weight of his as he'd let her, whilst he leaned most of it on his arms and used his knees to centre his rigid arousal at her heated, still-throbbing core.

Nodding frantically as she felt the weight and the potential and the potency of him, she let him raise her knees slightly and splay them to make her even more open for him, then she ran her hands over his striving body as he thrust into her and felt him shudder with delight and relief as she managed to take him, open to him even as the strangeness of being so full, so stretched made her marvel and exult in every extra iota he inched into her. He came up against the barrier he'd been testing for so carefully at last and she waited, trusting him with the taking of her virginity, waiting for it, longing for the loss of it even as she knew it would hurt. Using internal muscles she hadn't even known she had, she flexed about the fact of his starkly aroused shaft within her and heard him give a great gasp of half protest and half elation as he breached her maidenhead and buried himself in an intimate joining that took the jagged pain away in the sheer marvel of it. Cautiously she learned the full fact of his penetration and the potency of him so hard and deep and broad inside her, and then she met his eyes with wonder in her own and smiled a full, womanly, rather smug smile at him.

'Witch,' he told her with love and tenderness in his eyes, as well as what she now recognised as rampant lust, and he withdrew most of his length from her with a teasing look as she gasped reproachfully, then he gave her a wolfish, triumphant smile as he sank into her again and went even deeper this time, until she felt utterly possessed and filled and on fire for more, even while she wondered incredulously how there could be anything more than this.

Which he proved to her there definitely was, with as little treading on eggshells while he did so as she wanted of him. He thrust into her in a surging driving rhythm she learnt and matched and travelled with him as they strove for that beckoning fulfilment he'd taught her already, but this time it would be everything she'd felt wistful for not having the whole of last time, for this time he would be there, too. Kate felt her body begin that spasming of her inner muscles again that this time she knew indicated she was nearly at the peak of all this glory, but now she had his wondrous silky hardness fully engaged inside her to make them complete, drive them on together. He thrust more deeply as the beat of their bodies changed and went deeper and even more driven, until she cried out in desperation before finally, richly, witlessly she tumbled into deeply satisfied glory as he arched over her in an ecstasy that shook through them both with its fierce intensity.

Still taken to that somewhere wonderful he'd taught her was theirs by aftershocks of exquisite feeling, racked with delight such as she'd never dared consider possible even in her wildest dreams, Kate came back to herself with her lover slack muscled, love-shot and gloriously heavy against her tingling breasts as he laboured to catch his breath in her arms and reassemble himself somehow. She felt the delicious weight of him, still passion-dazed as he rested far too briefly on her satiated body and reviewed the last half hour with smug appreciation. Her love, her lover and her future husband stirred in her arms and shifted so he took his weight off her delightfully stretched torso, despite her incoherent murmur of protest. He raised himself from her and tried to disengage fully, until she locked her legs about his waist and refused to part with this new and astounding connection to him, although he was now but half-aroused within her and inclined to be far too gallant to do anything to remedy the matter.

'I'm too big for you, you'll already be sore in the morning, my love.'

'Maybe, but now I want you inside me, and I never want to let you go,' she told him seriously. 'We belong,' she managed to explain herself rather inadequately in her own eyes, but it seemed that he understood her as he flipped her over. She lay splayed over him, still locked together and content to just be so for a while, to feel and preen a little at their own extraordinary cleverness in finally finding each other, then wonder at what they'd just done so thoroughly and so very well every pore and sinew still sang with remembering such an exquisite shock of pleasure.

It didn't last above ten minutes, that state of half-spent contentment as she rapidly proved how right she was not to heed his warnings while she experimented with that novel position he'd put her in and found it was excellent for rousing half-exhausted lovers into reinvigorated, rampant and demanding ones. Lazily Edmund ran his hands over her hips and cupped her buttocks until he could push her forwards a little, bowed over him until he could recline against the pillows and plunder her breasts like some luxuriating potentate being fed exotic fruit by a doe-eyed houri, or so she informed him when she could find enough breath from panting at the new bloom of hot need his very skilled attentions were rousing in her all over again.

'Can you ride astride?' he asked wickedly and she flexed her lithe legs and arched her supple back to show them both that she could indeed.

It proved to be the most exciting and mutually satisfying form of exercise she had ever discovered. They were both far more breathless at the inevitable lovely end of it than she'd ever been from such a wholesome, almost innocently illicit pleasure as riding astride over the peaks and moors, when she was told she was far too old to run wild over her grandfather's estates in such a hoydenish fashion. Now she reflected, as she finally felt him disengage from her, then felt him tuck her slack and utterly relaxed body against him with a contented sigh, she knew that had been her way of keeping wild Kate Alstone alive until she could safely be herself again in her lover's arms. With a richly satiated murmur of assent she felt those arms close about her, as if he couldn't bear the thought of parting from her any more than she could of leaving him, as she surely must now the dawn was already lightening the sky.

'Why, my Kate?' Edmund asked her at last.

'Because there wasn't another way to let you know how I feel and have you believe me body and soul, Edmund,' she told him as she thought back to the very moment last night when she'd known she had to go to him. She'd had to prove that she now loved him absolutely, passionately and with every wild impulse and wayward emotion she'd smothered and denied for so long.

'I might have taken your word for it,' he told her as he ran his silver-green gaze over her as if he couldn't help looking and looking again, just to make sure she wasn't a very fevered fantasy, or a delicious, desperately dear dream who might still desert him.

'But one day you might have doubted us; you could have stood apart from our so-convenient marriage and your wildly passionate wife on that day and wondered what if? What if you hadn't been such a gallant fool and rescued me from my folly and loneliness that night, what if it was just as convenient for me to say "I love you" to my husband when we were bound together for life as it was to adore what we did together in our marriage bed? After I got past that awful thought and knew I loved you body and soul, Edmund, I had to find a way to let you know beyond any doubt that it's you I want and need and that I'll only ever be a shadow of a woman without you. I woke up to what we are to each other at last and how could I not come to you when you're everything to me?'

'Oh, Kate my love, you humble me. I had so many words stored up for you against the one-day fantasy I spun about you from the first moment I set eyes on you. You made the rest of that ballroom look like an etching in black and white compared with the full glorious life of you and I wanted you so much it hurt.'

'I know, I'm such an *idiot*,' she chided herself.

'You're my idiot,' he told her with an insufferable smile.

'I most certainly am,' she informed him just as smugly, 'and you're mine.'

'I'm yours, full stop, or your personal idiot?'

'Both,' she told him mock resentfully as he tipped her off the bed and stood up himself, knowing day was all but here and they had to part.

'I don't want to leave you, Edmund,' she told him with her feelings for him naked in her eyes, her body so changed by the love they'd shared that she felt every inch a mature and beloved woman as she stretched and yawned and met his eyes with her own full of sleepy sensuality.

'You have to. I don't know how I'm going to smuggle

you out of here without anyone knowing you've been here in the depths of the night as it is,' he told her and aimed a mock slap at her buttocks as she wiggled them as provocatively as she could while reluctantly retrieving her filmy chemise and donning it with a sensuous shiver as the fine silk caressed much-loved curves and whispered over sensitised breasts and hid her reverently manhandled body from his hungry gaze.

'Too late,' she told him without noticeable shame. 'I didn't sneak in here when nobody was looking and hide in corners to get here last night, Edmund. I walked through the front door and your butler and I had a very interesting conversation about interior decoration and future domestic arrangements while he conducted me impassively upstairs and informed me solemnly that all the staff would be retiring early and rising late.'

'The old rogue,' Edmund said, seeming quite torn between awe and indignation that the stately Lawson could be quite so devious, quite so complicit in such scandalous behaviour on the part of a single lady and his unsuspecting, if deeply delighted, master. 'I ought to pension him off.'

'That man is not going anywhere until he wants to. He's nearly as big a fraud as our Coppice under that chilly manner he cultivates so carefully and I like him extremely for it.'

'Not too extremely, I hope,' he joked and her heart danced that he could do so easily with her at last. 'Ah, well,' he went on, 'at least we'll still have him to help us out when we have to cook our own dinners and sweep our own floors, because the rest of my staff have discovered what a scandalous household they're going to be living in from now on and have left for more respectable quarters,' he said cheerfully.

'I'm never going to be able to go back to being coldly polite and proper with you, Edmund, even for the sake of your household and our personal comfort, so please don't ask it of me.'

'Of course not, how could I expect or want you to be anything other than who and what you are, my Kate? But I won't let you come to me like this again, love, for I care about your reputation even if you don't. I nearly cost another lady her good name and her prospect of a good marriage once because of a few indiscreet rumours and a careless act or two and I vowed never to do so again. Certainly not with the female who matters to me more than the rest of womankind put together.'

'She was the one Lady Tedinton pretended to be for some twisted reason of her own, I suppose?' she asked as coolly as she had it in her to risk questioning him in order to find out something she didn't want to know.

'Yes, and only for you would I risk telling a soul about it after that. Word somehow got about that I had been indulging in a liaison with a lady possessed of a Frenchified name and Selene Tedinton decided that I added to her standing in society as a lover very nicely, I suppose, and hinted that the lady was her. In reality I wouldn't touch her with a ten-foot pole, but Therese is a true lady and I couldn't refute Lady Tedinton's ridiculous posturing without revealing my one-time lover's true identity, especially now that Therese is very happily wed to another man.'

'Did you love her?' Kate had to ask, even if it might cost her more than she dared contemplate to hear an affirmative.

'Never. I still hurt so badly after making myself see I had not only lost you, but never had you to lose in the first place that I was incapable of loving another woman, then or now. But Therese was a widow and understood loss even better than I did at the time. We made the blankness easier for each for a while, that's all. I'm not proud of using another woman to block out my need of you, Kate, but you were very much unavailable on every level there can be between a man and a woman at the time.'

'I didn't trust what I had begun to feel for you then, Edmund, and it frightened me so badly that I managed to convince myself love didn't exist for me and that I would never let myself indulge in passion and its fell consequences as my sister had so disastrously. I suppose I needed to grow up and three years on, maybe I've managed to do enough of it to realise life is a gamble and, if you are to be my reward for taking a risk or two, then you're more than worth it.'

'Then you're willing to forgive me an *affaire* that was over two years ago, I hope, my love?'

'Only if you promise me solemnly never to look at another woman in that way so long as we both live on this good earth of ours and have each other to love,' she returned implacably, knowing she could trust him now as she should have then, but feeling that he needed her to be territorial and witchy about it all just the same.

'I'll promise never to do *more* than look if you like,

for I am a man, lovely Kate, and therefore fallible and foolish. But why would I risk doing more than feeling a brief moment of fleeting admiration for a lovely face or form as a wonder of nature, when I'll have the beautiful, passionate woman I've dreamt of in my wildest fantasies ever since I first set eyes on her in my bed every night for the rest of our lives?'

'I really couldn't say,' she managed demurely enough, but the look she slanted him beneath her eyelashes was pure invitation to take her to his bed once more and prove it to her very thoroughly.

'Stop it, witch. As it is, we can't risk any more daylight than this in case some fool coming home with the dawn sees me escort you back to the bed you should have been sleeping innocently in many hours ago.'

'I dare say I shouldn't have come,' she said, suddenly vulnerable and unsure of herself and him once more.

Kate wondered if she had shocked him by coming here, offering herself to him so blatantly that he could hardly refuse her brazen attentions without hurting her pride and her heart far more than he was capable of doing. He seemed suddenly able to read all her feelings and her fears though, for despite his stern resolution to get her home before daylight found them out, he strode over and took her in his arms to give her a reverent kiss full of promise as chaste as if they were both fully dressed and had a pack of interfering relatives waiting in the next room.

'Never say so, love, for I can't even begin to tell you how happy a man you made me by doing so, in defiance of all the conventions and your upbringing and that cautious heart you once insisted on keeping as close guarded as a miser would his gold. We'll find ways to be together again before we're wed somehow, without endangering your good name. I love you, Kate, with all of me. Don't you ever doubt it or forget it,' he vowed when he raised his head and watched her so seriously that she felt tears sting and threaten.

'And I love you, Edmund. Most of me has done so since we first set eyes on each other, but it took until tonight for it to let the last little bit know about it.'

'Then that's all that matters,' he said with a boyish, purely Edmund Worth smile she treasured and took with her to gloat over as they stole downstairs.

He urged her out through the garden door into the side streets and she fought the ridiculous urge to giggle all the time they flitted hand-locked and still dreamy and heavy limbed with such powerful loving, she covered with her cloak from head to toe like an illicitly escaping princess, as she whispered in his ear when they paused in a shadowy doorway to let a tradesman's cart go past. They reached Pemberley House by a route she doubted she could remember again if she tried, but as he urged her silently to the garden door she had stolen out of last night, she shivered and hated the very idea of parting from him now the time had come.

'I'll come to see you as soon as I have snatched an hour or two of sleep, then bathed and shaved, my lovely Kate,' he murmured as if he could hardly bear to part from her, either, and she leaned up to snatch a kiss that he gave her back with interest. 'Go, before I undo all the good we just did your previously pristine reputation by coming back here so early in the day by being discovered making love to you in the shrubbery by one of Lord Pemberley's astonished gardeners,' he urged her with a mischievous grin that made her heart turn over with love for him.

'Goodnight, Edmund,' she murmured with a fatuous smile.

'And a very good morning to you, Kate,' he replied with a wolfish look.

'Oh, go away, you wicked man,' she chided obligingly and flitted through the door and shut it behind her.

Chapter Seventeen

Now she had just had the wedding she'd once secretly dreamed of, before Miranda's elopement put her off the idea of marriage altogether for far too long, and it had been every bit as wonderful as she'd believed it would be in her childish fantasies and so much more besides. Kate walked down the aisle of Wychwood Church on her newly made husband's arm and marvelled how the rituals and heady frivolity of the joyous family wedding she'd thought she would never have until a few weeks ago had meant so much to her. At last she was very much married to the potent gentleman strolling at her side like a sleek-limbed predator, agreeing to be tame only in so far as he chose to be. The feel of Edmund's firmly muscled arm under her fingers reminded her that, in marrying him and agreeing to all this, she'd given all she was and could become into his keeping, and what a powerful and passionate lover she was getting in return, she recalled with a delighted shiver that had nothing at all to do with wedding-night nerves or being cold.

'Don't worry, Kate,' Edmund reassured her with a wry smile. 'You're not as easy to read as you seem to think, so I dare say almost half the congregation don't yet know you're wishing them at the devil so we can be rid of them all the sooner and be alone once more.'

'I'm not that transparent,' she told him with a fine imitation of her old vexed frown. 'I'm not really, am I, Edmund?' she added, hating the idea of hurting her nearest and dearest, even if she did want to be alone with her new husband rather badly after three whole weeks of not being lovers in aught but her memory.

'No, love, you're managing to disguise it very well from most of them.'

'Kit knows, even if he's said nothing to either of us. I swear he knew what I was about from the very instant I set out to compromise you beyond all hope that night I came to your house and lay in wait for you like an overeager houri.'

'You looked more like a scandalously ardent lady, recklessly in love and totally unashamed to admit it to me,' he chided proudly as they paused on the threshold of the church by mutual consent. 'And I was never more pleased to see anyone in my entire life,' he added wolfishly.

'Luckily I'd never have wed you if I wanted a tame husband,' she joked back, but there was too much reality in her words and she wished she'd learn to stop her hasty tongue with him of all people. Now he'd finally freed her from even wanting to be the once cool and detached Miss Alstone, who thought all she deserved from life was an arranged marriage and a complacent husband, her impulsive nature seemed poised to get her into trouble at almost every turn.

'I don't think, oh, dear wild wife of mine, that you would have wed anyone else when it actually came down to saying your yea or nay,' he murmured and lowered his head to kiss her and halt the eager throng behind them with a sentimental 'ooh!' that Kate was far too preoccupied to hear for eagerly kissing him back.

Far from blushing and becoming pricklingly conscious of so many eyes riveted on them from within and without Wychwood Church, she rose on tiptoes to meet him mouth for mouth, lip to lip, and press herself so close that they were body to body as well. He was quite correct, of course, and had been all along; she would never have wed anyone but Edmund George Francis St Erith Standon-Worth, Viscount Shuttleworth, when it came to the stark fact of actually having to do so.

'Maybe you're right,' she conceded as he reluctantly raised his head. She noted with distracted surprise that she'd so far forgotten herself as to raise hands covered in fine white kid gloves embroidered with silver to muss his immaculately cut and ruthlessly smoothed hair into the curling pelt she loved so much, making him look very different from the grave young lord who presented a composed public face to the world. She was beginning to realise how wildly that image flew in the face of his truly passionate and headstrong nature, but not as wildly as hers once had in the face of one equally wayward and just as wild.

'Don't expect me to meekly agree with you all the time, though, from now on, will you, Edmund?' she warned him unnecessarily.

'Now, where would be the fun in that?' he asked with his face alight with anticipation, as if he could already taste the joy of making up after the fiery quarrels they'd surely have.

'There wouldn't be any, not without you, my love,' she told him happily.

'Are you two going to stand there blocking the doorway all day?' her chief bridesmaid interrupted impatiently and Kate turned to give her little sister a smug look, for she was so full of insufferable pride in her own achievement after finally netting the love of her life and the most eligible ex-bachelor of the *ton* that she didn't mind who knew it today.

'Just you wait until it's your turn, Isabella Penelope Alstone,' she warned. 'Then perhaps you'll know why we're doing it.'

'I shall certainly manage the whole business far more handily than you two have done and not take three years to get myself to the altar,' her sister told her briskly. 'Now, are you finally going to move out of the way before I get crushed from the back by this charge of well-wishers behind me?'

'Aye,' said Edmund, just as smugly, towing his bride out of the church door and into the warmth of the glorious June day before she and her sister could start pulling caps and then standing with her to proudly show the world what a fine and fair viscountess he'd caught on his wedding day.

Laughing as he answered the cheers and frankly expressed encouragement of the wedding guests and the many spectators who'd turned out to wish Kate and her groom well, he bowed to his newly made wife and smoothed his own dishevelled locks, before solemnly resuming his fine top hat at a rakish angle. Then he seized her hand again and placed it in the crook of his elbow as if he had no intention of letting it go for a very long time.

After a rush of delighted kisses for her and congratulatory pats on the back that he weathered manfully, Edmund stood ready to hand Kate up into the open carriage the estate workers had decorated with hoops of lush flowers and ribbons and the odd wedding favour that should have made her blush, but didn't. Who would have thought when she went about her reluctant husband hunt at the beginning of this Season that she'd come home with the love of her life instead? Not her, she realised with a wry smile of self-knowledge, as she watched his eyes go silver-green with the very sight of her so frankly besotted with her newly wed lord.

'You really are a very *convenient* husband, Edmund,' she told him wickedly.

'Climb into this carriage and stop tantalising me and I'll show you just how wrong you are about that epithet, darling Kate,' he offered with a lecherous leer that made her laugh like a schoolgirl.

'I do love you, you know?' she told him very seriously as she moved her hand in his so he could help her up at last.

'Yes, I do know that at last, and rather better than

you did yourself at times, if I remember rightly. Now be quiet, woman, and hurry up and throw that infernal bouquet at someone so I can kiss you properly.'

'Your wish is my command, husband,' she told him with mock humility and hurled the lovely thing with apparent carelessness straight at Amelia Transome, her second adult bridesmaid, who blushed and tried her best not to look at Edmund's best man, even as Mr Cromer managed to look conscious and proud and resigned to the direction his future happiness was to take all at the same time.

'Why not Isabella?' Edmund asked with only vague interest as the carriage pulled away and they waved to their many well-wishers.

'Because she can look after herself from now on. If she wants to marry, I dare say she'll do as she says and go about it in her own way, and if she doesn't, then she'll manage that just as she pleases as well. She asked me when she came to town to leave her to live her own life now and just get on with mine, Edmund, so I'm going to take her at her word and do just that from now on.'

'You did a very fine job of guarding her from harm when she needed you to, Kate. You were painfully young when you were left to protect and bring up your little sister virtually alone by those who should have looked after you instead, but she's a wonderful, bright and happy young woman now and that's mainly thanks to you. So here's hoping we make half as fine a fist of raising our own daughters when the time comes.'

'I like the sound of them, Edmund, so long as you give me a son or two to spoil and chide and love as well,' she murmured and felt her heart sing at all the lovely possibilities in front of her and her new husband as they finally drew away from the village and could concentrate on kissing each other at last.

'How long will it be before they all go home, do you think?' he asked huskily as they emerged from that protracted and passionate interlude to find they were already at the Court and the horses were still and the coachman impassive, as if they'd all been waiting some time for the bride and groom to come to their senses.

'Well, they probably mean to stay for several days and celebrate the birth of Kit and Miranda's son and heir in proper style, now they're all assembled and more than ready for a family party,' Kate replied with an affectionate glance behind her at the laughing, joyously smiling guests piling out of their carriages behind them.

He groaned and looked hunted at the very idea of being called upon to forsake their marriage bed so often, or even put off getting into it in the first place for what seemed likely to be far too many hours. 'I love your family, Kate, I adore both your sisters and esteem Ben and Charlotte Shaw as if they were your true family as well, and that's not to forget Eiliane and her marquis also, of course, but when can we finally quit them all for the time being and go home, my love?'

'In about three hours, Miranda and I thought,' she said, taking pity on him and herself, for it sounded more like three days to her as well just now when she wanted her husband nearly as urgently as he obviously desired his wife.

'Thank heavens for that, then,' he answered brusquely

and Kate loved him even more when he was being such a man and refusing to admit how much having all this fuss and family around them while they made the most important promises of their lives had meant to him.

'I might need to change out of all this finery after an hour or so, though,' she offered with not very believable innocence, because three hours sounded far too long after three interminable weeks of abstinence to her as well.

'And I'm working on my skills as a ladies' maid, so I might even manage to master that row of hooks I can feel running down the back of this infernally proper creation if you keep still long enough.'

'Later, my love, and my very impatient lover,' she chided softly, then squeaked with surprise as he seized her and ran up the steps with her as if she weighed far less than she knew she really did. 'Put me down, Edmund, it isn't even our threshold,' she protested.

Edmund grinned and continued to cradle his new wife in his arms while he got his breath back, then turned to watch his host with a laughing challenge written all over his face.

'Feel free,' Kit told him equably from where he stood with his arm about his own wife, who looked about as joyful as a woman could be without actually weeping for it, and Edmund for one was profoundly glad she'd refrained from doing that. 'She's all yours, Shuttleworth,' Kit told his new brother-in-law with a wave at the flushed, distracted, lovelorn Kate Worth who was trying not to laugh as she squirmed in her husband's strong arms until he bent his head to snatch a quick kiss and she stilled to kiss him back with a passionate concentration he very obviously appreciated.

'At long last!' Edmund shouted back. 'At very long last, my love,' he murmured far more softly in Kate's ear and carried her over the threshold to pause once more and kiss her very thoroughly indeed with a silent promise never to let her out of his arms for long, ever again.

* * * * *

The Gentleman's Quest

Deborah Simmons

Chapter One

Hero glanced out of the window of the coach, but saw no sign of Oakfield Manor in the gathering gloom. The bad roads had caused delays; she had been confined in the conveyance for too long. Across from Hero, her companion stared ahead stoically, undisturbed by the stuffy, small space of the old-fashioned vehicle and the ruts that bounced Hero about. As usual, she couldn't help wondering whether Mrs Renshaw was with her strictly as a chaperone or as a spy, to make sure she concluded Raven's business satisfactorily.

Resentment flared before Hero tamped it down out of habit. She knew what was expected of her. No doubt Christopher Marchant would be old and shriveled and balding and smelly. And randy. And she would have to lean close, displaying her low-cut bodice. With a little cajoling, she usually escaped with the prize and her person intact, if not her self-respect. But she had learned long ago that such luxuries as pride were for the wealthy and secure, not for someone like her.

Any doubts that the world was a grim place could be easily vanquished by a glance at the windswept moors, the barren trees and darkening clouds outside. If Hero did not know better, she might think Raven had managed the weather, as well as everything else, and the idea unnerved her.

Another rut threw her against the worn and cracking leather interior, and she realized they had turned onto a sparsely graveled drive in little better condition than the road. She had only an instant to wonder whether they were at last approaching their destination when she was thrown again, harder, and grabbed uselessly for a hold. But it was the arrival of Renshaw in her lap that alerted Hero to the fact that something was amiss.

The imperturbable female uttered a surprised grunt, while her weight stole Hero's breath. When she was able to ease out from under her burden, Hero realized the coach had halted, tilting to one side. She cursed Raven and his ancient vehicle with its ancient fittings, for they likely had lost a wheel here in the middle of nowhere.

Scrambling to the door, Hero managed to jump out onto a thicket of grass, but there was little comfort to be found outside beyond escape from the stifling interior. Pulling up the hood of her cloak against the gusting winds, Hero took stock of their surroundings, and her heart sank. They were off the main road, black clouds chased across the sky, and a rumble of thunder in the distance presaged the coming storm.

Hero shook her head against the sense of doom that threatened and made her way gingerly to the rear of the vehicle where the coachman and footman were muttering amongst themselves. Even Hero could see the wheel was broken, and since both men were eyeing it stupidly, she could only fear the worst.

"If you can't fix it, one of you will have to go for help," Hero said, raising her voice against the wind.

They turned to her, their reluctance obvious. The village they had passed through was a long way back. "'Tweren't much traffic on that roadway, miss," the coachman said, scratching his head.

"There must be more there than here," Hero said with a glance at the overgrown drive. Were they even on the right path? Should she send one of the men ahead? If one went ahead and one behind, Hero would double the chances of their rescue. But that would leave her alone with Renshaw, two women in a broken vehicle on unfamiliar lands, not far from the infamous moors, with foul weather looming.

The thought gave even Hero pause.

Yet what could possibly threaten them in this barren landscape? Anyone with sense, including the residents, would be safely inside, prepared to ride out the tempest. Hero had a pistol in her reticule, and Renshaw had not been chosen for her feminine accomplishments. Wide of girth and taller than many men, she was armed with a cane she carried solely for protection.

Still, wariness was Hero's watchword, and so, in the end, she sent the footman forward, leaving the grizzled coachman to keep watch, while she climbed back inside the coach to wait as best she could. But the wind set up an awful moaning, and Hero wondered whether the vehicle would collapse entirely, falling upon its side and crushing its occupants.

Although Renshaw made no move to follow, Hero exited once more, and as she leaped down to view the scene around her, she considered the length of Raven's reach. Surely it did not stretch this far from his fortress, yet the situation smacked of his design. Was it a test? As she had so often in the past, Hero wondered if she would ever escape from the Gothic nightmare that she seemed so often to inhabit.

It was then that Hero heard something above the distant thunder and bluster. A glance toward the coach showed it swaying slightly, the coachman seeming to doze upon his crooked perch, but the horses had pricked up their ears. Whirling, Hero looked down the drive that disappeared into the growing gloom, but she could see nothing.

Then it seemed as though the sound was coming from ahead, and Hero turned around. Surely, the wind was playing tricks upon her, for now all was quiet behind, while she could hear a horse approaching from the other direction. Walking past the coach and the horses that tramped uneasily, she peered into the dimness. For someone weaned on tales of haunts and odd happenings, Hero felt an uncharacteristic trepidation.

And then she saw him.

Drawing in a sharp breath, Hero wondered whether her dormant imagination had conjured the sight, for he seemed to come straight from one of Raven's Gothic novels. A dark figure atop a black horse, cape billowing behind him, he rode as if born of the storm itself, fast and hard and directly toward her.

Hero was so transfixed that she did not even move and might have been trampled had the horse not stopped neatly. The figure dropped just as neatly to the ground, and only then did she feel he might be real, not a product of some unwitting fantasy, for he stepped toward her with a murmur of concern.

For once, Hero could not answer, having been struck dumb by his appearance. Tall and wide shoul-dered, his dark hair whipping about a face so handsome that Hero had never seen the like, he seemed the very embodiment of every young girl's dream of rescue.

But Hero was no longer a girl, and she knew that no one could help her, unless it was only to give her shelter from the approaching storm. Indeed, he was shouting something to that effect, and before Hero realized what he was about, he had taken her arm. Mounting easily, he reached down to lift her up in front of him.

Hero could only gasp in startlement as she felt her carefully constructed world spinning out of control. Before she could speak, he tucked her side against his hard chest, drew one strong arm around her and kicked the horse into movement.

Hero opened her mouth to protest this stranger's complete usurpation of her authority. Such nearness made her uncomfortable, and the warmth of his touch had an unwelcome effect upon her senses. But then he flashed Hero a grin, and she was struck speechless once more.

As Hero gaped, witless, at the face only a few inches from her own, she realized she had never been this close to anyone in her life. It was unnerving, and yet she had to resist an urge to touch the lock of dark hair that blew across his forehead, matching eyes the color of chocolate.

They held her own for a moment, then glanced upward, and Hero followed his gaze to where thick drops began hailing down upon them. Despite his efforts to hurry her to shelter, the storm had come, yet it was nothing compared to Hero's personal tumult as he pulled her close.

Heart pounding, dizzy and disoriented, Hero had the strange sensation that she could deny this man nothing. And that wild thought was more frightening to her than any Gothic horror.

Once deposited into the hands of Mrs Osgood, a cheery, apple-cheeked housekeeper, Hero felt more like herself. Obviously, the situation outside had worked upon her nerves until she was overwrought, imagining her rescuer to be some kind of superior being with an unexplainable effect upon her. Although Hero was not the overwrought kind, the only other possibility was too terrible to consider.

It was with some relief that she realized, through Mrs Osgood's chatter, that she had reached her destination and that she had only to meet with Mr Marchant in order to conclude her business. Who her rescuer might be, Hero refused to wonder or care. Yet, at the claim, her body shivered as if in denial.

She tried not to remember the feel of his hard form, wet garments slick against her own, as he helped her from the horse and into the house. A small Gothic, complete with battlements, its dark facade so evoked Raven that Hero again wondered what he had wrought, only to dismiss her suspicions.

Augutus Raven might have access to an astonishing variety of resources, but he could not control the elements. And Hero could hardly be surprised by the style of the building, considering Raven's penchant for such facades. Many of his fellow antiquaries shared his delight in the old and cold and moldy, probably because they were old and cold and moldy.

Not that Oakfield was moldy, but it looked sadly in need of improvement. Still, the fire was warm, and Hero was glad to be given her own room, with Renshaw nearby. As she bathed, dressed in dry clothes and brushed her hair by the fire, the incredible encounter with the handsome stranger gradually faded away. And by the time Hero went to join Renshaw downstairs, she was firmly focused on the task ahead.

That focus was only sharpened by her surroundings, for the housekeeper showed her into a rather threadbare library. Ignoring the gloom of the poorly lit room, Hero eyed the mostly empty shelves and the packing crates that were scattered about. *Was Mr Marchant selling all of his books?*

If so, Raven might be interested in a bulk purchase. You never knew what nuggets were hidden away, undiscovered and undervalued by their owner. Hero moved toward one open box and glanced inside. Some Latin and Greek volumes were piled in no particular order, and she was leaning down to read the titles when she heard footsteps.

Plastering a smile on her face, Hero turned in greeting, only to stare in astonishment at the man who stood in the doorway. Without his cloak and gloves he looked even more beautiful than she remembered, and Hero blinked in dismay. *Surely this was not her host?*

"W-where is Mr Marchant?" she asked, cursing her faltering tongue.

"I'm Christopher Marchant, at your service," he said, bowing slightly. Then he flashed her that winning grin, and Hero felt unsteady upon her feet.

She knew better than to dismiss all antiquaries as the grasping old fools they were often portrayed. Still, she rarely dealt with elegant, free-spending sorts like the Duke of Devonshire. And she certainly had never met any like this man.

Too late, Hero realized she was gaping, and she hurried to recover herself. Panic threatened—how was she to proceed when her heart was hammering and her wits scattered? But she could do nothing else.

"Thank you," she said, with a nod of her head. "I am Miss Hero Ingram, and this is my companion, Mrs Renshaw. I have brought a letter from my uncle, Mr Augustus Raven. I believe he corresponded with your father in the past."

Hero stepped forward to present the missive, while giving the man an opportunity to ogle her bodice. But unlike her usual hosts, Christopher Marchant was not ancient or shriveled or randy. And Hero doubted that anyone who looked like he did would be impressed with her small bosom, no matter how low cut her gown.

"I beg your pardon for barging in upon you like this," Hero said, reciting her usual patter. The lonely old men she most often dealt with were so flattered by her attention that they did not object to her doing business on behalf of her uncle, if they would even call it that. Most would label the transaction an arrangement between friends or acquaintances, among fellow collectors.

However, Mr Marchant was…different, and Hero wondered whether he would look askance at her sudden appearance at his remote residence. "I was in the area and thought to make a stop for my own convenience. You will forgive me?" she asked, her standard simpering sticking in her throat.

"Of course, please sit down," he said, with an easy gesture. His open and engaging manner further confused her, for the men she was accustomed to dealing with were often as secretive as Raven, hiding their thoughts behind pinched faces.

"I'm afraid the house is still at sixes and sevens," Mr Marchant muttered, his smile faltering. For a moment Hero thought he would say more, but he simply glanced around the room as though just realizing its disarray.

He did not appear to notice that Renshaw was seated in the most shadowed corner, which was just as well, for Hero could not depend upon her usual tactics. Thinking frantically, she decided to take a direct approach. "Are you selling some of your collection?"

Mr. Marchant looked at her rather blankly before glancing about. "Oh, you mean the books? No, we recently moved in, my sister and I, and have not yet arranged everything."

"Well, if you should wish to save yourself some of the trouble, I know someone who might well take these out of your way," Hero said, gesturing toward the crates.

Mr Marchant nodded, though he showed no interest, which was puzzling. Here, inside Oakfield, he seemed distracted, and Hero noticed shadows under his eyes. Was he ill? He certainly looked robust and not much older than she, but perhaps a long night of carousing had left him the worse for wear. Isn't that what handsome young men did, gamble, drink and seduce women? Hero could only guess, for her dealings with such were few and far between.

"If that's why you've come, I'm afraid I can't offer you any hope on that score," Mr Marchant said. "They were my father's, you see." Sadness flashed briefly across his features, and Hero cursed Raven's greed. How many times had he swooped down upon a grieving relative to break up and sell the precious volumes the deceased had spent a lifetime lovingly acquiring?

"I'm sorry," Hero said, and she meant it. But when his dark gaze met her own, she felt as though he were looking right into her, and she glanced away, unwilling to let anyone, especially this man, see her. Suddenly, she wondered whether he could tell how he affected her, and she straightened, determined to reveal nothing of herself.

"Certainly, I can understand your feelings," Hero said, briskly breaking whatever connection had been between them. If Christopher Marchant's only attachment to his father's collection was sentiment, then he shouldn't care about any of the individual items, which made her task that much easier. "I would not want you to part with so treasured an assembly, but perhaps you could spare one volume?" she asked.

At her words, Mr Marchant's open expression turned closed, making her wonder if he was as uninterested as he seemed. *Was he aware of what he possessed and its potential value?* Any collector would know that a book long thought lost would start a bidding war.

Hero gave no outward sign of her thoughts, though the change in Mr Marchant made her uncomfortable. *Did he realize she had hoped to dupe him?* He had seemed genuinely welcoming, but now there was an edge to the man, the kind that made her wary.

On occasion even the old and withered antiquaries were immune to her charms. Some miserly creatures were intent upon holding on to the meanest title even if it meant going without supper. But Hero did not intend to return to Raven empty-handed, so she chose her next words carefully.

"Perhaps you are aware of interest in the volume, a text by Ambrose Mallory?"

To Hero's surprise, Mr Marchant's handsome face darkened with anger, and she hastened to avoid any outburst that would destroy her chances entirely. "I'm afraid once word is out, there is no stopping them," she said, with a shrug of apology.

But he was not placated. Instead, he looked astonished by her comment. "You cannot mean to tell me that there are more Druids out there, intent upon evil?"

Druids? Hero kept her expression steady as she realized her host might not be in his right mind. Even as she shied from the possibility, she wouldn't put it past Raven to send her here, knowing of his condition. It was just the sort of twisted jest that amused Raven, who might hope to gain a bargain, as well.

Floundering, Hero cast about for some sort of reply and tried a conspiratorial smile. "Not Druids, sir, but something far more dangerous," she said, leaning forward. *"Bibliomaniacs."*

But Mr Marchant was not amused. Surging to his feet, he turned toward the doorway, and for one startling moment Hero thought he might forcibly evict her. She felt a tremor of fear. *Or was it excitement?* But Mr Marchant appeared to regain control of himself as he strode toward one of the deep-set windows.

Rain was lashing against the panes, pounding as fiercely as Hero's heart, and the very air crackled, like that which presaged lightning. She was on the edge of her seat, ready to make her escape, if necessary. Yet at the same time, she had to fight the urge to go to him, for he seemed in need of comfort.

When he finally spoke, he did not turn toward her, but gazed out at the storm. "The book you refer to is gone, burned in the conflagration that took my garden and stables. I cannot help you."

It was a dismissal, but Hero ignored it. Her mind was too busy working. *Was he telling the truth?* Books were often lost to fire or water, but it would not be the first time she had been handed a Banbury tale to divert attention from a prize—or to gain a higher price from another bidder. Perhaps Mr Marchant knew that some bibliomaniacs would go to any lengths to acquire an item, handing over outrageous sums for the rare and coveted.

Word had it that Snuffy Davie paid about twopence for a book that eventually sold for £170 to the Regent himself. Those with the means, such as the Duke of Devonshire, filled whole rooms, even entire houses, with their acquisitions. It was definitely a mania, one that Hero could not understand.

Although Mr Marchant had seemed indifferent at first, perhaps he was stricken, as well. *Was he playing her, as she had tried to play him?* Hero eyed him closely. "If that is true, then it is a sad loss to the collecting world, as well as to yourself."

"Hardly," he said. "My sister nearly died, and that accursed book was to blame."

With that, his gaze met hers, and Hero swallowed hard. Again, she felt out of her element. This man's grief and anger threatened to reach out and touch her, something that she could not allow.

Hastily breaking eye contact, she sought to regain control of the situation. "I'm sorry," Hero murmured. "But I believe I have some information that might be of interest to you, if you would hear me out?"

He turned to look out at the rain again, reaching up to run a hand through his dark hair, and Hero found her own gaze lingering on the thick locks in need of a trim. His clothes were those of a gentleman, though not of the most expensive materials, but his form was such that he could probably wear anything to his advantage. And Hero found his simple breeches and coat far more appealing than the London dandies with their gold embroidered waistcoats or Raven's friends with their old-fashioned wigs and silk breeches.

When he said nothing, Hero decided to press her

point. "You see, with that copy burned, any other would be the sole surviving edition, a very valuable volume indeed. And my uncle has reason to believe that another exists, perhaps in this very house—"

Mr Marchant cut her off. "I certainly hope not," he said. He turned his head to send her another probing glance. "Are you even aware of what you are seeking? This book that you want tells how to augur the future from the death throes of innocent people. And my sister was to be one such victim."

Hero sucked in a harsh breath. Was that the subject, or was Mr Marchant delusional? Hero cursed Raven for giving her so little information, but the thought focused her attention on her task. Druids and auguring, whether real or not, had little to do with it.

"I'm sure my uncle has no interest in the text," Hero assured her host. "It's the rarity of the work that makes it collectible." Without waiting for Mr Marchant's response, Hero pulled the paper Raven had given her from her reticule and held it toward him.

"My uncle found this in another book he acquired. Since all copies of the Mallory were thought lost until recently, he was most interested, of course."

For a long moment, Hero waited, hand outstretched, but Mr Marchant did not stir from his position.

"Perhaps I have not made myself clear," he said. "I have no interest in this work except to destroy it."

Now he was talking madness. "I can hardly believe you, the son of a scholar, would condone suppression of the written word," Hero said, hoping to shame him.

But he did not argue. Desperate now, Hero stammered out a protest before catching herself. She took a deep breath, then eyed him levelly.

"I assure you that Augustus Raven has no intention of letting anyone even see the book, except to admire its position in one of his presses. His collection is vast and varied, but it is the singular editions he particularly treasures, the pages being of no consequence, as long as they have not been gutted."

Mr Marchant simply shook his head, and Hero's heart sank. "Perhaps you don't realize the kind of sum Raven would consider paying."

But even that did not move him, and Hero tried to make some sense of his stand. It would be just her luck to find the only man in England with some sort of conscience. Usually, she was a good judge of people, but even she could not take the measure of Christopher Marchant. Was he a lunatic? A fool? That rarest of all creatures, a man without a price? Or had he simply received a better offer?

Hero studied him closely, looking for a telltale sign, a hint of how she should proceed. But she could see no hidden meanings, no deep dark secrets she could use against him, no weaknesses she could exploit, no promise of further negotiation. Or was her judgement clouded by the man himself?

Finally, he turned away from the windows to face her. "I would not send you out in this storm, so you are welcome to remain here for the night."

At his words, Hero didn't know whether to be relieved or not. Her instincts told her to abandon her mission now, while she could, and to run from this man who had such an effect upon her. But Raven's will was stronger than her own, and he had sent her here with a purpose.

Hero nodded her agreement, knowing that she would try again at supper, at the very least, at breakfast at the very latest. And if all else failed, she could search the place herself.

Kit pulled off his neckcloth with a sharp jerk, tossed it aside, and sank into a chair to stare moodily out at the darkness. But even he realized that he spent entirely too much time looking out into the gloom, and he forced himself to turn away from the window. Instead, his gaze was drawn across his bedroom to the decanter he now kept on a chest of drawers. There was nothing wrong with a glass or two to help him sleep, he told himself.

But he knew his sister Sydony wouldn't agree. She would not approve of his behavior, the nightly drinks and the brooding that she would say was not like him. *But he didn't feel like himself.* He hadn't since the fire.

He was the one who had brought Sydony here, insisting that the property willed to him from a greataunt was good fortune. And he had reveled in his new role as a landowner, ignoring her misgivings and suspicions. He'd even begun to wonder about her sanity when she prattled on about Druids and mysterious lights.

And then he'd nearly lost her. If it hadn't been for their old friend Barto, who had not ignored Sydony's suspicions, Kit would have woken up in a ditch, stupid and useless, his sister dead, his garden usurped by cloaked killers.

Kit shook his head at his stupidity. Of the two siblings, he had been the cheerful one. Syd certainly wasn't dismal, but she had always seemed more conscientious, perhaps because she had assumed control of the household after the death of their mother many years ago. Meanwhile, Kit had drifted through life with a casual contentment—until the fire.

Ever since he'd been unable to move forward, to tackle the rebuilding with his usual enthusiasm. He felt as though he'd been kicked in the gut and, angry and hurting, he questioned everything, especially himself.

Surging to his feet, Kit moved to the chest and poured himself a glass of wine. Just for another night, he told himself. Because of her. He took a big swallow and frowned at the wry twist of fate that had brought him a guest.

Visitors to Oakfield were infrequent, if not nonexistent, so he had been surprised when Mrs Osgood reported that a servant had arrived on foot from a broken-down coach. Racing against the storm, Kit had hurried out, only to come across a beautiful creature standing fearlessly against the wind, one hand holding the hood of her cloak against her streaming hair. *Just as though she were waiting for him.*

He had been so desperate for companionship that he had imagined… Hell, Kit wasn't sure what he was thinking when he saw her, probably that she was some sort of answer to everything that ailed him. And when she fitted so well against him, his hopes seemed confirmed.

Kit shook his head. Whatever conquests he had made had been left behind in his old neighborhood, while the female population around here stayed well clear of Oakfield and its owners, out of long habit. So he could hardly be blamed for letting his imagination run away with him when presented with a young woman who was as articulate, intelligent and opinionated as his sister, while making poor Syd look like an antidote.

But then he'd found out what she was about, this Miss Ingram. *Hero.* Kit swirled the name around on his tongue and found it bittersweet. If she had come for any other reason, he would have welcomed her into his home, perhaps even into his life. Instead, he had studiously avoided her company.

It had not been easy for a man so isolated to forgo such an opportunity, especially when his visitor was no ordinary female. Kit's mouth twisted wryly at that understatement. Unusual and intriguing, Miss Ingram was a puzzle that begged closer study. But more than that, she somehow had managed to stir him to life, as nothing else had.

Kit couldn't help remembering his first sight of her, standing like a beacon in the gloom, as though she could hold back the darkness. Tossing back the last of his drink, he shuddered. Looks could be deceiving, as he well knew, for it seemed that Miss Ingram had brought the darkness with her.

A knock made Kit lift his head, and for one wild moment, he wondered whether the beautiful siren had come to plead her case here and now. Drawing in a harsh breath, he surged to his feet and ran a hand through his hair. But when he opened the door, it was only to greet the new housekeeper.

"Pardon me, sir, but the coachman is downstairs, wishing to see you. I told him you'd gone up to bed, but he said it was important," Mrs Osgood added with a hint of disapproval. Obviously, she did not think much of the staff bothering her master at this hour.

But Kit nodded without hesitation, for Hob was his friend Barto's man and coachman was the least of his duties. Hurriedly placing his empty glass on a nearby table, Kit closed the door and followed the housekeeper downstairs. This sudden summons from Hob could not be good.

But what? Kit wondered. Those responsible for the fire presumably had all died in it, and the maze and book that had drawn them here were gone. Yet Barto had insisted that Hob stay on at Oakfield, and Kit had agreed, if only to placate his old friend.

Now he felt a new sense of foreboding as he slipped through the darkened house. Was his home doomed to disaster? Cursed? Kit had never believed in such nonsense, but he had never believed in murderous cults, either. His mood was bleak when he entered the dimly lit kitchen, where Hob stood waiting. With a nod toward Mrs Osgood, who disappeared into the servants' quarters below, Kit stepped forward.

"It could be nothing, sir," Hob said, as though gauging his temperament.

But Kit knew that Hob would not be here if he did not have a valid concern. "Go on."

"Well, it's their coach, sir, the one that arrived today."

"You mean Miss Ingram's?"

Hob nodded. "I gather it belongs to her uncle, Mr Raven, but she's the one who uses it the most, according to the coachman." He paused to eye Kit soberly. "We got a new wheel put on easily enough, but when we looked at the old one, well, it wasn't any ordinary break."

"What do you mean?"

"I mean it looked like a saw had been taken to it."

"What? You're saying someone deliberately tampered with the wheel, assuring it would fail?" Since his own father had died in a carriage accident, Kit was well aware of what could have happened, and he felt a sharp surge of anger. "Why would someone do such a thing? And who? Some stable hand intent upon a rich prize?"

Hob shook his head. "It's an old coach, worn and uncomfortable looking, hardly what one would expect from a wealthy man like Mr Raven."

"From what I understand, he's something of an eccentric," Kit said, then he glanced sharply at Hob. "Perhaps the break was not intended for Miss Ingram, but for her uncle."

Hob shook his head. "This was done recently, sir, and they're far from this Raven Hill, where they make their home."

"But if whoever did this wasn't drawn to the coach, then what do they want?" Kit mused aloud. He didn't like any of the possibilities, least of all the answer he got from Hob, who eyed him with a frown.

"Perhaps they want something inside it."

Chapter Two

Kit's mood was dark when he returned to his room. The candles he had left burning flickered as he swung open the door and closed it behind him. Without conscious thought, he reached for his glass, but it wasn't where he had left it. Glancing around, he found it had fallen to the floor, which was probably a good thing, for he needed his wits about him. He set the empty glass on the table and sank into his chair.

In the silence that followed, his gaze drifted to the empty seat opposite, and he realized that he missed having a sounding board. His old friend Barto's advice would be welcome now, as would Sydony's. Although the siblings had been apart before, this was the first time in his life that Kit had lived alone. And he'd better get used to it, for Sydony would be marrying Barto soon.

Kit had been so pleased at the news that he had not given a thought to the day when his sister would be gone, both she and Barto far away. But now that day loomed before him, and Kit glanced at the glass again before he caught himself.

He had a good home, which he planned to improve, property he hoped to make prosperous, and money he could draw upon to do both. So what if he was alone? He would just have to make more of an effort to meet the locals. Surely the gentry would come around, and there were some young people among them, for Kit had seen them at church.

The ladies he had chanced upon there, however, paled in comparison to the one who was under his roof. So why wasn't such a beautiful and intriguing creature married? Perhaps she was betrothed, Kit mused, but not many men would let her travel over the countryside making deals for her uncle.

As a rule, her gender did not conduct business. Although there had always been rich and powerful females who exerted their authority, often behind the scenes, a young woman usually did not call on gentlemen, even with a chaperone in tow. Perhaps Miss Ingram simply had been traveling in the area, as she claimed. Yet she spoke of her uncle's concerns so knowledgeably that Kit suspected this wasn't the first such errand she had undertaken.

He tried to remember all that he knew about Augustus Raven, but it wasn't much. The man styled himself after Horace Walpole, a dilettante of the past century who had authored *The Castle of Otranto*. As far as Kit knew, Raven had never dabbled in writing, but just as Walpole was famous for his Gothic home, Strawberry Hill, Raven had his own elaborate fortress called Raven Hill.

Unlike Strawberry Hill, it was shrouded in mystery, as was its owner. Augustus Raven was a collector, that much was known, and apparently, he had no compunction about having his niece acquire for him. And now he had put her in danger.

Kit frowned. At one time he wouldn't have given Hob's report a second thought, but he had learned the hard way not to ignore warning signs. The fact that someone had deliberately caused Miss Ingram's coach to break down so close to Oakfield was not a likely coincidence. And he could come to only one conclusion.

The wretched book had to be responsible.

It had drawn her here, as it had others before her, most notably a man named Malet, a latter-day Druid who had sought the text for some arcane ritual involving the maze behind the house. Both had been built by Ambrose Mallory, a mystic responsible for the writings that were wreaking havoc more than a hundred years after his death.

Had someone survived the conflagration? Or were there others out there who had not been caught in the blaze? Barto had the wealth and connections to investigate, but so far he had discovered nothing more than what they already knew, and Kit had begun to believe the whole business was over.

Until now. *But why Miss Ingram?* Kit shook his head. Whether someone thought she had the book in her possession or had information that would lead to it didn't matter. There were people who would stop at nothing to get their hands on that deadly nonsense.

Kit ought to know. They'd killed his father.

And after what Sydony had gone through, Kit wasn't about to let Miss Ingram meet a similar fate. Although he had pressing matters that required his attention at Oakfield and wanted nothing less than to be thrust back into the dark doings that haunted his new home, Kit had no choice.

He had been asleep on his watch once before, but he did not intend to let it happen again.

When Kit went down to breakfast, he found that his guests had already eaten and were waiting in the library. Although Mrs Osgood would have shown them there as a matter of course, Kit couldn't help wondering if Miss Ingram had been rifling through his father's books.

The thought sent anticipation buzzing in his veins, an antidote to the brooding melancholy that was his daily companion. But Kit was not willing to give it up easily, and he told himself that in the light of the new day, he would find his visitor wanting. Surely, no woman could be as beautiful and interesting as he had made her.

And yet, when he entered the library, Kit felt the same pleasure he had the day before. The pale light seemed to cast a glow upon her, just as when he had first seen her standing in the drive. And something about her pose, seated demurely by a window, hands folded in her lap, made his lips curve, for it did not seem a natural one.

Had she already rifled through the books or had she guessed at his suspicions? Kit wondered, not for the first time, what went on behind those eyes. They were a caramel color, as unusual as the woman herself, but told him nothing of their owner. Did she feel what he felt when he looked at her? Her impassive features argued otherwise and reminded Kit of the seriousness of the discussion ahead.

He looked around the room for Mrs Renshaw, only to find her seated at a distance that would make conversation difficult. But the stout female seemed to be nodding off anyway, so he did not bother to include her.

Turning his attention back to Miss Ingram, Kit spoke before she could begin reciting the usual pleasantries expected in such a social situation. "Show me what you have," he said, as he took a seat near her. "About the Mallory."

Kit saw a flicker of surprise, quickly masked, and he wondered how this woman had come to be so self-possessed. Sydony's feelings were always apparent, even if she wasn't voicing them, but Miss Ingram said little unless it related to her errand, and revealed even less. Showing no expression, she handed him a torn piece of paper.

"It is part of a letter from Mallory to one of his disciples," she said.

The paper obviously was old, and Kit handled it carefully. Although the hand was strong, the ink had faded and was difficult to read. Still, he could make out most of what remained.

I write to entrust you with this copy of my life's work to hold for safekeeping. Speak not of it to anyone, but secrete it well away from all prying eyes, so that the historical truths therein might be preserved. I have hidden a copy here, but, as you may have learned, the rest have been seized and destroyed. I blame the cursed printer who—

"*Historical truths,*" Kit muttered in contempt.

"Apparently, all other editions were destroyed because they were deemed sacrilegious, and Mallory was labeled a heretic," Miss Ingram explained. "He died shortly afterward, purportedly poisoned by one of his own."

Kit frowned at the thought of the murder, hopefully not done under this roof, although most likely deserved. "And who did he send this to?" Kit asked, trying to decipher the name.

Miss Ingram leaned toward him, an intent look upon her face. "Martin Cheswick, an ancestor of the Earl of Cheswick. Raven acquired some books, including the one in which this fragment was found, after the current earl's father died."

Kit nearly whistled at the idea of such a personage being connected with Mallory. Then again, every family had black sheep in their histories, including the Prince Regent himself. "But that's where you should be looking, not here," Kit said, returning the paper to her.

Miss Ingram frowned. "It speaks of two copies."

"But the one that was hidden here burned," Kit said. And that would be that, if not for the broken wheel. He could shout out to the skies that the volume was gone, but someone obviously thought Miss Ingram knew better. Were they looking for the piece of correspondence or the book itself?

"Who knew that you were coming here?" Kit asked.

Again, there was but a brief flicker of surprise before Miss Ingram spoke. "Raven, obviously."

"Perhaps some of his friends or associates, as well?"

To her credit, Miss Ingram did not balk at his questions, but answered with a trace of irony. "Mr Marchant, I assure you that Raven does not discuss uncompleted transactions with anyone. That is why I alone am here, without a host of others clamouring to outbid me."

"But you were lucky to reach Oakfield at all," Kit said, "considering that the wheel on your coach was carefully sawed so as to cause it to break."

This time there was no mistaking her startlement. And even the distant companion roused herself from her slumberous slouch. Perhaps she was not as uninterested as she appeared.

"What are you saying?"

"My coachman replaced the wheel, but there's no mistaking that the old one was cut."

Kit was so used to talking to Syd that he realized not every gently born female would take well to such news, and he braced himself for some kind of fainting spell or hysteria. But Miss Ingram again proved she was not typical of her gender. Evincing no fear or horror, she eyed him evenly.

"But why would anyone want to cause such an accident?"

"I would guess for the same reason you are here," Kit said. "Perhaps they've heard of your uncle's interest in the Mallory and think that you might acquire it or might know something that would lead them to it, such as what you just showed me."

Miss Ingram frowned. "I don't see how anyone could know about it when it has been hidden for years."

Kit shrugged. "Perhaps your uncle had occasion to mention it to someone, or the former owner of the book in which this was found might have spoken of it."

"Mr Marchant, Raven does not easily share his secrets," Miss Ingram said, yet there was a certain hesitation in her speech that made Kit wonder, especially when she refused to meet his probing gaze. Augustus Raven might be a man of mystery, but he was not particularly quiet about his possessions. Kit could well imagine a boast falling on the wrong ears.

"The fact remains that someone has gone to great lengths to stop you, and if you had not nearly reached Oakfield, you might have had unwelcome company."

That made her blanch, and Kit pressed his point. "Miss Ingram, it has been my experience that the kind of people who seek this text do not take well to disappointment. If they think you have something they want, they will kill you to get it."

Miss Ingram paled, but did not falter. "That seems a bit extreme, even for a bibliomaniac."

"For your protection, I insist upon escorting you home."

Miss Ingram cocked her head, as though considering the suggestion. "That is very kind of you, Mr Marchant, but if someone is seeking this paper or the book it mentions, they will not be satisfied until they get it."

Undoubtedly. "But you'll be safe once returned to

Raven Hill," Kit assured her, even as he felt a twinge of uncertainty. Hadn't his own property been invaded? His own sister attacked? But what else could he do, especially for a woman who was no relation? By all accounts, Augustus Raven was wealthier and more powerful, his famous house practically a fortress.

Miss Ingram shook her head. "If these people are as dangerous as you suggest, there is only one real option." She leaned forward, her caramel-colored eyes glinting as she looked at him intently. "We must find the remaining edition. Once Raven has it in his possession, no one will have cause to pursue me."

Kit was taken aback both by the suggestion and Miss Ingram's apparent determination. What she proposed was the kind of wild escapade that he and Syd and Barto might have planned in their youth, but not something that reasonable adults would undertake, especially strangers.

Kit had never followed the strictest codes of propriety, but traveling around the country with a woman who was no relation to him, even with a sleepy chaperone accompanying them, did not seem like appropriate behavior.

"I don't think your uncle would approve," he said.

But Miss Ingram showed no sign of demurring. She straightened in her seat and gazed at him directly. "Raven approves of any means that gets him what he wants."

It was the challenge glinting in her eyes that made Kit waver. Instead of hiding away, sunk in the dismals, he could do *something*, maybe even hunt down those connected with the bastards who murdered his father, threatened his sister and now stalked Miss Ingram. But as tempting as that notion was, Kit knew he could hardly chase suspected killers while protecting her. And he would not use a woman as bait to draw them out.

"It wouldn't take long," she said. "Cheswick isn't that far from Raven Hill."

"Cheswick?" Kit echoed. *The ancestral home of the earls?*

"Yes, just as you said."

"*I* said?" Kit was used to being confounded by his sister, but Miss Ingram was taking the practice to new extremes.

"You said we should look to the recipient of the letter for the Mallory."

Kit groaned at that logic. "I simply meant that the book wasn't here, but had been sent away. You can't hare off to Cheswick based on a hundred-year-old scrap of paper sent to a long-dead relative of the earl."

"Why not? Where else should we start?"

She was so serious that Kit could only stare in amazement. "Do you realize how many times that book could have changed hands?"

"If it had surfaced, the collecting world would know of it," she insisted.

Kit shook his head. "The fellow who received that missive might have hidden it or sent it away. Had he any sense, he would have destroyed it. Or it could have been confiscated with all the others."

"Maybe," Miss Ingram said. "But maybe not. The only way to find out is to look."

Again, Kit felt a leap of excitement at the dare, at

the opportunity to move against the dark threat that clung to his home. But he did not see how banging on the Earl of Cheswick's door would solve anything.

Perhaps once he got Miss Ingram safely home, Kit would ask Barto for an introduction to the earl. As Viscount Hawthorne, Kit's old friend moved among the *ton* and might even know the fellow nobleman. A few discreet inquiries could be made, though Kit doubted the book would ever be found. And as far as he was concerned, it could stay lost for ever.

Kit shook his head. "I'm just a gentleman farmer, not one of the desperate characters you described, driven by book madness." *Or worse.*

"But you must know more about the Mallory than anyone," Miss Ingram protested.

"I can't even tell you what the book looks like because I never saw it—none of us did," Kit said. "Which makes going after it a fool's errand and perilous, as well. You can pursue the letter's history through the proper channels, if you wish, once you are home, where your uncle can watch over it—and you."

For someone who had argued so passionately for her preferred course, Miss Ingram seemed to accept his decision with equanimity. Straightening in her seat, she gave him a slow nod of resignation, and Kit was too glad she had seen reason to question her response. Instead, he leaned forward.

"Now, here's my plan."

Since Mr Marchant's scheme required some time to organize, Hero took the opportunity to look through the house once more. Although Gothic, it was small enough to be made into a cozy home without much work. And as she walked through the rooms, Hero began imagining improvements, not the sort that Raven undertook, but the kind that would make it comfortable, inviting…

Hero shook her head at such fancies. What Mr Marchant did or did not choose to do with his property was none of her concern. Her only concern was acquiring the Mallory, and that was what she was doing, wasn't it? Hero conveniently ignored the small voice that told her she should have fled, broken wheel or not, refusing Mr Marchant's offer to escort her.

By ceding to him, hadn't she proven her fears were valid, that she couldn't refuse him? Hero shook her head, unwilling to consider any such possibility. She was only doing what she had to, and if he insisted on coming along, why not make good use of him?

Stepping into a parlor at the back of the house, Hero realized it was probably a later addition to the original structure, for tall doors led onto a terrace. Although it had been raining yesterday, she could see the rear of the property more clearly now through wisps of fog.

The sight was not heartening. The blackened stubble that stretched behind the house gave credence to Mr Marchant's story of a recent fire. Although Hero had questioned the servants about it, they claimed to be newly hired and ignorant of the facts. But something had burned back there. Had the book been destroyed, as well? Hero had only Mr Marchant's word on that, and she had learned long ago not to trust anyone.

And that included a man who could trip her pulse with one look. No matter how straightforward he might seem, Hero knew that his casual air could be deceiving. Christopher Marchant was smarter than he looked and far more observant. Despite his often heavy-lidded gaze, he was awake on every suit, and no matter how appealing he was, Hero could not afford to let down her guard.

As if to prove her point, Hero felt, rather than heard, him move behind her, and her heart pounded in response. Such quiet steps might be those of practiced stealth, she reminded herself as she tried to calm her clamoring senses.

"What do you think of the house?" he asked.

The question was not what she expected, and Hero turned to face him, an automatic response upon her lips. "It's very nice."

He sent her one of those probing looks that usually made her uncomfortable, but this time Hero did not dissemble. "Perhaps it could use a little work," she admitted. "Some paint, wallpaper and bright fabrics to lighten the atmosphere wouldn't be amiss. I'm sure whatever your sister has planned will be lovely."

Mr Marchant glanced about him, as if at a loss. "I don't know whether she got that far, and now she's gone. She'll be getting married soon."

"Oh," Hero murmured. "Congratulations."

Mr Marchant did not comment, for he was still studying the room, with its heavy curtains and even heavier furniture. "It needs a feminine touch," he said, and for some reason Hero's heart skipped a beat. He did not mean *her* touch, she told herself. She was definitely not the feminine ideal, for she could not watercolor or sketch or play the pianoforte. And a gentleman would have little use for whatever skills she did possess.

"You don't think the place gloomy beyond redemption, do you? Haunted by the history of its original owner? Far too eerie to ever be livable?"

Hero choked back a laugh. "Eerie? You can't know the meaning of the word," she said. "I live at Raven Hill."

"Oh, sorry," Mr Marchant said. "Your uncle does have a reputation for being eccentric."

That was putting it mildly. However, Hero had no intention of discussing Raven or his home, and she hurried to change the subject. "Shall we be leaving soon?"

Mr Marchant nodded, but his expression grew rueful, as though he were disappointed by the turn of the conversation. Had he hoped for more personal information? Hero had never met a man who evinced interest in something other than himself and his acquisitions. Indeed, such behavior was so unusual that she couldn't help wondering what had prompted that interest.

Was it curiosity for curiosity's sake or something more sinister?

Now that his plan was implemented and they were on the road, Kit felt a bit easier. If things went as he hoped, whoever was interested in Miss Ingram would be far away by now, traveling in the opposite direction behind Augustus Raven's old-fashioned coach.

Hob had agreed to drive it, taking a circuitous route along the moors and on to Burrell, where he could leave it with a fellow who owned an inn. Hob had wanted to continue on, making his roundabout way to Piketon, where they could exchange vehicles, but Kit was leery of dropping the charade too soon.

There was no reason why Miss Ingram and her companion couldn't ride in his more comfortable carriage all the way to Raven Hill, their driver and footman at the reins. Augustus Raven could easily send someone to fetch his coach, and should he not be willing, Kit would hire someone to do so.

Kit's main concern was Miss Ingram's protection, and if he managed to spend more time with her in the process, that was simply an additional benefit. But once she was safely delivered, Kit did not see how he could further their acquaintance, for they did not move in the same circles.

Miss Ingram was no country lass to be courted at local dances, flirted with during long walks with other young people or invited with relatives to visit. No doubt, her uncle would look askance at a barely landed gentleman such as Kit.

The idea was sobering, and Kit might have dwelled upon it, if the sound of another vehicle had not dragged him from his thoughts. Abruptly, he realized that the fog was becoming thicker, threatening to obscure approaching riders. Although he had traveled this section of roadway many times without concern, now the trees on either side seemed too close. Putting his hand on the pistol he had thrust into his bag, he urged Bay past the carriage to get a good look at whatever was coming.

At the sight of a horse and cart, Kit's tension eased, yet he remained alert, for just such a farm cart had been part of his undoing before the fire. Studying the driver and his load carefully, Kit saw nothing more threatening than a couple of old sows, but when it had gone by, he heard the echo of its noisy passage.

Too late, Kit realized that the sound was of something else. And by the time he looked behind him, the carriage had been stopped by riders who appeared out of the mist, kerchiefs obscuring their faces and guns in their hands.

Still, Kit might have prevailed with the aid of Miss Ingram's coachman and footman. But instead of presenting some kind of defence, the two cowered like frightened children, more frightened, in fact, than Miss Ingram, who was ordered to exit the carriage by one of the riders.

No wailing or sobbing or screaming ensued. Indeed, she stepped out with a composure that awed Kit, but made charging the riders impossible. He did not want her caught upon the ground among rearing horses.

"You stay in there," the taller of the two men ordered Miss Ingram's companion, who was more formidable than either of her male attendants. "We just want this one."

Kit tensed at the words that confirmed his worst fears. Highwaymen were mostly a thing of the past, and travelers were rarely robbed on today's busy roads. Although this was a quiet stretch that might be more prone to such thievery, why hadn't they taken Mrs Renshaw's jewelry or looked through the baggage?

More than likely, these two were responsible for the earlier accident, and they weren't intent upon questioning or searching, but kidnapping.

"Which one of those is yours?" the tall one asked, nodding toward the cases on top of the carriage. When Miss Ingram pointed to a valise, he told the footman to toss it down. Then he backed away, perhaps to avoid getting hit with the piece, an opportunity that the footman didn't have the good sense to act upon.

But Miss Ingram did. She glanced toward Kit, her gaze telling him everything before she dropped her head in seeming surrender. These men must know nothing of their victim, Kit thought, or they would have paid more attention to her, instead of training their pistols upon Kit and the men who cowered atop the carriage.

When Miss Ingram leaned down to pick up the baggage, Kit was ready. As she swung it round toward the tall man's mount, Kit kicked Bay forward. Reaching out an arm, he grabbed Miss Ingram and swung her up behind him as the tall man went down.

In the shouting and confusion that followed, Kit set off toward the woods on the opposite side of the road, hoping that the fog that had hidden his enemies would cloak their escape. Hearing a ball whizz past his ear, he ducked, pulling Miss Ingram down with him.

"Don't shoot her, you fool!"

The shout spurred Kit onward, with Miss Ingram clinging to his back and her valise flopping against them both. Kit nearly told her to drop it, but the way she hung on to it made him wonder whether there was something important inside that she didn't want taken.

Still, they were hampered in a way their pursuers were not, and Kit looked for some hiding place. Ahead, stones rose out of the mist that he soon recognized as an abandoned graveyard, its church looming beyond.

Kit did not hesitate. Heading toward the tall doors that were now worn and cracked, he leaned to the side, pushed one open and rode into the old building. Miss Ingram did not protest, but slid to the stone floor swiftly, and when Kit dismounted, he saw her slipping her valise under one of the old box pews, weathered, but still standing.

After leading Bay behind the fretwork at the rear of the small building, Kit stepped back to scan the dim interior. At first glance, the church still appeared empty, though anyone investigating thoroughly would come across the horse quickly enough.

But Kit had no intention of them getting that far.

He took up a spot at one of the narrow windows, his pistol in hand. The fog was growing thicker, which might work in their favor—or not, Kit mused as he squinted into the vapor. The heavy air blanketed the area, muffling sounds as he listened for movement outside, but all he heard was Miss Ingram's breathing, loud in the stillness.

Turning toward her, Kit braced himself for a delayed reaction to what she had just been through. But she did not swoon. Instead, her delicate brows lowered over caramel eyes that stared at him intently, her voice a whisper as she spoke a question.

"Where the deuce did you learn that?"

"What?" For a moment, Kit had no idea what she was talking about, then he shrugged. "My sister and I once saw some trick riding at a fair, and we practised until we could master some of what we'd seen. That was a long time ago, of course."

"Yet you managed to snatch up a grown woman, with baggage, and toss me up behind you with one arm."

"Well, not every woman would have the where-withal to follow my lead," Kit said, his lips curving in appreciation. In fact, most females would have fainted dead away at the sight of the masked men, instead of attacking one of them with her luggage. But Kit had the feeling that Miss Ingram had more than a few tricks of her own up her sleeve.

The crack of a twig outside drew Kit's attention back to the window as one of the riders came into view. The villain made a good target and Kit was tempted to shoot him through one of the broken panes. Better yet, he'd like to take the man down and beat some answers out of him, but he couldn't leave Miss Ingram alone and unprotected. And a shot would draw the other rider. But his choices were limited, and Kit lifted his hand as the man turn toward the church.

"Hey, you, get away from there!"

Kit jerked at the shout, which came from another direction, and as he peered through the mist, he saw a grizzled old man step out from behind one of the tilting gravestones. Kit was tempted to shout out a warning to the old man until he saw the fellow was armed with a rifle and appeared prepared to use it.

"This is a burial ground, not parklands! Off with you now, or I'll put a bullet in you," the old man shouted.

The rider paused, as though undecided, then kicked his horse and disappeared into the trees. When the sound of his passage faded away, Kit felt a measure of relief—until he heard the soft footfalls of the old man, heading toward the church. Perhaps the fellow was only securing the entrance, Kit thought, but he sank as low in the shadows as he could.

The creak of the door was ominous in the stillness, and Kit raised his pistol as the figure shuffled in. Dressed in worn and dirty clothes, his hair an untamed halo around his head, the old man had a wild look that made him appear not only dangerous, but possibly mad. No wonder the rider had been chased off.

Although Kit hoped the old man was making only a desultory check of the church, he turned unerringly toward the window where Kit and Miss Ingram crouched. Leaning close, Kit was ready to dive in front of her, should the fellow lift his rifle. But he only squinted and cleared his throat.

"Mr Marchant, is that you?"

Chapter Three

Since Kit could not remember seeing the old man before, he remained wary until the fellow lowered his rifle and grinned, revealing some missing teeth.

"I'm John Sixpenny, sir," he said. "I look after the chapel. It's been on Oakfield land as long as I can remember. So I guess it's yours now."

"John Sixpenny, I could not be more happy to make your acquaintance," Kit said, rising to his feet. He didn't know if the old man survived on donations or some other source of income, but he planned to provide a hefty bonus for this day's work.

"I've got a little place over there," Sixpenny said, with a jerk of his head. "I'd be honored if you'd come have a bite to eat or a bit to drink."

Kit nodded in thanks. A visit would gain them some time away from the riders who were searching for them. And another man, especially one armed with a rifle, was all to the good. Still, he glanced toward Miss Ingram, but she was already retrieving her valise, and he hurried to lead Bay out of the church.

At the sight of the horse, the old man frowned, so Kit slipped him a coin for any damage to the floor. Following behind Sixpenny, they moved as quietly as possible along a barely discernible path, Kit carrying Miss Ingram's baggage, while she clung tightly to her reticule.

They had not gone far when they came across a small structure overgrown with vines and plants. The crumbling remains of other buildings could be seen, but the forest had reclaimed whatever settlement that had once been here, except for the church and the home John Sixpenny had made for himself.

The house was an odd one, its stone base having been built up with timber and thatch. At some point, a lean-to for animals had been added onto one side, but it was empty now, and Kit tied Bay there, away from prying eyes. The inside of the home was odd, as well. For despite his wild appearance, Sixpenny kept it neater than a pin, and the fire burning in the hearth was welcome.

There were several simple wooden chairs, but Miss Ingram took a stance at the small window, as though to keep watch. She did not appear to trust their host, and her reticence made Kit refuse food and drink as politely as possible. Although he did not suspect Sixpenny of planning any mischief, his own bout with doctored cider made him leery of any offerings, no matter how innocent.

"Well, then, sir, is there anything else I can do for you?" Sixpenny asked, his blue eyes shrewd as he glanced up from poking at the fire. "I can't help but notice that you were hiding in my church, just when I chased a ruffian away from my graveyard."

"Our carriage was attacked," Kit said.

"The villains. A man isn't safe in his own home any more, let alone on the roads," the old man said, muttering a low string of imprecations. "Do you want to stay here?"

The question was one Kit had been mulling over himself. Sixpenny's home was well hidden, but if the riders decided to search the area carefully, they would stumble across it, and Kit didn't like the idea of being cornered—or putting the old man in danger.

The most expedient course would be to go back to the carriage, but one or more of their pursuers might be waiting there or watching for them. These riders were no ordinary footpads, who would scatter at the first sign of other travelers. They had not been fooled by the switched conveyances, and Kit could not count on the cowardly coachman to do anything, even wait for their return.

There was a third choice, and Kit looked toward Miss Ingram, wondering whether she would agree. John Sixpenny's introduction had reminded him that they weren't that far from Oakfield. Heading across open country, they could reach the manor without returning to the road. But they would have to ride together on Bay.

As if reading his thoughts, Miss Ingram glanced his way, and her calm gaze assured him that she could do whatever he asked. So while Kit thanked the old man, he refused the offer of sanctuary.

"I think we'd better keep moving," he said, though he did not mention their destination. And Miss Ingram's nearly imperceptible nod of approval told him he had made the right decision—for now.

Raven liked to claim he had trained her well, but nothing had prepared Hero for her current situation: riding behind Christopher Marchant, her arms wrapped around his torso. Given his startling effect upon her, it did not seem to be a wise position to be in. But she had refused to dangle sideways and insisted upon riding astride, her cloak tucked around her legs. And if Mr Marchant was shocked, he did not show it. In fact, the man seemed undisturbed by anything, from gun-wielding robbers to wild-eyed hermits.

His capability was appealing, and Hero had to fight the urge to lay her head upon his strong back and lean upon him, in more ways than one. She could feel his warmth even through their cloaks, and for someone who was perpetually cold, it was like cozying up to an oven, only better.

Yet she could just as easily be burned.

Despite her scattered wits, Hero realized that Mr Marchant was not what he seemed. At first glance, he appeared to be a simple rural resident whose every thought was visible upon his face, but he had surprised her too many times for her to believe that. And Hero did not like surprises. They were too dangerous.

Just who was this man? The shabby gentry did not own enough land to include an abandoned church-yard. Nor did they have the skills to snatch a women off her feet with one arm while riding on the back of a horse. Nor did they hide beneath their simple clothes and relaxed demeanor a body that was hard with muscle.

Her suspicions aroused, Hero wondered whether Mr Marchant was spiriting her away for his own purposes. But pressed so close to him, she could not muster any panic. For protection, she had her pistol, though she did not know whether she would be able to fire at him. And what else was she to do? Hero could only follow instincts honed through years of doing Raven's bidding.

Was that what he had planned? Surely, even Raven could not have anticipated her reaction to the attractive Mr Marchant. And yet, it was just the sort of thing he would find amusing, toying with her or testing her, safe in the knowledge that nothing could come of it.

"I'm going to ride right up to the house," Mr Marchant said. His low voice dragged Hero from her thoughts and sent shivers dancing up her spine. "So we can get you inside as quickly as possible."

"And then?"

"I'll have someone go for the carriage, but you should be safe at Oakfield. I'll send word to your uncle and hire some extra men to make sure we get you home as soon as can be arranged."

He turned his head toward her, and the nearness of his face made Hero's heart hammer. His skin was not pasty and pale like the antiquarians she usually met, but a deeper hue that bespoke time spent out of doors. His lashes were long and thick, his hair as dark as his eyes, and Hero wanted to reach up and push a stray lock from his forehead.

Instead, she shook her head. "What we need to do is find what they're after. The book."

Mr Marchant groaned. "Not that again! What of your coach, your footman, your *chaperone*?"

"I think we both know that we can't go back there, and they provided little in the way of protection," Hero said. "We're better off by ourselves."

Mr Marchant slanted her a dark look of speculation. "We can't travel, just the two of us, unrelated and unmarried."

"If you refuse to help me, I will have to go alone."

"You're not going anywhere alone," Mr Marchant said with sudden ferocity, and Hero had to suppress a shiver.

"I assure you that I won't accuse you of compromising me," Hero offered.

"I'm not worried about myself!"

"Well, there is no need to worry about me," Hero insisted. "I am a nobody with nothing to ruin."

"Except your good name and your future," Mr Marchant said. "Your uncle would hardly approve."

"Raven couldn't care less about my reputation," Hero said. And neither her name or her future were of any consequence. To anyone.

"But you're his niece," Mr Marchant protested.

"Of sorts," Hero said, though she did not elaborate. What was between her and Augustus Raven stayed between them. "He's more concerned with his collections than people, which is why we should go to Cheswick."

Mr Marchant sent her another speculative glance. "Let me make sure that I understand you correctly. On the basis of a fragment of an old letter that might never have even been sent, you want to go searching for a book that could have been lost, destroyed or hidden beyond reach more than a century ago?"

"Exactly."

Kit sat facing his guest, unsure what to make of her as he watched her pick at her supper. She didn't look addled and had proposed her mad scheme without batting an eyelash. But how else could he explain such a proposal?

And yet, Kit had been tempted to agree, to bow to an urge to take action against the unseen foe, rather than kick his heels at Oakfield as he had been, brooding and impotent. But recent events had made him vow to become more responsible, not less so. And chasing after a snippet of torn paper with Augustus Raven's niece was not exactly sensible behavior, especially after the ride to Oakfield had left him feeling a bit too close to the young woman for comfort.

Kit reached for his glass of wine, flush with the memory of Miss Ingram leaning close, her slender form pressed against his back, her thighs bumping against his own, and her throaty voice whispering in his ear.

He had ridden double with Sydony many a time in their younger days, but that, he had discovered, was not the same. During the quick trip to the abandoned church, they had been in too much danger for him to think about it, but on the longer jaunt to Oakfield, the difference became very apparent. And it was one more reason not to travel unaccompanied with Miss Ingram, her assurances notwithstanding.

Of course, in the eyes of society, the damage was already done. They had been alone together for some time, enough to ruin any proper female. In fact, most young women would be having hysterics or fainting dead away at the very thought, yet Miss Ingram, as always, remained composed. Kit shot a glance at her, but her color wasn't even high. Throughout the meal, she had said little, affirming what he already knew: Miss Ingram played her cards very close to her chest.

Kit frowned thoughtfully. He'd never been the suspicious type; that was Sydony's job. But after all his sister's wild theories had proven true, he'd begun to view the world differently. Instead of accepting everything at face value, he questioned what lurked beneath the surface. And as he looked across the table at his guest, he felt a twinge of doubt.

Hero Ingram could either be the most composed woman he'd ever met, or she could have some other reason for not turning a hair when her carriage was attacked. Perhaps she'd been unafraid because there was nothing to fear. Were the riders her uncle's men, intent upon forcing his hand? But there was no denying the ball that had whizzed past his shoulder, Kit thought, shaking his head.

Another possibility, even more insidious, kept nagging at his thoughts. After all, what did he really know of the woman before him? Was she even who she claimed to be? Some of her comments had been so jarring as to make him wonder about her relationship with Augustus Raven.

The letter she presented to Kit could have been written by anyone. Those who accompanied her had been odd, at best, and seemed to have disappeared, along with the carriage. Although he'd sent Hob's young helper Jack out to the road, the boy had found no sign of it.

Hob hadn't returned, either, and Kit frowned at the darkness outside the windows. It had been just such a night as this when everyone in the household had been picked off. One by one, they had been lured away or drugged until no one was left except Sydony. Kit looked down at the mutton he had been eating and felt the sudden loss of his appetite.

A sound from the doorway made him glance up warily, but it was only Jack, half-hidden in the shadows, an expression of urgency upon his face.

"Excuse me," Kit said, rising to his feet. He did not wait for Miss Ingram's acknowledgment, but hurried to where the boy stood, drawing him farther into the other room for a whispered conference.

"What is it? Has Hob returned?"

His eyes wide, Jack shook his head. "No, sir, but when I was making the rounds, I saw a party coming toward Oakfield."

"A party?" Kit echoed. His normally inactive imagination conjured up his worst nightmare, a cloaked group of so-called Druids intent upon a virgin sacrifice. Only this time, Miss Ingram would take his sister's place.

"What kind of party?" he demanded.

"It's the parish constable and a couple of his cronies, sir, and they're nearly here," Jack said, obviously agitated.

Kit felt some of the tension in his body ease. It was about time the local authorities, who had been noticeably absent before, stepped in to help. But something about the look on Jack's face made him pause. "What's wrong?"

The boy's eyes grew even bigger, if that was possible. "They're claiming to have a warrant straight from the magistrate for your arrest—on charges of kidnapping a lady!"

The idea was so outrageous, Kit might have laughed, but coming as it did upon the heels of their earlier peril, he was not amused. If he were taken away, Miss Ingram would have no protection at all as, one by one, those around her disappeared. *Just like Sydony.*

After giving Jack some hurried instructions, Kit turned toward the open doorway and called softly to his guest, "Miss Ingram, I'm afraid there's been a change of plans."

Although he had recently eyed her composure with dismay, now Kit was grateful for it. She evinced no alarm, but rose to her feet and moved toward him quickly, her golden brows lifted slightly in question.

"I've been told that the authorities are approaching with the intent of arresting me on a charge of kidnapping, presumably you. Now, we can either try to sort it out with the locals, who view Oakfield and anyone who resides here as in league with the devil. Or we can depart before their arrival."

Miss Ingram took the news with her usual aplomb. "By all means, let us avoid any confrontations, especially since they might have been engineered to destroy our alliance," she said. "Just let me get my things."

"You'll find a pack to use in my sister's room to the left at the top of the stairs, and feel free to take anything in there," Kit called after her. His own bag remained with Bay, so he took a moment to alert Mrs Osgood to the situation.

That stolid personage was more horrified than Miss Ingram, but agreed to tell any callers that no one had returned since setting out with the carriage earlier in the day. Exhorting the maid to clear all evidence of a meal from the dining hall, she went into the kitchen, returning to slip a package into Kit's hand before aiding the flustered maid.

Heading toward the stairs to hurry his guest, Kit had to look twice at the figure on the landing before realizing it was Miss Ingram. A vastly different Miss Ingram.

Instead of her cloak, she wore a heavy greatcoat that was a fitting garment for traveling, but not often worn by women. And beneath the hem, Kit could see a pair of scuffed boots, not dainty slippers, while her lovely locks were pulled tight and tucked up under a boy's cap that cast a shadow across her features. At first glance, she would seem a youth. Had she even dirtied her face?

Acknowledging Kit with a nod, she moved down the steps toward him. "It will throw off any who search for a missing woman—or the man alleged to have kidnapped her," she explained.

Yet she didn't meet his eye, which was understandable. Most men would have recoiled in shock, but Kit could only admire her cleverness, while trying not to imagine just what she wore beneath the coat.

"Let's try to avoid the servants," he said. "It's better if no one else knows of your new appearance." With that in mind, he led her to the parlor, where they slipped out the tall doors into the darkness outside.

The fog still lingered, casting a disorienting veil over the landscape, and the burned garden was rough going, with clumps of stubble looming up to trip the wariest of walkers. But Kit told himself that whatever hindered them would work even more upon their enemies, though he doubted any locals would willingly be out at this hour searching the grounds of Oakfield, a property steeped in legend and dread.

Kit set a good pace, and Miss Ingram kept up without her skirts to encumber her. She didn't harry him with questions, but silently followed his lead until they reached the barn that was being used as a temporary stable.

Jack had their mounts ready, and Kit set the boy to keep watch while he helped Miss Ingram onto Sydony's horse. Having not seen her disguise, Jack could not report it to anyone, should he be questioned after their departure.

Kit had no time to ponder the whys and whos of their predicament. Right now, his only concern was to put more distance between them and the party Jack had heard approaching the house, so he urged Bay into the night as quietly as possible. He had a lantern, but he was loathe to use it, at least until they were away from the barn. Oakfield's eerie history would keep the locals at bay, but any others might not be so easily frightened.

When he and Syd had first arrived at their new home, Kit hadn't seen a pressing need to map the countryside. But after the fire, he had ridden out daily until he knew these lands like the back of his hand, and that knowledge served him well as he found the small path that led toward the arable fields.

By the time he reached an abandoned tenant cottage, Kit was eager for a respite. They could not ride indefinitely in such darkness, and although the Druids had once used this building, no one had been near it since the fire. Kit and Hob had made sure of that.

Dismounting, Kit led the horses into a small barn. After tethering them, he turned to help Miss Ingram, only to freeze as his hands brushed against a solid human form. His normally even heartbeat skipped in its rhythm as he wondered whether to reach for his pistol or slam the figure against the wall.

"It's me." The familiar sound of Miss Ingram's throaty voice made him loose a sigh. She had dismounted without his aid, and there was no one else in the barn with them. No Druids, no authorities, no bibliomaniacs. Realizing that his gloved fingers still pressed against her, Kit dropped his hand away, but a noise outside made him stiffen.

They both remained still while an owl hooted and then fell silent. But as the sound faded away, Kit became aware of a more immediate and more personal danger. He was alone with Miss Ingram, standing only inches from her, in the dark. The lack of light seemed to heighten his senses, and Kit caught a whiff of her scent, delicate and intoxicating.

"We can spend the night here and ride out again at dawn," he whispered, expecting her to move. But she remained where she was, and in the ensuing quiet, Kit thought he heard her breath catch. Did she feel it, too?

Just as Kit was tempted to take the single step that would bring them together, a snort from Bay broke them apart. It probably was as succinct a comment as any on his folly, a rebuke for behavior that would hardly be welcome at the best of times, let alone now, when they were in jeopardy. And Kit took the message to heart: *Remember that you are a gentleman.*

With that in mind, Kit peered outside before leading Miss Ingram to the cottage, where they were met by the smell of dust and disuse. But Kit knew the place was sturdy and would keep out the worst of the night chill. There was a lantern by the door, and he lit it, turning the wick low, though the windows were tightly shuttered.

"I'll tend to the horses," he said, trying to ignore the sight of Miss Ingram's greatcoat falling open to reveal her slim legs, clad in breeches. "Will you be all right?" It was a foolish question, and, of course, Miss Ingram nodded.

Still, Kit did not dally. Returning with their packs and some wood, he shut the door behind him, only to find that his companion had already started a fire. For a long moment, he simply stood still, transfixed by her costume, which boldly delineated her long legs, while hiding her breasts under a boy's coat. It was a paradox that kicked Kit to life.

Thankfully, Miss Ingram showed no signs of succumbing to a similar passion. "I found some cut logs and thought we'd need the fire for warmth," she said. "Unless you think we'll be seen."

Kit shook his head as he put down the baggage. "I doubt the locals will search for us at this hour, and no one else should know of this place." In truth, he was grateful to be out of the darkness, with its inherent temptations, especially now that he suspected he had conjured their earlier intimacy out of whole cloth.

Jack had given him a blanket from the barn, and Kit spread it in front of the fire for Miss Ingram. With a gesture toward it, he took his own place, seated on the floor, his back against the door. The hard wood and the cold floor did much to help him gather himself—and his thoughts. Since they were safe for the time being, Kit took the opportunity to consider the events that had led him here.

And when next he gazed at his companion, he looked beyond the enticing form to the person inside. Up until an hour ago, Kit had thought Miss Ingram an independent and daring female in the mold of his sister. But during the course of the evening, she had proven herself to be far more unusual than Syd. Obviously, Miss Ingram was no ordinary young lady. But what, exactly, was she?

"So why does Augustus Raven's niece carry boy's garments with her while traveling?" Kit asked without preamble.

If Miss Ingram was startled by the question, she didn't show it. She glanced toward him, but her face was in shadow, making it difficult for Kit to gauge her expression. "I like to be prepared for anything."

"And just what sort of 'anything' were you expecting?"

She shrugged. "It's not what I was expecting—it's the unexpected that concerns me, Mr Marchant."

"And that includes having to masquerade as a male?"

She nodded, but told him nothing, as usual. And, as if the conversation were over, she spread her hands toward the hearth and turned her back to him.

But Kit was not prepared to be dismissed this time. "I'm a simple man," he said. "A gentleman farmer who wants nothing more than a quiet life in the country. Yet over the past months, I've been treated to my fill of deception and threats from everyone from cloaked intruders to my oldest friend."

She swung round then, perhaps shaken by the raw tone to his voice, but he was not adept at dissembling. And his gut twisted at the thought that this woman might be a thief or some kind of Captain Sharp, out to hoax him for reasons he could not fathom. Although she might deny it, Kit had to put the question to her.

"So you'll understand if I won't be played for a fool, Miss Ingram," Kit said. He paused to fix her with a probing gaze. "Are you even who you say you are?"

The light was behind her, so Kit could not see her eyes. Still, she did not look away, and he felt a measure of relief. She did not launch into any outraged protests or weeping admissions, but simply nodded. Then she cocked her head to the side, as though studying him.

"But if you doubt me, why are you here?" she asked.

Kit could have given her a number of different answers, but in the end, he chose the simplest one.

"Because, Miss Ingram, I am a gentleman."

Chapter Four

Wrapping herself in her heavy coat, Hero lay down upon the blanket Mr Marchant had so graciously put in front of the fire. Perhaps he knew she was always cold, she thought, before rejecting such a notion. The real reason for his behavior was more straightforward and required no personal knowledge of her.

It was the act of a gentleman.

The word was a common one, used to describe nearly all males except the poor, servants and those with money, but no lineage. And yet, Hero wondered if she'd ever met a gentleman in the strictest sense of the word—one who was decent, kind, thoughtful… *I'm a simple man*, he'd said. But Christopher Marchant was anything but.

Her back to the flames, Hero looked from under lowered lashes to where he was seated against the door. Presumably he had taken that position so that any attempt at entry would waken him, if he nodded off. But he couldn't be comfortable, arms across his chest, long legs stretched out before him. Although not normally bothered by such things, Hero found herself wondering about draughts, the hard surface of the door, the awkward position.

She could invite him to join her here by the fire.

The wild thought was born of drowsy warmth and set Hero's heart to pounding with both anticipation and alarm. Fully awake now, she knew she could not relax into a false sense of security just because her companion treated her far better than anyone else ever had. Manners made for a fine show, but what did she really know of Christopher Marchant?

Although the urge to accept this near stranger as a protector was strong, Hero knew better than to rely on anyone except herself. And hadn't he already proven many times that he was not what he seemed? That might include being the gentleman he claimed.

Roused to alertness, Hero was determined to keep one eye open through the night. She was a poor sleeper, at best, and vowed not let down her guard when alone with this man, no matter how tempting it might be.

Yet the heat of the fire relaxed her, making her lids heavy, and soon Hero had closed them. The tension in her body eased, reminding her of her ride earlier in the day, when she had held on to Mr Marchant's warm and solid form. Even as she tried to banish the memory, Hero's thoughts returned to the moments when she had rested her head against his strong back, leaning upon him.

And she slept.

A cock crowed in the distance, and Hero awoke with a start. She heard a thud and opened her eyes to see Mr Marchant jerk away from the door, rubbing the back of his head. The sight of him made her pulse quicken and not just because she had slept the night away alone with a man she barely knew.

It was the length of his fingers threading through the strands of silky dark hair that held her interest, the tilt of his head, the full line of his mouth as he frowned, and the way his brows lowered in annoyance. If Hero's heart hadn't been pounding so painfully, she would have smiled at his reaction. Simple. Natural. *Endearing.*

As if aware of her study, he suddenly looked at her from under impossibly long lashes, pinning her with one of his probing gazes. And all that Hero felt for him—and more—was reflected right back at her. Startled, Hero sucked in a deep breath as she realized that she was sprawled before the fire, her cap long gone, her hair falling in thick tendrils from where she had secured it.

In short, she was in deshabille, warm and languid and witless from sleep, and she hurried to rectify the situation. She would not expect her boy's costume to incite passion in any man, let alone one who looked like Mr Marchant, but she had seen something in his eyes that made her both wary and exhilarated. Glancing away, she rose to her feet as she pulled her coat close.

"It's light," she muttered. "We'd better go."

Turning her back to him, Hero heard his grunt of assent as he stood, yet the hairs on her neck tingled at his very presence. She waited, tense, until she heard him step outside. Then, and only then, did she release the breath she had been holding and reach for her cap.

She straightened and saw, to her dismay, that her hand was trembling. What next? Would she start stuttering? Hero cursed this man's ability to discompose her, senses running riot, wits scattered when she needed them most.

Kneeling before the hearth, Hero doused the lingering embers there, and shivered. Better to be cold, she thought, than so warm that she couldn't think properly. By the time she had finished, Mr Marchant had returned, and Hero turned to face him with a chillier greeting on her lips.

He didn't seem to notice, and they made a quick meal of bread and cheese from the packet he had got from his housekeeper. Then he went out to ready the horses while Hero tried to remove all evidence of their presence. After sweeping away their tracks on the floor, she stood at the doorway, giving the place one last look.

Still laden with dust, it was nothing more than a small farmhouse, but the single room was cozier than her bedchamber at Raven Hill. Hero's gaze lingered before the hearth, where she had slept so effortlessly for the first time in long memory. A surge of unfamiliar feelings kept her where she stood until a draught rattled the shutters. The noise finally spurred her to step outside and shut the door behind her.

The early morning light was filtered by the mist, which seemed ever present. Although the atmosphere would have suited Raven's sensibilities, Hero was more concerned with making her way as rapidly as possible. In this fog, Mr Marchant could lead her anywhere, and it would be difficult to keep her bearings.

"We'll stay off the main roads as long as possible," he said, as he helped her mount. "Then head east."

"To Cheswick."

"To Raven Hill," Mr Marchant said.

"Cheswick is closer," Hero pointed out. He groaned, and Hero suppressed a smile, for he made the sound whenever she pressed him. She was beginning to find his groans even more endearing than his grins. *And all the more dangerous.*

Hero could not afford to be distracted, and she forced herself to pay more attention to her surroundings than her companion. But there was little to notice. And the routes Mr Marchant took were hardly more than paths, where she saw no signs of life, only barren moors.

The fog did not unnerve her, for Hero was not the fanciful sort. One did not stay long at Raven Hill and give in to whimsy—not if one wanted to retain one's sanity. Still, when they traveled into a dell, the haze settled around them, making their movements echo strangely. And Hero began to wonder if what she heard was their own progress or something else, perhaps even the sound of pursuers.

Then suddenly, something loomed out of the mist, a tall silhouette, dark and ominous. Hero stifled a gasp and grasped the pistol in her coat, while Mr Marchant continued on his way in front of her. Suspicion roiled through her, chilling her to the bone and closing her throat. Yet, as she faced it the shape took form, mocking her fears.

How amused Raven would have been to see her start at a rock, but it was large and unnaturally shaped, making Hero wonder at its placement here in the middle of nowhere. Urging her mount forward, she called to Mr Marchant, "What is that, a road marker?"

"A standing stone," he said. "I've discovered that there are many of them in the area. Sometimes they are alone, like that one, or they can be grouped in circles, rows and by cairns. All are thought to be the work of the Druids who once lived here. Maybe that's why Mallory built his home in this land, with its references to sacred oaks and waters."

Hero glanced toward him, but could see little of his expression. She hadn't known what to make of his earlier remarks about Druids and had long since dismissed them. The resumption of the subject, here and now, did little to cheer her.

"And you think that they want his book back?" Hero asked.

"The ones who left these stones are long gone, their true histories forgotten," he said. "And most who call themselves Druids now gather for social or philanthropic purposes. But there were some others who embraced a more violent view of their forebears."

Hero did not find his explanation comforting, especially when he lapsed into a brooding silence that brooked no further questions. And as she followed blindly, she couldn't help the thought that returned to mind. *He could lead her anywhere.* And for any purpose.

She was not a timid creature, but the possibility of being caught alone on foggy moors with a powerful man obsessed with Druids was something even Hero found unsettling. She remembered his mention of death and debauchery based on the Mallory, and she shivered.

Yet she kept following, for what else could she do? And even uneasy as she was, Hero realized that the whole situation felt like something Raven would orchestrate. Although he had never written a Gothic novel, he enjoyed living like a character in one, with all the attendant terrors and dramas.

Had he arranged for the seemingly gallant Mr Marchant to accompany her? Or worse, had he arranged for a mad Mr Marchant to abduct her? Her companion's admission of a warrant for his arrest took on new meaning when considered under such circumstances. Was Mr Marchant the gentleman he claimed to be, or something else entirely?

Hero had made a life hunting and fetching and bargaining for Raven and ignoring all else, but now she felt her purpose faltering. Just what was she getting herself into?

The sun was setting when they rode into the courtyard of the Long Man. The inn was a simple one set in the middle of Longdown, a community large enough that their arrival would not be marked. Or at least that's what Kit hoped when he looked for a place to stop for the night.

Inside the common room was busy, and Kit's request for a room for himself and his brother drew little attention. He was not dressed in the sort of finery that would demand special service; nor was he the kind who might be refused admittance. His coin was good, and the horses would be tended to.

"Will you eat, sir?" the burly landlord inquired.

"Yes, but can you have it sent to the room? My brother is bone weary, and I'm for rest myself."

The landlord looked like he might make Kit pay for a private parlour, but then he nodded, perhaps fearful of losing the business entirely, for Kit's "brother" was slumped in the shadows near the door, as though waiting to see whether they would remain. With the meal settled, Kit motioned for Miss Ingram to join him, and the landlord led them to the staircase.

The room was decent enough, clean and neat, with a narrow window and a large bed not far from the fireplace, where logs were set. "I'll have that lit for you, sirs," the landlord said before disappearing back into the hall.

Kit nodded absently as he glanced around. He could have got two rooms, but he was loathe to leave Miss Ingram alone and unprotected, even if she was dressed as a boy. His own desire to stay in her company had nothing to do with his decision. Or at least that's what Kit told himself as he eyed the single bed.

While no one would think it odd for a couple of brothers to bed down together, Kit would have to look elsewhere for his berth. Unfortunately, the only chair was stiff and straight-backed, so Kit looked to the expanse of hard floor and told himself it was no worse than where he had slept the night before.

Miss Ingram was already drawing the curtains, and Kit reached for the candle, lest they be plunged into blackness until the chambermaid came to light the fire. It was one thing to share a room with Miss

Ingram, another to be alone with her in complete darkness, as he had learned last evening.

But a low word from her stayed Kit's hand. He lifted his head in surprise to see her silently motioning him toward the window, where something had drawn her attention. He stepped behind her, looking over her shoulder into the courtyard below. The Long Man was not a posting stop, so the cobbled area was relatively quiet, making it easy to spy the two men leaning against one wall in the deepening shadows.

Kit felt the tension in Miss Ingram's body and had to stop himself from drawing her back against him in comfort. "I don't see how anyone could have tracked us here," he assured her. "They would have had to follow us from the cottage, and we saw no signs of that."

"They could have been waiting on the road."

"For how long? And which roads?"

"Any road that leads to London," Miss Ingram said. She turned her head slightly. "If we go to Cheswick instead, perhaps we can lose them."

Kit stifled a groan at the familiar refrain, but he was not surprised to hear it. Someone as determined as Miss Ingram did not give up easily. And hadn't she told him earlier that she would go by herself, if necessary? The memory of that threat, coupled with her impassive features and the presence of the two men below, however innocent they might be, made Kit distinctly uneasy.

He might have been blind before, heedless of the signs of approaching trouble, but he was more observant now, and his observations told him that Miss Ingram might very well slip from the room the minute his back was turned, going from danger into danger. Alone.

And that's when the truth hit him. It didn't matter whether her chase was a foolish one, leading nowhere, and it didn't matter what his own feelings about the possible existence of a Mallory might be. It didn't even matter whether Miss Ingram was being completely honest with him. The only thing that mattered was keeping her safe. And since he could not force her to go home, the only way to protect her was to go with her.

Kit admitted there were other, less admirable reasons to remain in Miss Ingram's company, his own selfish desires among them. But first and foremost in his mind was the task he had undertaken when her coach had broken down on its way to Oakfield. He'd failed his sister, but he wasn't going to fail this woman.

"All right, we'll go to Cheswick," he said. If Miss Ingram was startled by his sudden capitulation, Kit did not see it, for his attention was fixed on the men below. Perhaps it wouldn't hurt to see what they were up to, he thought. But as he watched, the taller fellow pushed away from the wall, revealing not the nondescript clothing of their attackers, but livery. And very fine livery, at that.

Kit was glad he had not gone down to confront them since he was already plagued by one arrest warrant. "These two may be similar in height, but that's not the way our pursuers were dressed."

Miss Ingram turned her head, as if to argue, but a knock came at the door, and she moved quickly away. She slid into a shadowed corner, as though expecting the two men to burst in. Kit knew that was highly unlikely, but reached for his pistol nonetheless just as the door opened to admit a harried-looking chamber-maid.

After handing them a tray of food, she lit the fire and was on her way, leaving them to their supper. Kit let Miss Ingram have the chair and pushed the bed stairs between them, so that she could place her plate on the top step while he sat on the floor and used the bottom.

The room was dark but for the fire, and for a while they ate in silence, broken only by the crack of the logs. Kit told himself that the only difference between this night and the last was that their room was smaller and better appointed. Yet somehow this evening seemed more intimate. Perhaps it was the earlier hour or the fact that they were sharing a meal.

Last night Kit had leaned against a door, staring at a dark shape that was hardly recognizable. But tonight, the firelight danced across Miss Ingram's face, high-lighting the line of her cheek, the curve of her lips. Her skin glowed golden, and Kit wished she would take off that wretched cap, so he could see her hair...

"What?"

It wasn't until she spoke that Kit realized he was staring, and he looked down at his plate. He was tempted to tell her that she need not wear the cap in here, with only the two of them to see, but perhaps that wasn't such a good idea.

"Nothing," Kit muttered. He needed to gain more control over his thoughts, especially since his compan-ion appeared completely unmoved by their nearness, the firelight and the night outside. Yet when she reached for her wine, Kit could have sworn her hand was shaking. *Perhaps Miss Ingram was not unmoved, after all.*

"How can you be sure those weren't our two men?" she asked.

Kit barked out a low laugh. Now he was assured that Miss Ingram was not as entranced as he by their intimate supper. She was all business, a reminder that he would do well to heed. "Because they wore the livery of the Duke of Montford," he said.

"So?"

"So, I doubt that the duke's men are out searching for a book on Druid lore," he said, spearing a forkful of beef.

"And why not?" she countered. "The Prince Regent himself is a great collector, as is the Duke of Devonshire. The book madness strikes any and all, regardless of station. No less an authority than Reverend Thomas Dibin claims that it lasts year-round and through all of human existence."

"Perhaps," Kit acknowledged, "but I can't see a nobleman hiring thugs or arranging a kidnapping."

"Even to acquire such a rare book?"

"Even to acquire such a rare book," Kit said. He suspected that greed did not drive their pursuers, but something darker and twisted.

"I don't know. I've heard tales that you would not countenance," Miss Ingram said. "Stories of thievery and forgery, of collectors who have bought back their own books after having sold them or given them away, of despondent souls who killed themselves over lost libraries. One antiquarian actually bought a property that had been owned by the astrologer John Dee in the hopes that valuable books might be buried there."

Kit would have laughed at that example, if it hadn't hit too close to home—his home. Although the Mallory hadn't been buried at Oakfield, that hadn't stopped people from digging up the grounds for it.

"The most avid formed their own society, the Roxburghe Club, after the Duke of Roxburghe's collection went up for sale. And you must have heard of Richard Heber, who is filling several homes with books to the very ceilings, purportedly over a hundred thousand and counting."

"And I thought my father was devoted to them," Kit said with a shake of his head.

Miss Ingram paused to study him anew. "I'm surprised you did not catch his mania," she said, as though she suspected Kit of hiding his expertise.

"I never shared my father's singular fascination with study. I loved him, and I'm very grateful for his tutoring and his gentle wisdom, but he seemed to prefer the inside of his books to the world itself. And that wasn't for me—or Syd," he said with a grin.

"Syd?"

"My sister Sydony."

"An unusual name."

"She's an unusual woman," Kit said. He slanted her a glance. "Actually, you remind me a lot of her."

Miss Ingram ducked her head. "And your mother? Was she fond of books?"

Kit drew a deep breath. "She died when I was young."

"I'm sorry," she said. "Perhaps that is why your father sought to escape into his work."

The romantic suggestion coming from the pragmatic Miss Ingram made Kit look at her in surprise. But as always, her face, bent over her plate, revealed nothing.

"Perhaps," Kit said. He barely remembered his mother, so he could not recall if his father had behaved differently, and yet he'd always felt the loss. It might well be that Miss Ingram was right, and his father, always a scholar, had simply retreated further into his pages.

"What of your parents?" Kit asked. "Are they collectors?"

"They, too, are dead," Miss Ingram said briskly. Putting down her fork, she set aside her plate.

"I'm sorry," Kit said. "Have you been long without them?"

"Long enough," she said. "Now, before we head to Cheswick tomorrow, let's go over a few things."

The sudden change of subject took Kit by surprise. Had the conversation become too personal, or was Miss Ingram loath to reveal anything of herself?

"As you probably know, libraries are often arranged according to the owner's specifications," she said, and from her tone, Kit realized that the earlier intimacy would not return.

"A collector may group his prizes together by subject, date of publication, date of acquisition, or any other method that strikes his fancy or the fancy of whoever handles the purchase and cataloging of the books," she said.

"Well, that's helpful," Kit noted drily.

Miss Ingram's mouth quirked at that, and Kit realized just how rarely she smiled. Here in the glow of the firelight, even that gentle curve of her lips was delightful and alluring—and all too fleeting. What had made her so serious, and how could he coax more smiles from her when their situation was not exactly humorous?

"One famous collector housed his volumes in presses decorated with Roman personages, so there would be no way of knowing where to find something without looking through his 'emperor system'," she said. "And Samuel Pepys shelved according to size."

Her descriptions only confirmed Kit's opinion that their search was futile. But he knew that she would not be satisfied until she realized the truth: that they weren't going to find a copy of the Mallory. If he didn't know how dangerous the book was, he might even wish for her to obtain it, if only as reward for her dogged persistence.

"So how do you expect to find anything, let alone a volume that's been missing for a century?" he asked.

"I'll see when we get there."

Kit did not bother to ask how they were going to gain access to the Earl of Cheswick's library. Perhaps tomorrow, Miss Ingram would see for herself that her quest was impossible. And then…like the gentleman that he was, Kit would have to deliver her safely into the hands of her uncle. Unharmed. And untouched.

Kit might rue his earlier claim, but it was not something he could deny. Although honor was not much discussed in the Marchant home, his father had made his expectations clear, and his children did their utmost to live up to them. It had not required much effort on Kit's part. He had never been tempted by the dissipations that once had threatened Barto's future, and his most difficult challenge had been holding the Marchants together after the death of their parent.

But now, alone in a shadowed bedroom with a woman like no other, Kit began to sweat. Somehow, he didn't believe that this was the sort of test his father could ever have imagined.

Bringing Bay to a halt at the edge of the hill, Kit looked down at the house that lay nestled below. The afternoon sun lent a golden glow to the front of the neat stone structure and glittered off three stories of windows. Cheswick wasn't one of the grandest homes in the land, but it was grand enough to make Kit think twice about breaking into it.

"Well, here we are," he said, turning to his companion. "What do you suggest we do?"

Kit had expected that Miss Ingram might veer from her course when confronted with the sight of the ancestral home of the Earls of Cheswick. But she evinced no doubt or confusion, simply eyeing the estate with her usual calm deliberation.

Then, glancing around her, she frowned. "First, we need to find a place where I can change."

Kit swallowed a grunt of surprise. He could understand her wish to get out of boy's clothing, but how? He only hoped that she did not intend to march into Cheswick, demanding the use of a dressing room.

Thankfully, she did not. Nor did she attempt to use

any of the numerous outbuildings. "Too many servants. Too many eyes," she told him, turning away from the house. Instead, she rode into a copse of trees and dismounted.

Kit followed, dismounting, as well, though he was unsure of her intention until she shook out the blanket and flung it over some branches. The next thing he knew, her hat and coat were perched upon a limb, too.

Kit found himself staring at the sight of her head and shoulders visible above the makeshift curtain. Then he blew out a breath and promptly turned around. He had slept a few feet from her the past two nights, but he was not prepared to watch while she removed her clothing with only a thin piece of material standing between them.

His back to her, Kit could not see what was happening, yet he could hear well enough. And he tried not to picture what else was being removed. Her shirt? The breeches? Did she wear a shift beneath? She had to be cold, and the inevitable reaction of certain parts of her anatomy had certain parts of Kit's anatomy reacting, as well.

Drawing in a harsh breath, Kit concentrated on keeping a lookout, rather than taking a look behind. Just because the two fellows they saw at the Long Man were liveried servants in the employ of a duke, did not mean he could lapse into inattention. And the thought of anyone coming upon Miss Ingram in a state of undress kept him alert.

"I'm ready."

Although Kit was surprised to hear Miss Ingram speak so soon, he swung round only to gape in wonder.

Surely no female had ever dressed herself so quickly—or transformed herself so completely.

The boy with the cap was gone, replaced by a prim young woman, her gloved hands clasped in front of her, her eyes downcast. Having acquired a taste for the sight of those long legs clad in breeches, Kit was prepared for disappointment. But a glimpse of a revealing bodice, visible below the ties of her cloak, banished all such concerns. In fact, he could have spent some time savoring the view, but Hero was already turning away from the trees.

Abruptly, Kit was reminded of their whereabouts, and he realized that they still faced the problem of gaining access to Cheswick, no matter what Miss Ingram's guise. He shot her a speculative glance. "Now what?" And he didn't know whether to be encouraged or disappointed when she answered without hesitation.

"We take the tour."

Chapter Five

As Hero had hoped, Cheswick's housekeeper was authorized to give tours of the great house, and who could refuse Mr Marchant and his sister, two genteel tourists visiting the countryside?

Although Mr Marchant accompanied her without protest, he said little, and Hero was forced to comment admiringly on the elegant furnishings and works of art, while keeping her eye out for books. Yet as they moved from one spacious room to another, she didn't see any. Had she made a misjudgment? Although she knew the current earl was no collector, she didn't think he had sold off the family's library. But if not here, where?

Hero tried to recall what she knew of the man, including his other properties. Perhaps Cheswick was too new and had never housed the Mallory. When had the family gained the earldom, and where had they lived before? Hero wondered frantically. If the volume was not here, she would have to look elsewhere, for whether Raven had orchestrated this little jaunt or not, he would expect her to return with the prize in hand.

Despite her growing unease, Hero kept up a constant stream of chatter for the benefit of the housekeeper. But she must have given something away, for Mr Marchant shot her a speculative glance. Even as she ignored it, Hero felt suspicion roil through her again. Did he know something she did not? Is that why he hadn't wanted to come here?

Just when Hero was trying to work out what she might do next, Mrs Spratling stopped before a closed door, opened it and ushered them through, with a curt explanation. "His lordship doesn't often use this room, so it is usually kept shut, but it's a fine library."

Indeed it was. All four walls were lined with shelves, and all of those shelves were lined with books. Yet the room was open and airy, as was all of Cheswick, a relatively new house with none of the quirks of Raven Hill. Breathing in the scents of bindings, paper and beeswax, Hero felt her tension ease. She could have spent weeks browsing, but she knew they didn't have that sort of time.

Catching Mr Marchant's eye, she inclined her head toward the opposite wall, so that they might each search a section. As he had since their first acquaintance, Mr Marchant seemed to understand her direction without any speech passing between them. And when he casually strolled away, Hero turned to face the shelves. She paused, her hands behind her back, as though gazing in wonder at their contents. However, she was more interested in discovering their order, and she had to bite back a cry of dismay at what was soon evident.

The books in Cheswick's library were carefully arranged, but not by a system that would do Hero any good. As she stared at the great blocks of hues, Hero cursed the earl or his decorator or whoever had decided it would be stylish to order the library according to the color of the covers.

Since Hero had no idea what the Mallory looked like, her only option was to seek out older volumes. However, a book's condition depended upon a number of variables besides its age. If secreted safely away for a number of those years, it would bear few marks of usage, but if tossed in the cellar or worse, it could be damaged beyond repair.

Hero's heart sank as she eyed the shelves. While this collection was not vast, there were far too many books to search quickly. And the housekeeper already was making noises about returning to her work.

"Oh, but the books are all so pretty," Hero said. She turned to smile at the woman, then walked to where Mr Marchant was pondering the editions along the opposite wall.

"See how cleverly those are grouped," she said aloud. But her whispered message was far different. "We need more time."

"And how do you propose we arrange that?" Mr Marchant asked.

"Bribe the housekeeper?" It was no secret that most of the staff of these large homes were underpaid and overworked, but this one didn't have the slack-jawed look of desperation. Still, it was worth an effort.

Turning away from Mr Marchant, Hero walked the perimeter of the room, checking the rows for a volume that appeared old or pushed behind another. And all the while, she chattered away about her love of novels with the hope of distracting the servant.

Since Mr Marchant continued his inspection in silence, Hero could only deduce that he was unwilling to offer money to the woman or that he was waiting for the right moment. But it soon became clear that they could delay no longer.

With a loud harrumph, Mrs Spratling planted her formidable form directly in front of Mr Marchant. "I'm afraid I must insist that we move on."

"Oh, please don't say so," Hero said, with an expression of dismay. "Couldn't we just look around a bit longer? Christopher, give this wonderful woman a little something to let us linger. This is the most beautiful library we've seen yet."

But Mrs Spratling would have none of it. "His lordship doesn't allow for lingering," she said, her lips pursed. "He's having a ball tonight, and his party will be arriving soon."

"A ball!" Hero clapped her hands with feigned delight. "Did you hear that, Christopher?"

Behind the housekeeper's back, Mr Marchant shot her a pained look, which she promptly ignored.

"What kind of ball is it?"

"A masquerade," Mrs Spratling said, unbending a bit. "His lordship does love the theatricals and such."

"Oh, I can only imagine what sort of things they wear," Hero said. She donned her most ingratiating expression as she turned to the housekeeper. "I suppose you have a hand in arranging them all."

Mrs Spratling shook her head, but she smiled, obviously flattered. "His lordship does keep costumes on hand for those who aren't prepared, but I just have to lay them out, keep them all in good condition. It's the ball itself that I—"

Hero cut her off. "Oh, please, you must let us see! Just a peek," Hero wheedled. "I'll bet you have your favorites."

"Well, I…" Mrs Spratling smiled. "I do have a couple that I recommend, only if the ladies or gentlemen ask for my assistance, of course."

"Oh, you must show us, just for a moment, and they'll we'll be off, straight out the door," Hero said. She squealed with glee when Mrs Spratling nodded her agreement and hurried to the woman's side. Thankfully, Mr Marchant had the sense not to say anything, and as soon as the housekeeper marched ahead, Hero fell back, grabbing his arm to pull him close.

"We're going to the ball," she whispered.

When he turned to her with a dubious expression and a protest upon his lips, she shook her head to silence him. "You distract her while I get some costumes for us."

And before he could argue, Hero moved toward Mrs Spratling, more flattery upon her lips. It had been her experience that most people loved to show off what meant the most to them. Obviously, the housekeeper was proud of the grand home in her charge, but she also had a soft spot for fripperies, the creative bent of her master and her own opinion, all of which Hero used to gain entrance to the dressing room, where the masquerades were kept.

Mrs Spratling swung open the door, and Hero stepped inside just as a loud thump echoed behind them. Hero did not pause, but hurried forward, scanning the room for what she could slip inside her cloak. Unfortunately, most of the garments appeared to be housed in matching wardrobes, and she did not know how much time she had. Mr Marchant was quick-witted, but the housekeeper would not be diverted for long.

A domino with an odd mask that could be folded lay upon the arm of an Egyptian couch, perhaps in need of mending, but it would serve her purpose. Rolling it as quickly and tightly as possible, Hero tucked it inside her cloak. On a nearby table was a set of brightly colored garments. Hero snatched up the top items, then spread another on the couch in place of the domino, just as she heard Mrs Spratling's loud step behind her.

"Look at these," Hero said. "Did you make them yourself?"

But Mrs Spratling's mood had been ruined by Mr Marchant's stumble and subsequent complaints about the slickness of the floors.

"Certainly not. His lordship employs seamstresses for such tasks," she said. Hands on her hips, she surveyed the room with the look of a general inspecting his troops. Hero inched in front of the couch, hoping that the missing domino would not be marked. She held her breath, heart pounding, until Mr Marchant provided another distraction.

"Are the costumes in here?" he asked loudly, limping to one of the wardrobes.

"Don't touch that," the housekeeper said. Barreling past Mr Marchant, she opened the doors to display a variety of hanging items, as well as numerous masques and headdresses.

"There. As you can see, his lordship likes to keep a good supply on hand, especially for those he favors," she said with a sweep of a beefy hand. Obviously, she no longer intended to show them any contents of the wardrobes, Mr Marchant having fallen out of her graces literally. "Now, I have work to do, so you must be off."

Hero nodded, but waited for the woman to lead the way before moving from her position. Mrs Spratling's small eyes narrowed as she glanced behind her, as if looking for something. And Hero held her breath.

"I thought we were going," Mr Marchant said, coming to the rescue again. "I dare say I think I might need your help, ma'am, for I can hardly walk. If you could just let me take your arm until we reach one of the carpets. Sister, if you would assist me, as well?"

Hero would have smiled at Mr Marchant's posturing, if her heart hadn't been pounding so fiercely. Pulling her cloak close around her, she loosed a low sigh of relief at escaping the dressing room. She had maintained her composure in worse situations, with no one to count on except herself. But she wasn't sure that she could have managed this time, and she suspected that Mr Marchant had saved her from discovery.

As she took his arm, Hero was hard pressed to maintain her charade, for his effect on her was anything but brotherly. Fighting off the urge to press herself closer, she reminded herself that Mr Marchant was not what he seemed.

Nothing appeared to disturb him, not highwaymen, nor arresting authorities, nor difficult travels or accommodations. *Not even a sudden need for posing and deception.* On the contrary, he appeared to take everything in his stride, perhaps even thriving on their adventures.

Glancing surreptitiously in his direction, Hero noted that the dark circles under his eyes were gone. Had the grief and anger she had once seen been real, or had it all been a pose? And was Mr Marchant simply an actor playing a part?

As Sydony often said, there was very little that rattled Kit, but skulking around the Earl of Cheswick's property was one of them. After practically being thrown out of the home by the housekeeper, Kit was anxious to make their escape. But Miss Ingram insisted upon looking over the outbuildings and admiring the grounds, though nothing was blooming this late in the year.

"Haven't you seen enough, *sister*?" Kit asked, when a stable boy eyed them quizzically. He'd begun to wonder if she was like Lady Caroline Lamb, who was rumored to dress as a man, courting danger and pushing the boundaries of society. But Miss Ingram claimed she was checking out all available structures for later use.

"*Later* when?" Kit asked. "And *use* by whom?"

She only shook her head, smiled at the stable boy, and continued on her way. When, at last, she had seen her fill, Kit coaxed her back to the horses, eager to leave before the earl and his party arrived—or Miss Ingram's theft was discovered.

After they exited the graveled drive that led to Cheswick, Kit breathed a sigh of relief, for no shouts rose from behind them, and there were no signs of pursuing footmen. "Don't we have enough people chasing us without you stealing from the Earl of Cheswick?" he asked, slanting her a glance.

"How else were we going to get into the ball?"

Kit groaned.

"We need more time to find the book."

As if posing as brother and sister, conning Cheswick's housekeeper and outright theft weren't enough, Miss Ingram wanted to return? Kit shook his head. Her facility for deception made him leery, for a woman who fooled everyone else might be fooling him, too. If she were playing some sort of game, it could have deadly consequences that she didn't anticipate. And it made Kit's task even more difficult, for how could he protect Miss Ingram from herself?

Once Hero was back in her disguise, it was easier to get a room without dealing with maids—or separating. As difficult as it was to spend the night with her, Kit was not about to leave her alone. And he insisted they take time to eat a meal.

But as soon as the sun set, they headed back to Cheswick. The terrain was familiar now, and they tethered their horses in a stand of trees well enough away to avoid the footmen and grooms and arriving guests. Under the cover of darkness, they hurried closer to the house, Miss Ingram steering him toward a small shed.

Apparently, this is what she had meant by later use,

for she opened the door and slipped inside, motioning for Kit to follow. He swallowed a protest, for this trespass probably would be the least of his worries before the night was over. Still, Kit balked when he saw the shadowy shapes of a large table and various gardening implements.

"A potting shed?" he muttered. Were they going to take a turn at impersonating the earl's outdoor staff, as well?

"I was hoping there would be more room," Miss Ingram said, moving over so that he could join her inside.

"For what?" Kit asked. Stepping into the dark and dusty interior, he was assailed by the smell of soil and manure. His eyes were still adjusting to the lack of light when Miss Ingram shut the door, plunging them into pitch blackness.

"For dressing," she said. "We can change in here and walk to the house."

Kit blinked blindly. *"What?"*

"Here's your costume." She pushed something into his gut, and Kit grunted. Although he grabbed the bundle, he was still reeling from the idea that they should change clothes here. In the dark. Alone. Together.

"I should wait outside," Kit said, clearing his suddenly dry throat. "It's too cramped in here."

"Nonsense," Miss Ingram said briskly. "And we can't have someone seeing you lounging about."

Her apparent indifference was annoying, but if she didn't see anything untoward, then why should he? Kit vowed to pretend she was his sister and get on with it. *The quicker the better.*

Kit's disgruntlement only grew when he shook out

what she had given him and realized it was not a domino, the traditional hooded cloak worn with a half-mask that was the simplest of costumes.

"What the devil did you get me?" he asked, wishing now that he had taken a look in the light. Back at the inn. *By himself.*

"It's a Harlequin," she said. "And it was the only thing at hand. There were a pile of them, matching shirts and trousers, and I took the top set."

"I can't put this on," Kit said. Just from fingering the material, he could tell it would not fit over his clothes. And he had no intention of stripping down to his drawers in the cold shed, with or without Miss Ingram's company.

"Fine," she muttered. "You can have the domino, and I'll wear the Harlequin."

"No, you won't," Kit said. The thought of Miss Ingram traipsing around in nothing but the masque was even more repugnant than donning the outfit himself. At least in her current incarnation, her breeches were loose, and she was covered in layers of shirt and vest and coat. Harlequins, as a rule, were notoriously snug, making them a favorite of preening dandies who wished to show off their figures.

"Why don't you let me have the domino, and you can simply wear your boy's clothing?" Kit asked. "Women often masquerade as men, and vice versa, at these things."

"I don't want to be marked in my usual disguise."

"So you're wearing a costume over a costume?"

Kit felt a punch in his stomach as she shoved the domino at him. "Here, I'll trade you," she said.

"No." Kit held the Harlequin out of reach, though he enjoyed the touch of her hand, groping blindly against him. If it weren't so cold and their situation so peculiar, he would have leaned into it and…

"Then hurry," she whispered. "We need as much time in the library as possible."

With a groan, Kit turned around. They had traded their heavy traveling coats for cloaks, but he struggled with his coat and did not dare ask for Miss Ingram's help.

In polite company, men were rarely seen in their shirtsleeves. Did Miss Ingram even realize what she was asking of him? Kit was beginning to wonder if she'd been raised by wolves or in some foreign tribe that did not adhere to the dictates of society.

Folding his coat as best he could, Kit tried to pull the tunic over his shirt, but it was too small, requiring him to strip down to his skin. But he was already warmer than when he'd entered the building. And the more he took off, the hotter he grew.

Kit tried to concentrate on undressing, but it was difficult when he caught a whiff of feminine scent and heard his companion rustling beside him, much too close for comfort. In response, he inched away from her, lest she come in contact with an unexpected expanse of his flesh. But there was too little room, and he banged against something that was hanging on a hook. It tottered precariously, rattling in the silence.

"Shh!" Miss Ingram whispered, and before Kit knew it, her hands were on him, steadying him. It was far worse than the accidental brush he had feared, for her gloveless fingers were splayed full upon his bare chest.

"Wh-wh-what are you doing?" she asked, sounding decidedly unlike herself.

"I'm trying to put on a tunic that was made for someone half my size," Kit whispered. It wasn't as though he was taking off his clothes for any other reason. And if he were, he wouldn't be doing it here in the Earl of Cheswick's potting shed.

"I should have taken the Harlequin," she said. "I'm smaller than you are."

"Yes, but, no," Kit muttered, as he tried not to imagine Miss Ingram stripping down to her skin. And in the ensuing silence, he simply stood where he was, unwilling to move from beneath her caress. The air in the confined space seemed to crackle with the tension between them, and Kit was tempted to cover her hands with his own.

Since neither one of them seemed to be breathing, the silence was broken only by the distant sounds of arrivals and their servants until Kit heard something else. Was it a rat, scuttling around them, or was someone outside? The reminder of just where they were chilled him like a dose of cold water. Miss Ingram, too, was startled into action, for he felt the loss of her hands as she broke away. They both stood motionless, listening, but the scraping stopped.

Still, it was an impetus to be about their business, instead of dawdling dangerously. There was too much at stake, not the least of which was Miss Ingram's tattered reputation should they be discovered in a compromising position.

Tugging the tunic over his head, Kit leaned down to remove his trousers, then pulled on the bottom half of the Harlequin costume. But he could not rush, for fear of tearing the material, which was tighter than anything he had ever worn. Straightening, Kit inhaled deeply, just to make sure he could breath, then tried to adjust the snug areas of the material as discreetly as possible.

"Perhaps we should be husband and wife."

Kit froze.

"It might make a better story should we get caught *in flagrante delicto*," Miss Ingram said. "A brother and sister wouldn't be sneaking off to the library for an assignation."

Of course, she was talking about their masquerade; Kit had never considered any other possibility. And she was probably right. If the library were empty, then it would not be unusual for a couple to meet there, though they were more likely to be married to others. Still, a certain degree of intimacy would be implied.

"It's Kit," he said, abruptly.

"What?"

"No one calls me Christopher."

"Oh. Kit." She must have turned toward him because Kit could have sworn he felt the warmth of her breath when she spoke his name.

"Hero," she whispered. "My name is Hero."

"Out of the play?"

Kit could hear her shrug, though she did not reply. "You remind me more of Beatrice," he said, referring to the feisty heroine of Shakespeare's *Much Ado About Nothing*.

Of course, calling each other by their first names was inappropriate, but so was changing their clothes here in the dark together. *And so was planning to sneak into the Earl of Cheswick's masquerade ball.*

"Let's go," she said, as if reading his thoughts. Groping around in the dark, Kit found a dry bucket and stuffed his clothes in it. Hopefully, they would be there when they returned. Reminded of what he currently wore instead, Kit wrapped his cloak around himself.

Inching forward, Kit nudged the door open a crack and peered out. The scuttling sound began at once, and he froze where he stood, half-expecting an assailant to loom out of the darkness. But when he saw a squirrel dart up a nearby tree, and he loosed his pent-up breath and slipped from the shed, his companion not far behind.

By the time he shut the door, Miss Ingram—Hero—was already headed toward the house, and Kit hurried to follow. They skirted the stables, with its light and activity, yet Kit remained alert, lest someone notice them wandering the grounds. But no one marked their presence, and they reached the tall doors that opened onto the lawn, where the party would spill out in warmer weather.

Despite the cold, they could claim they were snatching a few moments alone in the moonlight, away from the colorful figures that could be seen moving about the glowing interior. Still, they chose the doors farthest from the assembly and made their entrance as discreetly as possible to avoid notice.

Inside, the vast room they had viewed earlier in the day sparkled with light and activity, and Kit blinked against the sudden change. People in outrageous costumes were milling upon, clutching glasses of punch and gossiping, while dancers took up much of the floor, moving to the music of an orchestra.

"A little chilly out there, isn't it?" a low voice asked. The man, dressed as a house, leaned toward Hero, dark eyes leering through the window that opened across his face. "I've got a fire going in here."

Ignoring him, they slipped past a witch, a monk and a man wearing a toga to disappear into the crowd.

"We should separate and meet in the library," Hero whispered, but Kit shook his head. Although he'd not been to many masquerades, he had just been reminded that some people were emboldened by their disguises. And this was no simple country gathering with its innocent pleasures. Kit knew from Barto that the higher ranks of society often displayed the lowest levels of morality.

"Go on," Hero urged.

"No," Kit said, even as she darted behind a tall character with a towering turban. He turned to go after her, but a hand on his arm stayed him.

"Do I know you?" a Columbine asked. She was dressed in extremely low-cut servant garb and might have been looking for her Harlequin. But Kit was not it.

"No," he answered, trying to get by her.

"But perhaps I'd like to," she purred, her fingers tightening on his arm. The woman's face was completely masked, which meant the bosoms bursting forth from her tight bodice were probably those of a female past her most alluring age.

Still, Kit would not insult her. He took her gloved hand from his arm and kissed the fingers. "Perhaps another time, fair Columbine," he said, and he moved past a shepherdess and her sheep before the woman could grab him again.

Having made his escape, Kit realized that Hero had disappeared from his immediate view. And his search for her quickly became frustrating. There were plenty of black dominoes, but as he scanned the crowd for a slight figure dressed in boots, he saw none with her lurid mask, at least none turned his way.

"Well, hello, there." A six-foot nun with a baritone sidled up to him.

"Pardon me," Kit said, making his exit before the fellow could become more familiar. Pushing past a bewildered-looking pair of Quakers, he realized that the longer he lingered, the more unwelcome attention he was drawing to himself. And still he could not find Hero.

There was nothing for it but to go to the library—and hope that she was there.

Chapter Six

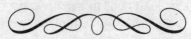

Hero moved easily through the rooms, drawing no notice on her way to the library. As Mrs Spratling had claimed, it was not in use, but a fire burned in the grate, casting a warm glow upon the tall shelves. Shutting the door behind her, Hero lit a candle and set it upon a drum table, so as better to see the titles.

When she heard the door open and close in stealthy fashion, she saw no reason to turn and greet Mr Marchant. *Kit.* They had only recently parted after being closeted together far too long, and Hero shivered at the memory of his skin beneath her fingers. Smooth and so very warm…

She heard his quiet footsteps as he neared her, and her heart began hammering at his approach. What was he about? He should be searching his own shelves, not looking over her shoulder. Yet that's just what he was doing. In fact, he was leaning against her, his breath hot against her cheek—and reeking of wine.

With a start, Hero turned around to face, not Kit

Marchant, but a stranger dressed in green, a great plume dangling from his cap. He was reaching for her, and Hero evaded his touch by stomping down hard upon his foot.

"Ow!" the man muttered. He seemed no more than a drunken guest, but Hero moved away quickly. Had he seen through her disguise, or was he indiscriminate in his tastes? Hero did not know, but she did not care to find out.

"I beg your pardon. I did not think anyone was here," Hero said in her deepest voice. She glanced toward the closed door and wondered where Kit was even as she cursed herself for relying upon him. Didn't she know better? She had become careless and witless and must face the consequences of her own inattention.

That meant dealing with this interloper so she could get back to searching. Hero glanced at the door, but she didn't want to leave the room, for fear she would not be able to return. Looking back at the man, she attempted to gauge the threat. He wasn't tall, but he was sturdily built. Just how drunk was he?

"Here now, Master Scarlet," he drawled. "What kind of greeting is that?"

He must have been referring to her bloodred mask, or perhaps he thought her someone else, for he was dressed as a fellow of the greenwood. "You must be mistaken," Hero said. "I know you not, sir."

"Well, let us remedy that, by God," he said, lurching forward. An elegant rosewood couch stood between them, but it provided little protection. Hero did not intend to participate in some French farce, but neither did she care to resort to her pistol. The success of her venture depended upon secrecy, and she did not want to cause any outcry.

Hero edged around the couch, but her companion was not deterred. In fact, he seemed to enjoy the game, grinning behind his half-mask and feathered cap. The green hose he wore beneath his short tunic left little to the imagination, and Hero was alarmed by what she saw.

"You are confusing me with another, sir," Hero said, backing toward the door. "I am not Will Scarlet. Now be off with you before I crack a cudgel upon your skull."

Hero heard the door open behind her and felt her heart constrict. If someone was blocking her escape, she was well and truly trapped. But instead of welcoming the newcomer, her companion warned them away.

"We are occupied here," he shouted.

"We are not!" Hero called out. Turning her head slightly, she glanced toward the entrance and felt a mixture of relief and joy at the sight of Kit Marchant.

As usual, he was completely unruffled by the scene before him. "Excuse me, but this is my assignation, Sir Robin, arranged earlier this evening," he said.

For a moment, Hero thought the interloper would argue. Kit must have, too, because he stepped forward, sweeping his cape out of the way, as though prepared to draw a sword, even though Hero knew he didn't have one.

What he did have was an extremely close-fitting costume, and Hero drew in a sharp breath at the sight. The shiny material with its garish red, yellow and blue diamonds seemed to hug every well-formed inch of Kit's body, revealing each sleek muscle, especially in the area of his groin, where a strategically positioned piece of red cloth called attention to that part of his anatomy.

Hero felt an answering rush of color flood her cheeks. Although she knew little of such things, her assailant's hose appeared ill filled by comparison. Indeed, as if echoing her thoughts, the man erupted in a loud harrumph and staggered toward the door.

"Well, I can see why you are wearing that, my friend," he said with a nod. "And I concede to my better."

When Robin Hood had quit the room, Kit turned toward her once more. "At least some good has come of this damned constricting costume," he said.

Then he looked down at himself for the first time, and despite herself, Hero found her gaze following his own. For a heart-stopping instant, her wits fled, and all she knew was the hot swell of what she could only guess was desire.

"Is it my imagination or is there a star on my—?" Kit began to ask, but he must have heard Hero's choked sound of dismay because he didn't finish. Instead, he lifted his head to slant her a glance, and in his dark eyes Hero saw a glint of seductive promise that robbed her of breath.

That look alone was far more dangerous than anything in Sir Robin's arsenal, and Hero had to struggle to keep a tenuous hold on her rioting senses. She tried to remember where she was, what she must do and, most of all, who she was, as her fingers clung, trembling, to the back of the couch.

A loud thump and raucous laughter from outside the room saved her from herself, for it seemed to call Kit to attention. Striding across the thick carpet, he easily lifted a heavy chair and put it in front of the door, so that they would have some privacy and warning, at least, of interruption.

Flushing, Hero ignored the giddy thrill that seemed to produce and turned her back upon the compelling figure of Kit Marchant. But he was not so easily put from her mind, and even as she scanned the shelves, searching for the Mallory, Hero was aware of his presence, both a comfort and a danger far more perilous than a host of drunken masqueraders.

Kit kept an eye on the hands of the ormolu clock, for he did not know how long the ball would continue. Usually, such events dragged through to the wee hours, but he had no wish to be found here after the other guests had left or sought their beds.

Already, he was weary of an activity that seemed pointless. And the sooner he got out of his costume, the better; he was beginning to feel as though blood was being cut off from necessary parts, parts that he might some day want in working condition…

Kit pushed aside that thought and all that came with it to concentrate on getting Hero out of Cheswick safely.

"The Mallory at Oakfield had been slipped between another cover to conceal it, which is why it remained hidden all those years," he said, hoping to put an end to the search.

As usual, Hero was undeterred. "We have no evidence that Martin Cheswick did the same."

Perhaps because half the instructions he received were missing, Kit thought, though he said no more. Even if the book was here, which he doubted, they would need to pull out each volume and examine it in order to find what they were seeking. And that sort of task was not going to be accomplished in one evening.

Still, Kit ran his fingers over the spines, looking for anything unusual, while the clock ticked, the only sound besides the crackle of the fire. When it came, the noise of something else was startling in the stillness, and Kit looked to the door, where the chair held fast despite being rattled.

Hero was already glancing his way, but she was crouched before another bookcase on the opposite side of the room. It was hardly the pose of two lovers, and Kit hurried toward the rosewood couch, motioning for her to join him.

Without hesitation, Kit pulled her down against the round pillow and leaned over her, all the while staring at the door. But after the initial rattling, it fell silent. In the quiet that followed, he waited, yet heard nothing else. Perhaps some other guests, seeking an assignation, had realized the library was occupied and moved on.

Kit loosed a low sigh at the respite and turned his head toward Hero. She had removed her mask, and had he seen his relief reflected on her features, he would have got to his feet and returned to the search. But in the candlelight, her beautiful face glowed, just as when he'd first seen her, like a beacon in the dark that he could not ignore.

Her hood was thrown back, revealing wisps of

golden hair that escaped their confinement to catch the light. Her usual cool expression was gone, her eyes heavy lidded, her lips parted and her cheeks flushed. Abruptly, Kit realized that he was bent over her, his chest nearly touching hers, his mouth only inches away from her own.

Without pausing to consider his actions, Kit lowered his head to brush his lips against hers, tasting, exploring and delighting in the soft curves. Beneath him, he heard Hero's low hum of surprised pleasure, and he smiled. For one long moment, they were in agreement, savoring their shared sense of discovery and the heat that flowed between them.

But even in his current state, Kit recognized a potential firestorm, and he pulled back slightly. Lifting his hand to Hero's throat, he stroked his thumb against the line of her jaw, teasing the corner of her mouth until it opened for him. Her eyes closed, his formidable companion looked oddly vulnerable, and Kit felt something expand within his chest. Leaning close, he kissed her again, more deeply, as if he could take her inside himself, hold her to him at last...

But this time, Kit heard no sigh of pleasure, only the jarring clang of the clock as it struck midnight. And like Cinderella of the old tales, Hero was transformed by the sound. Nothing turned into a pumpkin, but the warm and willing woman in his arms jerked upright, knocking her temple against his in her haste to escape his embrace. Rising in her wake, Kit rubbed his brow and wondered when his head had last suffered such repeated abuse.

"Are you all right?" he asked. But Hero was already

reaching for the books, her mask and domino in place, the telltale trembling of a hand the only sign of what had happened between them.

Kit was slower to recover, but it didn't take him long to realize the ramifications of his behavior. Rising to his feet, he returned to the search, cursing himself. He had been thrown together with Hero in more than one intimate situation, with just her coolness and his restraint standing between them. Yet when her coolness had wavered, his restraint had disappeared, and he had only himself to blame. Wasn't he supposed to be a gentleman?

"Now, isn't this interesting."

Kit swung round at the sound of speech. He looked at Hero, but she, too, had stiffened, and a quick glance at the door revealed that it held fast, the chair firmly lodged against it. Eyes narrowing, Kit scanned the room and was surprised to see a figure in a shadowed corner. Had it been there all along, unnoticed?

"You may bar the door of my own library against me, but I have more than one way to enter nearly every room in this house," the figure said, stepping forward. Behind him a section of decorative panel clicked shut, revealing the manner of his access.

Kit felt a moment's relief that the man had not been present earlier, but his appearance was still daunting, and his words had Kit thinking fast.

"My lord," Kit said, bowing slightly.

"You may call me your Grace, as I am good King Henry for this eve," the Earl of Cheswick said, with a regal nod. He was dressed in enormous purple robes trimmed in fur and wore a crown, presumably not of pure gold, upon his head, and surveyed them with a jaundiced eye.

"And who might you be?"

"I am but a simple Domino, your Grace," Hero said, in a deep voice. "And this is Harlequin."

The earl laughed as he moved farther into the light. "My dear young woman, I assure you that I can tell the difference between a youth and a maid," he said, waving about the sceptre he held in one hand as he paused to study them more closely. "Well, aren't you the loveliest couple."

"We're siblings."

"We're married."

Since Hero spoke at the same time Kit did, there was no recovering from their faux pas, especially considering the amused expression on the earl's face. At least he didn't call for some burly footmen to toss them out.

"How very interesting," he murmured. Moving closer, he lifted a quizzing glass and looked Kit up and down. When his gaze lingered on the red star that seemed designed to draw attention to a certain area, Kit frowned.

The earl dropped his glass with a sniff. "One wonders why a fellow who appears to be averse to attention would don such a masque."

"It's my fault," Hero said. "I chose it for him, not realizing it would be too small."

The earl turned his quizzing glass upon her. "A sad misjudgement for a *wife* to make," he said, and Kit groaned.

"You are right, my lord...er, your Grace," Hero

said. "We are married to others, and I persuaded him to meet me here for an assignation. I beg you to keep our secret."

But the earl wasn't having any of it, and he held up his hand as though to stop her speech. "You'll have to do better than that, child. And before you do, perhaps I should tell you that I do love my masquerades—so much so that I personally choose every costume that I provide for my guests. So you can imagine my surprise when I caught a glimpse of two of my favorites being worn by persons unknown to me."

The earl paused to eye Kit. "Not that I'm complaining, mind you. For I do like an intrigue."

Hero drew a deep breath, as if to tender a new explanation, but the earl waved her off. "I would like to hear what our manly Harlequin has to say. And don't try to hoax me with any talk of assignations, for that's hardly what you were doing when I came in."

It was time to lay their cards on the table, Kit decided, and he turned to face the earl without apology. "We were looking for a book," he admitted. He heard Hero's sound of distress, but he was not one to invent Banbury tales.

"A *book*?" the earl echoed.

"It was given to one of your ancestors, Martin Cheswick, for safekeeping," Hero said, in a not-so-subtle attempt to lay claim to the volume.

The earl dropped his quizzing glass with a look of annoyance. "Well, that's a sad disappointment. I had hoped for something a bit more interesting. A scandal broth, a bamboozle…a ménage à trois," he said, with a hopeful glance.

Kit shook his head.

Sighing, the earl waved a hand to encompass the room. "Well, you are welcome to it. I've no use for them, though they are pleasing to the eye. And really, what else can you fill the shelves with, except books?"

"I take it you aren't a collector?" Kit asked.

"Good heavens, no," the earl said, with a shudder. "Spare me from the dusty old mopes, although I do have an antiquarian costume that is rather amusing."

Obviously, the earl would have no idea what was or was not in his library, and while his offer was mag-nanimous, Kit didn't put much stock in it. Such a frippery fellow might be prone to whims and on to the next fancy before they could finish their search.

"Are they catalogued?" Hero asked, as though the same concern had crossed her mind.

"Lud, no!" the earl said. "I believe Father engaged a man to do that—Richard Poynter, was it? A waste of coin, if you ask me, and I have no intention of throwing good money after bad."

He looked around the room with a shrug. "I don't care what's here, as long as they look well. In fact, I think the architect had blank pages bound to his specifications in many cases. I certainly didn't want any of Father's old ones, horrid, musty, smelly things. That's why I sold them off."

"You sold your family's collection?" Hero asked.

"And why not?" the earl asked. "They meant noth-ing to me."

Kit could tell the earl was growing bored with the conversation, and he rushed to ask the most important question.

"Were the books sold at auction? Do you have a record of the buyers?"

"I don't need a record," the earl said. "I can tell you right now where they all went. We broke them up into four lots, very neat and tidy, and sold only to those among my acquaintances who like that sort of thing." He paused, as though proud of his own cleverness.

"The Greek went to Devonshire, for far too paltry a sum, I might add. The Latin I gave to Chauncey Jamison, a decent enough fellow I went to school with. Apparently, he's joined the antiquarian society and fancies himself some sort of scholar now," the earl said with a derisive laugh.

"And the rest?" Hero asked.

"The French went to Claude Guerrier, as he is known since his hasty exit from his own country, and the English to Marcus Featherstone."

"You sorted the books according to the language of the text?" Kit asked, trying to keep the surprise from his voice.

The earl gave a regal nod, obviously pleased with himself. "I couldn't be bothered with a protracted sale, so messy and time-consuming, dithering over every single volume."

"But I thought…" Hero began, only to pause, as if to reconsider her words. "That is, I had heard that one of the lots went to Augustus Raven."

"That queer fish? Certainly not," the earl said. "Why, the fellow has no taste. Have you seen that monstrosity of his, Raven Hill? Spare me from the Gothic lovers!" He shuddered.

"Thank you so much for your help…your Grace,"

Kit said hurriedly before Hero might betray her identity. "We have taken up far too much of your precious time when your guests are waiting."

"Yes, we should go," Hero said. Taking Kit's lead, she began backing toward the door.

"But you must stay! As king of all I survey, I command you. And a private audience with you, my mysterious Harlequin, is in order," the earl said, pointedly eyeing Kit. "Perhaps you'd like to get out of that tight costume. I own I fear for you. Constriction of the blood. We wouldn't want any…damage."

"Thank you, your Grace," Kit said. "But I'm afraid I can't leave my…sister."

"A pity," the earl said, putting his quizzing glass to his face once more to scrutinize his guests. Although Kit felt no sense of threat, he was aware of just how long they had been ensconced in the library as trespassers. And who knew what awaited them outside?

Hero was already at the door, and when she pulled the chair away from it, it burst open.

"My lord, are you all right?" A man stumbled over the threshold, a bit breathlessly. Kit couldn't tell if the fellow was a butler or simply masquerading as one, and he did not intend to linger long enough to find out.

"Of course I'm all right," the earl said, waving his scepter. "Behold my new subjects."

But Hero had already exited, and Kit was quick to follow. He hurried after her, hoping they could escape into the crowd before a hue and cry was raised against them. But no shouts erupted from behind, and they slowed their pace so as to draw no attention.

Yet they did not pause until they reached the tall

doors that led outside, and there only long enough to make sure they were not marked before they slipped into the night air. Kit blinked as his eyes adjusted to the darkness, a welcome cloak after the brightly lit, perfumed rooms. There was no one to note their movements on the lawn, and they veered away from the stables and any signs of activity.

Although the small shed seemed a veritable haven, Kit approached it carefully and nudged at the door, lest someone be waiting for them inside. But all was dark and silent, just as they had left it. Still, he did not intend to linger, and, once inside, he put his garments on over the Harlequin costume. He gave no thought to the closeness of his companion and didn't even care if his trousers were on backward, so eager was he to quit Cheswick.

Hero, who had only to remove her domino, was already finished and silent in the darkness, and Kit was struggling into his coat when he heard voices outside. He didn't need Hero's sudden grip upon his arm to stay his hand; he froze where he was, one sleeve on, the other off.

"They aren't here, I tell you."

It was not the man's voice, but his words, that chilled Kit, and he strained to listen.

"And how would you know when everyone's wearing costumes?" a second voice asked. The two must have been walking, for Kit heard the crunch of gravel growing closer, and he tensed. If men were searching the outbuildings for their unnamed quarry, he would be of little use, trussed halfway up in his coat.

"Because I talked to the servants, that's how, and there aren't any guests that aren't accounted for, with maids and valets all."

"What of those who aren't staying at the house?" the second voice asked. Were their steps slowing? Kit curled the fingers of his free hand into a fist.

"I've talked to every coachman here. You don't think they drove themselves, did you?" The tone was mocking, and Kit heard the other man curse as the footsteps resumed.

"Maybe," the other man said. "I wouldn't put anything past them. Didn't they ride—?"

Although Kit held his breath, he could not make out what else the fellow said, and he dared not lean toward the side of the shed, lest he blindly knock into something, calling attention to their presence. He waited, poised for trouble, but eventually, both the voices and the footsteps faded as the two men passed out of earshot.

When Hero finally loosed his arm, Kit tugged on the rest of his coat and stepped to the door, easing it open slightly. In the surrounding night, all was silent, and he saw no sign of a presence nearby.

"There! Look toward the stables," Hero whispered beside him.

Kit glanced in that direction and saw two men approaching the structure, but others milled about as well, coachmen, stable hands and the like. There was no telling if the two men Hero noticed were the same they had heard talking. But Kit could see why she had pointed them out.

Even in the pale lantern light, there was no mistaking the fact that the men wore livery, and Kit recognized the now familiar insignia of the Duke of Montford.

Chapter Seven

The exhilaration Kit had felt after their escape from the library was short-lived, deflated by the odd conversation they had overheard and Hero's concern over it. She hadn't even wanted to return to the inn, but Kit convinced her that they needed to get their things and rest the horses.

It was too late to set out upon the road to London and too cold to sleep in the open. And despite her insistence otherwise, Kit did not want Hero falling from her mount along some dark road. A fire, some food and some rest were what they both needed.

The hour was such that Kit was fairly certain they had not been followed back to their small lodgings. He had even been forced to wake a sleepy boy in the inn yard to tend the horses. And a quick exploration of the area revealed no one lingering suspiciously in the courtyard or beyond.

Even the common room was quiet, with only a few travelers or locals drinking ale before seeking their beds. Yet once ensconced in their room, Hero took up a stance at the window, as though she intended to keep watch all night.

"We don't know that those men were after us," Kit said.

She turned, her face in shadow. "Then who is?"

Although Kit wasn't sure himself, he doubted the Duke of Montford was responsible. Yet Hero seemed so convinced, he slanted her a speculative glance.

"You think I know?" she asked, as though taken aback.

Kit shrugged. Although he hadn't accused her of anything, even the most oblivious dolt would have wondered about his companion, who had proven herself adept at all manners of deception.

"You think this is all part of some elaborate scheme of *mine*?" she asked him sharply.

But Kit was not cowed by her anger, if that's what it was. "Let's put it this way—if you know anything that would be helpful, now's the time to tell me."

"I could ask the same of you," she said.

Kit bit back a laugh. "You don't trust me?"

"Should I?"

Kit snorted. "Then I'd say we are at an impasse." Yet suddenly, it didn't feel like one. In fact, their parrying had only seemed to heighten the tension between them, and Kit was struck with a want so powerful he didn't know whether he could contain it. He stood still, unwilling to move, lest he march across the room, take her in his arms and continue where he had left off in the library.

As if Hero could see his intent, she drew in a sharp

breath and turned to look out the window. When she spoke again, it was over her shoulder, her tone so distant that she appeared to put more than her back between them. "You cannot deny that the duke's men were there, just as they were at the first inn where we stayed," she said.

This time her coolness prevailed, and Kit was grateful for it, even though all of his senses screamed a protest. Running a hand through his hair, he ignored the clamoring of his body and tried to engage his brain.

"We cannot know that those two men we heard talking were discussing us," he said. "Or that they were the fellows dressed in the duke's livery. Or that those two were even the duke's men. They could have been wearing costumes."

"The earl's guests wouldn't be traipsing about the stables," Hero said. "And those were the same men we saw before. I recognized the livery."

"Perhaps," Kit conceded. "But the duke could be traveling, as we are, and attending the earl's ball."

"I don't believe in coincidences," Hero said.

Kit didn't, either, anymore, but he was not sure what to make of the sightings. "All right. Let's say those two are the ones pursuing us. Why would the Duke of Montford send a couple of thugs to kidnap you? Do you know him?"

"I know of him. He is a respected collector, so I can only assume he's infected with book madness and willing to do anything to get his prize." Turning her head, she eyed Kit directly. "Which makes it all the more imperative that we find the Mallory."

Kit shook his head at her stubborn certainty. It was

one thing to stop at Cheswick on their way to London, quite another to go elsewhere, continuing a lunatic search for something that might not even exist.

As if judging his mood, Hero continued. "I've found needles in haystacks before," she claimed.

Kit did not doubt her. "But this is different, unless you regularly tear around the country with a man who is no relation," he said, fixing her with an inquiring gaze.

"Of course not."

"Well, then, the longer we dally, the more hue and cry will be raised over your disappearance."

"Perhaps," Hero acknowledged, looking away. "Perhaps not."

"Your chaperone has gone missing, there's a warrant for my arrest, and you don't think your uncle will be concerned and alert the authorities?"

"He was not expecting me back for some time, so unless someone informs him of recent events, Raven will spare no thoughts for me," Hero said. "And even if he should become aware of the change in my circumstances, he would hardly raise a hue and cry. Raven's main concern always is the acquisition, and he will not question where I am or what I am doing until he is certain that I have not been successful."

Kit tried to absorb that bald statement and all it implied. He knew that not everyone shared his genteel upbringing. In a world where poor children were bought and sold and even royal progeny bartered away in marriage with no consideration of their wishes, Hero's situation was not that startling. And yet Kit was shocked and outraged. And if her uncle cared so little for her, where did that leave Kit?

Although he tried to mask his reaction, Hero must have seen it, for she returned her attention to the window. And when she spoke, she made it clear that the subject was closed. "What we must do is seek out the lot of English language books that went to Marcus Featherstone."

Kit groaned. "Do you even know the man?"

"I have heard of him, since he collects. He has a town house in London."

"But if all the English books were sold to him, then how did your uncle get the scrap of letter?"

Hero shrugged, but would not face him. "Perhaps Featherstone later parted with that volume or lost it in a game of chance. I understand he's an inveterate gambler."

Or, considering Kit's rapidly dropping opinion of Augustus Raven, there were other possibilities. A man who did not take care of his own niece might be unscrupulous in his dealings with others. Had he stolen the paper? Suddenly, the idea of continuing their quest didn't seem so insane. At least, Kit could continue to protect Hero from any who would do her harm—even her uncle.

"All right," Kit said. "Let's get some sleep so we can head to Featherstone's town house. But no more costumes, please."

Hero's lips curved slightly, whether in amusement or relief at his assent Kit wasn't sure. "I'm sorry about that," she said. "I'm not used to working with anyone."

Kit did not comment on her use of the word *working*, which only confirmed his earlier opinion of Augustus Raven. "Well, let's forge an alliance then."

Her delicate brows lowered, as though she was studying him with more than her usual care. "I can see how you would be of help to me, but what possible reason would you have for this alliance?"

Kit grinned. "I told you before. I'm a gentleman."

She did not seem well satisfied with that explanation, but Kit didn't know what else to tell her. Obviously, she thought he had his own reasons for staying with her, and he did, but they were not any he wanted to share at this point. And if he had not convinced her thus far of his honesty, he did not know how else to do so.

Instead, he turned his thoughts toward the morrow as he climbed into one of the two beds available, grateful for a soft berth after the last few nights. Trying not to listen to the sounds of Hero seeking her own rest, he focused on which roads would be best to take to London without alerting their enemies, whoever they might be.

The uncertainty was frustrating, and Kit felt as if he were groping blindly in the dark, unsure of what lay ahead or behind. Cut off from any source of information, he didn't know whether word had spread of the warrant for his arrest or if it had been quietly withdrawn, remaining a local matter. Despite what Hero said, had some hue and cry been raised about her disappearance? Kit had seen no broadsheets with his picture on them, but he did not fancy being carted off to prison by some sharp-eyed fellow on the lookout for felons.

But in order to get news, he would have to make contact with someone he trusted, a dangerous prospect at best. Still, Kit was tempted to appeal to his old friend Barto, a nobleman with the wealth and resources to provide aid. Kit and Hero could rusticate at Hawthorne Park while everything was sorted out. But how could he convince Hero, who already distrusted him, to abandon the search that drove her?

And as much as Kit would like to call a meeting of the knights of the round table of his youth, what would he tell his old friend, especially of Hero? Both Barto and Syd would have questions for him that he couldn't answer. And even feeling the way he did, Kit wasn't sure whether Hero was involved up to her pretty neck in some deeper deception. Was that really the kind of introduction he wanted to give to his sister and future brother-in-law?

No matter what the truth was, Kit did not want them to think ill of Hero. It was a petty reason, and so he added to it the fact that Syd and Barto would be deep in planning their wedding, and he did not want to disturb a happy time that had been so long in coming.

So, if not Hawthorne Park, where? Kit had few relatives, and his friends were clustered around where Barto lived. Frowning in the darkness, Kit knew they couldn't return to Oakfield, but there was another stop on the way to London that might yield up some answers.

"Hero?" Kit whispered, lest she already be asleep.

"What?" Her tone was one of caution, perhaps even tinged with alarm. And who could blame her after what had happened in the earl's library? Before, their dealings had been all business, but now a certain awareness seemed to have seeped into their every encounter.

Kit hurried to explain himself. "I'm thinking of stopping in Piketon."

"What?"

"That's where my coachman originally wanted to meet us."

"But I thought he was to leave the coach at Burrell?"

"He urged me to meet him at Piketon, where we could exchange carriages, but I didn't like the idea of dropping the ruse so soon. Not that it mattered," Kit added wryly. "But if something went awry with his plans or he returned to find chaos at Oakfield, he might go there, in the hopes of contacting us."

Kit paused to glance toward the other bed, but could see little in the darkness. "He's more than a simple coachman."

"Just as you are more than a gentleman farmer."

Hero's statement sounded like an accusation, and Kit snorted. "Hardly. Or I would have prevented my sister's abduction."

"What happened?" Hero asked softly.

During the ensuing silence, Kit heard a creak in the room next door, and lifted his head. But it was nothing, only an excuse for him to remain silent. For once, he was the one who did not want to conduct such a personal discussion, and yet somehow the words came spilling forth.

"It began, for us, with my father's death. He and our neighbor Viscount Hawthorne were killed in a carriage accident. We found out later that he had received a shipment of books from the household of my great-aunt, and among them was the Mallory."

Kit heard Hero's indrawn breath, but she said nothing, so he continued. "Father had no idea of its rarity or its significance, but he knew the viscount belonged to some latter-day Druid society. The group was nothing more than an excuse for wealthy landed gentleman to socialize, but at least one other, led by a man named Malet, was not so innocuous. Malet had been searching for the Mallory at Oakfield, driving my great-aunt mad with his efforts to find it and his midnight trips through the maze there. Of course, we knew nothing of that. She died before Father, and I then received the legacy of Oakfield."

Kit winced at the memory of his delight in the inheritance. "From the moment of our arrival, there were strange happenings, but I ignored Syd's concerns. Thankfully, Barto was not so blind, and it is due to him that Syd lives."

"I don't believe that you were that stubborn or heedless," Hero said.

"Oh, I finally believed her when Barto told us of his own suspicions," Kit said, taking no pride in the fact.

"And then?"

"Then Malet picked us off, one by one. He knew that none of the locals would remain at Oakfield on Samhain, and I did little to hold them there. He arranged for some tainted cider to knock out the rest of us. Barto found me along the road."

"If your friend Barto was so clever, why didn't he stop everyone from drinking the cider?"

Kit paused, for he had never really questioned Barto's whereabouts at the time. "He wasn't there."

"Perhaps he was simply luckier than you."

"Perhaps." But Kit couldn't see Barto downing the home-brewed drink even had he been at Oakfield. *Because he was smarter than that. More cautious. Less oblivious.* Kit felt his anger and frustration return.

"Or perhaps his own suspicions made him more wary, and you could hardly be privy to his information or thoughts," Hero said.

That was true, but still, Kit should have paid more attention to what was going on around him.

"So Barto saved your sister?"

"No. Yes," Kit said. "We both rode back to Oakfield, but Syd managed to set fire to the great oak in the centre of the maze, and it spread."

"She sounds like a resourceful woman—who saved herself," Hero said.

"But if I had just believed her from the beginning, she wouldn't have been there, scared to death by hooded Druids intending to murder her." Kit's regret threatened to choke him.

"What happened to them?"

"We assumed they were all killed in the fire, but now I'm not so sure." The admission was a harsh reminder that he needed to stay alert, to protect Hero from such madmen, perhaps even to redeem himself, at least in his own eyes.

"You're taking the blame that should be directed at those responsible," Hero said, absolving him in her usual brisk tone. "Your anger is festering, probably because you never faced the men who did this to your family."

She might well be right, but what good was that realization? Kit could hardly raise Malet from the dead.

"And you may never be able to face them," Hero said, as though reading his thoughts. "But you might make do with those who are chasing us."

Kit's lips curled at the thought of some measure of retribution. He would gladly dole it out if he could get his hands on them, especially since they might well be one and the same.

As they approached Piketon, Hero watched for anything unusual. Although the town was on the way to London, she didn't like veering from her goal, and she was leery of meeting up with anyone else. There were too many variables, too many chances for surprise.

But Hero could hardly refuse to stop unless she was prepared to quit Kit's company, which she was not yet ready to do. The roads presented too many threats to the solitary young man she appeared to be, and though she had many skills, she did not overestimate her abilities.

Nor could she fool herself, Hero admitted bitterly. For no matter how many pragmatic excuses she might give, truth be told, she remained with Kit Marchant because she could not bear to part with him. He had proven to be just as dangerous as she first expected, wielding a power over her that Raven never had possessed.

Hero flushed at the memory she had tried most to banish: the night in the dim library when Kit had leaned over her, pressing his mouth to hers. He had taken her unawares, but like someone under a spell, Hero had let him, overwhelmed by the unexpected sensations, her innate caution abandoned in the heat of the moment.

If that was his sole effect upon her, Hero might have been able to dismiss the incident as a sudden weakness of her gender. But Kit Marchant was insidious, luring her with his gentle touch, his warmth, his humor... *Everything about him.*

Nothing seemed to disconcert the man. He remained calm in every situation, keeping his head while he took appropriate action, all solid strength and reason. Indeed, he was so remarkable, that it was easy to see him as her rescuer, and not just from the storm. But Hero could not take shelter with him permanently.

Raven would not allow it, of course. But more importantly, she could not allow it. Her circumstances were such that she could never form an attachment to anyone, for the risks were too great. For everyone.

And when that knowledge threatened to overcome her, Hero told herself that Kit Marchant could not be what he claimed, that no one would help her unless they had their own motives for doing so. *Even a gentleman.*

And yet... She thought of the tale he had told her last night in the closeness of the room they had shared. For a moment in the dark she glimpsed what she had seen at Oakfield, a man who was holding in anger and grief. And despite her best intentions, Hero had been affected.

No doubt, that was what he intended. Hero frowned, uncertain, but unable to dismiss her suspicions. Perhaps someone else could accept Kit Marchant's help and his explanations for it without question. But she had been raised differently, as a pawn on Raven's chessboard. His machinations had so altered her outlook that, even now, she wondered what part he played in all of this.

Hero shook her head. All she could do was move toward the goal and hope that she was on the right path. Nothing else mattered, she reminded herself. And yet, when Kit turned his head toward her, her pulse leapt, her gaze settling upon his handsome face with an eagerness she could not deny.

"This is the place," he said, nodding toward a tall brick building ahead. A large sign proclaimed it the site of the Crowned Head, and belatedly, Hero scanned the area for anything suspicious. The inn was a large one, which meant that they could blend in with the crowd, but others could do so, as well.

Once inside the courtyard, they gave their horses over to a stable lad and walked among the bustle of grooms, postilions, coachmen and servants, all providing for the mail coaches and post chaises, horses and passengers.

Hero looked from the hurrying throng to Kit. "Where would he be?"

Kit shrugged in his usual casual manner, though Hero doubted he was as unconcerned as he appeared. "Let's just look around."

Although Hero felt a measure of safety in her disguise, she still kept a wary eye out, for Kit was recognizable and anyone with him would garner scrutiny. "Perhaps we should separate," she suggested, but he gave her a black look. Was he being protective or laying a trap? Hero slowed her steps, hanging back just enough to avoid any sudden entanglements.

They had nearly completed a circle of the perimeter when Kit paused. "He's here, all right, there by the door to the kitchens."

Hero glanced in that direction and saw a stocky fellow, his cap slung low, lounging against the brick wall.

"I'll keep my distance," Hero said. "I'd rather he not see me dressed as I am." At Kit's nod, she sauntered toward a farm cart that was rolling to a stop nearby. "I'll take care of this for you, sir," she said to the driver, ducking her head.

"Molly usually doesn't need tethering, lad. Just make sure no one steals my goods," the farmer said. Dropping to the ground, he unloaded a large crate of apples, passing by Kit on his way into the kitchens.

Standing silently at the horse's head, Hero kept her face turned away even as she inched closer to the man Kit had pointed out. Although loath to be recognized, she wanted to be privy to the conversation. And as long as the two didn't whisper, she was in a good position to listen.

"Are you all right?" the man called Hob asked.

"Yes, and you?"

From the corner of her eye, Hero could see the fellow nod. "I left the coach in Burrell. Didn't see a sign of the two men, sir, and began to think perhaps they were just a pair of thieves looking for something to steal." He paused. "Then I went back to Oakfield. It appears they raised the stakes."

"Are the authorities still looking to arrest me?"

"I don't know. When I found out about the warrant, I didn't stay around to be questioned. I sent word off to the viscount and decided to come here. I didn't know where else to catch up with you."

"Obviously, they were not fooled by the switch in vehicles."

"No, and they seem to mean business, sir. What of the young lady? Is she all right?"

"She's safe," Kit said.

"Really? And just where might that be?"

At the sound of the new voice, Hero did not turn, but kept her eyes resolutely fixed upon the ground.

"Here, now, put that away before someone gets hurt," Hob said.

Only then did Hero glance surreptitiously toward Kit. He and Hob were pinned against the wall, facing a third man whose back was to her. Obviously, he had some weapon, a pistol or a knife that kept them at his mercy, and Hero's heart hammered violently at the sight.

They had been threatened earlier, but that was before she had come to know Kit Marchant. In fact, the assault on the carriage seemed a lifetime ago, so far in the past that Hero could not believe she had once thought he played some part in it. Now, his life was in danger because of her, and Hero felt a horror that even the worst of Raven Hill's frights had never induced. For an instant, she could do nothing except stare, stricken numb.

"Tell me where the girl is and no one will get hurt," the man said, and his words finally roused Hero to action. Although she could not see his face, she heard the sneer in his voice, the falseness of his promise, and she knew that no one would come out of this unharmed by co-operating with him.

"And just in case you're hesitating, my friend is across the courtyard, ready to join us," he said. "He's still smarting from the tumble off his horse, so if I were you, I wouldn't annoy him."

Tugging on her cap, Hero glanced up and saw that a tall man, hat shadowing his face, was approaching. She had no time to draw her own weapon, and the horse and cart stood between her and Kit. So she gave Molly a smack, sending the animal charging toward the doorway.

Kit and Hob moved out of the way, but the other fellow, obviously counting on his cohort to watch his back, was taken unawares. Knocked aside, he was soon being pummeled by Kit, who exhibited the kind of boxing men paid to witness. Hero had only a startled moment to admire his skill before she maneuvered the horse and its load backward, putting them between the kitchen and the approaching man, who had broken into a run. A quick shove to the cart sent it careening into him.

"Here, now, what's going on?" The farmer, emerging from the kitchens, shouted in annoyance.

"He ran into your cart," Hero called.

The farmer might have been more forgiving if the fallen man had apologized. Instead, the villain lurched to his feet and shoved the approaching farmer out of the way, intent upon reaching his companion. Not taking well to such treatment, the farmer tackled the tall man and an brawl ensued.

By the time Hero reached Kit, he had his assailant shoved against the wall, trying to get some answers. But even as Kit pressed him, the fellow sank to the ground, unconscious. Seizing her opportunity, Hero darted forward and grabbed Kit's arm. He swung round, ready to strike her, before recognition flashed in his dark eyes. Then he shouted for Hob, but a stream of men and boys were pouring from the stables to watch the fight, and they had pushed the coachman into the doorway.

Hob waved them away even as he backed into the kitchens, unhurt, and Hero pulled at Kit, dragging him beneath the cart. Exiting on the other side, they dodged the growing throng and ran to where their horses waited, making good their escape.

Chapter Eight

Hero did not know her way around Piketon, so she followed Kit as he took a circuitous route through the narrow roads and lanes. Perhaps he was sighting from the sun because it soon became apparent that they were heading north, not east. She could only guess the change in direction was to escape their pursuers, who would be watching the road to London when they recovered.

But for once, Hero did not care where Kit led her. She was simply glad that he was unhurt and astride his mount, his familiar form only feet away from her. Although she had learned long ago how to hide her fright, her hands were still shaking after what they had been through.

Before her fear had always been for herself—for her safety, for her sanity, for her ability to evade a situation or to complete a task. But when Kit was threatened, Hero had felt a panic such as she had never known. And it lingered, making her cold and queasy.

She kept her gaze on his wide shoulders, as if he might suddenly disappear from the saddle. *From her life.*

When Kit finally headed off the road toward a sluggish stream, Hero was grateful for the respite. She dismounted quickly, driven by an urgent need to touch her companion, as if the feel of his solid form might assure her of his safety. But she did not know how to approach him, and simply stood by, uncertain, while he watered the horses.

As she watched his graceful movements, Hero felt her throat thicken, as though clogged with some kind of violent emotion. But Kit's casual demeanor was not conducive to dramatic declarations. Nor was she accustomed to making them.

Hero took refuge in a less personal observation. "Y-you handle your fists very well for a gentleman farmer," she said. And he did. She had caught only glimpses, but she was certain that not every member of the landed gentry would be able to acquit himself so admirably in a fight.

"I know a bit of boxing. Just enough to protect myself from someone who doesn't," Kit said, in his usual modest fashion. Then he turned his head to flash her a grin. "You were right. I do feel better after thrashing one of them, though I wish I could have got some information from him first."

Hero might have been gratified by his statement, but she was too horrified by the sight of blood on his mouth. "You're hurt."

He lifted a hand to finger his lip gingerly. "That's to be expected, I suppose, but at least the fellow didn't nick me with the blade he was brandishing."

Hero felt the earth sway beneath her feet. Not only had Kit been in danger, but he had been injured. He was so capable that she had thought him invincible, and the realization that he was not filled her with alarm.

"Don't tell me the imperturbable Miss Ingram swoons at the sight of blood?" he teased.

Hero shook her head as she searched for a handkerchief. It wasn't the blood that made her uneasy, but the fact that it was Kit's blood. The knowledge that he could have been knifed or killed terrified her, making her throat tight. She had blithely traveled with this man, using him just as she would any convenience to meet her ends. And she had justified her actions with the assumption that he was using her, as well.

But suddenly that wasn't important anymore. What was important was Kit's well-being, Hero realized, as she dipped the handkerchief in the cold water and moved toward him. Stepping close, she lifted the cloth to dab at the drop of red, but she was so near that memories of his kisses rushed over her, threatening her tenuous composure.

Hero's trembling fingers slipped, her thumb brushed against his lower lip, and she thought she heard Kit groan. Had she hurt him? Abruptly, he had her wrist in a tight grip, and her gaze flew to his dark one. For a long moment she stood there, her pulse pounding under his touch, before he released her hand.

"Thank you for your quick actions," he said. "I'm glad you didn't leave."

Did he think her so heartless that she would abandon him to his attackers? Hero felt stricken.

"The men didn't know you were there, dressed as you were. So you would have been wise to go since it was you they were after," Kit said. "But as much as I wanted you to get away safely, I wondered how I'd ever find you again."

In the silence that followed his admission, Hero could hear her heart thundering. The husky tone of Kit's voice hinted at something that so closely echoed her own feelings that she was afraid to look into his eyes for fear he might see her thoughts. Yet she stood rooted to the spot, unable to move away, fighting the urge to touch him that had somehow turned into an urge to throw herself into his arms. And stay there.

Even in her current state, Hero knew that no good would come of that desire. Pursuing any sort of relationship was impossible because of what she was, where she had come from, and what her future might hold. That bitter reminder finally spurred her to turn away. All that she had left unsaid would have to remain so, for Kit's sake and for her own.

It was time to resume their journey, to return to her quest and the life that had no place in it for anyone like Kit Marchant. Mounting, Hero watched him do the same, the emotional interlude seemingly forgotten. But her hands shook as she took the reins, proof that she could not so easily put it from her mind.

Kit frowned when the rain began. They'd had unaccountably good weather for days, so it was to be expected. But that didn't make the cold pelting any more comfortable. Hero turned up the collar of her greatcoat and donned a wide-brimmed hat to replace her cap, yet Kit couldn't help worrying about her, and when they came upon a private home that had been converted into a country inn, he was more than ready to retire for the day in front of a blazing hearth.

Unfortunately, all inns were not created equal. Some had terrible food, abusive proprietors, poor servants or those who did little or stole or demanded coin for any service. Others had rooms that were dirty and bug-ridden or cold and damp, without even the meanest of comforts.

Kit should have recognized their fate when the private parlour where they ate boasted only a meagre fire, and their sumptuous meal consisted of hard pota-toes, undone mutton and even less palatable fare. As they sipped their watery wine, Kit tried not to imagine what would have been awaiting him at Oakfield— good, simple food and a hot bath. Thoughts of the latter made him sigh into his plate.

"What is it?" Hero asked, looking up.

Kit shook his head. She must be chilled to the bone, but had not complained at all, so how could he voice his grievances?

"Are you feeling all right? How is your lip?"

Was that concern that shadowed her face? Kit grinned at the thought and touched his mouth gingerly. "I'm all right."

And he was. Despite the discomforts, Kit realized that the dismals and moodiness that had plagued him after the fire were gone, banished perhaps by time or the pummeling he had given his assailant or Hero herself. But now that he felt a bit like his old self, Kit was ready for a little less excitement. And the home he had viewed so dimly just a week ago now seemed a veritable haven, where he could make a life for himself—if he had someone like Hero to join him there.

The thought brought Kit's attention back to his companion, and he frowned at the damp spots on her sleeves. "If you're finished, we should get you out of those wet clothes," he said. The words came out differently than he intended, and Kit pushed away from the table rather than face Hero's reaction. He walked to the small window, where daylight was fading into darkness, but the thrumming of the rain continued.

"I don't want you catching a chill," he explained, something seizing within him at the notion.

"I'm very hardy," Hero said in a wry tone.

Kit turned round to look at her. Certainly, she was taller than most women and seemingly capable of just about any task, but that didn't mean she could not be felled by the illnesses that struck everyone. "Perhaps we should think about taking a coach."

"Passengers on the stage have been known to die from exposure," Hero stated baldly.

"Those on the outside, yes, but I was thinking of hiring a coach, so we could be out of the weather."

"What of the horses?" she said. "And I don't like the idea of being dependent upon anyone else."

Kit frowned. Nothing except their own mounts would give them the ability to escape quickly when necessary, as well as to go about their business without anyone taking note of them or their whereabouts, an important consideration after what had happened at Piketon.

"All right, but if the weather gets too bad, we'll stop for a while," Kit said.

"The sooner we get to London, the sooner we can find the Mallory and foil our pursuers," Hero argued.

Kit felt a twinge of annoyance at her eagerness to end the journey, but he pushed it aside. Right now he had more pressing concerns, and there was something that neither one of them had mentioned.

"The men in Piketon weren't wearing livery," Kit said. Although he'd never believed there was a connection between their pursuers and the Duke of Montford's staff, still he had to admit that such men would be recognizable.

"Maybe they took off their livery, the better to avoid notice."

Kit snorted, unconvinced.

"Or maybe the men in livery are waiting outside."

Kit would have laughed if she hadn't been so serious. Indeed, her calm expression was so alarming that he posed the question even though he knew he would receive no answer.

"Just how many people do you think are chasing us?"

Hero breathed in the moldy odor of the small room and sighed. Although they had asked for two beds, there was only one, and the paltry fire in the small grate produced little warmth. Circumstances had forced her into worse places, but not often. Yet what else could they do unless they were willing to travel by night in the rain?

While Kit went out to call for a chambermaid, Hero

took his advice and quickly changed her breeches and socks. She had no other coat, so hung it up as best she could, though the room's dampness boded ill for anything drying during the night, especially two great-coats and a variety of lesser garments.

She had just finished dressing when Kit returned with a belligerent girl who obviously did not intend to be of much help. She carried a poker with which she stirred the fire, but she did not add any wood until Kit promised her good coin. And even then, the room did not heat.

It was a gloomy night, and Hero might have been excused for being sunk in the dismals. But instead, she felt as though something hard inside of her had crumbled, freeing her from its grip. And even the grim accommodations could not dispel the odd sense of lightness in her chest.

They were alive and well and together for now, and perhaps that was enough, Hero thought. Glancing surreptitiously at her companion, she studied his mouth, where his beautiful lower lip was cracked. Fighting back the urge to touch it, she contented herself with helping him off with his coat.

"Did you change your clothes?" he asked, and his protective manner warmed Hero far more than the wretched blaze. No one had ever cared for her welfare, and no matter what the reason behind his concern, she delighted in it.

At her nod, he began rummaging through his own pack. "Better get into bed then. It's got to be warmer in than out, and I don't want you catching a chill."

Hero didn't pause to wonder just why he cared, but

enjoyed the proof that he did and crawled under the covers, trying not to think about the general cleanliness of the place. What she wouldn't give for a bath. Instead of curling up to sleep as she usually did, she turned over, peeking out at Kit, who was sitting on the lone spindle chair and pulling off his boots.

Hero knew she should look away, but after what had happened in Piketon, she found it difficult to let the man out of her sight. And her view of him in his shirtsleeves, his wide shoulders straining, was arresting. As she watched, he set his boots aside and then stripped off his socks, and there was something about the sight of his bare feet that made her heart trip.

When he covered them with a dry pair of socks, Hero wondered if he would change his breeches, as well. And although she flushed at the thought, she didn't look away when he stood and turned his back to her. He peeled away the buckskin to reveal a brief white garment that clung to his behind and thighs hard with muscle before donning another pair.

They had been sleeping in their clothes, but Hero wondered what he wore when alone. A nightshirt? Nothing at all? Hero stifled a bubble of hysterical laughter at questions that only a week ago would have been unthinkable.

Kit must have heard something because he paused in his circuit of the room, perhaps looking for the driest bit of floor. "What?" he asked.

Without pausing to consider the reckless thought that came to mind, Hero moved over and threw back the blankets. "Here," she said. "As you pointed out, it's the only warm place."

For once, the easygoing Kit appeared startled. "No, I'll be fine in front of the fire."

Hero shook her head. "It's the only sensible solution."

Kit looked right at her, that dark and dangerous glint in his eyes. "I don't think sharing a bed is a good idea."

Hero shivered at his low tone, husky with promise, and she knew she was on treacherous ground. She had no business encouraging any closeness between them, but neither did she want him to lie freezing upon the filthy floor.

"Huddling together might be the only way we both fend off illness," Hero said. "And I don't see a problem because, as you so often point out, you are a gentleman."

Kit's mouth twisted at the reminder, and he put a hand to his split lip, with a grimace. "Even a gentleman has his limits."

Hero shivered again at the stark admission. Although they were both fully clothed, something in Kit's gaze hinted at a different arrangement, should he join her. And her heart thundered in response. For one wild moment, Hero wanted nothing more than to give this man her all, to deny him nothing.

And then? All actions had consequences, and it was the knowledge of what they might be that kept Hero from succumbing to the temptation Kit Marchant presented. Swallowing a groan, she pulled the covers over her head and turned to face the wall, her lightened spirits abruptly dimmed.

But then Hero felt the bed dip and a sudden warmth

by her feet. Peeking out once more, she saw that Kit had taken up a position at the other end. He was sitting up against the bedstead, his long legs stretched toward her, and the last blanket tossed over them both.

"You can't be comfortable," Hero protested.

"I'm all right," he said. Hero would have argued further, but the comfort of his closeness and heat made her shut her eyes.

"Tell me more about this uncle of yours," he said, his voice low in the darkness. "Why does he have you fetch books for him? Is that how he adds to his collection?"

"He never leaves Raven Hill," Hero said. *Like a spider at the middle of his web, he sends his minions out to do his bidding.* "He looks at the auction catalogues and knows booksellers, but he usually won't pay what they are asking. He prefers contacts who look through the various booths and backstreet sales and report what is available."

"Why doesn't he just have them buy it?"

"He doesn't trust anyone."

"But he trusts you?"

Hero would have shrugged, had she not been tucked against Kit's solid form. "To a point," she muttered. She often arranged buys, especially whenever Raven thought her wiles and attractiveness might sway a client. And he always said she was smarter than anyone else, though it was hardly a compliment. *Cleverness and cunning will out every time, my girl,* he often said.

But he had many other resources. "He sometimes sends my, uh, cousin, Erasmus Douthwaite Raven,"

Hero said. But Raven claimed Erasmus was too stupid and too greedy to be depended upon not to take his own portion out of the dealings. Which didn't sit well with Erasmus.

"He was for the law, but he would rather be a gentleman of leisure, like Raven. Unfortunately, he doesn't have the necessary funds."

"And where did Raven come by his fortune? What are his connections?"

"I don't know," Hero said. "He probably inherited most of it, for he bought Raven Hill many years ago. Perhaps he sold other property in order to do so. He does have a man of business, so he might well have other investments."

"But he spends it all on books."

"He has done a lot of work on Raven Hill over the years," Hero said. *So-called improvements that suited Raven's fancy.* "That continues, but his main interest now is books and other acquisitions. He's a member of the antiquarians."

However, he hadn't joined in order to write papers or see lectures, but to show off that which he owned and try to obtain that which he sought. Collecting was Raven's mania. Sometimes Hero thought he considered her part of his collection, a pretty decoration no more valuable than the least of his possessions.

At the reminder, Hero frowned and feigned a yawn in order to put an end to the discussion. But she could not return to her earlier ease, and sleep was long in coming. The conversation had cast a pall over her mood, as though Raven, like his namesake, was spreading black wings over her, even here, and reaching out to steal her from her cozy nest.

The next morning, Hero woke to the sound of rain pelting against window panes. Snuggling deeper into her bed, she became aware that she was not at Raven Hill, for she had slept long and well. And she was more comfortable than she ever had been in her life.

The reason for that condition soon became apparent, for when Hero opened her eyes, she saw that she was clinging to a large lump of blankets. Since it was solid and gave off an enormous amount of heat, she realized that Kit must be in there somewhere.

Heart thudding, she glanced around to view the room crookedly. Sometime during the night she must have migrated to the other end of the bed in search of Kit's warmth. Although he was still on top of most of the bedding, it was a tangle, and Hero struggled to extricate herself. For in the bright light of day, the dangers of sharing a bed were far more glaring than in the seductive darkness.

Thoughts of what might have happened—and the dire consequences—robbed Hero of her breath, and she pulled at the material trapping her, only to hear the distinctive sound of it ripping. In an instant, she was staring into dark eyes, alert above her, and for a moment she felt the full weight of Kit's hard body.

"What the devil?" he murmured.

Hero did not care to make her explanations while lying beneath warm, muscular male, and she slid out as best she could, trying not to think about the way he looked, the way he smelled, the way he *felt* against her.

Stumbling to her feet, Hero clasped her arms about her, as though to ward off the man's potent allure.

"I—I think I tore your shirt," she said.

Having discovered no outside threat to either of them, Kit leaned back against the pillow, a lazy smile on his handsome features. "Did I miss something?"

"No!" Realizing that she was reacting far too strongly, Hero tried to compose herself. Where was her cap? She grabbed at her hair, pulling it up tightly once more.

"Look at how late it is. We've slept away half the morning," Hero said, only to choke on the words. "We'll have time to make up."

A grunt signaled that Kit was finally stirring from the bed, though Hero studiously avoided looking in that direction. She busied herself putting on her boots, donning the guise of a boy when she felt less like one every day.

"It's wasn't my shirt that tore, just a bit of pillow-case," Kit said, and Hero sighed in relief. She did not want to waste time trying to find someone to mend it in this awful place, while her own sewing skills were definitely lacking.

She just wanted to leave, to escape the confines of the room, although she knew that the danger did not lie here, but would be traveling with her, ever present, ever tempting… Still, she turned to hurry Kit along, only to find him standing unmoving, a thoughtful expression on his face.

"What?" Hero asked. For once, she couldn't divine his mood. In fact, the man who usually was so relaxed appeared tense and awkward, and Hero braced herself for the worst.

"I have a proposal for you," he said.

Hero drew in a sharp breath at the bald statement and what it might mean. Was Kit finally going to admit to some ulterior motive? Did he want to split the profits from the book when they found it? If so, Raven would never agree, and she could not return to Raven Hill empty-handed.

"What is it?" Hero asked, despite the panic that threatened.

"A proposal," Kit said, as if the word explained itself. He cleared his throat. "Of marriage."

Hero felt the world spin again, and this time, she was so startled that she reached out to the wall in order to right herself. Surely, she had not heard Kit correctly?

"Wh-what?"

Kit smiled. "That's not exactly the reaction I was hoping for," he said. "I know I should be talking to your uncle, but these aren't the usual circumstances, and knowing you, I assume you'd want a more straightforward approach."

But that was just it. *He didn't know her.* So why was he asking her to marry him? The answer came to Hero all too quickly. *It was the act of a gentleman.*

"Is this because of last night, because we shared a bed?" she demanded. But before he could answer, she remembered what else had occurred during the evening. Had she revealed too much of herself—and Raven—in drowsy conversation? "I don't want your pity, thank you," she said turning away.

"I'm not offering you pity," Kit protested.

Although Hero didn't believe him, the reasons for

his proposal mattered little. She could not marry him—or anyone—and she answered automatically. "Thank you for doing me the honor, but I must decline."

"May I ask why?"

Kit's voice was curiously flat, and Hero wanted to explain, but how could she? Perhaps she had caught a chill after all, for she felt the same queasiness that she had yesterday, along with a sudden thickening of her throat that made speech difficult.

In the end, she simply shook her head. Although another male might have stormed off, indignant or angry, Kit was no ordinary man, and perhaps his proposal was not typical, either. As though unaffected by her denial, he nodded curtly and turned to put on his coat.

Hero told herself the offer had been a sham, an act of pity or some ruse to obtain the Mallory. Yet the very notion of wedding Kit Marchant made her chest hurt and her eyes sting. She hurried through the doorway past him, so that he could not see her weakness.

Fighting back a sniffle, Hero realized that she truly was ill, but it was not a chill that afflicted her. She was heartsick. It was an ailment that she never expected to have, but she never could have anticipated Kit Marchant and his power over her, a power that rivaled Raven's.

Chapter Nine

The foul weather didn't let up, so they rode through a drizzle most of the day. Kit kept trying to veer east, but it seemed that the roads curved, turning back on themselves, and by the time the day was fading, their route had become a muddy track that seemed to lead nowhere.

The proliferation of inns in the past decade had done much to eliminate the time-honored tradition of seeking shelter at private homes, but when Kit glimpsed a light in the distance, he did not hesitate, for soon they wouldn't be able to see their way at all.

The prospect of a night spent in the open put his own disgruntlement in perspective. But he could still not shake the mood that had settled over him after this morning's ill-fated conversation. Obviously, he had learned nothing from Syd and Barto's idiotic behavior, for he'd made a mess of things that equaled their own.

He had spoken too soon. If he'd had time to consider his words, Kit would have handled the situation differently. But when he woke up in bed with a woman, a gentleman tried to make things right.

Although nothing untoward had happened, any reasonable person would view their entire association as untoward, improper...scandalous. Kit's motives were good, but this morning even he realized that things had gone too far and he must do the honorable thing.

Of course, it was not as though he hadn't toyed with the idea ever since first setting eyes upon Hero Ingram, so his heart was in perfect agreement with his head. And the rest of him wasn't averse, either.

But he had spoken too soon, tipping his hand when he should have bided his time, especially considering how little he had learned about the mysterious woman. There was a reason for her refusal, Kit was certain of it, unless he was entirely wrong in his perceptions, which was possible considering what had happened at Oakfield.

Kit shook his head, only to dash his face with cold water from the brim of his hat. He was chilled to the bone, so he could only imagine how Hero must feel, and he spurred Bay forward, past farm fields, low stone fences and a barn. Finally, the light revealed itself to be a rambling farmhouse, with windows glowing and wafts of smoke trailing from its chimneys.

Dismounting, they followed slippery flagstones to the worn door, and Kit knocked loudly to be heard above the rain. A sturdy, genial-looking fellow answered, and Kit doffed his hat, explaining that he and his brother were hopelessly lost.

He had barely finished speaking when a stout female appeared, wiping her hands on her apron. "Oh, let the poor gentlemen in. They'll be drowned out in that, I'll warrant, if not frozen to death."

With a nod, the genial fellow motioned for them to enter, and Kit stepped inside, trying not to drip on the wooden floor inside the entrance.

"Tad, see to their horses," the woman said, and a scrawny lad ran past them like a blur. Two more hastened to follow, but the woman put out an arm. "Did I say Luke and Bill?" she asked the two boys, who were smaller than the blur. They shook their heads. "Then off with you!" But the youngsters, obviously curious about the arrivals, hung back, eyes wide.

"You've got out of the way, that's for certain. We don't see many travelers here," the woman said. "I'm Min Smallpeace, by the way, and this is Bert."

"Christopher Marchant," Kit said. "And my brother Sid."

"Sid," Bert said, with a nod. But Min only gave Hero a sharp glance and continued on. "As it happens, our nephew Clyde is away."

"Off trying to woo a young lady," Bert said, with a chuckle.

"So his room is empty, for the time being."

"Perhaps forever," Bert said.

"Nonsense. I told him he could bring Sal back here," Min argued. "You two get out of those wet clothes, and I'll see what I can find for you to wear. Where's Cassie?"

"Here, ma'am." A young woman appeared, probably some sort of hired girl, and gaped at them, unable to hide her interest in the strangers.

"See what you can find for these two to eat, some of the pork pie and potatoes and apple tart for starters."

"Oh, we can't impose on you," Kit said.

"Nonsense! We can't save you from drowning just to let you starve."

And before Kit knew it, they were in a cozy room under the eaves, with a fresh fire burning in the hearth and a pile of clean, dry clothes in hand.

"Let me have all that you've got with you. I'll wash everything tonight and string it up in the kitchen," Min said, reaching for Kit's pack. For a moment, Kit thought the woman was going to rifle through their things, which might prove awkward.

"We'll bring them out to you," Hero said, stepping in front of the stolid female.

Without pausing, Min turned away, heading toward a low cupboard. "See that you do, and I'll have the boys bring up some hot water." Pulling out a small tub, she eyed Kit up and down. "Not big enough for the likes of you, young man, but perhaps you can squeeze in with your knees up to your chin."

Kit laughed with delight. "Ma'am, if you were not already married, I'd have to propose to you right now, for surely you are the most wonderful of all women," he said, sweeping into a low bow.

"Oh, get on with you," Min said, waving him away with a smile. Her cheeks flushed, she bustled out, shutting the door behind her.

Kit sighed with pleasure in anticipation of a thorough wash, though Hero appeared less enthused. Perhaps she was concerned about his presence, Kit thought, his chill body surging with heat at the notion. But he had no intention of lingering. There was a limit to his control and sharing a bath definitely went beyond it.

Kit slanted a speculative glance at her, for she was rooting through her pack, her back to him, curiously silent. And when she did speak, she tossed the words over her shoulder with a carelessness belied by the tone of her voice. "You've been busy with the proposals today, haven't you?"

"And twice denied," Kit said. "I must be a poor bargain."

For a moment, he thought she might say more, but she shook her head, as though confused by his nonsense. But she needed more nonsense in her life, and Kit would be happy to provide it. *If she let him.*

"Anyone who offers to feed me, clothe me, give me a clean bed *and* provide a bath deserves my devotion," Kit said.

"I don't trust her," Hero said, turning to face him. "And I'm certainly not giving her all of my male clothes."

Kit snorted, rolling his eyes heavenward at her suspicions. "Oh, yes, you are," he said, stepping toward her purposefully. "Even if I have to remove them myself."

Fortunately—or unfortunately—it did not come to that. When the water arrived, carried by a troop of boys of varying sizes, Kit insisted that Hero take advantage of it, while he waited outside the narrow door. When she appeared, she was dressed in someone's cast-offs, complete with a clean cap, and carried her own clothes in her arms.

Ducking inside, Kit made sure that she had left nothing behind, then stripped down to his skin and poked one arm out the door to hand over his wet things, as well.

Although the small tub provided the basic of necessities, Kit vowed then and there to install a bathing room at Oakfield, smaller and less grand than the one they had seen at Cheswick, but a room devoted to bathing nonetheless.

Tossing the dirty water out the window, he could see little but blackness outside, where night had fallen and a steady rain continued. His garments were worn and ill fitting, but dry, and Kit heaved a sigh of relief at the turn in their fortunes.

The neat farmhouse with its hospitable occupants loosed the tension that had gripped him for most of the day, and he was reminded of his childhood home. This place, with its tilted floors and narrow hallways, might not be as well-appointed, but it was comfortable and welcoming.

As if in confirmation of his thoughts, Kit found a couple of boys waiting for him outside the room under the eaves, and they led him down the narrow stairs to the kitchen. When he did not immediately see Hero, Kit felt a momentary panic. Had she been right to suspect even these simple people lodged in the middle of nowhere? But before he could act, Min pushed him into a hard chair and nodded toward the line where Hero was helping Cassie hang up their wash.

"Your brother is quite handy in the home, isn't he?" Min asked.

Kit could only nod. He might have given some explanation for Sid's helpfulness, but then Min set a steaming plate in front of him, and all else left his head as he relished a hot meal that put any inn's offerings to shame.

"Your husband is a lucky man," Kit said between mouthfuls.

"Oh, go on with you," said Min.

Hero lay in bed, staring at the window where a subtle glow gave evidence to a new day, but the sound of raindrops continued. From the direction of the hearth, she could hear Kit's soft breathing, as she had throughout the night, and she felt a sudden pressure behind her eyes.

If she had not slept as well as the night before, Hero blamed her strange surroundings. Inns, with their impersonal accommodations, whether shabby or elegant, were a known commodity, while this place and the quiet farm life it represented was as foreign to her as an Indian dwelling.

Even though the cozy space was warm and dry, the bed as clean as Hero was herself, she had tossed and turned all night. But she suspected it had more to do with what was missing than anything else. Lying there in the half-light, she had to admit that no number of blankets could produce the heat generated by Kit Marchant, who had chosen to bed down upon the floor.

It was the only sensible decision, and yet Hero decried it. Even now she was tempted to join him on the floor, just to be beside him, a mad impulse that set Hero's heart to pounding at the possibility that what she most feared was finally happening. Was she losing her heart or her mind?

A knock on the door made her start, and she reached for the pistol tucked beneath her pillow, but no one tried to enter the room.

"Breakfast is on," the woman of the house called. "Come while it's hot or go without."

Weapon at the ready, Hero watched the door for a long moment before her attention was drawn to the man in front of the hearth. The sound had woken him, and he rolled over, looking delightfully disheveled. His dark hair hung over his eyes, and Hero felt her throat thicken. The worn shirt he wore only made him look more appealing, more manly, more *real. Or was it all part of her fantasy?*

"Ah, breakfast on the farm," he said, his voice deep from sleep. "Who could want more than that?"

Hero shook her head, though she had many more wants, all of them impossible and most of them generated by the man who rose to his feet with such casual grace. Wildly, she wondered whether he could hear her heart pounding at the sight of him, but he seemed oblivious.

"Hurry, I don't want to miss a bite," he said, flicking a dark lock back from his face. "That tart last night was better than anything we've had on the road."

Food didn't interest her at all, but Hero knew she could not remain in bed. Slipping out from the covers, she did the best she could with her hair, thankful for the cap that covered it. If questioned as to why she wore one in the house, she would claim that a scalp problem required constant covering and hope that fears of contracting it would silence the family.

Kit was out the door before she had her boots on, and Hero hurried to keep up with him, following as he veered toward the sound of voices. There, they found the whole family seated at a long table in a dining room, and Hero paused on the threshold to stare at the sight of children eating with adults. Min and Bert or one of the older boys were helping the little ones, but the six youngsters seemed to talk in unison and wiggle as though unable to keep still.

Kit did not hesitate, but stepped forward, while Hero lingered, uncertain. In her dealings with Raven or his antiquarian acquaintances, she had never faced anything like this.

"Here, come sit by me, sir!"

"No, me!"

It took Hero a moment to realize the boys were shouting at her. She looked around for Kit, but he was sandwiched between two of the older ones.

"Settle down, now, lads," Bert said. "Sid can find his seat without any help from you."

Sid? Again, it seemed like a good minute passed before Hero realized they were referring to her, and she hastened to the nearest spot, tucked between two of the smaller fellows.

But her heart was hammering, for when was the last time she had forgotten her role? Although she had never masqueraded as a youth for long, she had always been able to keep her mind on her task. *Always.* Without such concentration, she was liable to make a mistake, a dangerous liability.

Focusing her attention, Hero resolved to eat as quickly as possible in order to soon make her escape from the Smallpeace household and its sharp-eyed matriarch. But the boys kept trying to serve her helpings, and she had to stop them from slopping food all over the table. The one on her right, Max, even dropped a piece of toast in the milk she had been given.

Although Hero tried to follow the adult conversation, there was too much going on around her, too many voices raised in high spirits. She heard something about clothes not being entirely dry and the rain continuing. Was Kit agreeing to remain here?

"We really need to reach our destination, brother," Hero said, dodging a bit of food that flew from Ty's mouth while he talked beside her.

"Nonsense! You'll not get far in this weather. Better to rest yourselves for a day," Min said, and Hero shot her a suspicious glance. She did not trust these seemingly innocent people, though she could not figure out what possible connection they could have to the Mallory.

"Sir? Sir? *Sir!*" Hero gasped as the boy on her left, Danny, tugged on her shirt sleeve. Unlike Kit, she had been given an old waistcoat that hid her breasts, though not as well as her usual costume. But she did not need anyone pulling on her clothes and revealing her secret.

Detaching his grip, she leaned toward the boy's dark head. "What?"

"If you stay, you can meet Harold and George."

For an instant, Hero imagined liveried assailants hiding in the barn, waiting until she and Kit had been lulled into a false sense of security. "Who are Harold and George?"

The boy mumbled an answer, his mouth full of food, and she was forced to duck her head closer to his own.

"They're my kittens."

Hero's face was only inches from the boy's, and instead of viewing him as a strange, vaguely threatening creature, she realized he looked more like an angel, his eyes shining brightly as he spoke. "Kittens," Hero echoed.

"Yes, they're lovely," he said. "You'll love them, too." He reached up to touch her cheek as if in reassurance, and Hero felt the now familiar pressure at the back of her eyes. And for the first time, it had nothing to do with Christopher Marchant.

Maybe she *was* going mad. And yet, the sensation was not frightening. In fact, she lifted a hand to awkwardly pat the boy's head. And when she glanced up, she found Kit watching her so avidly that she blinked.

He raised a finger to point to his cheek. "Um, you've got a bit of jam…"

Embarrassed, Hero swiped at her face with her napkin, removing a splotch of red.

"You'll do well when you have children of your own," Min said approvingly, but Hero jerked in alarm. That could never happen. *Must never happen.*

To cover her reaction, Hero finally resumed eating her breakfast, which tasted as good as Kit had predicted. And after the meal was finished, the youngest dragged her into the main room of the house, which was cluttered with a variety of clothes and toys and implements, none of them collectible, but all more important to these people than anything Raven possessed.

Again, Hero was reminded of her duty, and she realized that she needed to talk to Kit about leaving. But he had promised to play with the children, and they were leaping around him as though he were the Pied Piper, shouting so happily that she could not be heard above the dim.

While they played some kind of game involving marbles, Hero took the opportunity to watch her companion, noting his loose-limbed grace, the wide shoulders that filled out the simple shirt, and the crinkles at the corners of his eyes that proved how often he smiled. His laughter rang out repeatedly, as did that of the boys, until Hero felt as though she had stumbled into a fairy story, where all was warmth and ease.

She knew that the lot of the farm family was not as appealing as it seemed, dependent as they were upon weather and hard work. But there were no harsh words spoken in this house, no machinations, no deceptions, no vying for power. What was treasured was character and goodness and willingness to complete chores, not some trinket whose value was set by greedy old men counting their coins.

Strangers, instead of being judged upon their business acumen, were welcomed and dragged out to the barn to meet Harold and George. Part of a seemingly enormous population of felines, the two were Danny's favorites, an orange tabby and a calico that were smaller than most of the others.

Danny instructed her carefully on how to pick them up. "You mustn't hurt them," he said. "But if you are nice to them, they'll be nice to you."

Such wisdom from such a little fellow, Hero thought, and advice that she should heed more often. Despite Raven's claims otherwise, not everyone was out for their own gain. And Hero recognized that Kit just might be one of those who acted out of charity, not selfishness. Perhaps it was time to let her suspicions go and accept him for what he was, a gentleman.

Lost in thought, Hero was surprised when Danny pressed one of the kittens to her face. The soft fur tickled her skin, as did the gentle purring, and she felt her heart lurch in her chest. Although there were cats on the property, Raven did not believe in pets, so Hero had never befriended them. And, no doubt, he would prevent her from doing so.

That realization left Hero feeling pensive as they returned to the house. Once inside, Danny asked her what she would like to see now, and Hero automatically asked if the family owned any books. The boy excitedly led her to an area in the kitchen where there was a comfortable chair and a small cupboard that held a variety of titles.

"Because of the heat and smoke and moisture, this isn't the best place to keep them," Hero warned.

"Oh, we don't keep them, we read them," Danny explained, which made Hero smile. *As well they should*, she thought.

Crouching before the cupboard, she had just begun to look through the volumes when Kit came to join her. He leaned close to whisper in her ear. "Tell me you aren't going to steal any rare editions from these people."

Startled by his words, Hero jerked her head up, nearly knocking into him. Surely he did not think so little of her? But his mouth was twisted into a wry grin, and she shook her head. Would she ever grow accustomed to his teasing?

It was after he had turned away and Hero was left holding one of the Smallpeaces' older volumes in her hand that the idea came to her. She nearly flinched at the audacity of the notion, but refused to dismiss it outright. After all, she knew how much Raven was willing to pay for the Mallory, so she could guess just how much the edition was worth.

The question was whether she could use the book as a bargaining chip—and gain something for herself for the first time in her life.

While the boys raced outside, Kit stood in the doorway of the stone farmhouse, lingering in order to slip Min a payment for her hospitality. Although she waved him away at first, he persisted, for no inn would have provided such good care.

More importantly, the doubts that had nagged at him since his first glimpse of Hero Ingram had faded away in the midst of the farm family's friendly embrace. Hero might have behaved awkwardly at first, but Kit watched her now as she reached down to hug the youngest, and he could envision his own dark-haired boy in her arms.

"Tell me you'll be marrying the lass."

The words that so mirrored his thoughts made Kit suck in a sharp breath. He turned to see Min's shrewd gaze upon him, leaving him no opportunity to dissemble.

"Of course," he answered simply.

"When?" Min demanded.

"She's a bit reluctant," Kit said, though that was an understatement. Sometimes, he felt like one of those fellows who tamed wild horses, using lots of patience and a gentle hand in order to coax a ride from the most wary. But Kit's recent experiences had taught him that the important things in life were worth the effort.

"What? Why?" Min asked. "Surely you're a prize to please even the most discerning."

Kit studied the unusual creature before him, dressed as a youth and knee-deep in little boys. Although she was out of her usual habitat here, Kit had never seen her behave more naturally. "I don't know," he muttered. "But I'm going to find out."

Hero picked at the meat pie they had sneaked into their room, hoping to eat in silence. Lately, Kit had been asking her all sorts of probing questions about her childhood, her interests, what music she liked, and what books she'd read. But with the exception of the last, she had little enough to share.

Tonight, presumably their last before reaching their destination, Hero longed to just enjoy the company that she would not be keeping much longer. But, as had become his habit, Kit turned to her with a curious glance.

"Have you ever been to Almack's?"

Hero nearly choked on her dry forkful at the question. The thought of Raven making an appearance at the exclusive assembly rooms was laughable. As was the idea of him sending her there. Unless she could complete a book transaction in some secluded alcove, while the *ton* danced around her, there would be no reason for Hero to venture into that world.

"No," she answered, without elaborating. "Have you?"

Kit shook his head. "I understand that you have to be invited to attend, and I've only been to London a few times."

The thought of Kit among all the marriageable young ladies gave Hero a pang, but she pictured him looking dashing in his finest clothes and dancing with the skill he evidenced in everything else. "Since your sister is marrying a viscount, she should be able to gain you admittance."

Kit laughed. "I can't quite picture Syd there, following their strict social rules. And she would have no need to go," he said. "I thought the main purpose of the dancing there was for young ladies to make a good match. Isn't that why it's called the Marriage Mart?"

"I wouldn't know."

"And why should you? You've no need of their services," Kit said. "A beautiful, clever young woman like you could have your pick of suitors. They probably trail after you eating out of your hand, though perhaps not when you are dressed like this."

"No," Hero said, smiling at his lifted brows. No one in society would approve of her disguise or her duties. But then, she didn't aspire to such company.

"No, what?" Kit asked, not to be diverted from his probing.

"No, I don't have any suitors," Hero said. "Where would I make such conquests?" She hesitated to admit that Kit was the first eligible young man she had really met.

"You've never been to balls, dances, country house visits?" Kit asked, his expression dumbfounded.

Obviously, the gentleman farmer had an unrealis-

tic view of her position. Even in the wealthiest of
households, poor relations served as retainers, com-
panions, nursemaids or other drudges. At least her occupation was a more interesting one, and in dealing
with antiquarians, Hero had met far more unfortunate
females—wives, sisters and aunts relegated to unpaid
service.

But Hero had no interest in discussing the plight of
women. Suffice to say that Kit was wrong in his assessment of Raven as the sort of person who attended such
activities or hosted them. "Raven doesn't believe in pur-
poseless socializing," she explained. "He has no interest
in others unless he can acquire something from them."

"So he only lets you out to do his bidding?" Kit
asked, giving her a sharp look.

Perhaps she had said too much. "You make it sound
like I'm a prisoner," Hero protested, her tone light.

"Are you?" Kit's usual careless demeanor was
gone, and he suddenly looked dark and dangerous.

Hero's heart pounded, for she had no wish to en-
tangle this man any further in her problems. Raven's
reach was long, his resources many, and she did not
want his machinations to extend to Kit Marchant.

"I am grateful for the home Raven's given me,"
Hero said. Rising to her feet, she signaled an end to
the conversation.

Kit looked as though he would like to say more,
but, as usual, he respected her wishes, and Hero knew
a measure of relief for that. But her uneasiness
lingered, and suddenly, she hoped that Raven had no
idea where she was or who she was with; a hope, like
so many others, that was probably in vain.

Chapter Ten

Once they reached London, they were able to find Marcus Featherstone's home without much trouble, blending into the bustle of town, crowded with conveyances and horses and people hurrying about their business.

"This is it," Kit said, inclining his head toward a tall brick facade in one of the less fashionable squares.

His words seemed sadly prophetic, for this *was* it, perhaps the end of their search and of so much else, Hero realized. Swallowing hard against the sudden thickness in her throat, she knew she must focus on the task at hand, for she would need all her wits about her if she were to carry out her plan.

And that plan meant she was loath to contact Raven, as she once might have, for information about Marcus Featherstone. But without Raven's supply of facts, secrets and rumours that might be used to her advantage, Hero would be going in blind. So she remained leaning against the wrought-iron railings, hesitant to take the next step, for she suspected that Featherstone was not as careless as Cheswick.

"Once we speak to him, word will get out we are looking for something," Hero said to Kit. "And then we'll not only have the duke's men, but every collector in the city in pursuit."

Kit appeared dubious, for he was not convinced of the power of book madness, but he said nothing. And with a frown, Hero finally pushed away from the fence and headed toward the steps to seek out the owner of the Mallory.

A rather worn-looking butler answered their knock, only to inform them that Mr Featherstone was not at home.

"But we've come from Cheswick," Hero said, inching inside before the door could be closed against them. "The earl himself sent us upon an errand."

The butler looked them up and down and shook his head. "You may come in, if you insist, but he is not here."

Featherstone didn't appear to be all that was missing, Hero noted as she looked around. The foyer was empty of furniture, paintings and other decoration, and a glance through doorways into other rooms revealed little else. Was Featherstone moving? Hero felt a stab of panic.

"Is there a man of business we can speak to?" Kit asked.

"All creditors should present a detailed account," the butler said. "If you have one, I can take it."

"We aren't creditors," Hero protested. "We're here on an important errand, referred by Cheswick himself."

The world-weary butler did not appear impressed.

"It concerns a book from the earl's collection," Kit said. "If you would show us into the library—"

The butler shook his head. "The library is empty, sir."

"Empty? But what happened to all the books?"

"I couldn't say, sir."

Hero had an inkling. *Creditors.* Perhaps the collection had been sold to pay them off, she thought with a sinking feeling. But she drew herself up and donned her most businesslike expression. "Then it is even more vital that we speak to Mr Featherstone at once, for the offer I have for this edition could go a good deal toward paying off any debts he may have incurred recently."

The butler appeared skeptical, but shrugged. Perhaps he had gone without his own wages for some time and was long past caring. "You might look for him at the Three Aces," the fellow said.

"The Three Aces?"

The butler pursed his lips. "I believe it is a gaming establishment located on St James's Street."

"Thank you," Hero said. "We will seek him out there."

"No, we won't," Kit whispered as they made their exit. "It must be a gambling hell," he added, once outside. "A wretched establishment designed to part the green or desperate from their money. More often than not, the poor devils can't even win fairly, and if they do, hired thugs are on hand to dispute it."

When they reached the railings, Hero halted. "You are probably right, and normally I wouldn't choose to visit. But this could be our only chance to talk to Featherstone."

"We can wait here until he comes back," Kit suggested.

"*If* he comes back," Hero said, turning to face Kit. "We could kick our heels here indefinitely while Featherstone disappears to the Continent or elsewhere, fleeing one step ahead of his creditors."

"But you can't just walk into such a place and talk to him," Kit said with more vehemence than usual. "These sorts of dens frown on idle chatter."

"Then we'll have to join in the play, if that's the only way to speak to Featherstone."

Kit looked pained. "And what are you going to use for a stake? Those with empty pockets aren't welcome."

"I have some money from Raven to use for expenses, if necessary, in order to procure the Mallory."

Kit frowned. "Fine. I'll go," he said. "We'll find somewhere safe for you to wait since genteel young ladies don't frequent St James's, and I'll talk to Featherstone."

Hero was touched, as always, by his protectiveness. The fact that he still saw her as a genteel young lady after all they had been through said more about Kit than herself. But she shook her head. They were too close, and this was too important for her to take any chances.

For a moment, Hero thought Kit might argue, but he groaned, a sure sign of his capitulation, and she took comfort in the knowledge that he would be with her a little bit longer.

"It could be worse, you know," she said as they headed for St James's.

"What could be worse than marching into a gambling hell with you dressed like that?" Kit asked.

She flashed him a smile, eager to prove that he wasn't the only one with a sense of humor. "At least it isn't a brothel."

Kit stood in front of the Three Aces, eyeing the facade with a jaundiced eye. Although not as elegant as some of the other establishments, such as Crockford's, it gave an appearance of gentility, which probably was why it drew the likes of Marcus Featherstone.

The two massive "gentlemen" at the door looked them up and down with such disrespect that Kit moved closer to Hero, wary that her disguise had been penetrated. It was one thing for her to ride upon the roads dressed as she was, quite another to travel about the city, where all manner of villains were ready to prey upon women and young men alike.

"Are you members?" one of the giants asked, and Kit choked back a snort. Surely, they weren't required to join in order to lose their fortunes at the shady tables inside?

"Marcus Featherstone wanted us to meet him here," Hero said.

"We don't allow creditors to bother our patrons," the other fellow said, studying them through narrowed eyes.

"We're here to recoup our losses…or perhaps not," Kit said, adopting a bored tone.

"He must have a private game going on upstairs," the one fellow said to the other as he ushered them inside.

The interior of the Three Aces was spacious, boasting several salons with high ceilings, chandeliers and mirrors that reflected the scene. Men crowded around the green baize tables of hazard, faro and the decidedly illegal E.O., while servers provided tea or stronger brews. The more serious players wore odd coats or leather protectors upon their sleeves and bizarrely decorated hats in order to conceal their eyes from the light and their thoughts from each other.

When a loud bang erupted from above, Kit wondered what kind of "private games" were to be had there. Some of these places were supposed to be run by famous abbesses, who dealt not only in cards, but in female flesh. The thought that he might have brought Hero into a brothel after all made him wince, and he was all the more eager to complete their business.

"Do you have any idea what Featherstone looks like?" Kit whispered.

"No, but didn't the man say he might be having a private game upstairs?" she asked, glancing in the direction of the curved staircase.

Kit shook his head. "Oh, no, you're not going up there."

But Hero was already moving away from him, toward a drunk stumbling down the steps. "Is Marcus Featherstone up there?" she asked.

"Just blew his head off," the man said. Then he proceeded to cast up his accounts.

Pulling Hero out of the way, Kit wondered if the fellow's words were some kind of gaming cant. A servant came to clean up the mess, but most of the players were too sunk in their own dissipation to even notice the disturbance. The turn of a card, the roll of the dice or the spin of the wheel held them enthralled. Surely, this really was a madness, Kit thought as he surveyed the room.

When he glanced back at Hero, she was again moving toward the stairs, where a couple of white-faced fellows were stumbling down. Whatever the Three Aces was serving up there, it must be strong. Or perhaps the party had been imbibing all night, for when questioned by Hero, they simple shook their heads, hurrying for the exit.

Catching up with her, Kit managed to catch her arm before she could bolt upward. And he was grateful for his hold upon her, for the next two men who appeared were not foxed, but sharp-eyed, shifty-looking fellows. At the sound of Hero's query, they headed straight toward her, frowning and intent.

"I don't think that's him," she managed to say before Kit dragged her away. By the time they reached the exit, Featherstone's name had traveled from one end of the club to the other, voices rising above the usual din of conversation and gambling. And the men who were following them had stepped up their pace.

The burly fellows at the entrance had abandoned their post, perhaps called to more important duties, so Kit and Hero threw open the doors and began to run, trying to disappear into the throng on the street.

"You there, stop!"

The shout that rang out only fueled Kit's steps, and he cursed his height, which made him easier to spot. Ducking, he sought a cart that he and Hero could jump on in order to make their escape. But before he found a likely candidate, Hero surged ahead to where a couple of young men stood with Dandy Horses, or whatever such apparatuses were being called. Knocking one of the fellows aside, Hero climbed on the thing and took off.

Kit could do little else but follow her lead, pushing aside the youth who protested the loss of his fellow's contraption, only to watch himself fall victim. "Excuse me, but I need to borrow this for just a moment," Kit said, as he hopped into the saddle and pushed off as hard as he could. The wheels sent him careening away from his pursuers, and soon he had left both them and the owner of the machine behind.

Kit had seen such things the last time he was in London and knew that young men liked to race them along the thoroughfares, adding to the congestion and crashing into anything and everything. But viewing the contraptions and propelling one were two entirely different things. Without reins, there was no way to change directions, and the two wheels did not respond to nudges, as did a living, breathing animal.

Keeping his balance as best he could, Kit tried to remain upright and propel himself forward, but eventually, he hit a bump in the road and tilted sideways. Although he managed to stop himself by using one leg, he ended up on his side on the ground, his body bruised and battered. Rising to his feet, Kit counted himself lucky not to have caused worse damage.

Kit had been too busy hanging on for dear life to notice what was going on about him, but now he looked frantically for Hero. Although he saw no sign of her, the other Dandy Horse was propped against a shopfront up ahead. Kit put his own beside it, for retrieval by the owner, and looked inside the small shop, but Hero was not there. Stepping outside again, he scanned the crowd to no avail, his worst fears realized at last.

She was gone.

Kit hurried to the inn, afraid of what he might—or might not—find there. Just in case their meeting with Featherstone could not be conducted at once, they had taken a room on the outskirts of the city. It was genteel enough to pass as long-term accommodations for visitors, but out of the way in order to avoid any acquaintances. *Although it didn't sound like Hero had many.*

Kit amended that thought. Hero didn't have the experiences of a typical young woman in society, so she could not count upon such friends for help. But such friends probably would be of little help anyway, especially if she made an afternoon call while wearing boy's clothing.

But Hero might well have contacts throughout town, collectors, book dealers and even seamier sorts that might serve her better. Kit only hoped she was somewhere safe and hadn't been snatched off the streets. No matter how capable she seemed, she was still a woman alone in a dangerous city, harried by at least two villains.

Kit went up the stairs of the inn as fast as he could without drawing attention to himself. Upon reaching the door, caution made him knock softly before opening it. But there was no answer to his summons, and the room, when he entered, was empty.

Cursing under his breath, Kit walked the length and breadth of the space, as though Hero might be hidden behind the curtains or beneath the bed. Unable to face the emptiness, he left as quickly as he had come, hurrying out to check the common room and the courtyard for signs of her low-slung cap. But soon it became evident that Hero was not skulking anywhere around the inn under any guise, male or female.

Kit considered returning to the area where he'd last seen her, but he guessed she hadn't stayed around there any longer than he had. He could go looking for her at Raven Hill, but she appeared extremely wary of returning home, and Kit had no desire to explain to Augustus Raven how he had allowed her to go missing.

The inn was the only meeting place that they had agreed upon, and there was little sense in heading back out to comb the city. Finally, Kit was forced to accept that he had only one choice.

So he sat down to wait.

Hero didn't pause to look behind her. When her velocipede crashed into the rear of a moving cart, she dropped it to the ground and clambered into the load of hay in front of her. Hoping someone would retrieve the abandoned apparatus, she burrowed deep and leaned against the rear panel. It was only after she'd finally caught her breath that she realized Kit had not joined her.

Frantically pushing aside some of the hay that cushioned her, Hero peeked through a crack in the wood, but she could not see him. Even the buildings looked different, and she realized the cart must have turned, its different route taking her farther away from Kit.

A sharp stab of panic nearly sent her leaping from her berth, but the wariness that had served her well in the past kept Hero from moving. If she left her hiding place, there was no guarantee that she would locate Kit, who might have traveled past her in the traffic or fallen behind. But there was a very real danger that she might be found by those who had chased them from the Three Aces.

She could not go back.

With a map of the city in her pocket, Hero could take a sedan chair or some other conveyance back to the inn. But she needed to get her bearings, and the next time the cart slowed, Hero climbed out, slipping into the shadow of the nearest building.

Her first thought was to hurry to the inn, if only to make certain Kit was all right. The fear that he wasn't created a knot in her chest to match the one in her throat. But she needed information, and returning to their room would do little to aid her cause, especially when time was of the essence.

For the first time in years beyond count, Hero felt hope, a fluttering, glimmering glimpse of something beyond the walls of Raven Hill. It was that hope, and the plan it depended upon, that gave her strength of purpose. Hailing a passing boy, she gave him a coin to find out what had happened at the Three Aces in St James's, promising him another coin upon his return.

The sun would be setting soon, so Hero urged him to hurry. And just in case he should be waylaid, she glanced across the street for a place to wait and watch for his return. As fate would have it, there stood a bookshop, William Strong's, and Hero headed toward it.

These days the retail book trade was centred in Picadilly, Pall Mall and St James's, with new shops springing up to cater to the customers living in the most fashionable new sections of London. But Hero rarely did business in such public places, so she did not know them all.

Still, the moment she entered, she was assailed by the familiar smells of ink and paper and leather bindings, as though being welcomed home. Inhaling deeply, Hero wandered the premises, looking over the newest publications, as well as the many reprints of older titles, while glancing periodically out of the bow windows for the boy.

William Strong's had nothing for the serious collector, unless such offerings were kept behind the counter, and Hero resisted the temptation to ask. The less contact she had with others while in her current guise, the better. Such thoughts set her nerves on edge, and at the sound of a door opening, Hero flinched. Since she heard no corresponding tinkle of the bell, she glanced up warily.

The front of the shop was still and quiet, so she looked over her shoulder. Behind the long counter, a door had opened, perhaps leading to a storage area or select stock. The latter was probably likely because the man who exited clutched a wrapped parcel to his breast. He was short, with dark, stringy hair and shifty eyes, and Hero was struck by the sensation she had seen him before.

Quickly, she turned her head and hunched over a book to avoid notice. Was he one of Raven's minions, or just a fellow buyer she had glimpsed during some past encounter? Either way, he should not recognize her, dressed in her boy's costume.

Yet, somehow Hero felt his gaze upon her. Refusing to look up, she ducked her head and tugged on her cap, pulling it down over her face. Hardly daring to breath, she waited for the sound of footsteps to go past her, but they did not, and suddenly she was nearly knocked down by a hard jolt.

"Excuse me…sir." The man's voice sounded odd, and Hero did not respond, but crouched to retrieve the volume she had been holding, her eyes focused on a pair of worn boots.

"How clumsy of me," the fellow said. "I hope you are not hurt."

Shaking her head, Hero cursed herself for stepping into the shop. She should have known better, for the book world was an insular one where most serious players knew each other by name, by reputation, and perhaps even by face.

When the man finally shuffled away, Hero still kept her head low, refusing to lift it until she heard the tinkle of the bell over the door. Only then did she sur-reptitiously peek around the cover of the volume she held to her face. She was in time to see the back of the shifty-eyed man's coat as he stepped outside, confirming her suspicions that he was the one who had run into her. But was the action deliberate?

Putting aside the book, Hero walked to the bow windows, but the man had already disappeared into the street. Had theirs been a random encounter, or was he even now hurrying to alert Raven to her presence in town? Hero knew only that she could not afford to linger here where she had been marked.

Slipping from the shop, she glanced up and down the street, taking special note of any shadowy corners where shifty eyes might be watching. Although she did not see him, she saw the boy she had paid approaching their meeting place. Again, Hero scanned the area for any signs that he might be accompanied or followed, then hurried across the roadway to meet him.

"Sorry I'm late, sir, but I'm not used to finding out the news, just handing it out. I'd sold all my gazettes when you saw me. But now, I'm thinking I might just become a reporter someday."

"Maybe," Hero answered, too nervous to smile at the boy's bravado. "What did you find out?"

"It was a shooting," he said. "A gentleman killed himself right in one of the gambling places, not one of the fancier establishments, mind you, but still, the kind where they aren't used to that sort of thing. It's called the Three Aces. He'd lost his fortune, they said."

Hero felt a stab of panic. "Killed himself? Are you sure he's dead?"

"Saw him for myself, sir," the boy said. "Or what was left of him as they carried him out. I guess his brains are splattered all over the salon where he did it. And on some of the patrons, too, I'll warrant."

Hero felt sick. Perhaps men, even boys such as this one, could handle such frank talk, but her stomach churned and bile filled her throat.

"You all right, sir?" the boy asked.

Hero nodded, trying to fight off the nausea that threatened, along with the emotions that Raven claimed she didn't possess. He was wrong, of course. She simply had learned to keep her feelings to herself, and now she used that skill to dismiss visions of Marcus Featherstone, a young man in the prime of life, reduced to debris on the mirrors of the Three Aces. She had never met him, but he was a lover of books, a collector, someone's friend, someone's relative, and Hero felt the loss.

Fighting against the thickness in her throat, Hero managed to catch her breath only when her own loss became glaringly apparent. Without Featherstone, how was she to follow the trail of the Mallory? Her sorrow over his death twisted into despair, as all the hopes and plans she had so recently devised were dashed.

Was she doomed to resume her old life, hunting and fetching at Raven's beck and call, prey to his increasingly bizarre whims? Hero's heart thudded at the thought of returning to that world of darkness and gloom, greed and deception. Helpless. *Hopeless.* After her brief escape, it would only be that much harder to endure.

As would Raven's displeasure at her failure.

Perhaps Kit was right about the Mallory. It certainly

had a history of bringing misfortune to all those who owned it—from the murdered author through to poor Featherstone, dead by his own hand. In that case, Raven would be a fitting owner for the calamitous volume, Hero thought, though she instantly regretted it. Despite all, she did not wish Raven ill, just that she might be free of him.

If only there was a way to satisfy him without actually proffering the book, but how? If the Mallory had been among Featherstone's possessions, it would eventually make an appearance. Unless, if Kit was correct, and there was no copy to be found, then…

Suddenly, Hero thought of Thomas Laytham, a respected bookseller and collector whom Raven dismissed with contempt. Although Laytham hadn't a hint of scandal to his name, Raven didn't trust him or the hundred-year-old pamphlets that he was famous for procuring for his wealthy clients.

"He's a clever one, I'll give him that," Raven had told her. "And as long as he does me no ill, I'll keep my suspicions to myself. But it takes one to recognize one, my dear, and I think someday the truth will come out when it comes to the revered Mr Laytham."

The idea that came to Hero now was so audacious, her breath caught. Surely nothing could come of her wild notion, yet the urge to pursue it was so strong that she could not easily dismiss it.

"Are you all right, sir?"

Absorbed in her own thoughts, Hero had nearly forgotten the boy standing before her until he spoke. "Yes," Hero answered, handing him the coin she had promised.

"Will there be anything else, sir?"

Glancing at the waning day, Hero was filled with a sudden urgency. "Yes, you may fetch me a hackney coach."

While Hero watched the boy set off with a nod, she realized she wouldn't have time to return to the inn. But perhaps that was just as well, for she suspected that Kit would not approve over her plan. *It was not the act of a gentleman.*

But Kit could not understand what this opportunity meant to her. He'd never been desperate, for even stripped of his property, he had opportunities. He could join the military, take up a trade, cast himself in with friends or relatives. Hero could do none of that. Still, she did not want him to think poorly of her—or see her for what she was: what Raven had made her.

In an instant, Hero decided to pursue this scheme alone, though her pulse pounded at the thought. Raven's presence in her life had been omnipresent and stifling, but the realization that she had no one, not a chaperone or footman or companion of any sort at her side, was more alarming than freeing.

The wisest course would be to send a message to Mr Laytham, but Hero could not risk anyone learning of her interest. Nor did she have the time to wait for an appointment. If the shifty-eyed patron at William Strong's recognized her and reported her presence to Raven, it wouldn't be long before his minions were out looking for her.

Her heart hammering, Hero hesitated, but the stakes were too high to give in to personal fears. When the hackney coach arrived, she straightened her spine, stood tall, and gave the driver the address of Thomas Laytham, Bookseller.

Chapter Eleven

Mr Laytham was not in the habit of working behind the counter in his shop, so Hero spoke to one of the men in his employ. Since her clothing hardly marked her as the sort of wealthy client with whom Laytham normally dealt, she had to convey that it was a matter of urgency and importance, involving one of the hundred-year-old pamphlets he so prized.

The ploy worked. Hero was immediately shown into an office where Laytham conducted his more mundane business. He was an older man, his middle grown thick, with a shock of white hair and the air of a scholar about him. At the sight of his solemn demeanor, Hero felt her resolve weakening and took a deep breath.

"And what is so important, pray tell, Mr…?" Laytham looked askance at her obvious youth and ill-fitting clothes.

"Sidney Marchant," Hero answered automatically. "Thank you for seeing me, sir."

By all appearances, Mr Laytham was just what he professed to be, a gentleman, a collector and a purveyor of books, and yet Raven was rarely wrong in his assessment of people. And despite Laytham's studied air of annoyance as he looked down his nose at her, Hero thought she detected a bead of sweat upon his brow. Either way, there was only one way to play this.

"I'm here for a favor, actually," Hero said in her most businesslike manner. "I'm looking for a book by Ambrose Mallory."

Laytham grunted in surprise. "Aren't we all?"

Hero smiled. Leaning forward, she steepled her hands in front of her. "Yes, but all I need is a facsimile."

Did the man twitch? Hero saw a flash of something in his eyes before the white brows lifted, and she was grateful for the years of experience that kept her own face impassive.

"I don't know what you mean," he said.

"It's a prank," Hero said, falling back against the elegant cushion of her chair. "Nothing that will be sold, of course, but it must be able to pass initial scrutiny."

Laytham's brows fairly leaped off his face, which was growing ruddy in color. "You are asking me to…find you an edition of a book that is not authentic? A…hoax?"

Hero nodded. "It shouldn't be difficult." Indeed, she could do it herself, if she had access to an antiquarian library, except for printing the title page and the cover. After all, no one knew the contents except for some dead Druids. "Since there are no reliable sources as to the contents, any old occult text would do."

Laytham's skin turned beet-red. "And why on earth should I agree to this preposterous request?"

Hero met his angry stare without wavering. "I think you know why."

Laytham held her gaze for a long moment before looking away. "If you mean to tell me that you have chosen Laytham's for its ability to acquire the unusual and meet its customers' expectations, I will not disagree. However, what you are asking for is hardly within our purview."

Hero said nothing, while Laytham fiddled with his watch fob, then grunted, as though coming to a decision. "If it is to be used only for amusement, I suppose I could ask one of my contacts within the book business to prepare something for you." He paused to eye her directly. "No money would change hands, of course."

"Of course," Hero said, though she had not foreseen this development. She had been prepared to use some of Raven's funds in order to deceive him, an irony that was not lost upon her. But obviously, Laytham was more concerned with whom she might be working for, and it was not Raven or any other collector who had him worried. Someone in authority or a wealthy patron could well have put her up to this game in order to catch Laytham at it.

"I'll need the volume as soon as possible," Hero added.

Laytham winced, but nodded. "And where shall I have the parcel delivered?"

"I'll come to pick it up," Hero said, unwilling to give out an address, even that of the inn. "Tomorrow."

"That's absurd," Laytham sputtered. "It might take weeks—or months—to find an appropriate text."

I don't have months or weeks or perhaps even days, Hero wanted to scream. But she schooled her features to reveal none of her panic. "The day after."

"The ink will hardly have time to dry upon the page!" Laytham protested.

"Then let it smear," Hero said. "I'm sure you don't want long, drawn-out dealings in this matter."

Gaping at her, Laytham shook his head in honest reaction. Then he rose to his feet and ushered her from the room, displaying only the barest civility, his relief at her departure obvious.

Once outside the bookshop, Hero felt her knees shake, and she leaned against a nearby fence in order to right herself. She was playing a dangerous game—one that could cost her everything, for she shuddered to think of what would happen if Raven found her out. But when fright threatened to overcome her, Hero told herself that she would use what Laytham provided only if absolutely necessary.

Meanwhile, she could still try to track down Featherstone's books. With that in mind, Hero went over all that had led her to this point, considering any pieces of the puzzle that she might have missed. But she came up with nothing, except the oddity of Raven having the scrap of paper that referred to the Mallory, but not the book itself.

Perhaps Raven alone knew the answer to that mystery. And yet…there might be another who could help. Straightening with new determination, Hero pushed away from the fence and began looking for another hackney coach. By now it was full dark, and she had no intention of walking the streets of London alone, even in boy's garb. Besides the various men who had trailed her since Oakfield, she wanted to escape anyone who might have followed her out of Laytham's.

For Hero was not so witless as to savor her triumph over the bookseller. A lifetime of wariness told her that despite the seeming ease of her transaction, she might have made a powerful enemy—to add to those already in pursuit.

Kit was pacing. It was something Barto might have done while Kit watched askance, sprawled in comfort, with no real worries of his own. But now he understood the need for movement, the urge to do something to alleviate the fear that pressed down on him like a weight. *Fear for Hero.*

Looking back, Kit wished that he had not left St James's, but had combed the area for her. He had thought the Dandy Horse proof of her escape, but anyone could have retrieved it and propped it there for its owner—even the two men from the Three Aces.

The thought of Hero being manhandled by those thugs and discovering that they had a young woman, not a boy, in their clutches was enough to make Kit's blood run cold. They were after money, he told himself, not anything else, yet that sort could easily turn from bad to worse.

And here he was, useless and helpless, just as he'd

been at Oakfield. Swearing under his breath, Kit swung a fist in the air, nearly punching a hole in the wall. At the thud of a knock, he looked at his own hand, as though it was responsible. Then he turned toward the door, where a chambermaid probably waited to light the fire.

But when he thrust open the worn wood, Hero stood before him, and without conscious thought, Kit snatched her up in his arms, hugging her to him with bone-crushing zeal. He might have kissed her, too, if not for the sound of a throat loudly clearing itself down the hall. A glance revealed a large man with expansive mustaches eyeing them with disfavor.

"It's been a long time, brother!" Kit cried, before dragging Hero inside.

And then he did kiss her.

Slamming the door shut, he pushed her up against the smooth surface and lowered his head, taking her mouth for the first time since those brief moments in the library at Cheswick. And this was no tentative exploration, but a white-hot possession, an exultation that she was here and unharmed.

When his lips touched hers, Kit felt her startlement, yet she was soon clinging to him, returning his greeting in kind. Her arms wrapped around his neck, and her body, dressed in boy's clothes, strained against his own. He kissed her until they were both breathless, his blood running loud and fast in his ears, and still he did not stop. The cold room, bereft of light and fire, dropped away, leaving only heat and scent and sensation.

The darkness had always been his downfall where

Hero was concerned, for it was easier to ignore the promptings of his conscience when nothing existed except the two of them. Running a hand up the back of her neck, he knocked aside her cap and loosed her hair, wrapping his fingers in the smooth silkiness, just as he tried to wrap himself around every bit of her.

In fact, he might have tried to take her to the bed, stumbling across the unfamiliar floor to grope for its soft surface, if not for the knock that soon sounded. Kit was of a mind to ignore it, but he felt Hero stiffen in his arms, and then her palm came up to cover his mouth, a silent warning not to forget their situation.

Kit stepped back, prepared to tackle anyone who would gain entry, all his unspent passion now changed to fury. But it was only the chambermaid, coming to light the fire. Mumbling uneasily, she cast an odd glance at the darkened room seemingly occupied by two men, for Hero stood behind Kit, her hair and cap restored.

If only Kit could regain his senses so easily. As soon as the maid left, he turned on Hero. "Where the devil have you been?" He lifted a hand to run through his hair. "I nearly went mad with worry!"

"I was trying to find out what happened to Featherstone."

"Featherstone!" Kit wanted to throttle her. "Don't tell me you went back to the hell."

She shook her head. "I paid a boy to nose around and report back."

Kit felt a tumult of anger and relief. "You should have come directly here," he said, even though he knew remonstrance was useless. Hero would always follow her own course, risking her life over what seemed senseless to him. With the taste of her still on his lips, Kit wondered whether she would ever be content to sit back, out of harm's way, with no dealings to make, no mystery to unravel, no treasures to search out.

The thought sent his mood deflating like one of Montgolfier's balloons, all his emotions spent. Perhaps the answer he'd been seeking had been before him all along, a realization that left him stunned and gaping, while Hero prattled on about Featherstone.

"What?" Kit asked, his voice strained, as he tried to marshal his wits.

"They're saying Featherstone shot himself, supposedly despondent over losing his fortune."

"I imagine his fellows think ill of him for dirtying up their table," Kit muttered. He had not known Featherstone, but lost fortunes and even deaths were little regarded in a world where gaming was encouraged without thought for the consequences.

"Probably," Hero admitted. She wore an expression Kit had come to know too well, and he stifled a groan.

"What?" he asked.

"I'm sure the boy faithfully reported what people were saying, but what if Featherstone didn't shoot himself?" Hero asked. "Perhaps those men who started chasing us killed him over the Mallory."

"In a roomful of gamesters?" Kit asked. "I doubt it."

"We don't know who else was in there."

"I'm guessing the fellow who cast up his accounts at our feet," Kit said drily.

Hero frowned. "But if Featherstone shot himself, why were those two men chasing us?"

"We have a sign over our heads asking two men, not one or three, mind you, to chase us at all times?"

Hero was not amused, and Kit sighed. Sometimes, her logic was more convoluted than sensible, for he could not imagine how two thugs from a gambling hell could be connected to an old book that probably did not exist.

Kit shrugged. "They heard us asking about Featherstone and thought we might be friends or relatives from whom they could squeeze the money he owed them."

"What?"

"Some of these cent-per-centers are quite capable of ungentlemanly actions," Kit explained. "Murder would do them little good, but seeing their hopes of repayment dashed, they might look to their victim's heir. Some hells provide their own unscrupulous lenders in order to better fleece their clients."

Hero appeared unconvinced. "Why would such fellows give chase?"

"To get a name, an address, a payment, a promise. If Featherstone has nothing, they have little chance of recouping their losses, but they might press his acquaintances to make good his name. The entire world doesn't revolve around your quest," Kit said, more sharply than he intended.

"No, but sometimes I think the entire world revolves around Raven," Hero muttered.

"So now what?" Kit asked, before realizing that his words could be interpreted in many different ways.

Hero sat down in the room's only chair, and Kit realized just how tired she must be. He had been so consumed with his own fears and frustrations that he had forgotten that Hero, despite her often stoic bearing, was not invincible. She leaned forward wearily to stare into the fire.

"Obviously, Featherstone cannot tell us the fate of his books," she said. "And we could spend weeks trying to hunt them down, interviewing his servants, his friends, his family."

Was she giving up? The suspicion startled Kit, but her features soon took on the cast he well recognized.

"But I was thinking that there's someone else who might be able to verify where those lots went, someone we might approach first." She glanced up, her gaze intent. "Only the people who arrange the sales can really account for the whereabouts of the volumes under their care."

"You think Featherstone had someone in charge of his collection?" Kit asked, dubious.

"No," Hero said, waving a hand in dismissal. She eyed him intently. "I'm talking about Richard Poynter."

"The man who handled Cheswick's library?"

Hero nodded.

"Do you know where to find him?"

"The world of books is an insular one. And more often than not, the only place one leaves it for is the grave." Leaning over to tug off one of her boots, Hero rubbed the sole of her foot. "These days Mr Poynter works with the London Institution."

Kit shook his head at her determination. There was no stopping her, ever, which meant if she really wanted something, she would surely go after it with the same single-mindedness she exhibited in her search for the Mallory. The thought was a discouraging one.

"Here, let me do that," Kit said. Kneeling before her, he brushed away her protests and unrolled her sock. Her foot was pale and smooth, delicately formed, and cold to the touch. He rubbed it briskly with both hands, then began to gently knead.

"Y-you prove your skills yet again," Hero said softly. She cleared her throat. "For a gentleman farmer you handled the velocipede very well."

"I assume that you didn't see my ignominious dismount," Kit said. "And where did you learn to ride such a beast?"

"One of the antiquarians," she said with a faint smile. "A member of the society gave one to Raven, who had no use for it, of course."

"And you quickly mastered the technique."

"I don't think there is much technique involved," Hero said.

She groaned at his touch, and Kit had to remind himself that the massage he was giving her was therapeutic, not erotic. Removing her second boot, he set to work on the other foot. "Though I imagine one would have an even more difficult time trying to ride side saddle."

Hero made a low sound of amusement that turned into another groan. "I don't care to know how you acquired this skill, gentleman farmer," she said. "But is there nothing you can't do?"

Yes, Kit thought. *I can't seem to capture the one thing I want.* But he didn't voice his thoughts aloud.

Hero leaned back her head and sighed. "Kit..."

"Hmm?"

"You'll remember that you are a...gentleman."

"Yes," Kit assured her, despite his ministrations.

He'd forgotten that for a while, earlier this evening. But it was a momentary lapse in judgement, a mistake that he would not make again.

It felt good to take off the breeches.

Although there was a certain freedom to be had in wearing boy's clothing, Hero was happy to don her feminine garb. And Kit's surprised delight in her transformation only added to her contentment. For a moment, Hero felt nearly normal—until she had to sneak out of their room, which was supposed to be occupied by two brothers from rural environs.

Once they were outside, Hero relaxed into her role and Kit gave her his arm. "To what do I owe the pleasure of your company, miss?" he asked.

Hero tucked her gloved hand over his sleeve, and she was surprised to feel her cheeks grow pink at the gallant gesture. Although they had spent a lot of time together, little of it was in her current guise, and even less engaged in the typical pursuits of a young man and a young woman.

"And where shall we go today, to see the sights of London?" Kit asked, inclining his head toward her.

Hero laughed, though she suspected he might be serious. She was reminded again that her quest was not his, and she was grateful for his continued company. "I live on the outskirts of town, so I am no visitor."

"Well, then, perhaps you would show me the city?"

Hero shook her head, but could not stop her smile. She was glad to see the return of the careless charmer that was Kit. Last night, he had been moody and sulky, unusual behavior for which she felt accountable. Hero didn't know much about what went on between men and women, but she knew that they should not have kissed as they had.

Warmth flooded Hero's cheeks at the memory, a wild, wonderful interlude in which she had thrown caution to the wind, along with most of her wits. But she could not afford to do so again. And walking about the streets of town, where anyone might mark her steps, would not be wise. As she had discovered, Raven's contacts were everywhere.

"I'll be happy to show you the Institution, which is in the house that once belonged to Sir William Clayton," Hero said, focusing upon her goal. "And it is to Richard Poynter that you owe the return of Miss Ingram, for I hope to trade upon my connection to Raven."

The gamble was a risky one, of course, for Raven would soon hear of it and know of her presence in town. *If he didn't know already*, Hero thought, the memory of the shifty-eyed fellow from William Strong's shop still fresh in her mind. But with Featherstone dead, Hero was counting on Richard Poynter's help, and he was far more likely to meet with Miss Ingram than Sid Marchant.

Suddenly, Hero slanted a glance at her companion. "But how shall we introduce you? We can hardly pass you off as my brother."

"Perhaps I could be your cousin, Erasmus."

Hero laughed aloud at the thought of the handsome, dashing and kind Kit impersonating the stooped, balding and grasping Erasmus. She could only hope that Mr Poynter had never met Erasmus before—and that Erasmus would never discover the charade. If she obtained the Mallory, it would matter little, for Raven would handle his nephew, and then…

Hero drew in a sharp breath. *If she obtained the Mallory.* But she refused to consider the possibility that she would not, and she marched up to the Institution, just as though Richard Poynter was expecting her to call.

He wasn't, but they were shown into the small salon, where Hero began to hope that he would see them. She perched nervously on the edge of a cabriolet armchair, while Kit roamed the room, looking at the books that were scattered about.

Hero idly wondered if they had traded places, for she should be the one searching out some rare title in the hopes of bartering it from its owner. And then she wondered at the changes in herself, for not that long ago she would have suspected her gentleman farmer of searching among the volumes for his own gain.

But Kit was no bibliomaniac, and when he spoke, it was not to marvel at some obscure edition, but to quote from it. In the original Greek. Hero glanced up at him in surprise. "You *are* a scholar."

Kit laughed. "Hardly. I just had a good teacher."

"But you are still a reader?"

"Of course, though I've pretty much abandoned the ancient texts that so consumed my father. I'm more interested in the new fields of science, especially agriculture these days," he said, flashing her a grin.

"That doesn't make you any less of a scholar," Hero said, the need to defend him nearly sending her to her feet. Admiration for him swelled, then turned into something else so strong that it nearly frightened her. But she was never one to shrink in fear, and she would not do so now.

"You are a gentleman and a scholar," Hero said, her voice cracking with the force of her emotion.

Kit must have noticed, for he shot her a speculative glance, but Hero was saved from any questions by the arrival of an elderly man. Slender and gray-haired, he introduced himself as Richard Poynter and greeted them graciously. But after a perfunctory glance at Kit, his attention settled upon Hero, his pale blue gaze lingering with interest.

Hero did not flinch under the scrutiny, for she was accustomed to the curiosity of the antiquarian community. Women with aspirations to join the ranks were limited by their lack of education and their inability to travel freely, whether their destination be libraries or ruins. Exceptions, such as Dorothy Richardson and the notable book collector Richardson Currer, were rare, and Hero often had to deal with contemptuous and dismissive colleagues.

But Richard Poynter was not one of those. Gesturing toward the chairs, he took a seat himself, setting aside a pile of papers. "Excuse my haphazard housing here, but I am only providing some aid to the current librarian." He eyed Hero again. "A fact which is not well-known."

"Raven likes to keep well informed."

"I dare say," Poynter said. "I have heard that you

often act for him these days, Miss Ingram. Is he not well?"

"He is fine, but perhaps more reclusive."

"Ah." Poynter nodded, and the simple word implied that he knew far more about Raven than he might say.

"Actually, I'm here on my own," Hero explained. "I was hoping that you might clear up something for me."

Poynter appeared surprised, but he nodded in agreement.

"We've been trying to track some lots from the Cheswick library and have met with a discrepancy. The current earl told us he directed that the volumes go only to certain individuals, yet it appears that Raven possesses at least one."

Hero assumed a suitably puzzled expression. Hopefully, Poynter did not know Raven well enough to suspect he might have obtained the book through questionable means.

Poynter sighed. "Well, you have found me out."

Since Hero had expected him to suggest that Featherstone had sold or gambled away his lots, she tried not to appear shocked at his admission.

"The current earl had some eccentric notions of how to handle the distribution," Poynter said. Though the elderly gentleman maintained his gentle demeanor, Hero suspected he was putting a polite gloss on the experience. However likable the current earl was, he had no respect for books, and a devotee such as Poynter would be appalled, not only by the breaking up of the collection, but by the cavalier instructions.

Pausing, Poynter glanced toward them both. "I

assume you heard of the unfortunate passing of Mr Featherstone."

Hero nodded, as did Kit.

Poynter shook his head. "The earl wanted only those few collectors he liked personally to buy the lots, but I soon came to realize that Featherstone was not in a position to make such a large purchase. Not wanting to go against his lordship's wishes, I suggested to Mr Featherstone that he act as an intermediary, accepting the lot on the behalf of someone else, while taking a small payment for himself to do so."

Poynter paused then, as if assessing his audience. "Naturally, I would not wish to earn the earl's ill will, should he hear of this."

When Hero and Kit both nodded in confirmation of their silence, Poynter eyed Hero with that same look of curiosity she had seen earlier. "Mr Featherstone gladly accepted the commission, handling receipt of the lot that then went to Augustus Raven."

Hero drew in a sharp breath. Did Raven already own the Mallory? She knew that it took time for some buyers to organize and catalogue their purchases, but not Raven, who was meticulous enough to have found the torn scrap of paper that had sent her on this quest.

Was it all some bizarre jest or test, yet another piece of drama orchestrated by Raven? Or had the man finally gone mad, putting her through the paces of a Gothic novel only he envisioned?

"I see you appear baffled," Poynter said. "Isn't that the mystery you were trying to solve? How Raven ended up with the lot that was to go to Featherstone?"

Numbly, Hero nodded.

"Is it possible that someone else might have bought some of the titles?" Kit asked.

Poynter shook his head. "I had dealings with Raven, only, and he is unlikely to have shared his spoils." Poynter then paused as if in thought. "At the time, I was also approached by the Duke of Montford, but too late. The arrangement had already been made with Raven."

Ignoring Kit's startled glance at the mention of the man she so often claimed was pursuing them, Hero kept her attention focused on Poynter, in the hopes that he might reveal something else of interest.

Although Hero had come to think of Montford as a threat, Poynter's expression left no doubt that he would rather have dealt with the duke. He frowned, a look of disapprobation on his face. "I thought perhaps Raven would be willing to concede out of loyalty to his old employer, but he was not."

"Old employer?" Kit echoed, while Hero sat in stunned silence.

"Why, yes," Poynter said, eyeing them curiously. "Your uncle and I once both worked for the duke, years ago when his Grace was first in the thrall of bibliomania. Of course, that was before your uncle was known as Raven."

"What?" Kit blurted out.

Hero was just as stunned, but she was more aware of their roles as niece and nephew to the man and schooled her features accordingly.

"Why, yes," Poynter said, with the faintest of smiles. "He was born Augustus Tovell, or at least that is how I knew him. That was before he became enamored of all things Gothic, changed his name and acquired his castle."

"And when did that happen?" Kit asked. Hero wanted to stop him, to stop her ears, but her own raging curiosity kept her silent and immobile.

Poynter frowned, as though considering dates, then shook his head. "I am not sure when, for it was after I had left the duke's employ myself."

The wry twist of his mouth told Hero that his move probably had not been voluntary. More likely, his fellow staff member had forced him out. Had Raven got his first taste of power and abused it, or was he already orchestrating the fates of others so long ago?

"But it would have been several years later, after he parted ways with the duke, as well," Poynter said.

"Did they have a falling-out?" Kit asked.

"I don't know, but he did not seek another position when he left. It might well have been around that time that his elder brother died. Augustus took over the family fortunes, sold the home in Surrey, bought Raven Hill, and began his retreat from the world at large."

Poynter smiled apologetically. "But you must know all of this. Indeed, you must have changed your name to Raven," he said to Kit.

"He did," Hero answered, before Kit could speak. "We are both distant relatives, and Raven has been kind enough to help establish our futures."

"Ah," Poynter said. "I had wondered at your connections, for I knew of no other siblings besides his brother, and yet here you are." He nodded in approval, for it was not unusual for wealthier members of a family to provide for those less fortunate. Those without heirs might even adopt those they favoured, whether relations or friends.

That was certainly what had driven the real Erasmus to change his name and curry Raven's favor. He wanted Raven Hill and all that went with it. But unless Hero was mistaken, Erasmus had no more love for his uncle than she did. And his position was not secured, which explained his increasingly desperate offers to do Raven's bidding without question.

"Well, Augustus should take great pride in such a fine pair of young people as yourselves," Poynter said with a smile. Hero was hard pressed not to snort a disclaimer, for Raven took no pride in anything except himself and his acquisitions. But then, weren't she and Erasmus little more than puppets, human additions to his growing collection?

"Thank you," Kit said, when Hero did not comment. "Obviously, you harbor no ill feelings toward him."

Poynter's mouth twisted again. "Life is too short, and collecting too cutthroat a passion to carry grudges. Indeed, my path has crossed many times over the years with both Raven and Montford."

He paused to shake his head, his expression sad. "Indeed, I was most grieved to find out that his Grace is gravely ill."

"What?" Again, it was Kit who had the presence of mind to speak, while Hero sat still, stunned.

"Yes, one of the great antiquarians of the age is near death, from what I hear, though I pray God will spare him yet."

"I'm sorry," Kit said. "We had not heard these bad tidings. In fact, when we were at Cheswick, I thought I saw the duke's men or those dressed in his livery."

Poynter shook his head, apparently as puzzled as they by the sighting. "Perhaps they are on some final mission at his behest," the older gentleman finally said with a wistful smile. "I'd like to think his Grace still pursues his final prize, that most rare of volumes, a collector to the end."

Chapter Twelve

Hero was so dazed, she let Kit lead her from the London Institution without thought to who might see them. Her mind was in a whirl, trying to take in all the information that Richard Poynter had imparted and make sense of it.

"Shall we find a place to sit?" Kit asked, ever solicitous.

Hero shook her head. "No, I'd rather walk."

Taking her gloved hand, Kit placed it in the crook of his arm and patted it, as though to comfort her. "Well, that's it," he said. "Obviously, the book was never part of the old earl's library. Martin Cheswick buried it or burned it or somehow disposed of it. The Mallory is lost, and I can't say I'm sorry."

"Maybe," Hero said. "Maybe not."

Kit slanted her a speculative glance. "The only other possibility is that your uncle already possesses the book. And he sent you off on a mission to fetch it from himself?"

Although Hero had considered that possibility, she did not share her thoughts with Kit. But when she did not reply, he eyed her sharply.

"Perhaps you'd like to break into Raven Hill and look for it," he suggested. "That's the only way we'll know for sure."

"You can't break into Raven Hill," Hero said.

"Why not?" Kit asked. "I thought it was possible to tour all the great homes, especially one patterned after Strawberry Hill."

Hero smiled, though not in amusement. "Unlike Walpole, who wrote a guidebook and gave out tickets to view his home, Raven does not open his house to visitors. But his secretive behavior seems to incite more curiosity about the place, causing him to employ several footmen to chase gawkers away from his property." And because of Raven's Gothic fancies, those footmen were armed with swords.

Hero shook her head. "Despite Raven's determination to outdo Walpole, there are few similarities between the two houses. Strawberry Hill is full of innovative designs and wallpapers and original use of colors and light. But Raven is no visionary." He was not interested in creating a showplace, only in feeding his own twisted fantasy.

"While both buildings have vaulted archways and hidden passages, Strawberry Hill is like a fairy castle, with pinnacles, quatrefoil windows and intricately carved staircases. Raven Hill is more an actual castle with battlements and dungeons. It's made of real stone and filigree, not wallpapers that cleverly depict such materials."

Hero never spoke of her household, but once begun, she could not seem to stop herself. "It's like a tomb, cold and dark and uncomfortable. And deliberately frightening," she muttered.

"What?"

Hero nodded. She couldn't begin to count the times she had come across some faux horror, even as a child, that Raven had added for his amusement. "I learned long ago not to scream at the sight of a falling axe or start at some ghoulish sound emanating from nowhere, but to keep on eating my soup in silence."

"What?" Kit halted his steps.

"There is not one comfortable chair, not one warm spot in which to read a book, just presses full of protected volumes or cases stocked with medals or other antiquarian follies." Hero drew a breath, intending to go on, only to realize that Kit was standing in front of her, a look of shock upon his face.

"The devil ought to be horsewhipped," he said, making Hero rue her words. She did not want to set Kit against Raven, now or ever. The knowledge that the man had been born an unassuming Tovell did not lessen his power. A Raven by any other name…

Hero shook her head, as though to make light of Kit's charge. "No doubt he deserves such punishment, but for crimes against others far more serious than the lack of desirable furnishings."

"I'm serious," Kit said, with such ferocity that Hero drew in a sharp breath. "I don't want you to go back there. It sounds like you are little more than an unpaid servant at the whim of a madman."

Although Kit was not far from the truth, Hero was

not about to confirm his suspicions. And she certainly did not want his pity, especially if it prompted another proposal. *Because this time she might not have the strength to refuse.*

"Perhaps I won't," Hero simply said. But she couldn't meet his probing gaze. And she did not share with him the desperate scheme she had devised to win her freedom.

Aware of the attention they might be drawing with their public argument, Hero began walking once more, forcing Kit to join her. And she forced a change of topic in the conversation, as well.

"If the Mallory truly is lost, why is Montford searching for it—and us?" she asked.

Kit groaned. "The Mallory *is* lost. And we don't know that the men were Montford's, and we only saw them once."

Hero sent him a questioning look.

"All right, twice, but that's no indication they were chasing us."

"Perhaps Montford heard rumours of the Mallory surfacing," Hero said. "Because of their past connection, the duke might be aware of Raven's interest and had his men follow me as a matter of course."

Kit shook his head. "I still can't imagine a duke's servants trying to kidnap you, and the fellows who did weren't wearing any livery."

"They might have changed their clothes, so we wouldn't be able to identify them," Hero said drily.

Kit snorted. "So what do you suggest we do, march up to Montford's family seat, demanding to see a dying man so we can accuse him of assault?"

Hero frowned at Kit's tone. When he put it that way, the idea did sound absurd, but Poynter understood. He knew that bibliomaniacs were consumed with the madness, whether down to their last coin, last thought, or even last breath.

"If Montford thinks we are on track, perhaps we should continue the search. We could talk to Featherstone's servants and friends and try to discover what happened to his books."

"But the lots went to Raven," Kit said.

Hero paused, struck by a sudden thought. "Yes, but how?" she said, glancing intently at Kit. "Were they delivered directly to Raven or did they pass through Featherstone first? If so, Featherstone might have lifted a few choice gems for himself."

"By cracking open a couple crates and going through every volume?"

"And picking the best for himself? I know I would have," Hero said.

"But Featherstone was sunk too deep in dissipation by then," Kit argued. "He probably was more interested in the money than any of the books."

"Book collecting is as great an addiction as gambling."

Kit shook his head. "You're assuming that Featherstone took delivery of the lots, which more than likely went directly to the purchaser, meaning your uncle."

Hero almost snapped at him not to refer to Raven as any relative of hers, but she caught herself. Instead, she said, "There's only one way to find out."

This time Kit did not groan, and Hero held her breath, for the ties that bound them were tenuous, at best. He had no good reason to continue to help her, and yet…

Finally, he halted again, turning to look at her directly. "You can't give it up, can you?" he asked.

Hero couldn't tell if his expression held dismay or pity, but she shook her head. "No," she answered.

There was too much at stake.

By the time they had returned to the London Institution, Poynter had gone, so they were left with little to do the rest of the day. And Kit refused to return to the inn, which might be for the best, considering what had last happened there. The thought of this man massaging her feet or any other part of her made Hero's face heat and her heart pound.

As long as they didn't draw attention to themselves, she was willing to go along as he dragged her to Madame Tussaud's Wax Museum and Week's Mechanical Museum. Steering clear of stationers, booksellers and circulating libraries, they wandered through a variety of shops, looking at toys and prints and elegant silks. They visited a clockmaker's and a perfumery. And they enjoyed delicate pastries purchased in a bake shop, as well as gingerbread from a street vendor.

For Hero, it was like a dream. After a lifetime of cold duty and a week of masquerading as a young man, the afternoon spent as Miss Marchant, about in London with her attentive brother, was a holiday. But Kit was not her sibling, and though he conducted himself as such, sometimes Hero caught glimpses of a dark glint in his gaze, a sign that his feelings for her were not brotherly. And she felt an answering shift inside, a hot surge of yearning that threatened to rob her of breath, before it faded into the less dangerous manner of easy companionship.

But when they finally approached the inn, the sparkle of the day began to fade into twilight, and Hero's buoyant mood with it. Recalled to reality, she was reminded that she was not Kit's sister. Nor could she ever be anything else to this man whose time with her was rapidly coming to an end.

To add to her distress, Hero was forced to wait in a shadowed corner of the hall while Kit got her great-coat, bundling her up so she would be unrecognizable before hurrying to her room. The reason for the ruse remained unspoken: she did not want to be taken for a prostitute or sent to jail because of some such mis-understanding.

Once inside the darkened room, Hero shivered while Kit lit a lamp. Her boots were damp, but before they called for a fire, she needed to change. Reaching for her pack, Hero put a hand inside for her shirt, only to realize that it was not on top of the clothing she had placed there, folded and ready for rapid donning.

Drawing in a sharp breath, Hero turned to survey the room. There were few enough of their own belongings about, but her boy's boots were not where she had left them. Although in the same general area, their position was subtly altered, a discovery that made her heart hammer.

"Someone's been in here," Hero said softly.

"What?"

"Someone has searched our room."

Kit looked around at the spare, neat space and sent her a startled glance. "Perhaps the chambermaid…"

Hero shook her head. "She might have moved my boots, but she would not have been inside my pack."

"Unless she's a thief," Kit muttered.

"Try to remember exactly where you put everything and see if it is not slightly changed," Hero said.

Kit must have seen that she hadn't the energy to argue with him, for he turned to look through his own things, then swung round with a grim expression.

"She's not a thief, for I left some money hidden in an old sock. It is still there, but has been shoved farther down into the toe." He paused to shake his head. "Who would go through them only to put them back?"

"Someone looking for the Mallory," Hero said, and, for once, Kit did not argue.

They discussed what to do, then called for the maid to light the fire, conducting themselves as usual. Whoever had been in their room had gone to great lengths to avoid notice, and for now, they would play along. But Kit slept in a chair in front of the door, and Hero tossed and turned in the bed.

The bright, shiny day that she had spent with Kit in carefree excursions had been tarnished. With the coming of the night, Hero's thoughts grew dark, and she wondered at what price she had bought those precious hours.

The next morning Hero was back in her boy's clothing and so quiet that Kit cursed the circumstances that conspired against him. Yesterday she had been delightful company—warm and witty and beautiful in her feminine guise. A strong and independent woman, Hero also possessed a deep well of tenderness just waiting to be tapped. Their silences were comfortable, while their discussions were far ranging, going beyond books to houses, politics and even agriculture. And Kit knew her passion matched his own.

In short, she was everything he might want in a partner. *A wife.* Kit shook his head. He had all but given up hope until yesterday when everything between them was so easy and natural. But it had all gone awry. Hero had turned cold and distant, while they faced unknown threats yet again.

Now, Kit could spare no thoughts for anything except her protection, and he kept his pistol close as he packed his few belongings. Wary of watchers, they were going to slip away before first light, and they spoke in hurried whispers. Kit suggested they look for a place to lease, where they could disappear into the mass of London residents. But Hero shook her head.

"Time is running out," she said in a way that made Kit balk. "Another inn would be better, perhaps a larger one closer to the heart of the city."

Although in the past few days Hero had revealed more of herself, there still was too much missing for Kit to solve the puzzle. "People have been chasing us since we left Oakfield, so why is time running out?" he asked.

Hero hefted her pack. "Because we're on Raven's ground, in his neighborhood, and he will grow impatient for his prize."

"What? Surely you don't think your uncle is the one who searched our rooms?"

"Not Raven himself, but he may well have ordered it," she said.

Despite Hero's earlier revelations about her uncle, Kit was dumbfounded. "Why?"

Hero opened her mouth, then closed it again. Finally, she drew a deep breath. "I don't know," she said. "One never ever knows with Raven."

This was madness. It was an insane way to conduct business, and even more lunatic manner in which to live. There was very little that roused Kit to anger, but his rage toward Augustus Raven had been building for some time.

"Perhaps we should stop haring around town on this fruitless errand and go directly to Raven Hill," he said, giving Hero a hard stare. "I'd like to have a word with your uncle."

Ducking, she shook her head, but Kit was not prepared to let it go. Thus far, he had ceded to Hero's wishes, to her greater knowledge of the situation, but he could be stubborn, too. And he had no intention of letting her return to her uncle's control.

Even if he had misconstrued her interest, even if she would not accept his proposal, he could find somewhere else for her to go. Barto had connections. A post as a companion to a decent gentlewoman had to be preferable. Surely, when Syd met her, she would…

Suddenly, Kit realized just how long it had been since he had been in contact with his sister. Vaguely, he recalled some mention of a Christmas wedding, and he felt a different sort of alarm. Startling as it might seem, the holiday was not that far away, and he had no idea of what the arrangements might be.

Somehow, today he was going to have to get a message to his sister, whether Hero approved or not. The thought of whisking her away to Hawthorne Park was a tantalizing one, but unless he planned to drag her there bodily, Kit was not sure how to accomplish it.

As if sensing his mood, Hero turned toward him, pack in hand. "Perhaps we should separate."

"No." Kit spoke with such deadly vehemence that Hero did not argue. Still, when she moved into the narrow hall, he did not let her out of his sight.

They saw no one but sleepy grooms as they made their exit, taking the most winding route from the inn and sticking to the shadows. For the time being, they left their horses behind, fleeing on foot and climbing into a passing cart before debarking to slip through some alleys, until even Kit was confused over their location.

But in the breaking dawn, Hero pointed out the Maple's Inn, a busy place that was a far cry from their previous small, out-of-the-way lodgings. Since coaches came through at all hours, their appearance would not be marked, and after eating an enormous breakfast, they settled into a more spacious and neat room boasting two beds and a roaring fire.

When Hero made no move to change her costume, Kit looked a question at her. "Are we returning to the London Institution?"

"Not yet," Hero said, without meeting his gaze. "I've an errand first."

"And what might that be?" Kit asked.

When Hero did not immediately reply, Kit planted himself in front of the door with no intention of moving until he got some answers. If time was running out, so was his patience. At one time, he might have returned to his old life without taking action, but those days were gone. Now, he was determined to fight for what he wanted.

Although she had planned to come alone, Hero was grateful for Kit's solid presence as she stepped into Laytham's. She had not admitted as much, but the search of their room had unnerved her. Despite their various escapes, their pursuers had never seemed that close. And somehow, the thought of someone handling her belongings was worse than being threatened with a weapon.

It was more personal. More invasive. In fact, the more she thought about it, the more Hero began to think the secretive manner of the examination was one of Raven's touches. Surely, the kind of men who attacked the carriage or cornered Kit and Hob would engage in haphazard rummaging, not the eerily discreet violation that Hero had discovered.

Did Raven think she already had the Mallory, or was this one of his tricks to make sure she was alert and wary? Hero shook her head, for she knew there was no use trying to determine his motives. But perhaps, she would never have to puzzle over them again…

Heart pounding, Hero approached the counter at Laytham's, knowing full well what was at stake. Yet she managed to keep her face expressionless as she asked to see the owner.

"Mr Laytham is not here," the man said, eyeing her less-than-elegant attire with disdain.

Hero sucked in a breath. She had not anticipated this, but now she saw that Laytham's easy capitulation could have been a ruse. He might be on the Continent by now or, worse, explaining to some magistrate why *she* should be arrested.

"Did he leave anything to be picked up?" Kit asked, while Hero faltered.

"Your name?" the disdainful fellow inquired.

"Marchant," Kit said, taking control with his usual ease, and Hero could only be thankful for his quick command.

"Ah, yes," the man at the counter said. "Just a moment, please." He turned away, opening the door that led to Laytham's office, and Hero waited, her breath caught in her throat.

She wasn't certain what she expected, perhaps authorities swarming from the private area to arrest her or the salesman himself, returning to brandish a weapon. But both outcomes seemed unlikely when there were other customers about. This was a busy shop, a respectable business, in spite of the commission Laytham had agreed to undertake.

When the man returned with a thickly wrapped object, tied with string, Hero simply stared at it for a long moment. For surely none in her long history of acquisitions had carried the importance of this, the least costly.

"Thank you," Hero said, barely restraining herself from snatching up the parcel. Instead, she took it carefully, holding it against her chest as they made their exit. But once outside, she slipped it within her heavy greatcoat, where a large interior pocket was designed to hold all but the largest of volumes.

Now it could not be knocked from her grip or dropped into a puddle. And Hero looked no more than a young man bundled up against the cold, without anyone the wiser as to the prize in her possession. Still, she did not dawdle, and they hurried to the relative safety of Maple's Inn, so that she might take a look at what she had just received.

The walk was long enough for Hero's euphoria to ebb as she considered the contents of her pocket. Despite Kit's influence, hers was a suspicious nature, and she wondered whether she even held a book. The heavily wrapped item could be anything. A piece of wood. A title of no consequence or worth, given to get rid of her, while Laytham covered his tracks, refusing to meet with her ever again.

That fear gnawed at her until panic eroded her good sense, making her careless. And it wasn't until Kit had her halt at their door, in order to check the room, that she became aware of her inattention.

Suddenly nervous, she saw a man down the hall whose stance seemed vaguely familiar, but he stopped in front of another door, and Hero turned back to her own. Still, she was not as wary as usual, and when Kit waved her inside, Hero paid the price as she felt the barrel of a pistol pressed into her back.

"Quietly, now, let's go into your room. I'm sure you don't want any trouble." Hero recognized the voice as one of the two men who had attacked the carriage and threatened Hob, and if that wasn't enough, a poke of the weapon urged her to do as he said.

At the sight of their company, Kit started to reach inside his coat, but the man stopped him with a warning.

"Don't move, or I'll shoot her," he said. "So you just keep your hands were I can see them."

Behind her, Hero heard footsteps, followed by the ominous shutting of the door. A second man came into view, his pistol trained on Kit. It was the tall fellow, so the short one must be behind her, Hero reasoned. What she didn't expect was the appearance of a third man, and she drew in a sharp breath as the vaguely familiar figure from the hallway stepped into her line of sight.

"Erasmus! What are you doing here?" Hero gaped at her so-called cousin. Had Raven put him up to this?

"It has taken some doing, I admit," Erasmus said, his dark eyes birdlike hollows in the whiteness of his face. "You've led a fine chase, but one of Raven's underlings reported you were in town. And luckily for me, he was so startled to see you in that garb that he followed you."

Hero gaped. She'd made sure…

"Or he paid some youth to do some," Erasmus said. "I don't know or care. Nor did your disappearance this morning concern me. For, you see, I had spoken with the dependable Mr Ridealgh at Laytham's, who discovered that you, or rather Mr Marchant as you are now calling yourself," he added with a sneer, "would be back in a day's time. So all I had to do was wait."

Hero spared a moment to regret that all her precautions and wariness had been for naught. Despite her efforts, she could not control those outside her influence, such as Mr Ridealgh, whether he was Laytham's assistant or some lowly salesman eager for a bribe.

"But if you hadn't secreted the parcel inside your

coat, we could have avoided all this," Erasmus said, shaking his head. "A quick knock against you, and I could have been off with the Mallory."

"Why?" Hero asked. "If you plan on stealing from Raven, you've sadly misjudged your opponent."

"Oh, Raven will have his previous volume all right. When I give it to him. While you, after so much time and money, will return a failure."

"And when I tell him what you did to get it?"

Erasmus sneered. "I don't know what you're talking about, cousin."

"It was you who searched my room, wasn't it?" Hero said, and Erasmus's thin smile told her she was right.

"And you sent these brutes to kidnap me, waylay me, and delay me. Dangerous doings, Erasmus," Hero said. "All designed to prevent me from completing my mission, which is not something that Raven will take kindly."

"I don't know what you're talking about," Erasmus repeated, his lips curling in contempt. "I can account for my whereabouts, while you? It seems that you've been traipsing across the country on a romantic fling, spending more time on your lover than your mission, hardly the sort of thing of which Raven will approve."

Hero sucked in a harsh breath. There was no point in arguing, for they both knew the truth. It would be her word against his when they faced Raven, and Erasmus was well aware that those who came bearing gifts were always rewarded.

But just what sort of gift was he intending to present? Hero's knowledge of the parcel was the ace up her sleeve. So instead of the dread she might well have felt, she knew only a cold anger that this inept would-be usurper should ruin her one chance for freedom.

Hero eyed him coolly. "It will do you no good, Erasmus," she said. "Raven doesn't trust you. He knows you're only out to get what you can."

Erasmus's expression turned black with hatred. "Well, then we are two of a kind. While you? I don't know what you are. I've never understood why you're the chosen one when I've done everything to please him, even changing my name to his. I've got his blood. *Do you?*"

Hero did not flinch at the taunt. Nor did she dwell upon the fact that Kit was only a few steps away, listening to it all. Instead, she focused on the skills and experience that had served her well, while Erasmus… As usual, his emotions clouded dealings, which was one of the reasons Raven did not favour him.

She could almost hear Raven in her head. *Cleverness and cunning will out every time, my girl,* he whispered. *No one expects a female to think so cold and clearly.* Lately, Hero had discovered he was wrong about her lack of feelings, but she knew well how to hide them, and she did so now, her lack of reaction spurring Erasmus's rage.

"Everyone knows you're no relation, that you were bought, just like one of his acquisitions, though far more cheaply, I'll warrant."

Hero kept her expression impassive, as though he was discussing the weather, not the most hurtful of truths. But he could not know it all, she told herself. He could not know the worst.

"Where did he get you?" Erasmus said, stepping closer, his pinched face twisted by years of disappointment and jealousy and ill usage. "I've searched through his books, his private correspondence and found nothing," Erasmus spat. "Which proves just how little you are worth."

Erasmus took another step, standing so close now that Hero could see the spittle on his lips. "Did he find you on the streets, a beggar, a thief?" Erasmus demanded. He smiled then. "I don't think so. There's only one place where he could have bought a girl child like you, for the meanest coin. And that was a brothel, where your mother was the lowliest of whores."

Erasmus was staring so fixedly at Hero that he paid no heed to Kit or his hired men, who were gaping wide-eyed at the conversation. And at the word "whore" Kit launched himself. Taking Erasmus unawares, he knocked the smaller man to the ground, while Hero elbowed the fellow who held the pistol at her back. The third man swung his weapon toward them, and a shot rang out, sending Hero dropping to the floor.

"Stop, you idiot! Are you trying to kill me?" The man who had held Hero shouted at his compatriot, whose shot had gone wide, but was sure to draw attention. Hero took advantage of his panic by leaping to the window and pushing up the sash, thankful they had chosen their location for its easy access to a low roof. Whirling, she pulled her own weapon, ready to stop her assailant from following.

But he was busy trying to help his fellow, who was struggling with Kit, while Erasmus lay on the floor, abandoned, his rage replaced by fear. Ignoring him, Hero seized a wooden chair and brought it down hard on the back of the shorter man. With a grunt, he fell, and she retrieved the pistol he dropped.

"Ahhh!" A pained wail rose up from the taller of the two brutes as his pistol, too, dropped to the floor, and he clutched at his sleeve, where a bright spot of red gave evidence of his injury.

In an instant, Kit hurried her to the window, wiping a bloody knife upon the curtain.

"Where did you get that?" Hero demanded.

"My boot."

Hero sent him a startled glance. "And to think you're just a gentleman farmer."

The sound of footsteps alerted them to the imminent arrival of others who had heard the shot, so they clambered over the sill. There was no time to gather their things, only for one last glance at the room, where the two villains lay groaning and the door stood open.

Erasmus was gone.

Chapter Thirteen

Crouching, they slid, more than walked, along the slippery roof that covered an overhang near the kitchens. Kit dropped to the ground easily, then turned to catch her. Again, Hero was grateful for his quiet strength. But she didn't even have time to savor his touch as he quickly pulled her through the stables and out into the street.

Once among others, Kit slowed his pace to avoid notice, but Hero still had to hurry to keep up. Her mind in a whirl, she could not think where to go, for it seemed that she was watched even more than she suspected. She felt an urgency to get to Raven, but she did not want to appear before him in her current guise. And all her other clothes were gone.

Suddenly, Hero felt as if she had come out the loser in the fight, bruised and battered by the implications of Erasmus's actions. If she could not use the Mallory to her advantage, then her already difficult position would be made worse by Erasmus's enmity. It would be just like Raven to pit them against each other in an endless struggle for his favour.

So caught up was she in these bleak thoughts that Hero barely blinked when Kit hustled her into a hackney coach. He leaned toward the driver to give directions without shouting, then slid in beside her.

"Where are we going?" Hero asked.

"Somewhere safe," Kit said, patting her arm in an automatic gesture of comfort.

At one time, Hero would have viewed his words with suspicion or doubt. But now she simply leaned back her head and closed her eyes, too weary to protest. Her thoughts went round and round, but her lack of sleep and the closeness of Kit's warm body had her nearly nodding off until the coach stopped and he helped her out.

Glancing around, Hero had no idea where they were as they slipped through a shop, exited onto another street, and walked another street before heading up to a neat town house. After a few words from Kit, they were ushered into a cozy parlor, where they were soon greeted by a handsome young man Kit introduced as Charles Armstrong.

"Kit, it's a pleasure to see you!" Armstrong said. He was as fair as Kit was dark, yet he seemed to possess the same friendly nature. "How many times have I invited you to town? But you're a gentleman farmer now, I suppose, with little interest in our doings?"

Hero nearly laughed aloud at that, for among his other skills surely Kit was the only such fellow who kept a knife in his boot and was able to subdue two villains at once. And yet, looking at him, he seemed little different from Armstrong, if a bit disheveled.

He still had that easy grace and untroubled countenance that belied the measure of the man, whose inner strength and abilities made him more formidable than just about anyone. In fact, the juxtaposition of his demeanor and his capability made Christopher Marchant all the more…dangerous.

Swamped by a sudden surge of emotion, Hero swallowed hard and tried to focus on the conversation between the two men.

"And how is that lovely sister of yours?" Armstrong asked, his tone showing more than idle interest.

"She is to be married soon, to our old neighbor, now Viscount Hawthorne."

"Oh, that is…good news, of course. I hope you will tender my heartiest congratulations when you see her."

"Actually, I was hoping that I could post a brief letter to her while here. Pardon our appearance, but we've run into a bit of trouble here in town," Kit said.

He drew his host aside, and they held a whispered conversation punctuated by Armstrong's exclamations and furtive looks her way. At one time, Hero might have distrusted anything she couldn't hear, but Kit appeared to have it all well in hand, while her own mind and body seemed to have reached their limits.

Once they were finished talking, a genial housekeeper led them upstairs, showing Hero to a lovely room before taking Kit on to his. For a long moment, Hero simply stood and stared at the cheery surroundings, decorated with bright chintzes and soft chairs.

Gauzy curtains were drawn back from wide windows, and Hero knew she ought to shut them, but she didn't have the heart.

A low knock heralded Kit's entry, and Hero's weariness was replaced by dread. She had hoped to be gone from his life, without him ever knowing, but Erasmus's accusations made that unlikely. Now it would all come out, Hero thought, her head pounding along with her heart. Although she wanted nothing more than to flee, she could not, and so she walked around the room, admiring the ewer and basin and small comforts that a stranger freely offered her.

"I've explained that you are in disguise," Kit said. Without standing upon ceremony, he sank into one of the upholstered chairs. "He's going to have a maid bring you some of his sisters' clothes. In case you'd like to change," Kit added.

Hero choked back a laugh. Now that they were in Kit's world, she felt her own lack. A strange female who dressed in boy's garb, she did not fit in here. It was just as well…

"Shall we have a look at it?" he asked.

For a moment, Hero had no idea what he was talking about. And she nearly laughed again when she realized how far her thoughts were from her singular purpose. It didn't seemed possible that she had forgotten the Mallory, the most important thing in her life. Or so she told herself.

Unbuttoning the heavy greatcoat, Hero reached inside and pulled the parcel from her pocket. "It's not real," she said. "I had it made up."

"What?"

"It's a forgery," Hero explained as she walked across the room. "Raven always hinted at the authenticity of Laytham's pamphlets, so I gambled on him being right." She did not mince words, for what could it matter now? "I blackmailed Laytham into creating an edition that might fool Raven, at first glance, at least."

"Clever," Kit said. Startled, Hero glanced toward him, but his expression held no hint of the disapproval she'd expected. A bit dumbfounded, she set the parcel upon a drum table that stood near his chair.

"We'll see," Hero said, for her success remained to be seen. Raven was far more clever, and she was still uncertain what she would find beneath the wrappings. Putting shaking fingers to the string, she was confounded until Kit reached into his boot for the knife, slicing clean through it. And suddenly, her whole body seemed to shake as she moved the paper aside to reveal what was nestled inside.

It was a book, and Hero let out a low sound of relief. The bindings were old, a hundred years at least, and the title barely legible. Whether accidental or deliberate, that was a nice touch, Hero thought as she gently tipped open the cover with one finger. Inside, the title page looked just as old, and Kit rose to his feet to stand behind her.

"It looks real enough," he said.

"Believe me, it isn't," Hero said. "Or else Laytham would never have parted with it."

A knock on the door made Hero start, and she quickly rewrapped the volume as a pert little maid entered the room, carrying several garments.

"Mr Armstrong said you'd be needing these, uh, sirs," the girl said.

"Yes, thank you," Kit said.

She laid the items on the bed. "And I'll be bringing up a tray for you. Will there be anything else?"

"A bath?" Kit suggested.

"Of course, sir," she said, with a nod, and was soon shutting the door behind her.

A bath. And clean clothes. And some good food, not purchased at an inn. Thinking of the pleasures that Kit so valued allowed Hero to avoid the inevitable.

But she knew it could not be staved off for long. Wrapping the book as neatly as possible, she slipped it into the bottom of a heavy wardrobe, beneath a chamber pot, which she would never have cause to use, just as she would never use the pretty bed with its thick coverings.

"Will your uncle be fooled?" Kit asked.

"Don't call him my uncle." The words were out before Hero could call them back.

For a long moment, Kit was silent. "Surely you don't believe any of that rot your cousin was spouting, vitriol that was born of jealousy?"

"No," Hero said softly. "It's worse than that." She turned to face him. He was seated again in the upholstered chair, looking so at home in such surroundings that she felt an interloper. She *was* an interloper.

"Raven bought me at an asylum. My mother was a madwoman."

Although Hero braced herself, the horror and judgement that she knew Kit would be unable to hide did not appear. In fact, he simply shook his head. "I don't believe it. From what you've told me, that's just the sort of tale he would concoct to frighten you and keep you tethered to him."

Kit paused to eye her directly. "Maybe he's your father."

Hero shuddered at the possibility, which would still make her the offspring of a lunatic. *Perhaps two lunatics.* But the idea that Raven had engaged in intimacy of any sort with anyone seemed highly unlikely.

Hero shook her head. "I can't imagine him having a child with anyone. Ever."

"Even in a fit of passion?"

"Raven's fits of passion aren't the kind that would result in childbirth."

"Have you ever asked him about it?"

Hero laughed humorlessly. "Question his word? You don't understand. Conversation with him devolves into hints and mysterious intrigues, while disputes are met with stony silence."

Kit lifted his dark brows as if she had just proven his point for him. "If he talks in riddles and is known for his intrigues, why would you take his word about this?"

Because Raven appeared to revel in her origins, subtly hinting that her own eventual madness was a foregone conclusion.

When Hero didn't answer, Kit pressed her. "Why would he go to an asylum to shop for children to adopt?" Kit asked. "That makes no sense."

"I assumed he wanted someone no one else knew about, with no connections, who would be grateful..."

"He could do that anywhere on any street, without

the possibility of spending his time and money on someone who might not be grateful or useful."

"Maybe the idea appealed to him," Hero said. "It would certainly fit into his sense of Gothic melodrama. He could use me until I went mad, then lock me in the tower, where my shrieking and wailing would only add to the atmosphere of Raven Hill," Hero said, shivering at the very real possibility.

"The idea might appeal to him, but would a recluse actually visit such a place, inviting into his private home someone who might not be as easily governed as he might wish?" Kit shook his head. "I think he's concocted the tale out of whole cloth."

Hero opened her mouth to argue, then shut it again as she stared at Kit's open expression. He spoke with such absolute certainty that for the first time in her life, doubt crept into her mind.

Raven had never talked of her antecedents outright, but in a cryptic manner that left Hero to divine the truth. Not even Erasmus had guessed the real story, and Hero had kept it hidden, dark and festering, from everyone until this very moment. Yet, now she wondered if, in his own twisted way, Raven hadn't dropped the hints purposefully so that she might draw the wrong conclusions.

But if her entire history was a lie, then where had she come from? And who were her parents?

As Kit dressed in fresh clothes, he silently thanked Charlie for his generosity. A cousin of the Armstrongs who had once been Kit's neighbors, Charlie wasn't a close friend, but he had provided the two who had showed up on his doorstep with good food and the luxury of an enormous copper tub, in which Kit had enjoyed a good long soak.

He also provided them with a safe haven, for Kit couldn't envision Erasmus and his hired thugs venturing into this genteel neighborhood. Kit loosed a low sigh, relieved that the villain harrying them had turned out to be nothing more than a disgruntled relative, not deadly followers of Mallory's writings.

Kit had no doubt that Hero's cousin was dangerous, for his ranting smacked of someone with a tenuous hold on his wits. And the men he'd hired had brandished their pistols alarmingly. But once Hero was removed from Erasmus's orbit, he would have no further reason to threaten her.

And Kit had all intention of removing Hero from his reach, as well as from Raven's. He'd had no chance to say as much when the maid had appeared with her bath water, but he hoped to receive a different answer when next he tendered his proposal. For, at last, the final piece of the puzzle that was Hero had fallen into place. And the deep, dark secret she had so zealously guarded seemed nothing more than a Gothic tale from the master of Raven Hill.

Although Kit was fairly certain Hero had not come from an asylum, he was just as certain that Raven had wanted her to think so. What better way to keep her tied to him? He permitted her no friends, no social life, no interaction with other women or potential suitors. And if, by chance, she should form an attachment, his ugly lie would keep her from pursuing it.

Kit shook his head as he closed the door behind

him. Although many women had few choices in life, this man had made sure that Hero had none. With a combination of threats and lies and virtual imprisonment, he had maintained a stranglehold upon her, body and mind. It was a measure of Hero's strength that he had not broken her spirit, as well.

As he walked toward Hero's room, Kit's steps slowed, but the sight of a passing maid spurred him onward. Now that they were at Charlie's, it wasn't prudent to make himself a frequent visitor to a bedroom occupied by a young, unmarried miss. Ruefully, Kit realized that circumstances had forced them into behavior that had become habit, but that society would not condone.

Although, by necessity, Charlie had been apprised of Hero's disguise, he had been told little else. Kit had kept to himself the fact that the two had been traveling alone together. The servants might suspect something odd, but they had all been told that a woman was to occupy that room.

Charlie had even contacted his dowager aunt to come serve as chaperone, a gesture Kit much appreciated. For Hero's sake, he did not want her reputation tarnished in any way in the eyes of the world. Barto and Syd wouldn't put stock in gossip, but it had a way of following one, even to the farthest corners of the countryside, and preventing acceptance into genteel society.

In fact, Charlie's aunt might already have arrived and be meeting with Hero, so Kit hurried down the curving stair to the floor below, where he found Charlie seated at a writing desk in the parlor.

"Oh, hello! You said you wanted to post a letter to your sister," Charlie said, rising to his feet.

"So I did," Kit answered. "Thank you for the reminder, as well as all else you've done for us."

Charlie waved away the gratitude. "Next time I need rustication in the country, you shall simply have to open your new home to me."

Kit laughed. "I'm afraid you won't find the place as entertaining as your cousins'."

"I'm sure it would be less taxing than London," Charlie said. "Rest and relaxation amongst nature, eh?"

Kit smiled in reply, and for the first time since the fire, he began to think about the landscape that had been denuded behind the house. He certainly did not want to revive the hedge maze that had burned down, but he would like a garden, the kind of area that would be a welcome refuge, such as Charlie mentioned. With walkways and trees and plantings bright with flowers. Perhaps he could call in a designer…

But he was getting ahead of himself. There was business to be taken care of first, and one of the matters that most required his attention was Syd. Taking the place that Charlie had vacated, he wrote her and Barto a brief assurance that he was safe and would like to introduce someone to them. Unwilling to get ahead of himself again, Kit did not explain why, but promised to head to Hawthorne Park as soon as he tied up a few loose ends in London. That one of those consisted of Augustus Raven, Kit kept to himself.

He had barely given the missive to a footman when Charlie's aunt arrived. Short, pudgy and wearing a variety of shawls and fur muffs, she was ushered into the parlour in an endless stream of chatter, involving her conveyance from her own town house to Charlie's. As the butler helped her from her heavy cloak and various fur pieces, Charlie shot Kit a glance that spoke volumes.

Kit realized he was even more beholden to his friend, for he suspected that Charlie's aunt was not a frequent visitor, for reasons that were rapidly becoming obvious. Once relieved of her heaviest garments, she snatched back a brightly colored shawl.

"And then, it began a cold drizzle, which at my age is the very worst of conditions," she was saying. "I admit, Charles, that I would only have ventured out for you and the most urgent summons."

Having finally situated her garments to her apparent satisfaction, the stout female turned to survey the room. "Ah, there are you are, Charles," she said, acknowledging her nephew with the fluttering handkerchief.

Squinting in Kit's direction, she paused to pat her enormous bosom, from which general area she produced a pair of spectacles. "And who is this?"

"This is Mr Marchant," Charles said, throwing Kit another glance of apology. "He's a friend of mine, a former neighbor of William and Elizabeth's."

"William and Elizabeth! That brood," she said, heaving herself on to a chaise longue. "I've told her time and time again of the need to rein in those children. And how often has that youngest scamp of theirs gotten into trouble, I ask you?"

Although Kit knew the family well, it wasn't long

before he had lost all track of the conversation, if one could call it that. Charlie tried to look attentive, while Mrs Armstrong kept up her ceaseless prattle. She didn't seem mean-spirited, simply eager for a chance to give her opinions on all and sundry.

Kit realized that she would probably drive Hero to distraction, but he had often been trapped with his father and his father's scholarly friends, so he had developed the skill of judicious nodding when listening to long-winded discourse. In fact, he had practically nodded off when a sharp change in the pitch of Mrs Armstrong's voice had him jerking to attention.

"Mr Marchant! I say, this young woman you wish me to accompany, where is she?"

"She's resting, Aunt," Charlie said. "She requested not to be disturbed."

The combination of Charlie's last words and the lengthening shadows outside made Kit surge to his feet, abruptly alert. "I'll go check on her."

At Mrs Armstrong's horrified gasp, Charlie stood and summoned a maid for the task, but it was all Kit could do to remain where he was.

"Really, young man, you cannot expect me to act as a chaperone when you make such outrageous remarks. Why are you looking so pale?" the older woman demanded, lifting her spectacles, the better to peer at Kit. "She isn't ill, is she?"

Having discovered a new topic for discussion, she launched into a long, detailed account of a young lady who had suffered most violently from what they claimed was gout. "But that hardly seems likely, now, does it?" she asked no one in particular.

The maid, who had been urged to hurry by Charlie, soon reappeared, shaking her head. "No one's in the room, sir," she reported.

"But I don't understand," Charlie said. "Did anyone see her go out?"

"No, sir," the maid said. "I can ask the kitchen staff, but I'm sure they would have told the housekeeper, if the young lady had gone that way."

"But then, how?" Charlie asked to the room at large. Swinging toward Kit, he sputtered a protest. "You don't think someone managed to gain entrance to the house and...make off with her, do you?"

At Charlie's horrified expression, Kit shook his head. "She probably climbed out the window."

"Climbed out the window? In winter?" Mrs Armstrong's voice rang out as she looked from her nephew to Kit, her eyes wide behind her spectacles and her jaw slack with astonishment.

Without answering, Kit rushed past her, but he heard her speak to Charlie in a scolding tone. "My dear boy, I can see that this charge is going to be more difficult than you let on."

Bounding up the stairs, Kit headed to Hero's room, where a quick check confirmed that she had made her escape in her borrowed female clothing. But why? Kit threw open the doors of the wardrobe, searching for the book she had hidden there, only to find it gone, as well.

The doubts that Kit had once entertained came surging back, fuelled by the memory of his poor judgement at Oakfield. That experience had made him distrust his own instincts, and now he wondered whether he had been wrong about Hero, as well. Perhaps she had been playing him all along, and, having found the real Mallory, was off to collect the huge price it would bring.

But even as such thoughts flashed through his mind, Kit dismissed them. Whether right or wrong, his heart held sway over his head, and he was not about to let Hero go until things were settled between them, once and for all.

Swearing under his breath, Kit realized he should never have left her alone. In the future, he might consider tethering her to him with a chain. With a lock. *If there was a future.*

The thought spurred Kit to action. He needed to borrow a horse from Charlie and head…where? Kit could only guess that she had gone home, which meant he would have to do the impossible: break into Raven Hill.

Chapter Fourteen

The cold drizzle Mrs Armstrong complained about had stopped, leaving only a few slick patches in its wake. But as twilight descended, a mist appeared, making Kit's first sight of Raven Hill enough to give anyone pause.

He had barely turned onto the long lane when he saw Hero's home ahead, an old castle rising out of the fog as night gathered around it like a cloak. The size of the place was not imposing, for it looked to be a keep that had been added to in an odd fashion. But a high stone wall surrounded it, culminating in a massive iron gate and a gatehouse whose window blinked in the coming darkness.

At least there wasn't a moat.

But the gatehouse light might indicate a presence, and just in case Raven's defences included keeping a lookout atop the battlements, Kit veered off the lane, though he was still far away. Tall trees added further gloom to the setting, and Kit headed toward them, hoping to avoid being seen.

Too late, he wished that he had pressed Hero for more information about the home she claimed no one could breach, patrolled by guards and perhaps even filled with traps for the unwary. Hadn't she said something about falling axes?

Tethering Charlie's horse to a tall sycamore, Kit stood at the edge of the stand of trees and studied his target. As he surveyed the daunting stone structure looming before him, he took a good, long look past the obvious. And he realized that Raven's fortress was designed to intimidate, to convey a Gothic atmosphere, a melodramatic mystique nurtured by its owner and intended to keep the curious at bay.

Like the facade that Augustus Tovell had assumed, it was based more upon perception than reality. For no matter how wealthy Raven was, he could not afford an army to patrol the grounds or workmen to repair the ancient structure. Raven Hill was showing its age, and while that might add to its eerie impression, the cracks in the walls and crumbling stone would provide Kit the footholds he needed to gain entry to the grounds.

What he would find inside was anyone's guess.

It was better this way.

That's what Hero had told herself all the way from the Armstrong town house to the massive great room of Raven Hill. Although she hadn't wanted to leave Kit without a word, she needed to face Raven alone, to try to bargain for her future with the book she carried with her. She did not need the distraction Kit would bring to herself—or to Raven.

The owner of Raven Hill would have been outraged by the presence of an outsider in his sanctum, hardly a good beginning to any dealings, let alone the most important of Hero's life. And he would have been in no mood to give her what she wanted.

Although that consideration had been the deciding factor, Hero had another, more selfish reason for coming here without Kit. He was from a different world, where there were such things as gentlemen and kind strangers and welcome refuges, a world that Hero wanted to keep separate from the one ruled by Raven.

And here, Hero did not need the protection Kit had so ably provided. Raven would easily handle Erasmus, should he arrive to make trouble for her. In fact, her only fear lay in the chance that she would not succeed in buying her way out of this place for ever. But she kept that concern well hidden behind an impassive countenance, lest it be marked.

For Raven was here. Hero could feel it. He was probably in one of the upper galleries, spying upon her during the long wait that was intended to shake her composure. But Hero did not bother looking for him. She could see little in the perpetual gloom, for only one torch had been lit, and its feeble glow did not reach far beyond its placement at the rear of the hall, near the dais where Raven liked to hold court.

Even though she could see little of her surroundings, Hero knew them well. The tiles stretched out on all sides to walls hung with threadbare tapestries and ancient hauberks. Swords, axes and other weapons were displayed, although Raven did not keep any valuable collections here. *Too public*, he said, though he rarely allowed anyone to enter, let alone members of the general population.

Alongside the armaments stood the trappings of war, whole suits of armour assembled to stand freely upon unseen frames. They were placed in the shadows, so that at first glance, they might be mistaken for menacing figures. Long ago, when Hero had become inured to their presence, Raven had arranged for someone to don the old metal and step toward her from the darkness.

Hero had been hard pressed not to react. But after that, she came to expect most anything, including the rising of the dead from Raven's prized effigies, which occupied an alcove added for their presentation. That had never happened, and Raven claimed that the tombs were empty, probably because trading in the dead might be illegal.

Although the effigy alcove was the largest, there were many smaller ones that the odd piece of furniture or marble statue occupied. And some dark recesses contained a curtain or a hidden door that Raven had added over the years. Even Hero didn't know all of the castle's secrets.

Above, there were hiding places, as well, where Raven could look down, unobserved, upon all he had wrought. A wooden panel, carved in an open pattern, rose from the floor behind his dais nearly to the ceiling and could easily obscure him, while allowing him to see the pool of light below. And there were other spots behind cleverly designed walls, along galleries, or under decorative bays.

Waiting below, Hero expected him to send some wisp of silk flying down or sound a boom of cannon-like proportions by way of twisted welcome. And to see her reaction. But nothing fell from the darkness or broke the silence except for the ticking of the massive old-fashioned clock that marked the time.

And just when she wondered when he would show himself, Raven suddenly appeared, stepping from the shadows as if a part of them. He certainly did his best to be indistinguishable, his tall, thin figure cloaked in black, his eyes and cheeks unseen hollows, his ebony cane ever present. "You've taken your time," he said, by way of greeting.

Hello to you, too. "I ran into some difficulty," Hero said.

"I take it Marchant did not have the book?"

"That copy was destroyed."

"Unfortunate."

"But the letter spoke of another, and that's the one I found," Hero said, evenly.

"Did you, now? Clever girl."

Was there some inflection in his voice that hinted otherwise? Hero's pulse picked up its pace at the thought. She did not trust herself to speak, but she had to take her chance. "I-i-it was a treacherous errand, and since the book is worth so much, I would like something in return."

Now that she was here before him, eyeing his pale, gaunt face, Hero felt her determination weaken.

"And what would that be?" His back was to the light, so Hero could not discern his expression, and his tone gave nothing away, not anger or annoyance or amusement. "A new hair ribbon? A gown? Perhaps a new boy's costume?"

Hero winced at that, but she could hardly have conducted all of his business the way she was dressed, especially after what had happened to her coach. The memory of that, and the circumstances that had thrown her upon the mercy of a stranger, made her stand up straighter.

"I want more than that," Hero said. "Not only did I have to hunt down the missing volume myself, but I was delayed and threatened throughout by Erasmus."

"An annoyance," Raven said, in dismissal.

"He hired men to shoot at me, more than once," Hero said, her voice rising. "I could have been killed. And for that I should have my freedom."

The word hung in the air like some kind of obscenity. But before Raven could react, Hero went on. "I ask only for a small stipend, a settlement that would allow me to live elsewhere while troubling you little," she added, lifting her arm to take in Raven Hill and the valuable collections he had amassed, often with her aid.

"If I wanted to be robbed, I could have Erasmus handle it with more delicacy—and venality," Raven said. His voice was low, his anger obvious. "At least he is not an ingrate. Do you remember where you came from? Or perhaps you would care to go back there."

"Back where?" Hero asked. "You've lied about so much, why should I believe your innuendos about my origins?"

The stillness that followed vibrated with his rage,

and he took a step forward. "Make no mistake about my power," he said. "I can arrange to have you put away in such a place, and no one will ever find you again."

"I don't think so." The sound of that familiar voice, calling down from above, bolstered Hero's wavering strength and made Raven start in surprise.

Against all odds, her gentleman farmer had managed what no one else had ever accomplished. He had made his way unchallenged—and unnoticed—into the heart of Raven's realm. Although she had spent a lifetime cowed by Raven's seemingly otherworldly powers, they faded in comparison to Kit's very real skills. And at the moment, Hero was convinced there was nothing the man couldn't do.

But before she could gloat, Raven called to his guards, and one soon appeared in costume, complete with sword and helm. "We have an intruder. See to him," Raven said.

"That's not an intruder. He's my guest," Hero said. But the guard did not obey her, and Raven told the other who appeared to light the torches in the upper gallery, where Kit was hiding. Hero called out a warning, and she heard Kit's footsteps running lightly above, followed by a thud.

Hero cursed the darkness as she craned her neck. Then light blazed forth from one of the torches set into the wall, illuminating two silhouettes armed with swords, one of which Hero easily recognized. It appeared that Raven's personal protectors were more decorative than effective, for Kit must have got his weapon by overpowering the first guard.

And now he harried the other. As Hero watched in awe, Kit thrust and parried, driving the second guard back along the gallery and up against the wall. It was no surprise to Hero that, in addition to all his other skills, Christopher Marchant was an excellent swordsman.

Since Kit obviously had the upper hand, Raven needed no prescience to predict the outcome. "Close him off," Raven shouted to his startled butler. "Shut him up there!" While the elderly servant hurried to do Raven's bidding, there was a grunt and a clatter from above, as Kit disarmed the guard.

Kicking the fellow's weapon aside, Kit knocked him to the floor, where he disappeared from view. Then, rather than find the exits bolted against him, Kit leapt on to the carved railing, tugged at one of the fading tapestries, and swung from the gallery to the floor in one fell swoop.

Hero squeaked out a protest, for fear the old material would crumble in his hands, dropping him to the hard tiles below, but he landed on his feet, ever graceful, like some latter-day Robin Hood. Hero didn't know whether to laugh in delight or swoon at the arrival of her champion, who turned to Raven, weapon in hand.

But Raven ignored him, as though he were no more than a pesky gnat, and fixed Hero with his hooded gaze. "You are mine, and I won't be handing you over, now or ever."

Hero shuddered at the statement, but it was too late and the taste of freedom too strong. "I'm not part of your collection, Raven," she murmured.

"I acquired you, didn't I?"

Hero flinched, but Kit stepped forward. "If you did, she has repaid your investment many times over. Now, she's of age and marrying me, so you will just have to find someone else to handle your dealings for you."

Hero didn't dispute Kit's claim of betrothal, though she had no more desire for his pity than she ever had. She simply could spare no thought for the future when the present was so precarious.

"She's not going anywhere with anyone, least of all a penniless, upstart intruder," Raven snapped, visibly angered.

But the lapse was a brief one, and when he spoke again, it was to Hero, his tone low and derisive. "Perhaps this young man, Mr Marchant, I presume, is unaware of your family…legacy."

Before Hero could respond, Kit stepped forward. "I don't care where Hero came from, and I'm certainly not going to believe your version of events, *Mr Tovell.*" Swinging the sword in the air, he spoke over his shoulder to Hero. "He never struck you, did he? Because if he did, I'll run him through right now."

"No, Kit," Hero said. At one time, she might have enjoyed the sight of someone toying with the great Raven as he had toyed with so many others. But Kit was too much the gentleman to employ Raven's tactics. "I don't want any trouble."

"You already have it," Raven said, his voice harsh with promise. "Trespassing, menacing, assault, at the very least. Mr Marchant will enjoy a long stay in jail."

Hero's heart pounded at the threat, which Raven,

with all his seeming resources, might well make good. And for once in her life, Hero felt faint. All the childhood terrors and horrors of this place were as nothing to the frightening power Raven now wielded: power over the man she loved.

It was an admission she had failed to make, even to herself, but one that Hero could not deny, and she stood, trembling and uncertain. Such was her fear that she might have thrown herself at Raven's feet, begging for a mercy she knew he would not grant. But Kit must have sensed she was wavering, for he put himself between them.

"And what about imprisonment of a young woman not related to you?" he asked, no hint of his own courage faltering. "There are laws in this land against slavery."

Raven laughed, a chilling sound in the hollowness of the hall. "You can't touch me. I'm above the law."

And then, as though to prove his claim, footsteps sounded from one of the passageways. Whirling, Hero was not sure what she expected, at the very least additional guards summoned from outside. But the lone figure that appeared made her loose a shaky breath of relief.

"Erasmus, rid the hall of this intruder," Raven said, lifting an arm to extend a bony finger toward Kit.

Obviously startled by the directive, Erasmus stopped to gape at Kit, armed with the sword, but made no effort to evict him. He had tangled once with the gentleman farmer and had come out the worst for it.

"He's of no consequence to me," Erasmus said dismissively. "All I want is the Mallory."

Raven laughed. "Ah, the Mallory. It seems to have been an ill chance that set me lusting after it." He paused dramatically, as though to make certain he had the attention of his audience before continuing.

"I admit to being ruled by my passion for the arcane, the unusual, the singular, so I could hardly resist the lure of a missing book, especially one with—what shall I call it?—a Gothic tone."

"Not Gothic. Druidic," Kit said, his expression tense.

"Yes, so I heard," Raven said.

Knowing Raven as she did, Hero was wary of his sudden desire for speech. She opened her mouth to warn Kit not to listen, but Raven was already talking again. "I found the scrap of letter as soon as I purchased the lot, of course. I knew the significance of such a find, so I sent out some discreet inquiries."

Raven paused to fix Kit with his hooded gaze. "I even wrote to the woman who owned Mallory's old home, to no avail. Oakfield, I believe it is called? But then she must have been a relative of yours?"

Raven's words had their intended effect, and before Hero could intervene, he lifted his cane and knocked the sword from Kit's hand to clatter upon the tiles. Although Raven's cane had always seemed an unnecessary affection, now Hero wondered if it held a blade. And she slipped her hand into her reticule.

It was Erasmus, however, who proved to be the greater threat, for he retrieved the sword before either Raven or Kit could move. "Now, if you will just hand over the Mallory," he said, backing toward Hero.

Raven laughed, and Erasmus swung toward him.

Waving the blade wildly, he was all the more dangerous for his lack of skill. "I've wasted enough years
toiling for no reward, kicking my heels at your beck
and call," he said, his pinched features twisted with
anger. "It's time I established my own reputation. And
the Mallory will do it."

Hero swallowed a gasp of surprise at Erasmus's unexpected defection. His previous plot having been
thwarted, he was gambling everything, his present and
his future, on a book that was not even genuine. But
Hero was not about to enlighten him, and she held out
the volume she had carefully rewrapped.

Erasmus snatched it from her, his beady eyes alight
with avarice, yet his triumph was short-lived.

"Go ahead and take joy of it," Raven said. "It's a
fraud."

The flush of victory faded from Erasmus's pale
face. "You lie."

Raven laughed. "This is why I put my faith in the
girl, you fool. You were always too stupid to understand the intricacies that came so easily to her."

Wanting only to be left out of this, Hero took a step
back, and she was relieved when Erasmus turned the
sword toward Raven.

"Put that thing down," Raven ordered. "You don't
know how to use it, any more than you know how to
use the information at your fingertips." He paused to
point his cane toward Hero, and she tightened her hold
upon the pistol she kept hidden.

"She was seen getting the book from Laytham's,"
Raven said. "Not from Oakfield or Cheswick or
Featherstone or even Poynter. From Laytham."

"So?"

"So," Raven said, sneering, "if Laytham had such a rare book, he would be crowing to the skies like the rooster he is. Your precious edition is as authentic as one of his pamphlets, a fake, a forgery fit only to fool an idiot like you."

At Raven's words, Erasmus whirled toward Hero, the sword slicing violently through the air. "Is this true?" he demanded, turning the full force of his hatred upon her.

If he hadn't been so dangerously volatile, Hero might have found amusement in the reversal of their roles. For right now, Erasmus seemed far more likely to carry the taint of madness. But out of the corner of her eye, she saw Kit move closer, and she was not about to lose him.

"Stop right there," Hero said, raising her hand inside its silken covering. "Don't make me ruin a perfectly good reticule."

Erasmus halted, as if frozen, and in the ensuing silence, Hero noticed an odd crackling noise. She cocked her head to listen, but it was soon drowned out by Erasmus's shouts.

"This is all your doing! You played with me, toyed with me," he screamed, lunging at Raven. Hero sucked in a sharp breath, certain he would draw blood, but Raven lifted his cane to ward off the blow.

"Stop! Look!" Kit called. At first Hero thought he was trying to put an end to the struggle, but he was pointing to the corner of the vast room, and what Hero saw there made her blanch.

The tapestry that Kit had used to swing from the

gallery had fallen against the lighted torch, and fire chased up the old material, catching the other tapestries ablaze, as well as the carved wooden screen that covered most of the rear of great hall. The smoke that drifted upward in the huge space, now could be seen—and smelled.

It took a couple more shouts to capture the attention of both Erasmus and Raven, who were grappling upon the tiles. But when they fell apart, they both gaped at the blaze that was racing through the furnishings.

"My books!" Raven screamed, rising to his feet. "We must save my collections!" He turned to run toward one of the alcoves, Erasmus not far behind.

"No! Save yourselves!" Kit called.

But they paid him no heed, and Hero had one last look at the two men who had so ill used her before they disappeared into a shadowy passage, fire at their heels. Hero knew that their mania and greed would surely be their death, but she took no joy in it. When she lifted her hand to her mouth, she wasn't certain whether she was stifling a cough or a sob.

"Hurry!" Having given up on the others, Kit grasped her arm and pulled her toward the entrance. The heavy bolt was slid home, and as he wrestled with it, Hero wondered what other exit they might seek among the maze of passages, for already the smoke hung thick in the air, and she heard something crash to the floor behind them.

"Kit, through the back," Hero said, trying to judge how swiftly the blaze was traveling and in what directions. But at that moment, Kit managed to push the massive wood aside and to fling open the door.

They raced through the opening, gulping in great breaths of the chilly air that met them. Outside in the foggy darkness, Hero caught a glimpse of eerie figures dashing into the night, and for an instant, she wondered whether Raven had made his escape, after all. But she realized that, like rats abandoning a sinking ship, his meagre staff were fleeing their master and his Gothic nightmare.

Chapter Fifteen

Kit dragged Hero away from Raven Hill, but the eerie landscape that met them firmly reflected its owner. The rising moon lent a pale glow to the expanse of open ground ahead, illuminating tendrils of fog that veiled any path—or trap—that might be there. Kit could only hope that Hero would alert him to pitfalls.

But they made their way without incident to the gatehouse, which stood unmanned, its door hanging open. Either the guard had hurried to aid Raven or he had fled at the first sign of trouble. Kit halted to catch his breath, and as though she could go no further, Hero stepped inside, sinking wearily on to the heavy wooden bench.

She probably was in a state of shock, for despite everything, Raven Hill had been her home, and the people inside the closest she had to a family. Glancing back at the castle, Kit saw the tall windows gleaming brightly, like some kind of leering pumpkin, consumed from the inside out. And he was struck with a sense of the past repeating itself.

Kit didn't know whether Raven's interest in the Mallory had roused the attention of Malet and his followers or simply coincided with their own search. But the end was the same. Just as the maze went up in flames, taking those who would kill with it, now Raven Hill was burning, claiming its victims.

Kit shook his head, unwilling to believe in some kind of curse that could follow even a forgery, but his surroundings did not lend themselves to coherent thought. The sooner they left here the better, he realized, but Hero had reached the end of her resources, and the empty building was as good a landmark as any in the mist.

Kit knelt before her. "I've got to fetch Charlie's horse, so I want you to stay here until I come back."

Hero lifted her head. "Where would I go? I have n-n-nothing."

"You've got me," Kit said. He took her face in his hands, forcing her wide eyes to focus on his own. "I love you, and I think you love me, too."

She did not deny it, and for once, all that she felt was visible on her face. The outpouring of emotion was nearly Kit's undoing, and he kissed her with all the force of a claim laid. She clung to him, and when Kit stepped back it was because he knew they could not linger.

"Stay here," he repeated. Exiting the gatehouse, Kit ran round the wall that enclosed Raven Hill's inner court, glad that he had not been forced to climb it again. He was heading for the woods, trying to get his bearings, when a sudden crashing in the brush had him backing against a black trunk.

But it was only a deer, scared up by the smoke, and Kit went on, though his pace slowed considerably as he groped through the trees, the mist rising to obscure his way. Finally, he heard a whinny nearby. No doubt, Charlie's animal had smelled the smoke, too, and was restless.

Still, Kit approached slowly, wary that someone else might have come across the horse, someone fleeing the fire. But the animal was tethered where he had left it, and he led it out of the woods toward the wall. The looming gray curtain was the only solid marker in an increasingly misty world, and he followed it, even though the massive stone seemed to disappear into the distance.

So thick was the fog now that Kit was upon the gatehouse before he realized it. Breathing a sigh of relief, he led Charlie's horse right up to the open door and called softly to Hero. When she did not appear, he wondered whether she could even stand, considering the state she'd been in when he left her.

Dragging the reins, Kit stepped inside, only to bite back a cry of alarm. For even in the near darkness, it was obvious that the seat was vacant, and a search of the shadows revealed the small gatehouse was empty of all life, Hero having vanished into thin air.

Kit shook his head to clear it. As tempting as it was to blame the ghoulish atmosphere in which he found himself, Kit knew that this was no Gothic trickery. There was a logical explanation for Hero's disappearance, and he quickly dismissed the most obvious one—that she had fled from him yet again.

And then he heard it.

Stepping outside the gatehouse, Kit laid a calming hand upon Charlie's animal to still it, then cocked his head to one side, listening. Now that the horse was quiet, there was no mistaking the creak of wheels and muffled hooves. Looking down the long lane, Kit could see nothing in the fog, and he realized the noise could be coming from anywhere, a path back to the stables or along the acres of property that surrounded Raven Hill.

Raven or Erasmus could have come to their senses, left the burning building and come upon Hero. A servant might have offered rescue—or taken her back toward the blaze. Kit only had moments to decide, to make the gamble of a lifetime as he swung into the saddle.

In the end, he chose to move forward, heading down the lane and putting Raven Hill behind him.

Hero sat back in the luxurious coach, so tired that she felt as though she might lose consciousness. Weeks of tension and danger, lack of sleep and the events of the last hour had robbed her of her strength. And her wits. They had left her completely, or else she would not be here now.

The wariness that had served her well for so long had deserted Hero as she sat slumped in Raven Hill's gatehouse, trying to make sense of all that had happened. Even if she hadn't been distraught, Hero would have seen little need for caution, with Erasmus and Raven both…gone.

So when some dark figures appeared, gently urging her from her seat, Hero thought them servants or neighbors who had seen the fire. Dazed, she had let them lead her to the coach. At some point, she'd had the presence of mind to ask about Kit, and the vague assurance she received belatedly roused her suspicions. But by that time, it was too late. She was inside a vehicle far too comfortable to be Raven's, the door firmly shut behind her.

Hero could only think Erasmus responsible, but he was dead, wasn't he? Or had he left his mentor to burn in order to claim the inheritance? If so, he would have no qualms about doing away with her, as well. But Hero's last sight of him, fire close behind, was too fresh in her mind to imagine any other outcome for the man she had called cousin.

For a moment, Hero wondered whether Kit had been right all along and some black-caped Druids were kidnapping her. But even that possibility could not rouse her to action. She was too tired to keep up the carefully cultivated facade that Raven had insisted upon, let alone muster her waning resources. All she wanted to do was to crawl into Kit's arms and stay there.

But even the thought of the man she loved filled Hero with despair, for Raven had taken the facts of her birth with him to the grave. Now she would never know whether her parents had been insane, eager to sell their child to a passing stranger.

Although Kit claimed that he didn't care, Hero did. How could she marry him, knowing that she might turn on him? Christopher Marchant, gentleman and scholar, deserved the best of everything, and that did not include becoming caretaker to a madwoman.

Hero closed her stinging eyes and choked back a moan. She could not take the chance that she might make him miserable or turn violent. And worst of all, loomed the possibility that she might some day sell her own child in a lunatic act, repeating her sordid history.

Swallowing hard, Hero realized that she should be grateful that fate had spirited her away from Kit and the temptation he presented. If Raven had given her a stipend, some kind of future, she could have tried to make a life for herself. But now, with Kit all that was left to her, she might have given in.

It was better this way, Hero told herself, though she had no idea how she would make her way in the world. But perhaps that would not be a concern for long, she thought, as she peered out into the night with no knowledge of her whereabouts.

Yet Hero soon recognized the lights in the distance as those of the great estates that Raven had so coveted. Raven Hill was as close as he could get to the homes of the country's nobles and most wealthy, and though they had done business with him, they had never welcomed him into their ranks.

The darkness and fog made it difficult to determine her exact location, but once the coach passed through gates and turned toward a stylish facade, where rows of windows appeared out of the mist to wink with light, Hero realized her destination. And she laughed.

Although she had never been here, Hero knew that the elegant residence was built during the last century in the classical mode, with four stories of cream-colored stone and slender marble columns marking the entrance. When the horses drew up before the stairs, Hero did not even bother to seize her pistol or try to escape. She simply stared as a footman appeared and hurried toward the coach.

Upon opening the door, he bowed and held out a gloved hand to assist her descent, a treatment so different from her arrival at Raven Hill that Hero stifled another laugh. Unlike her old home, which was sadly neglected in favour of Raven's collections, this place was neat and well kept and well staffed. But then the owner was wealthy beyond even Raven's dreams.

Inside, the marbled foyer was ablaze with light, in stark contrast to Raven Hill's miserly darkness, but the mood was sombre. The footman handed her off to a grim-faced butler, who showed her into the study, an enormous circular room with carved ceilings and a door that seemed to disappear into the woodwork. The walls were hung with pale silk and the accents all painted, which made the space bright and airy even at this hour.

Several lamps were set about, chasing away any shadows, and the furnishings were white and gilt, probably French collectibles worth more than some libraries. But Hero didn't know much about furniture. Instead of inspecting it further, she walked to the pier glass to have a look at herself.

Even to her jaundiced eye, she did not appear as though she had but recently escaped a conflagration. Thankfully, she had kept on her cloak at Raven Hill, and she kept it on now, as well, not knowing what was in store. Her boots were wet from her run through the grass, and she settled into a delicate chair near the marbled fireplace, where a roaring blaze warmed her cold feet.

Compared to Raven Hill, with its petty horrors and perpetual discomforts, this home was the epitome of fine taste and opulence. And yet, her very presence here confirmed that the owner could be no better than Raven himself.

However, as a prison, this place was preferable, and the absence of any guards made escape a simple option. In fact, Hero was tempted to go to a tall window and check the drop to the ground below, but she could not rouse herself. Besides, she was too interested in what her host intended.

She did not have long to wait. Soon, the subtle door opened, and a slender older gentleman entered. He was dressed all in black, and although there was nothing lacking in his costume, it was not of the quality Hero expected. It took her a moment to realize that he was not the master of this house.

"Miss Ingram," he said, with a polite bow. "I apologize for the abrupt manner of your arrival. I understand it was quite the hurried undertaking, but I assure you there was cause for haste." He turned away, walking toward a large ormolu desk that sat in the center of the room.

He made a careful show of pulling out his chair, taking a seat at the desk and folding his hands in front of him. In the light, Hero could see that his face was pale, the shadows under his eyes attesting to some strain. When he spoke, his voice cracked under it, and he was forced to clear his throat.

"You see, we had hoped, but…" He paused, as though to gather his composure. "Again, I apologize for my erratic behavior. My name is Fiskerton, and I'm the secretary to the…late Duke of Montford."

"Late?" Hero asked.

Fiskerton nodded. "His Grace passed away earlier today."

Hero shook her head. "I'm sorry." Although she had never met the man, he was a fine collector whose presence would be missed in the book world. And despite his liveried servants harrying her over the past weeks and practically forcing her into his coach, Hero forgave him. As Poynter had said, he appeared to be in pursuit of one last, great find. And how could she begrudge him that?

Fiskerton cleared his throat again. "The timing is most unfortunate because his last wish was that he speak to you." He drew a deep breath. "But you are a difficult young lady to find."

Hero blinked in surprise.

"When his Grace made his intentions clear, we wrote repeatedly to you at your home, I believe it is called Raven Hill?"

Hero felt a cold chill dance up her spine. She nodded, then shook her head. "But I never received any messages."

"Yes," Fiskerton said, frowning. "I suspected as much. I even sent one of my representatives there in the hopes of speaking with you in person, but he was denied admittance." He sighed. "As his Grace grew more ill, my queries became more insistent, but then Mr Raven claimed that you were no longer living with him."

Hero drew in a sharp breath.

"Unfortunately, a great deal of time was wasted before we came to the conclusion that Mr Raven might not be forthcoming to us." Fiskerton frowned. "That's when we were forced to make some alternative inquiries, and we discovered that you were traveling, but your whereabouts, again, were difficult to determine. During this time, we also set a, ahem, watch upon Raven Hill, should you return at some point."

Hero could only gape in astonishment at this revelation, which explained why the coach had been so quick to retrieve her.

"Unfortunately, since time was of the essence, they might have been a bit abrupt. Indeed, I believe they were prepared to enter the house, if need be," Fiskerton said, with obvious disapproval. "Thankfully, that was not necessary, though I understand that a fire was reported?"

Hero nodded numbly.

"In that case, their abruptness may be excused, for their intention was to get you safely away, and to bring you here, of course."

It was the "of course" that finally prompted Hero to speak. "But why?" she asked, in confusion.

At her question, Fiskerton assumed a more businesslike expression. "That was for his Grace to explain, but when it became clear that we might not be able to locate you, he did empower me to notify you as to the, uh, circumstances."

Looking down at a sheaf of papers on the desk, Fiskerton began shuffling through them, as though he was not eager to explain further. "And from your curiosity, it appears that Mr Tovell...er, Raven, kept his part of the bargain in that you are unaware of your relation to his Grace."

Hero blinked, uncomprehending.

Fiskerton cleared his throat. "You are, ahem, the duke's natural child," he said. "Of course, inheritance laws and entailments apply, so that his Grace did not intend to, uh, formerly recognize you. A cousin will inherit the title and estates, but his Grace did want to make certain that you received something."

Hero felt as though someone had struck her. She tried to draw in air, but her stomach roiled, and her lungs did not seem to be working.

"Miss Ingram? Are you all right?"

Fiskerton rose from his desk to come round to her chair. "Put your head down," he advised, obviously agitated. "Perhaps I should send for a maid or Mrs Ferguson. She will know... Shall I call for smelling salts?"

Hero shook her head and swallowed a hysterical laugh. She had seen and heard it all, Gothic horrors that would set any sane woman to screaming, yet now she threatened to swoon at something that was not even frightening.

"Are you certain?" Mr Fiskerton asked. When she nodded, he awkwardly patted her arm. "I wish you could have spoken to his Grace directly, for...I know that when he neared the end of his life, he rued his earlier decision."

Hero's head shot up so quickly that she almost knocked the older man aside. "He gave me to Raven!" she said, as the realization struck.

Fiskerton frowned. "Actually, the man was then Augustus Tovell, and he served the duke's library well. It was only, uh, afterward that he assumed his, uh, new character."

"Why?" Hero asked numbly. Although legitimacy counted for much in society, many fathers, including the royal heirs, provided for their natural offspring, setting them up in households without acknowledging them officially.

Fiskerton shook his head. "Again, that was for his Grace to say. I was not privy to the decision."

Hero looked at the man long and hard until he finally glanced away. "I believe pressure from the dowager duchess was involved."

Pressure from his mother, Hero thought dismally, then she drew in a sharp breath. "Who was *my* mother?"

Fiskerton shook his head. "His Grace never named her."

Again, Hero gave him a hard look, for servants knew everything that took place in their households and were privy to every bit of rumour and gossip. She knew it, and Fiskerton knew it.

Frowning, he finally spoke, with obvious reluctance. "There was talk that she was a princess royal. But I know nothing for certain, and you will find little to gain should you pursue that avenue."

Hero reared back in outrage at such a suggestion.

As if fearing he had said too much, Fiskerton returned to his seat at the desk, put the massive piece of furniture between them, and resumed his business-like manner.

Shuffling through the papers, he did not look up when next he spoke. "As I said, his Grace's final wish was to talk with you, but he made arrangements on your behalf, should he be unable. He was most pleased that your interests echoed his own, so his bequest reflects that shared appreciation."

Hero felt like her weary head was spinning. What was he saying?

As if she had spoken aloud, Fiskerton lifted his head to eye her sombrely. "His Grace left you his library."

Again, Hero reeled as though from a blow, unable to comprehend what she had just heard. "Wh-what?"

"You have inherited his Grace's collection of books, which is worth a great deal of money—" Fiskerton began, but he was interrupted by the sound of a commotion beyond the confines of the quiet room.

Hero heard muffled shouts before the discreet door burst open to reveal a familiar figure, followed by the butler and assorted footman, who appeared to have been shaken off in some sort of altercation.

"What's going on here? Hero, are you all right?"

But by the time Kit spoke, Hero had already leapt to her feet, intent upon throwing herself into his arms. They were a haven that she would never have to leave, she realized, as she cried out in relief.

"Oh, Kit, my parents weren't lunatics."

Chapter Sixteen

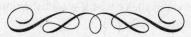

Once Hero identified Kit as her betrothed, the footmen trooped out, leaving the two of them alone with Fiskerton. However, the duke's secretary eyed Kit up and down with some disfavour, as though the new arrival did not quite meet his approval.

Hero swallowed a bubble of hysterical laughter at the suspicion that Kit might be after her money. Not long ago she had been homeless, penniless and of dubious parentage, and still he had pressed his suit. At the memory, she wanted nothing more than to throw herself back into his arms.

However, Fiskerton frowned upon such displays, so Hero restrained herself, for the time being, and tried to appear impassive. But the facade that had served her so well in the past was unattainable. Despite her best efforts, Hero felt her lips curving and her cheeks flushing. Happiness, long denied, filled her so completely that it threatened to spill out.

Of course, Fiskerton could not know that her joy

came from his news, not of her inheritance, but of her ancestry, and with it, her ability to accept Kit's proposal without reservation. She had kept him at arm's length for his own sake, as well as her own, and now she would close any distance between them.

"Perhaps you don't realize, Miss Ingram, the value of your bequest," Fiskerton said, frowning at her seeming giddiness. "His Grace's library is a great responsibility and will make you a wealthy woman, should you choose to break it up."

"I can well imagine members of the Roxburghe Club salivating at such an opportunity, but I don't intend to put the collection up for auction," Hero said. She nodded toward Kit. "Mr Marchant is planning some improvements to his estate, and perhaps that will just have to include the library."

Although he had not been privy to the earlier discussion, Kit took her cue, as usual, and nodded in agreement, while Fiskerton looked dubious.

"Oh, yes, Mr Fiskerton," Hero insisted, her smile wide. "Perhaps his entrance here gave the wrong impression, but I can assure you that Mr Marchant is both a gentleman and a scholar."

If Fiskerton still was not convinced, he kept his opinion to himself and included Kit in the ensuing conversation. There were details that had to be seen to and papers to sign, as well as questions about the fire at Raven Hill to be answered. But Raven's reputation for being reclusive and eccentric made for little inquiry, as did the statements from the Duke of Montford's liveried servants and Hero's presence in his Grace's home.

* * *

It was late by the time all the business was concluded, and rather than see them off into the cold at that hour, Fiskerton offered them accommodations for the night in the dowager's residence tucked into the woods nearby.

"It's not staffed at this time, since her Grace passed away some time ago, but I had the housekeeper prepare some rooms and light fires," Fiskerton said, giving his papers a final shuffle.

Although Hero would have liked to see more of her father's home, the true heir would be arriving soon, and, understandably, Fiskerton wanted to avoid any awkwardness. When presented with the prospect of setting out for Charlie's in her current state of exhaustion, Hero was eager to bed down anywhere.

Still, she was hardly prepared for the lavishness of her destination. Although not built on the grand scale of the main residence, the dowager's house was larger than Oakfield and beautifully appointed. While the fires were being lit, Hero wandered around, running a finger over the dusty surface of a gilt writing desk and a medallion-backed chair.

Her presence here, in the home of the woman seemingly responsible for her life, made Hero feel oddly off balance. Although the dowager duchess might not have arranged Hero's placement with Raven, she had made sure the duke never knew his daughter. And she had been Hero's *grandmother*. That thought was startling enough, but then Hero considered just who her other grandparents might be, and she had to stifle another hysterical laugh.

Wasn't the king himself rumoured to be mad? It seemed that Hero could not escape that taint, but it was enough that she had not be purchased from asylum inmates—and that she was not related in any way to Raven. Although Hero regretted his stewardship, she found it difficult to envision any other existence, especially one as the illegitimate daughter of a duke, and her steps faltered.

On the surface, the idea seemed ideal—the dream of every orphan who ever pondered her ancestry. But upon reflection, Hero felt an uneasiness far different from that engendered by Raven and his Gothic home.

In truth, Hero was not sure she would have liked the stigma of natural birth, even with such an exalted pedigree. And what kind of world would she have inhabited? She could not have lived with either parent, and would never have known her mother, for though there were rumours, the royal princesses did not acknowledge any scandals.

Would her caretaker have been any better than Raven? Probably. But who would have made up her circle? Would she have been pursued for connections, her influence? Hero could not imagine anyone like Kit in that setting, someone kind and decent, who wanted her only for herself, without name or coin attached.

And suddenly her parents seemed poor, despite their wealth, concerned only with their position, with no thought for love or what was right. Glancing up to where Kit was speaking softly with the housekeeper, Hero realized that her gentleman farmer was worth more than the lot of them.

As if sensing her attention, Kit looked up and

flashed Hero a smile that chased away the chill in the air. The house was cold in more ways than one, she realized, hugging her cloak close. For all its luxury, it held no life or hospitality, and the expensive furnishings were as brittle and meaningless as Raven's elaborate collections.

"You're cold, miss," the housekeeper said. "Here, let me show you to your room, and you, too, sir, then I'll be off. If you need anything else, just give a ring, for I'll have one of the maids stay in the quarters here."

Ushering Hero into a bedroom where a fire burned brightly, the woman closed the door, leaving her to stand in the middle of a vast space, occupied by an elaborate bed decorated with heavy hangings. As in the other rooms, the dowager's taste tended toward French furnishings and gilt, taken to extremes.

Although elegant, the place had none of the appeal of the Armstrong town house or even the Smallpeace farmhouse. But it would do for tonight, Hero thought, bone tired as she removed her cloak. She had barely laid it upon a painted couch when the door burst open and Kit strode in unceremoniously, a determined look upon his face.

"What?" Hero asked, as he made a point of eyeing the curtained windows. For a moment, she fell into her old habit of wariness, but who could be after them now?

"I just wanted to make sure you weren't planning your escape," Kit said, slanting her a speculative glance.

Hero smiled, and the odd mood that had settled upon her since entering the dowager's domain lifted. "I'm not going anywhere."

"Well, I'm here to make sure of that," Kit said, advancing upon her, his lips curved in a devilish fashion.

Hero took a step back, her weariness forgotten as a frisson of excitement danced up her spine. Suddenly, she realized just how alone they were in this strange house, without even a staff of servants to gossip. "You'll just have to learn to trust me, even though it may take a lifetime."

"I'm counting on that, but in the meantime I was thinking about a chain to tether you to me. With a lock," Kit added, coming so close that Hero found herself up against the curtained bed.

Had she thought the house cold and dead? Kit brought warmth and life with such force that the very air around her crackled and her body roused itself in response.

Kit gave her a jaundiced look as he inched nearer, his hard frame almost touching her own. "But by the time I find one, you might be gone."

When Hero opened her mouth to protest that he needed nothing to keep her to him, Kit put a finger to her lips. And the sensation was so powerful that she lost all train of thought.

"I could try to get a special licence, so we might be married immediately, but again, I don't have enough time, especially since we need to leave for Hawthorne Park as soon as possible to attend my sister's wedding," Kit said.

A subtle nudge from him had Hero falling back upon the soft bedding, and he leaned forward. "So I'm going to have to do something else to make sure you never leave me again."

"And what's that?" Hero whispered, even though she recognized the dark intent in his eyes.

Kit grinned as he moved over her. "I'm going to thoroughly compromise you."

Hero felt her pulse leap at the warning, but instead of protesting, she sighed in anticipation. "Well, in that case, I'm definitely not going anywhere."

Hero arrived at Charlie's town house in far more elegant fashion than before, in the Duke of Montford's coach, his liveried footmen in attendance, and Kit riding Charlie's horse alongside. Although Charlie was out, they were shown to their rooms and settled in for an overnight stay before leaving London.

This time, Kit threatened to remain in Hero's bedroom during her bath, but when she invited him to join her, he left, muttering something about Charlie's aunt. While Hero lingered, enjoying a perfumed toilette for the first time in her life, he arranged for their horses to be retrieved from one inn and their packs from another.

It was all over, and yet, Hero felt like her life was just beginning. Although she was inclined to toss out her boy's clothing, Kit insisted she keep it in case she wanted to muck about with the new landscaping that he planned for Oakfield. Hero smiled to herself, certain that his reasons had less to do with work than play. Hadn't he whispered something to that effect last night, about the look of her legs, clad in breeches?

Hero flushed as the memories rushed back of his long, slow seduction, intent yet playful, sweet yet fierce, a tangle of limbs and smooth skin, and Kit's mouth moving upon her. He had whispered of his love over and over until Hero had haltingly spoken herself, stuttering at first, as she choked with the force of her emotion. It returned now, and she had to swallow hard as she packed away her boy's clothes for some future romp with her future husband.

Although Hero insisted that quid pro quo demanded Kit keep his Harlequin costume, he balked, claiming that he had already arranged for the earl's purloined masquerades to be returned to Cheswick. However, when pressed, he reluctantly agreed to wear something similar should Hero devise it—as long as no one else was involved in its construction.

Hero's cheeks grew heated at the thought, and she realized the project would be as good a reason as any to perfect her meagre sewing skills. But she said nothing to Kit as he escorted her to the parlour for some biscuits and chocolate. The hot drink was a delight that Hero had never known before, and she finished her own cup and then half of Kit's, while he complained about the missing Mrs Armstrong.

"It appears your would-be chaperone has fled," Kit said, leaning back in a chair near the fire. "So we'll have to see about obtaining another." Putting his feet up on a nearby hassock, he looked as though he might nod off, which was not surprising, considering how little sleep either of them had got the night before.

That memory not only made Hero flush, but seemed to negate her need for a chaperone, and they were in the midst of arguing the point when a commotion erupted in the foyer. Charlie's butler arrived one step ahead of a pair of guests, but he did not have a chance to announce them before the woman rushed forward.

"Kit!" she called out. He rose to his feet in response, and Hero felt a stab of alarm. But as the lady flung herself toward Kit, the uncanny resemblance between them became apparent, and Hero realized this must be his sister, Sydony. At the discovery, Hero's alarm turned into a kind of queasy feeling that had nothing to do with the chocolate she'd consumed.

"Where the devil have you been?" Sydony demanded, and for a moment, Hero didn't know whether she was going to strike her brother or throw herself into his arms. "I've been worried sick!"

"As I wrote in my letter, we had a bit of adventure," Kit said, ruefully.

"A bit of adventure!" The woman scoffed. She nodded toward the dark, silent man, who stood distant from the siblings. "Barto and Hob have been out searching London for you! They stopped short of storming Raven Hill only to learn it burned to a hollow shell last night!"

Kit looked apologetic. "I'd forgotten about Hob."

"Yes, Hob! He came to us with tales of knife-wielding assailants, kidnappers, warrants..." Sydony paused as though to catch her breath. "I didn't know whether to go on with the wedding, or if you'd be there, or even where you were or if you were hurt..." She trailed off, a stricken look on her beautiful face, and Kit soon was patting her back in awkward comfort.

Although Hero could understand the woman's agitation, it did little to ease her own queasiness. For it was she, a total stranger, who had put Kit in danger and wrought havoc in all their lives. Would they hold her responsible?

As if sensing Hero's thoughts, the woman turned from Kit to look at Hero, her dark eyes missing nothing. "And you must be Hero," she said. "Are you all right?"

The question was not what Hero expected, and it took a moment to respond. When she nodded warily, Sydony moved to take both her hands. "Well, then, welcome to the family."

"What?" Kit asked, looking startled. "How did you know?"

"Perhaps it was the undertone of your letter." The dark man stepped forward, his tone wry. "I'm Viscount Hawthorne."

"Just call him Barto," Sydony said, pulling Hero down into a chair and taking a seat beside her. Now that she had found her brother in good health, she appeared more composed and less daunting.

Yet Hero remained uncertain. Her stomach seemed to have settled, but she was not accustomed to being the center of such attention and her dealings with women, especially those near her own age, had been few. Her anxiety was not eased by her sudden realization that she was destined to call the future viscountess her sister.

Although Sydony leaned forward, as if expectant, Hero had no idea what to say. She knew nothing of the traditional female occupations and could not watercolor or play the pianoforte. Nor did she even trust herself to conduct a proper conversation on feminine topics until Sydony put her at ease with a smile and a single demand.

"Now, tell me everything."

Epilogue

Kit stood on the threshold of the barn from which he and Hero had once made their escape and smiled, for the view before him was much changed. Then, it had been cold and dark, an eerie fog veiling the bleak landscape devastated by the fire behind his home. But now, the summer sun shown upon neat lawns that stretched up to Oakfield's rebuilt terrace.

The property was a far cry from the one Kit had inherited. The lands that had lain fallow were tilled, the formerly empty tenant farms bustling with life. Sheep grazed not far away, and he could see a horse and plough off in the distance, growing crops that had made the estate a success and bounty that made his table groan with good food.

The house that had seemed cursed now glowed in the afternoon light, its stone stripped of dark growth. The stables had been rebuilt, bigger and better than before, and the blackened remains of the maze had been cleared away, replaced by clipped grass and new trees and plantings. Kit had helped in the design himself, disdaining the old formal beds for bright spots of colorful flowers scattered among gravel paths.

It was a place to walk and linger and sit upon benches tucked in the shade, and sometimes Kit couldn't believe his good fortune. Immediately after the fire, he would have never imagined this outcome, and he knew who to thank for it all. But for the arrival of Hero, he might still be stuck in the dismals, drinking and brooding, while his holdings further deteriorated around him.

Now, he could look back without flinching. The fire had changed him, but it had not scarred him, becoming nothing more than a bad memory. Afterward, he had matured from a careless boy into a responsible man, shedding the guilt and tension, with Hero's help, until he felt like himself again, at home in his own skin.

Although she claimed that all he needed was to pummel someone insensible, it was more than that. By protecting Hero, Kit had redeemed himself, and now he felt he could handle just about anything. Although he had stopped looking over his shoulder for Druids, he stayed alert, intent upon guarding his own.

Those experiences had also taught him to savor every moment, and Kit did so now, taking a deep breath scented with grass and flowers. Ahead, on one of the gravel walks, he could see the figures of Sydony, Barto and their son Max gamboling with the dogs, carefree and happy, and he felt the same.

Behind him, he heard Hero's light footfalls, and as she moved to stand beside him, Kit slipped an arm around her. His hand immediately moved to rest upon the swelling that marked the child who would be coming soon.

"How are George and Harold?" he asked.

"And Missy and Clyde and Thomas and Toby…." Hero's recitation trailed off into a laugh. "All the cats and kittens are well. In fact, I've another who wishes to come to the house with me."

Kit groaned as she lifted her hand to reveal a tiny, orange ball of fur, purring contentedly. "It's not sleeping in our bed," he said.

"I love you," she whispered, knowing full well that the admission, so long in coming, was bound to bend him to her will.

"I love you, too," Kit said, because he knew she never got tired of hearing it. Turning his head to nuzzle her silken hair, he resigned himself, with a smile, to yet another cat.

But how could he deny his wife anything when she continued to surprise and delight him? Once distant and secretive, she had proven to be warm and giving, and laughter filled their days. She had made their home welcoming and comfortable, a haven for all who came to visit, not just Syd and Barto. Why, the last time Charlie had been here, he threatened never to leave.

The library was filled to overflowing with her inheritance, and she had been named Raven's heir, as well. Although Hero had sold off what little was left of Raven Hill as quickly as possible, she had decorated Oakfield with the "blood money" that her father must have paid her caretaker over the years.

But after updating the catalogue and parting with

some volumes, Hero had shown little interest in the books that had once been such a part of her life, and Kit sometimes wondered... He slanted her a speculative glance. "Do you ever miss your adventures?"

She blinked at the unexpected question. "I never had any until I met you."

"What about all your book dealings?"

Hero shook her head as she put the kitten to her cheek. "Those were usually boring transactions made with dull antiquarians, hardly something I enjoyed." She looked up at him, her lips curving. "Are you saying life with you isn't an adventure?"

Kit shrugged. "Well, I am just a gentleman farmer."

Hero laughed. "I don't think so," she said, slipping an arm around his waist. "You might have the rest of the world convinced, but you can't fool me, Kit Marchant." Her eyes shining, she gave him a teasing smile.

"You're a gentleman and a scholar."

* * * * *

The World of Mills & Boon®

There's a Mills & Boon® series that's perfect for you. We publish ten series and with new titles every month, you never have to wait long for your favourite to come along.

Blaze Scorching hot, sexy reads

By Request Relive the romance with the best of the best

Cherish™ Romance to melt the heart every time

Desire™ Passionate and dramatic love stories